$\mathcal{I}$ WILL MEET *you* THERE

S. M. HARDING

Bella
BOOKS
2015

Copyright © 2015 by S. M. Harding

Bella Books, Inc.
P.O. Box 10543
Tallahassee, FL 32302

All rights reserved. No part of this book may be reproduced or transmitted in any form or by any means, electronic or mechanical, including photocopying, without permission in writing from the publisher.

This is a work of fiction. Names, characters, businesses, places, events and incidents are either the products of the author's imagination or used in a fictitious manner. Any resemblance to actual persons, living or dead, or actual events is purely coincidental. The publisher does not have any control over and does not assume any responsibility for author or third-party websites or their content.

First Bella Books Edition 2015

Editor: JoSelle Vanderhooft
Cover Designer: Linda Callaghan
Cover Photo: S. M. Harding

ISBN: 978-1-59493-466-7

PUBLISHER'S NOTE
The scanning, uploading, and distribution of this book via the Internet or via any other means without the permission of the publisher is illegal and punishable by law. Please purchase only authorized electronic editions, and do not participate in or encourage electronic piracy of copyrighted materials. Your support of the author's rights is appreciated.

About the Author

S. M. Harding has been a teacher at grade school, high school and college levels, a cab driver in Chicago, a secretary, an art director and a chef. She started writing fiction in the mountains of northern New Mexico during a long winter when the roads were closed by snow, and has been writing ever since. She lives in Indiana and revels in a retirement that centers on writing, editing and teaching writing.

You can find her at www.smharding.webs.com, www.storytellersfire.wordpress.com, and www.facebook.com/pages/S-M-Harding.

Dedication

For the Bloomers crew of many years ago in Pittsburgh: Kathy, Patty, Sally, M.G., Linda, Deb, and in memory of Gray.

Acknowledgments

My deepest thanks to Bella Books and Linda Hill for not only realizing a dream for me, but for continuing to hold the banner for lesbian publishing; to Karin Kallmaker for plucking this book from the slush pile; to JoSelle Vanderhooft, my editor for her guidance; and designer Linda Callaghan for such a lovely cover.

The one constant in my life since I returned to Indiana has been "In Mysterious Company," a critique group that has shape-shifted a number of times over the last ten years. For all of those who've come and gone, but especially for the core, Diana Catt, Marianne Halbert and David Reddick, I am grateful. I also give my thanks to the Indiana Writer's Center and the Antioch Writers Workshop, Yellow Springs, Ohio, for scholarships that gave me so much: new skills, better craft, and support. My thanks also to early readers Kieran York and Chris Paynter for their encouragement and Lena Smith for her enthusiasm and technical assistance.

If you look at a map of Indiana, you'll never find McCrumb County. It's an amalgam of various areas in the southern part of the state, though certain place names or roads may be familiar. In a like way, the story is set in 2013 before the tide of marriage equality swept across the country. The purpose is for purely dramatic purpose—and the following stories.

I sincerely hope you enjoy this tour through McCrumb County with Sarah and Win.

"Out beyond ideas of right doing and wrong doing, there is a field. I will meet you there."

—Jelaluddin Rumi, *The Essential Rumi*, translated by Coleman Barks

CHAPTER ONE

Sarah

One kiss can change your life.
A soft brush of lips that flames desire for union with the other. Two lives entwining, growing together. All that in one kiss—that both of us drew back from, as if lips had been hot irons. One kiss.
I'm growing weary of this constant contradiction between feeling delicious expansion and fearsome contraction. I dare not breathe.

When people hear the word *sheriff*, they conjure up the romantic haze of gunslingers in the Old West or a posse chasing bandits through the Badlands. But to me, *sheriff* means reams of paperwork to get through every day, a dwindling budget and some sixty people under my command to keep McCrumb County's fifty thousand residents safe. As a third-generation sheriff, the word also signifies power restrained by the law and one hell of a lot responsibility.

A tap on the doorframe and I looked up to see my chief deputy examining the mess on my desk—tons of paper and a dozen file folders.

"Should I come back later?" Caleb asked.

I motioned him to sit. "I've been going over grants—Homeland Security, DOD, the whole damn alphabet of governmental agencies. You think we could use a SWAT team?"

Caleb eased down in the chair, rubbed his jaw. "Honestly, Sarah, we need money to run the department as it is, not military hardware or gung-ho soldiers. Or am I missing something?"

"Grandpa eliminated rank in the department because he didn't want us confused with the military—that's not what or who we are. We're peacekeepers. But we need more deputies on patrol, and the county commissioners aren't going to give us the money. We need to find outside sources, like the federal government."

He looked at me glumly, but then a smile cracked his face. "New hires? Who are on patrol most times, not doing SWAT stuff?"

I grinned back. "I think we can swing it. We have to, because after all this snow, we'll be lucky if the commissioners don't cut more of our budget and send it to Roads. It damn well better stop snowing or we won't have the budget to put any deputies on patrol until summer."

"I think we should take our commissioners on a week of ride-alongs." He shifted in the chair. "You sure we ain't making a deal with the devil?"

"No." I leaned back in my chair and rubbed my neck. "Drugs flood the county, weapons follow. We're already outgunned. I don't know, Caleb. We'll just have to proceed with care."

"Why don't you run the SWAT idea by Win Kirkland? Ex-Special Forces, isn't she? Probably could head the team. At least, might know of some good hires who aren't rabid."

"Uh, that's a thought." I got busy sorting the files into meaningful stacks.

He brushed his mustache. "You *are* running for sheriff again?"

I fussed with the files on my desk. "Haven't really thought about it yet."

"Sarah, you better start thinking real fast. We're getting close to the time when you'll have to declare." He gave me a hard look. "Mac and his crew are running someone. Not Mac."

"Hell. After the disaster Mac made this office, does he really think anyone in the county would vote for his candidate?"

Caleb nodded. "'Cause no one's gonna know he's backing the candidate. We need to get ahead of them."

Caleb rose, put a folder on the edge of the desk. "The week's crime and closure stats. We can't get a new boat for rescue and those commissioners are considering building a fucking ten mil waterpark!"

What could I say? Everybody in McCrumb County knew the commissioners were a band of nitwits—and kept voting them into office. I watched Caleb weave his way through the bullpen and slam into his small office.

I went through the stacks of paper, stuffed all the SWAT material into one folder, then put all of it in my briefcase. Time to go home.

* * *

I drove with one hand on the steering wheel and half a mind on the road. My headlights were small ripples of light that bounced off five-foot snowbanks and made the road feel like a tunnel to Alaska. Maybe it was and if I just kept going, I could mail my badge and all its weight to Caleb with a note: *Run!*

A night like this, cold with snow, Hugh made a traffic stop on I-65. He ended up on the berm, a bloody mess, still bleeding out when Dad found him. Could it really be fifteen years ago? I'd tunneled everything into work, the only area left I had passion for. Was the passion waning?

I slowed, pulled into the rutted drive of the Barrow family homestead. Family legend had it that this was the fourth incarnation, the others burned down by a renegade band of Shawnee, Morgan's Raiders and lightning. Built around what was left after the last fire in the 1880s, it was a nightmare to maintain. But it was home, where I'd come when Hugh died and where I'd stayed when Mom got sick. When she died, I thought I'd lose Dad too, through those long nights when he'd paced through the hours.

I pulled into the area Dad had cleared of snow, turned off the engine and sat. I didn't want to go down this road again, raking through the past to find my present or my future. Screw it all.

When I opened the back door, I was almost knocked off the stoop by the aroma of beef, onions and garlic. I closed the door quickly and got out of my outerwear. I padded into the kitchen in time to see Dad put the lid of the roaster on the counter.

"Smells wonderful. What is it?"

"Braised oxtails."

"Oh wow—it's been ages."

"Yep," Micah said. "Since Lizbeth last made it. Finally found her recipe. Hurry up an' wash up, I'm dishin' up right now."

He could say my mother's name without hesitation, as a familiar landscape of his life, viewed and touched every single day. I still avoided talk of Hugh, as if I inhabited a subterranean chamber that distorted sound. Hell.

After dinner, I handed him the SWAT folder as he popped up his recliner's footrest. As I built a fire, I could hear him flipping through the pages.

"Is it advice you want, Sarah?"

I told him my plan and watched as his eyebrows inched upward. I settled on the couch with the department's budget request, but I couldn't keep the figures in focus. My thoughts kept slipping to Win Kirkland.

I'd known Win since first grade, and as friends do, shared secrets with her. She'd told me she was gay our sophomore year in high school. Win dropped out of college after her freshman year, joined the marines and when she retired from their Intelligence Agency, had come home. She'd also brought the war home in the form of David Paria, who'd tried to kill her. The case had brought us back together.

Last week, she'd invited me to see the new house she'd designed and finally moved into. We'd ended up talking about Hugh. For the first time, I didn't hear the warp in my voice, the reluctance to say his name or tell his death. Win, in return, had given stories of Afghanistan, Iraq, places all over the Middle East and North Africa. Not adventures, but journeys of understanding.

The warmth of the fire in the fieldstone fireplace against the snow outside, the openness of Win's face and the way she listened all combined to make me relax. Not think about work, but to say things I'd only thought.

As I took my leave, we stood at the same height by the door.

"What do you want the next chapter of your life to read?" Win asked.

"No idea, I just keep reading word to word. You?"

"To stop ducking at every backfire. Otherwise, it's a blank page."

We hugged, but instead of stepping back, she pulled me close and kissed me.

"You run this past Win yet?" Dad asked.

His voice shocked me back from a bewildering cascade of feelings. The budget schedule spilled from my lap. "Uh, no."

"Do it, Sarah Anne." He closed the folder. "Got no experience with half of them agencies, you mebbe could pick up a few deputies thanks to the largesse of the United States Government."

He looked at the papers strewn over the couch and floor. "You okay?"

"Budget time. You know I get twitchy." I collected the papers, carefully sorting them into the proper order.

He didn't say anything, just examined my face.

"I'll call Win, see if she can meet tomorrow."

He took off his glasses. "Win's a good woman, smart, big heart. Guess she don't talk much 'bout what she went through, but I reckon the wounds are slow healin'."

"Was she shot?"

"Internal injuries, Sarah. Scars of the psyche." He flicked on the TV. "Be a dang good addition to the constabulary of McCrumb County."

* * *

Win's military bearing brought her into Beans aBrewing with easy strides. She acknowledged me with a nod and made for the counter. She wore her blond hair short and spiky, and I had a feeling she could be prickly as her hair. She would be a formidable foe. Or friend? Had been. Could be again? Or had I ended our friendship with my rapid retreat? Did she think it was a slap at who she was?

I shook my head to clear it. It wasn't like I'd been celibate since Hugh. Why the hell had this one brief kiss shaken me to my root cellar?

The other chair at the table scraped back, and I looked up into eyes as blue as mine. And as searching.

"I want to apologize, Sarah. Not only was I out of line, but I've thrown you a fastball you never saw coming." She took a sip of some variety of latte that smelled like fall. "Anyway, I value our friendship. How easy it was to pick up after all these years. How comfortable it was to talk to you. I had to screw it up. It'll never happen again. Promise."

"Why did you? Kiss me, I mean."

Win ran her hand through her hair. "You looked so alone. I just wanted to…" She wrapped both hands around her coffee cup.

"So, you wanted to run an idea by me? About a SWAT team?"

I exhaled and told her my idea. She said she'd go over the material and asked if I wanted her to write up the grant applications.

"Really? You'd do that?"

"Don't have a lot on the schedule, Sarah. I'll drop them off at the station when I get them finished."

"Sure. Great." I handed her the file folder. "I, uh, I didn't mean to flee. I mean, I didn't even say anything." I remembered my shaky descent of her porch steps, dropping my car keys. I could feel a flush spreading from my neck.

"What would you have said, Sarah?"

"I've no idea."

"Then maybe fleeing was the best thing. We'll keep it business. When I prove true to my word, maybe we can be comfortable again." Win scraped her chair back. "Besides, I never get involved with straight women. Nothing but a whole heap of trouble."

She stood, gave me a small salute and left.

What the hell had she meant, "I looked so alone"? Forlorn? Wimpy? Not the picture I had of myself. Did others see her version or mine? Again, she'd left me disturbed.

I took a sip of coffee. Cold. Batting a thousand. Nothing but distance from Win, cold coffee and budget time. Damn.

Jerry, one of the owners, exchanged my cold cup for a fresh one. "Couldn't figure out if you were going to leave or you just wanted some quiet time before you headed back to work. Sorry to make you wait."

I pulled the fresh cup toward me. "Day off and I just passed off some work. I can loiter."

"Do you always carry a gun?"

I pulled my blazer in place over my shoulder holster. "Yep, part of the job."

"How awful for you because you can never get away from the job. When are you starting your campaign for reelection?"

"Been too busy doing the job to think about it."

He sat in the chair Win had vacated. "Well, I heard the opposition's going to run some Navy SEAL who's going 'to bring the sheriff's department into the twenty-first century.'" He closed the air quote and leaned in. "They say it's pitiful we don't even have a SWAT team."

I drew a deep breath, exhaled slowly. "We're running on a shoestring right now, and until the economy and the weather really turn around, the commissioners have very little to dole out. That's the reality. SWAT teams consume funds we don't have unless we can get outside funding."

"Well, we don't need SWAT people, do we?"

"If drugs keep flooding into the county, we might." I took a long sip, then scooted my chair closer. "I haven't heard about a SEAL running, but I did hear Mac's behind the candidate."

"Rob McKenzie?"

"Shhh. That's for your ears only."

"That awful man. God help us all! He hates gays." Jerry stood. "You know me—the soul of discretion. This news will never pass my lips."

I watched him march back to the counter, the growl from his corduroy trousers increasing with every step. If Mac wanted to play games over law enforcement in McCrumb County, he was going to have to deal with gossip central.

* * *

The completed grant applications landed on my desk two days later. Caleb brought the manila envelope and sat in the visitor's chair. "Win said to tell you, if you got any questions, here's her email address." He handed me a Post-It.

God, she didn't even want to talk to me. I stuck it on my computer monitor. "You have time to go through these now?"

He nodded, and I pulled out the thick pile of paper and handed him half. We read in silence. After two pages, I knew I could never have produced such compelling and cogent reasons for funds. As I worked through the pages, I realized she'd found several grants I'd missed. Damn. Maybe she should run for sheriff. Or had Mac already tapped her talent?

"DOD should love these," Caleb said, sliding his stack toward me.

I handed him my finished reading. "She's done a much better job than I could've."

He scanned a page, flipped it. "Whoa—two Zodiacs. How'd she know we needed a new boat for Water Rescue?"

"Maybe she heard the groans every time we took our boat out. Caleb, I didn't find any way to get the money for one. Here she comes up with an application for two, plus scuba gear and more training."

"When all this snow starts melting, we'll need Water Rescue at peak performance." Caleb rubbed his jaw. "Think we ought to leave the forensic lab in the basement?"

"I've been thinking about that too." I massaged the back of my neck. "That warren of small rooms on the third floor? What if we knocked out a few walls and moved the lab up there?"

Caleb did more jaw rubbing, this time with his knuckles. "We have money for it?"

"Volunteer labor and supplies. I could get Dad started on organizing it."

He grinned. "Let's go up and show me what you're thinking."

I took the rough plans I'd drawn up and rose. "I think Vincente and Leslie should be in on this from the get-go."

Vincente was out on patrol, but Leslie joined us. We spent the next two hours working through the plan, with Leslie throwing in her suggestions. Since she was half of our CSI team, we listened.

"We've gotta get this junk out before we do anything else." Caleb brushed dust off his black uniform. "Shall we?"

By the time I got home, I was covered in dust and achy. We'd moved a ton of stuff down three flights of stairs to our Dumpster.

"You have a rough collar in a bakery?" Dad asked as I hung up my parka.

"You remember the third floor?"

"Oh my." He quickly turned back to the stove and began dishing up.

Over dinner, I explained my plans and asked him if he'd be in charge of the project.

"Depends," he said, beginning to clear the table. "On if you're plannin' on bein' 'round long enough to reap the benefits of such labor." He put the dishes in the sink with a loud *clink* of china. "Signatures is all collected, paperwork all filled out. Waitin' on the dining room table for your signature. All of that paper is goin' into the fireplace tomorrow. You don't want the job, you don't deserve it."

Rage swept over me, churning my stomach, clenching my jaws shut. Didn't *deserve* it? After the years of bone-hard work? The sleepless nights, working or worrying about work? *Deserve?* The hell with it!

I shoved back my chair, left my plates on the table and stomped into the dining room. Without even turning on a light, I scribbled my signature. Threw the pen down and marched upstairs to bed.

The tears came after I'd tucked myself in. I'd always worked so hard to gain Dad's approval, not that he'd ever begrudged it. He'd always given it freely, sometimes lavishly. Okay, it was me, not him. Except, he'd hovered a bit when I first took office, but he'd gradually backed off. Which allowed me to seek his advice from time to time. Ah, pride.

I wiped the back of my hand across my face. He'd said if I didn't *want* it. Did I? I'd kept pushing that question away the whole past year. I felt the weight of that badge every moment I was awake and a few in dreams. When Dad was sheriff, he made time for us that he didn't have. I had no family but Dad. So maybe too much of me got funneled into the badge.

Last year, Dory had taken a long up-and-down look at me from her seat at the dispatch console. "When you gonna get yourself a boyfriend?"

"Too old for boys," I'd replied, blushing.

"Can't grow nothin' in a garden ain't gettin' watered."

I'd walked away from the cryptic comment, didn't ask what she'd meant and didn't want to know. I kept myself wrapped in the cocoon the badge provided. Everyone was distanced by a sheriff's need for neutrality and objectivity to maintain the wall against discrimination.

Is that what made me look so alone to Win? I wished I could ask her.

A tap at the door and it opened. The hall light let a slash of light in. "Sarah Anne? You awake?"

"Dad, I—"

"Just wanted to apologize for rilin' you up so. I surely didn't mean to offend. But your election committee is gettin' a tad bit nervous. 'Fraid you won't run 'cause you got too much sense to suffer 'nother four years of stress an' bein' the butt of ever body's anger and frustration. They wouldn't blame you, neither would I. You do what fits you, Sarah Anne."

"We'll talk about it in the morning."

"Anytime you want to talk, 'bout anythin', I'm here to listen. Good night, Sarah Anne."

The door closed softly and I was left in the dark.

CHAPTER TWO

Win

One kiss can change your life.
Deliciously soft kiss that can ignite two souls, envelope them in that precise moment of longing.
Until the kiss ends. I never meant to stray over the line I'd drawn. Or I would never have drawn it.

My therapist's waiting room was painted a warm gray and the furnishings upholstered in a nubby burgundy material. I liked running my fingertips over the arm, the feel changing as I varied the speed. I never played with the miniature rock-and-sand garden she had sitting on the coffee table, though evidently others did because it had been changed every week I came. Other patients used the tiny rake to quell their anxiety. Establish control. My only impulse was to dump the sand and rocks out the window, toss the black lacquer box and its wee rake back on the table. Control is illusionary.

So I had destructive impulses. Fuck. The world wasn't a sand-filled rectangle that I could comb and make into an ordered beauty. The world was a place of traitors, ambushes. Of exploding human flesh.

Breathe, Win, breathe.

The office door opened and Dr. Emily Peterson leaned out. "I'm ready if you are." She left the door ajar and disappeared into her office.

I followed. Stiffly. I could feel my defenses rushing into action.

Relax, Win, relax.

I took a chair across from her in the cozy conversational area. Her desk was an unobtrusive table and chair by the window. I worked through the relaxation technique she'd taught me. She waited silently until I'd finished.

When I opened my eyes, I found her examining me through half-closed eyes. Some kind of alternative weirdness I didn't understand. But she wouldn't take my bullshit, threw it back at me with her own spin on it. I'd come to trust her.

"Something's happened," she said. "What?"

I nodded. "I'm not ready to talk about it."

"Yet?"

I nodded. How could I talk about a kiss of betrayal?

"Having to do with your war experiences, or something here?"

"Here." Betrayal of a friend.

It was her turn to nod. "We'll put it on the back burner, then. But just be aware, whatever it is, it's big. You can't ignore it. Don't stuff it down." She opened my file. "So, how are the nightmares?"

"They must be getting better because they don't wake me up and I don't remember them in the morning. No night sweats in a month."

"I want you to keep trying to remember them—and control them like I taught you. All that stuff's still there, churning at night. It's good the intensity's gone down. Good you're sleeping through the night. But the shooting's bound to have triggered something, and I want you to be cognizant about that threat."

"I thought we were working to reduce my vigilance."

She stared at me, her eyes growing so dark in the low light they could've been two gun muzzles. "Talk to me, Win."

I looked out the window. "On the day David Paria made his third attempt on my life, I cowered behind a wall, my hands so sweaty I could've dropped the gun. I let Sarah and her dad take all the risk. Micah wasn't even armed. He's in his late sixties, early seventies. He could've had a heart attack."

Emily sighed. "God, it must be comfortable to take all the world's woes and put them on your own back."

"Comfortable? Shit, it's hell. I just feel such goddamn guilt that I put them into that position."

"The same kind of guilt as when you put those Afghani villagers in danger?"

"*Yes!*" Tears came unbidden, rolled down my face untamed. I couldn't control them anymore.

Emily sat with her eyes half-hooded, didn't offer tissues, let me struggle through the surge of guilt and shame.

I gradually calmed down. "I should've told you that before."

"Yes. You want results, for the haunting to stop, but you won't expose the bone. You need to keep your image intact—and I'm telling you right now, you've got to destroy that warrior to become a new one. A whole one. That old image hoards the guilt, drapes it over a shoulder like a cartridge belt. That's what's crippling you." She glanced at the clock. "What I want you to do for homework is to write out the shooting of your would-be assassin. I want you to put in every detail you can remember—sounds, smells, feelings. Email it to me, I want a chance to go over it before we meet next week. We are meeting next week?"

"Yes." I looked at the nubby arm of the chair. "But is that really a good idea? Having to live those moments over and over? Making sure I didn't leave out a floorboard squeak?"

"You're incorrigible. This would be so much easier for both of us if you'd just surrender."

Withdrawal is permissible, surrender isn't. Ever. Well, mostly ever.

* * *

I'd managed to postpone my assignment for two days, but I had no more chores to do. I gathered the tattered remnants of my courage and sat down at the computer to write a police-action shooting. Then I could go back and drop in a few appropriate sensory details.

My hands shook so much that a series of unrelated letters marched across the screen. I hit the Backspace key and erased them all. Why, God, didn't you give us a Backspace key for our lives?

I felt clammy. I got up and fed another log to the fire. Paced from window to window to window. Okay. At least I could put myself back in Sarah's kitchen, eating lunch that day. In silence, both of us wondering what David Paria's next move would be. I sat down again and did deep breathing.

Amid the pops from the fireplace, I heard a truck engine straining up my drive. I went to the window, wondering if I should grab my

Glock. Had a dead Paria sent someone else to kill me? The truck, a new cherry-red F-350 pulled up in front. A beefy man with graying hair got out and looked around. What the shit was this man doing in southern Indiana?

I went to the door, opened it. "General Lester."

He looked up at me. "I'm in civvies, so please call me Scotty."

"Yes sir."

He marched up the stairs, and I closed the door behind him. "Nice spot here," he said as he bent over to pull off his boots, placing them carefully in my boot tray. He padded to the fireplace and held out his hands. "A good place to retire."

"Yes sir. Would you like coffee?"

"Yeah." He followed me into the kitchen area and settled onto a stool at the island. "Real nice place."

I served his coffee, leaned against the counter. When was he going to get to the point of his visit? I waited while he took a sip.

"You healing okay from your wound?"

I nodded. "Back to full mobility. It was a through and through."

"Good. Good." He took another sip. "Miss the action any?"

"No sir."

"Please call me Scotty. I must admit I'm surprised. Adrenaline surges, you feel alive. Hard to get off that particular horse."

I crossed my arms.

"What languages are you fluent in?"

"I think you know that."

He took another sip. "A number of dialects of Tajik and Pashtun, a bit of Turkmen, some Uzbek. That about it?"

"A few more. What is it you want?"

"Want you to come back in the translation section."

"No."

"You could come in as an independent contractor," he said, pushing the mug away. "Good money. What other job could you do now where you'd have seniority, complete autonomy with no one supervising your every move?"

"No. I'm retired."

He stood. "You've already got satellite Internet. We could arrange an encoded uplink, you could work when you wanted."

I glared at him.

"You stay here, we only send you the important stuff. Good offer. At least think about it."

I didn't move, kept my arms crossed and my mouth shut.

As he put his boots on, he looked at me. "I'll be back. Remember, you can always be called back to active duty."

What I'd been waiting for. The threat.

* * *

Most people don't think about drones and collateral damage. But that night, my dreams were an unbroken loop of missiles and fire and the cries of people I knew. The one peaceful spot came when Sarah appeared in the mountain landscape, dressed as an Afghan woman. She reached out her hand to me. As I moved forward to take it, we heard the engine of another drone.

I forced myself awake and found the sheets drenched in sweat. I sat up in the dark, my head held in my hands. Slowed my breathing. More than a month since I'd awakened in a panic, ready to kill. Scotty waltzes in and I'm reduced to a puddle of terror again. No. Not quite right. I'd known I was dreaming and I woke myself up. Maybe there was something to Emily's alternative mumbo jumbo.

As I changed the sheets and took a shower, I tried to form a battle plan. I had one primary ally, Colonel Bill Keller at Camp Atterbury. My old CO. I looked at the clock as I waited for coffee to brew. He'd be up and about by six o'clock and I had his home phone number. But paranoia tapped me on the shoulder. My phone would be tapped. Ditto my computer. How could I contact anyone without some analyst at Quantico writing a summary of the conversation?

I poured a cup, spilling some as my hand shook. Breathe, Win, breathe.

Okay. I could outmaneuver them with older technology. I packed paper and pen in an old backpack, poured the rest of the coffee into a thermos. I checked my wallet for cash, picked up my truck keys and left.

The Rise 'N' Shine diner was one of the few places in Greenglen that still had a pay phone. I wasn't sure it was open until I tried the door. It swung open, and I stepped into a nil zone.

Not one fluorescent tube was on, the whole place small pools of light provided by wall lamps with low-wattage bulbs.

"You come to eat or gawk?" Tillie Dietz, esteemed proprietor, asked.

"Gawk. I've never seen this place with low lighting. Or so quiet." Only four men, each at his own table, and one woman in a back booth.

"Folk don't wanna get sensory overload early in the mornin'. If you were up an' about early, you'd knowed that a long time ago."

"It's nice, Tillie. Actually, I came to use the pay phone."

"Ain't workin'. Think the fancy telephone company gives a damn? 'Course not. Nathan said he'd look at it when he got some time. Ain't holdin' my breath. That boy's out all over the county, fixin' his network problems. Them satellite dishes are kinda fragile." She turned away, then turned back. "Go ahead, use my land line. By the register. Just leave money to cover the call."

I went behind the counter and was treated to a heavy black phone with a handset. The surprise was that it wasn't rotary. I punched in the colonel's number and listened to three, four rings.

"Keller here."

"Bill, it's Win. Sorry to disturb you so early, but Scotty dropped by yesterday."

"The general? Scott Lester?" he asked. "Social call? No, that old buzzard just picks at bones."

"My bones this time." I explained the general's proposal, including the big bucks and secure uplink.

"Sonofabitch."

"I cannot go back. I was just getting past the nightmares and all the other crap."

"Paria's shooting couldn't have helped. Good police action as I read it. You seeing a shrink or somebody?"

"Yeah. Started when I got back." I shifted the phone to the other ear. "I'm thinking the general's put a tap on my phone and computer— and wondering how paranoid I am."

"He might have, Win."

"Anyway, tell him I won't come back. I'm out. He tries to recall me to active duty, I'll eat my gun."

"He threatened that?"

"Yes."

"Rank and all, I can't go at him straight on. But I sure as hell can outflank him." He paused and I could hear liquid poured. "Don't dare hurt yourself, you hear me, Win?"

"Last option, Bill. The very last option."

"It won't come to that. Promise."

"I'll get a burn phone, text you the number."

"Good. I'll stay in touch."

"Thanks, Bill. Thank you."

I set the handset in the cradle and left a five-dollar bill by the phone. My next task was going to take some fortifying, so I slipped into a booth and studied the menu. Tillie took my order, and I eased into my "assignment" by imagining myself in Sarah's kitchen, eating lunch the day Paria came for me.

I saw her face, tension pulling down her eyebrows to a frown. Her strong hands building a BLT in quick, sharp motions. Her glances out the window to the snowy hills beyond, alert for any sound that wasn't part of country living.

Tillie brought my pancakes and the memory vanished. A thought remained: with the arrogance of a battle veteran, I'd counted our arsenal. Sarah had thought about Paria's strategy, trying to move one step ahead of him.

I ate without tasting. When I finished, I pushed the plates aside and got out paper and pen. I didn't have time to screw around with this.

Sarah and I had finished lunch when we heard tires on the frozen gravel of the drive. Sarah cocked her head and said, "Dad's home. I've been wondering where he was." She took her plate to the sink and looked out the kitchen window. She ducked out of sight, told me to get my Glock and stay upstairs. She was grabbing her gear and I didn't know what was happening. But she'd given me an order, so I raced upstairs and got the gun. I heard the back door open, Micah's voice, though I couldn't hear what he said. Then another man's voice. Paria. I crept back downstairs very carefully. I heard Micah say something about "upstairs sleeping." Paria must've asked where I was. I moved to the wall by the door into the kitchen. Stood still. I heard something drop to the floor, bathroom tissue or a head of lettuce. Something soft. Micah groaned. I heard Sarah give the police warning. Two shots. Then she said, "Clear," and I went into the kitchen. Paria was dead.

As I folded the paper and stuck it into an envelope, I thought about what I hadn't written. The terror that had frozen me to the wall before Sarah had said that magic word. *Clear.*

* * *

I glanced at my watch. An hour until my appointment with Emily. Took a sip of coffee.

The day after my visit from the general, I'd tailed her from her office at lunchtime to a sprouts eatery. I waited until she'd ordered, then sat at her table.

"I'm not stalking you," I began. Then I gave her a sketch about the general's pitch. "I know this sounds paranoid, but I think he's probably monitoring my phone and computer. This is a safe number." I handed her the envelope where I'd written my new cell number. "My assignment's in the envelope. I wrote it longhand."

Emily put the envelope in her purse, then scanned my face. "You want an appointment today? I have a cancellation at five."

I nodded and left. That evening we talked about specific techniques to help me handle the extra stress. At my next regular appointment, she assessed my progress with a long series of questions. Then I showed her my old friend's analysis of the wiretaps on my phone and computer. Nathan ran a wireless service in the county. Could've been a world-class hacker but was too honest. "I've been using the computer to write a romance novel."

"Lesbian romance?"

"What else?"

"You think someone reads it?"

"Oh yeah. The guys should get their rocks off on it."

"Is any of it based on your own experiences?"

"No way. Main characters are suburban housewives. Not one gun anywhere around."

Emily laughed. "Oh Lord, Win."

She let me go early, and I felt like she'd let me off the hook. So she could set the hook today and reel me in later?

Fuck. I wished I could surrender. Open up and light those caves where my demons hid. Recognize and name them, then send them on their way.

I glanced at my watch again. Took the last sip of coffee. I drove to the nondescript office mall that housed professionals. I'd no more than opened the waiting room door when Emily opened her door and told me to come on in. My watch said I was a half hour early. I didn't even have a chance to assess the changes in the sandbox.

"Win," she said once we were seated, "we've got four things in play. One, your war experiences—particularly the one that sent you into retirement. Two, the recent attempt at coercion by a high-level marine officer that's got you scared to death." She held up a third finger. "Three, Paria and his plan to kill you. All of them connected to your military duty."

I waited. "And the fourth?"

"Whatever happened after the shooting that you haven't told me one word about. Whatever it is, it scared you and you're grieving it."

She held up her hand like a traffic cop. "That seems to be separate, so when you're ready to talk about it, bring it up."

I squirmed in the chair, played my game with the nubby material. I hadn't forgotten how much the kiss had shaken me. How much I missed Sarah. I'd spent a long afternoon with Nathan, reliving our travails and triumphs as a rural version of the Three Musketeers. It had felt as warm and comfortable as an old quilt.

"But," Emily continued, "I need to know the precipitating incident. What drove you back home. If you can't share that, all I can do is keep the demons at bay from moment to moment."

"I can't talk about it—national security."

"Fuck national security," Emily said. "It's you I'm worried about."

I fought tears and searing pain and a feeling I'd fly apart if I told the story. The silence stretched.

"Your nightmares are about it," Emily said softly.

I couldn't even nod. Swallowed hard. Looked out the window and saw, instead of the snowbanks, mountains of the Hindu Kush where spring had made the sound of water dashing from rock to streambed an enchanting melody. The beauty of the place. The warmth of the people. The tears spilled over and I had no control over them.

"Friendly fire," I forced out. "Fucking friendly fire from some joystick jock in California playing with his fucking drone."

Emily handed me the tissue box.

I took the box, cried like I hadn't done. Ever. When the fit finally abated, I took a deep breath.

"Can you set up the situation for me?" Emily asked. "Without spilling any national secrets."

"Fuck it all. All the fucking games." I took another deep breath, called memories back. "We'd been in a small village in the Hindu Kush—mountains, really high mountains with beautiful valleys. Breathtaking country."

"You were there on assignment?"

"Gathering intel. In an area where Afghanistan, Tajikistan and Pakistan border one another. We ended up using the village as our base about nine months—a long time for one place. But the people took us in, protected us. Good people, had been part of the Northern Alliance."

"You said 'we' and 'us.' Were you part of a team?"

"Three men and me. They posed as three brothers from another village. Depending on the circumstances, I either played the youngest brother or a village widow." I could feel my voice tightening. Tears threatened again.

"The village supported this disguise?"

"Yes."

"With you as both woman and boy?"

"Clothes were a lot alike. Fabric was different. I only put on the boy outfit when we were on ops. Farther up in the mountains, scoping out travel routes. Keeping an eye out for Al Qaeda and the Taliban."

"The villagers viewed you as female? Where did you sleep?"

The crying jag started afresh and I couldn't catch my breath. How the fuck had this woman and her slitty eyes zeroed in on the heart of my pain? The only heart I had left. Fuck her. Fuck this process. I tried to stand but my legs wouldn't hold me. I collapsed in on myself, rocking in the chair, holding myself together with both arms.

"So you didn't billet with the men." Emily left the statement hanging.

I did deep breathing until the room came back into focus. Spit it out, Win, be done with it. "I stayed at a house a widow owned. The widow was Azar. She was so beautiful with these huge eyes. Light hazel, but almost green in some light. She was funny, I don't know how. Deep. We'd talk philosophy stuff, some nights until dawn."

"You developed a relationship with her, a close one."

"No. I fell in love with her and she with me."

I remembered the afternoon when we'd sat beside the stream that eventually flowed into Kowkcheh River. The water moved slowly, tinkled with misappropriated drops. Azar leaned toward me, put her hand on the back of my neck and pulled me into a kiss.

One kiss can change your life.

I pulled myself into the present. In my shrink's office with balled-up tissues cascading off my lap and onto the floor like the snow outside.

"Had you ever been in love before?" Emily asked.

"Maybe. My freshman year in college, but when I dropped out, we drifted apart."

"Nothing in the years between?"

"Too fucking dangerous if I wanted a career. Gays weren't welcome. Remember?"

Emily steepled her fingers, tilted her head. "Were you celibate all those years?"

"Hell no. Some one-night stands—always off base. Quickies in bar bathrooms. Partying when I was on leave."

"Sex without attachment."

"The shadow life has that effect."

"Until Azar?"

I closed my eyes, saw her face again in the soft glow of an oil lamp. "Until Azar."

In the silence, I could hear the traffic outside. An occasional shout. My watch ticking.

"I know this has been rough, Win. You must be exhausted."

"Yes."

I could hear her move in her chair, felt her hands on mine.

"Your nightmares exhaust you at night as much as telling this today, though I don't think you realize it. You're running on empty, Win."

I felt a jolt in my hands, then a steady tingling. I didn't pull back.

When Emily leaned back into her chair, the tingling ceased but I felt...not so dark. Not so heavy.

"I know the painful part of your story is still to be told," she said. "But you made a truly important beginning. Keep doing your exercises. Call if you need an extra session. I'll do anything I can for you. Just ask."

* * *

I white-knuckled it through three days, but the third night made it unbearable. Every part of my life entered the dreamscape of explosions and fire. I recognized a young girl kneeling in the dirt, sobbing, as the version of Sarah I'd met in first grade. Annie, my first lover, terrified and on fire. Micah, one of the village's casualties, his skin seared. Women officers I'd known, biblically and to salute. All maimed by missile after missile. The bombardment wouldn't stop.

Even in the daylight, these wraiths would float at the periphery of my vision. All in tattered clothing, all bloodied and burned, all begging for me to stop the attack.

I punched in Emily's number, waited through a couple of clicks.

"Doctor Peterson."

"I need to see you."

There was a pause. "Do you realize it's Sunday?"

"No. Crap. I'm sorry. I'll call back—"

"Hold on, Win. I was just leaving for the *dojang*. Could you meet me there in two hours?"

"You do tae kwon do?"

"For a long time. You know where Kim's is? Walnut Street, south of Market?"

"Okay." Weird place for therapy.

"Wear sweats and bring a change of clothes." She disconnected.

What the hell? She thought she'd beat the demons out of me? Good luck, Emily. I showered and searched for a sweatshirt that didn't say USMC. Didn't find one.

I walked into the *dojang* at one on the nose. The large room, painted white with a shining hardwood floor, seemed to dwarf a tiny, older man dressed in his *dobok*. I wondered if this was Mr. Kim and if he was the *kwan-jang-nim*. The grandmaster. The one who could flick an attacker away as if a pesky fly. He bowed and I responded.

"Emily will be out soon," he said in slightly accented English. "I give her one good workout." He smiled.

I didn't need to be polite to this man, I needed to rant at Emily, throw the damn sandbox out the damn window. She'd raised the demon, now she needed to slay it.

"You do tae kwon do."

From his inflection, I couldn't tell if it was a question or a statement. "A little. I've moved around a lot, so I've never studied with one teacher for very long."

"Could be good. Could be disaster." He shrugged and smiled.

"Good, you're here," Emily said, emerging from a door at the back of the room. She wore a sweatshirt and jeans and carried a gym bag. She dropped it by the door and walked over. "This is Mr. Kim, our *kwan-jang-nim*. I thought some strenuous exercise might help you."

"You want a match?"

"Mr. Kim has agreed to give you a workout. He's promised not to hurt you."

I knew the appearance of a *kwan-jang-nim could* belie tremendous skill and power, but the top of Mr. Kim's head came to my breasts. Christ, all I wanted to do was talk. I peeled off my coat, shoes and socks and met Mr. Kim in the center of the room. We bowed and I thought I heard him say "Good luck."

Luck! In the next forty minutes, I landed only one kick and two punches that were only semideflected. I'd needed an army of flying legs and feinting fists.

He bowed again at the end, not a hair out of place, not a breath that needed to be pulled into burning lungs. "You pretty good. Come to class, I make you better." He smiled again and left through the door Emily had come through.

I leaned over, hands on my knees and breathed.

"You're quite good," Emily said. "I've never seen anyone land anything on him. Go shower, then I'll feed you."

I followed her Jeep to a tree-lined street at the edge of town. She pulled into the driveway of an extended A-frame with weathered cedar shingles. No restaurant I'd ever visited. Home? I pulled in behind her and followed her into the house. It smelled of woodsmoke and fresh-baked bread.

"I never bring clients home," she said, hanging her jacket on a coatrack made of antlers. "You're the exception because you made it through three days on your own and then had the sense to call. I really didn't want to go to the office." She took off her boots, walked into the kitchen.

I left my parka and shoes by hers, gawking at the house as I followed. It was as if two other A-frames intersected the primary one. The interior was mellow pine boards soaring up to intersecting ridge beams.

She turned up the gas under a large pot and began to pull bowls and plates from a cupboard. "I was letting the soup simmer, shouldn't be but a moment."

"Can I help?"

"No. Sit." She motioned to a kitchen table that reminded me of Sarah's.

I sank into a chair and realized how tired I was. No solid sleep in four nights and the wraiths chasing me during the day.

Emily brought two plates to the table and a breadboard with what looked like a home-baked loaf. "You bake too?" I asked.

"No, my partner's the baker. She's teaching a seminar this afternoon and won't be home until six or so." She brought two steaming bowls. "So we'll have time to do some good work."

Until I sipped the first spoonful of soup, I hadn't realized how hungry I was. I wolfed it down along with three pieces of bread.

Emily brought me a second helping. "How long since you've eaten?"

I shook my head. "No idea. I remember grabbing a burger on the way home from your office."

The carbs hit as we cleared the table, and my eyelids wouldn't stay open.

"No you don't," she said, rinsing the china quickly. "We've work to do. Just pretend you're on guard duty."

She led me into a study lined from floor to ceiling with bookcases. What looked like a massage table stood by the window.

I sat on a couch and leaned back. "The nightmares have been horrible. Same scene, but just about everybody I've ever known is running or on fire or dead. Even Micah."

"Sarah's dad?"

"Yes." I took her through all the scenes I remembered, each face I recognized. Begging for the barrage to stop.

"Interesting. The night of the drone attack—it *was* a drone?"

I nodded.

"That night, how many missiles were fired?"

"Two."

"Were you ever engaged in an artillery barrage?" She looked up at me. "I began life as an army nurse. Desert Storm."

Surprise. Then she had a hint of what combat was like. "At the beginning of the war, I was in a team that was spotting artillery fire. One of our guys screwed up the coordinates and they hit our own men."

She pulled her feet up under her in the chair. "Another case of friendly fire. Do you see why they're related in your dreams?"

I felt sick. Neither occurrence had been my fault. Not that it helped. The California jock had inverted numbers. He was supposed to hit a village on the other side of the mountain.

"Was anyone on your team injured by the drone attack?"

"Two seriously enough we had them airlifted out. Nolan went with them."

"So, on both occasions, men were seriously injured and you remained unscathed?"

I nodded. "Please don't hand me that crap about survivor's guilt."

"It's not crap. You saw your own side injured twice when you were supposed to be handling intel. Why the hell wouldn't you feel guilty?"

Fuck it all, I could feel myself slipping into the cave of the demons.

"Win, it's not weird that you've transferred some of the guilt you felt from the barrage to the drone attack. Whatever residual feelings you had from the first misdirected attack superimposed itself on the drone attack. Can you understand? Images you saw the first time seeped into what you dream about the second attack."

"What difference does it make?"

"Once you really understand that, you can control the dream. You can say to yourself, 'No, that doesn't belong here.' The extra carnage *will* go away."

"Don't I need a magic word? Shazam!"

Emily stared at me. Eyes wide open.

"Okay, okay. I see the logic."

"Perhaps you'll be fortunate enough to experience the logic." She shifted her feet to the other side. "Azar died in the drone attack?"

I squeezed my eyes closed and nodded. Couldn't stop. I heard her move, felt her weight on the cushion next to me. An arm around me. "I'm so sorry, Win."

I grabbed her shoulder and couldn't control the sobs that racked my whole body. I held on tight for a long time. Finally I leaned back and wiped my face with the backs of my hands.

"Exhausted?" she asked.

"Utterly."

"Go ahead and stretch out." She rose and spread a blanket over me.

"You'll sleep now. Without the nightmare. But remember, you have the ability to control the outcome of your dreams."

"Can I bring Azar back to life?"

CHAPTER THREE

Sarah

I drove back to Greenglen in the thin sunlight of early spring. We weren't quite to the budding stage for trees, but there was a green fuzz around them if you squinted. I had the window open, and the smell of fresh-turned earth filled the cruiser. I watched a great blue heron swim majestically across the sky and knew spring had formally arrived.

I hadn't seen Win alone since our coffee meeting, but I couldn't get her out of my mind. I'd started fantasizing about what it would've been like if I hadn't fled. Maybe, if I sprung a surprise visit on Win at her house, we could talk about what had happened.

My phone rang and I pulled onto the berm. Dispatch wanted me back ASAP. Dory didn't say much except she had a victim in my office who needed to report a rape. "Her older sister brought her in, and the girl's ready to bolt."

"ETA ten minutes," I said, pulling back on the road. "Anybody leaves, it's on your head, Dory."

I watched the landscape pass, thinking there was little evidence to the heavy snows we'd had. The floods had come, not as bad as we'd feared because the thermometer bounced between periods of twenty degrees and fifty. The Zodiacs had arrived in time too. Blew everyone in the county away. Though generally well-intentioned, the federal government never responded promptly to anything resembling a grant.

I'd called Win to thank her and ended up leaving a rambling message. Though she'd been scarce around Greenglen, I often found myself wondering about what combat had done to her, how many friends she'd lost. I worried that David Paria's shooting had set her back. Win had seemed fragile when she'd come into the kitchen, her hands wrapped around the Glock, trembling just a tad.

Counseling was finished now for me. I'd had no second thoughts about putting two bullets into a man who'd walked into my house with my dad as hostage and revenge killing on his mind. Em had let me go after two sessions.

My life now was full of breakfast, lunch or dinner with Rotarians, Lions, Elks, Masons, Shriners, Knights or Oddfellows and every other organization the county produced. I could run through my stump speech without thought. Dad said that was a dangerous condition. I handed out a sheet of crime statistics at every meeting. That's what I wanted them to concentrate on: some crime had gone way up, but so had our arrest rate. Not hard after Mac's term.

Mac's secret candidate was indeed a former SEAL, but Mac's backing wasn't secret anymore. I'd told the editor of the Greenglen *Sentinel* that he really should hire Jerry or the talents of one of the best gossips in the county could be put to nefarious purposes. The SEAL turned out to be Willy Nesbit, a quiet man built like a bulldozer. I had no doubt he could run special ops, but the day-to-day running of the sheriff's office seemed beyond his ken. Besides, he hadn't lived in McCrumb County for thirty years. All I could do was do my job to the best of my ability, speak the truth and let the voters decide.

I slowed down at the edge of town, waited impatiently for one traffic light and pulled into my spot behind the department. As I walked down the hall, Dory intercepted me.

"Little girl's destroyed, Sarah. She don't know what happened, got no memory of the night."

"Then how do you know a rape happened?"

"It's all over Facebook. Kids posted pictures on her wall, sister took 'em down, but they got shared all over."

"Damn. She has no memory? She was drunk?"

"You need to ask her, but as far as I know, she's a good girl with good grades and a future. Oh, and in case you need a blood draw, the EMTs are eating our doughnuts in the break room."

"A blood draw? For alcohol level?"

"That and roofies."

Dory left me standing in her dust as she galloped off to save the damsel in distress. All that was missing was "Hi-yo, Silver." I just hoped this case didn't involve a sports team and YouTube videos.

When I entered my office, I saw a teenaged girl curled up in a visitor's chair and an older version perched on the arm talking to her quietly. A kind of rhythmic chant.

"I'm Sheriff Pitt. Call me Sarah." I eased down into the other visitor's chair. "What can I do for you?" God, I sounded like the greeter at Wally World.

"I'm Brittany Elder and this is my sister Natalie. She went to a party last night. There were these awful pictures on her Facebook timeline this morning. She was raped at the party."

Natalie started crying and didn't try to wipe away the tears. She buried her face in her sister's shoulder.

"Has she been to the hospital?"

"No, I brought her straight here."

"We need to get...her there right now. We've got an ambulance on site, we can go now. Okay?"

"No," Natalie said. "I just want to die."

I looked at Brittany, waiting for her to understand the urgency in my message. She nodded and helped her sister from the chair. I motioned to Dory, who'd been hovering. In ten minutes, the sisters were headed out and I was behind them.

I needed to talk to the older sister alone, get some facts and permissions. But she seemed to be the only thing holding Natalie together. I wondered where the parents were. When I walked into the ER, I saw Brittany standing outside a curtained cubicle.

"They won't let me stay with her," she said as I approached.

"I know it's hard, but it doesn't take much time." I pulled her a little farther away. "I need some facts. Where was the party?"

"I never should've let her go, but she's such a good kid. I never—"

"Stay with me, please. Whose house? What's the address?"

She gave me the information while she periodically looked over her shoulder.

"Where are your parents? Have you notified them?"

"No. I didn't call them because they're at a trade show that's really important for their business. They'll be home tomorrow." She hugged herself. "I'm twenty-one, so I've been signing all the paperwork."

"Brittany, I need permission for our computer consultant to go in and document the photos you took down from your sister's page. It's important evidence. Will you sign a release form?"

"She can't see those—"

"No one will. He won't repost them, just retrieve them for the investigation. We need the evidence." I opened my folio, handed her the release form and held my breath. She didn't take time to read the document, just scribbled her signature. I'd have to do this again when the parents got home since she wasn't a legal guardian. "Tell me about last night. Were you home?"

"No, I was on a date. But I told Nat to call if she needed a ride or anything. If something went wrong."

"She didn't call?"

Brittany shook her head. "When I got home, I checked on her. She was in bed, asleep."

"What time was this?"

"Around one thirty."

"How did she get home?"

"She has no memory. Somebody brought her home, put her to bed. I've no idea who. Nat didn't know anything was wrong until she woke up. She hurt and her underwear was missing. Oh, God, I should've—"

"Hey, you're her one support right now. You don't have the time for blame or guilt. You need to keep it together. Can you do that?"

She nodded.

The curtain opened slightly and a nurse motioned to me. "Her genitals are pretty messed up. We're going to have to take her to surgery."

"God." My stomach flipped. "I won't try to talk to her now, but let the office know when she's out of surgery and is able to have visitors." I turned to Brittany. "Stay with her as much as you can and let her find you there when she wakes up. Here's my number, call if you need anything."

I drove back to the office in a rage, but I should've saved it for the photos I saw. John Morgan, my head detective, had searched other pages and places for photos and found plenty. I looked at the images he'd compiled as a slide show.

"At least five boys raped her, but they're all wearing the same ski mask. We decided on five from body build and body hair. Then they started getting pretty damn sick."

I couldn't take more. "Here's the address where the party took place. Find the location where these were taken and get the CSI unit on it. Search for the ski mask. We need a list of people who were at that party and then their cell phones or cameras. I'll see warrants are waiting for you."

"I can't believe our kids are capable of this kind of shit," he said as he turned to leave. "Do they really think this is cool?"

* * *

Sick. That was the word that described these kids, those who did it and the others who stood by and didn't stop it. *Sick.* The other meaning reflected the feeling I and my deputies had, that stomach-churning experience of complete and utter disgust. Pain and humiliation dealt in public was something high school kids shouldn't have to face, ever.

I'd called Natalie's mother, met her at the hospital when she'd arrived that night. She'd been very gentle with both girls. I asked Natalie for a statement, but the memory she had left was fragmentary at best. She'd asked for a cola, received it in a plastic cup with ice. She remembered a ski mask lunging, a horrible green-and-purple knit. She remembered sounds. I left the three of them crying, holding on to one another.

We were now four days into the full-out investigation, and we'd made progress. Leslie had found the ski mask, taken it to a lab at Indiana University and stood by to witness the initial testing. We couldn't afford cross-contamination or any other legally questionable occurrence. Ditto on the rape kit. Results on both would take another week. Leslie analyzed the blood draw, found no alcohol but a Special K cocktail. Ketamine, the animal tranquilizer, had immobilized Natalie.

Meanwhile, John and another detective had gotten a somewhat complete list of partygoers, pulled more photos from those Facebook pages and had begun to both question the kids and collect images from cell phones. Part of what John was doing was trying to reconstruct a timeline for the party and identify the watchers.

I found myself wanting to choke the kids who sat across the table from me in the interrogation room. Their parents and lawyers too. Caleb and John felt the same. It was so hard to keep the disgust from our voices, and sometimes we didn't succeed. Lloyd Dowd, the *Sentinel*'s editor, had kept the lid on it, but gossips hadn't.

I felt like I'd fallen into a pile of coyote shit.

The campaign appearances I made felt the same way. Of course I couldn't talk about an ongoing investigation, but that didn't stop the questions. It was a delicate balance. I didn't want to be accused of sweeping this under the carpet, but I didn't want to go public until the DA was ready to prosecute the case. Cases. Theoretically, a number of these kids could be charged with disseminating child pornography since Natalie was underage.

In the office, I tried to maintain objectivity, but Jesus Christ! I knew the kids were defensive because they understood what they'd done was monstrous, but I'd moved from wanting to throttle them to a great desire to pound their heads on the table, walls and floor.

Meanwhile, McCrumb County bloomed its glory. Redbud trees splashed small swaths of magenta through the light green forests. Daffodil, crocus, forsythia and hyacinth had begun to joust for attention in people's yards. Tulips and flags would come later. Even the air smelled new. To cleanse myself, I walked at lunchtime, visited the creek on our farm after work.

"We've got one of them," John said as he entered my office. He plopped down an open yearbook on my desk, his finger on the picture of a wrestling match. "I think." He pointed to a large scar on the thigh of one contestant, then laid a photo from the rape next to it. Same scar. "Enough for probable cause?"

"Yes. I'll walk it over to the courthouse right now. I want the damn judge to see the goddamn rape pictures."

* * *

It had taken damn good work from the detectives, but we had five suspects and enough evidence to get DNA testing done. When the matches were made, I'd take the case to the prosecutor.

Natalie refused to go back to school. I didn't blame her.

I went to bed early one night, worn out by all the stress of preparing for a trial. Waiting for the media to pick up on the charges. Mom wouldn't have called it stress. Mimicking Dad's accent, she would've said, "You're just plumb tuckered out from worry."

I jerked awake around three a.m.

I'd been dreaming. A party with loud music? I'd dreamt I couldn't move, felt like I was going to pass out. Someone helped me into a bedroom. David Paria. He stood at the end of the bed and began to undo his belt.

I controlled my racing heart and said out loud, "Paria, you're dead." I slipped back into an uneasy sleep, afraid to go too deep.

As I drank my morning coffee, I mulled over the dream. I understood what it was about: powerlessness. But I also knew I had not only the power to stop a rape but the power to end a life. With power came responsibility, a weight that was always with me.

I would've waxed philosophical about it except I had the same nightmare for the following two nights. The fourth morning, I called Emily and asked for an appointment. The problem for me wasn't understanding the symbolism, it was stopping the nightmare.

She gave me a slot late that afternoon without asking any questions.

I sat in Emily's waiting room, playing with the sand-and-rock garden on the coffee table. Someone had made a squiggle through the space, and raking the sand back to its pristine condition seemed soothing to me. Emily opened her door and beckoned me in. I made two final neat rows with the rake and walked to the open door.

I sat in the comfy chair and took a deep breath. "I'm having nightmares, well, one nightmare three nights in a row."

"Seems to be going around. We may have to smudge the whole county," she said, opening her notebook. "So tell me what it's about."

I did. "I know this is about stress. We've had a rape case, really brutal multiple rape. When the charges are made, it's going to be a media circus. That stress combines with shooting Paria, and so I dream Paria raping me. I just want to know how to stop it."

"So you've gotten your shrink degree when I wasn't looking?" She scowled at me, then flipped a couple of pages in her notebook. "Any other stressors in your life?"

Win, but that was another issue altogether. "No. The job is the producer of stress."

"All the time?"

"It's a ton of responsibility."

"What about campaigning?"

"What about it?"

"God, Sarah, you came in here looking for a pill that doesn't exist. Oh, I could give you something that would knock you out for the night, but that's not a resolution."

"Hell, Em, they're just dreams. Can't you teach me how to stop them?"

"It's not just a dream, it's your anxieties slipping out because you won't acknowledge them. Now, answer my question. How do you feel about the campaign?"

I sighed as noisily as I could. "I like talking to people, but I hate the idea of a campaign. Why, if I'm doing a good job, should I have to take time away from the job to convince a bunch of people that I'm doing a good job? It's stupid."

Emily laughed. "So you want to be installed as the sheriff-until-you-get-tired-of-it? Sarah, didn't you want to run for another term?"

"I really hadn't decided and time ran out."

"What a load of bullshit. You've known for the past three years you'd have to run again. So what'd you do—flip a coin?"

"Not funny, Em."

"Wasn't meant to be." Emily closed her notebook, eased back in her chair. "Who's your best friend?"

I blinked. Emily sure was good at throwing curve balls. "Dad, I guess."

"You couldn't disappoint him?"

I shook my head. "That's probably part of it, but I do a damn good job. Some days, it's just overwhelming and it seems like all I'm doing is sticking a finger in the dike, waiting for the next leak."

"The weight of responsibility," Emily said, nodding. "If it's twenty-four-seven, it's too much. You take days off?"

I nodded. "Tuesdays."

"Who do hang out with?"

"Um, Dad. I had a good time at Win's. She's built a beautiful cottage up on Tyler's Ridge." Wrong direction. "Mostly I sleep in late, do chores and read."

"You and Win getting reacquainted?"

I wished we could, but that seemed overwhelming too. "I haven't spent time with Win since I visited her new house but I keep meaning to give her a call."

Emily stared at me, her eyes at half-mast. "Mmm. There's a few techniques I'll give you for controlling the dream."

CHAPTER FOUR

Win

The spring sun felt so good on my arms and neck as I dug a garden, the loamy smell reminding me of home and planting the garden each spring. Mom had despaired of keeping me in clean clothes. The earth between my toes and caked on the knees and seat of my jeans had never felt dirty. I thrilled at the first green sprouts, mourned at a late frost, reveled at each new miracle of spring.

I glanced at the sun and figured I had a good three hours before I was due for my appointment. Emily said we were making progress, though it was going to be a long road. I still had some nightmares, but I was getting better at reeling them back. Herding them in another direction.

I'd slept twenty-four hours straight after my dissolution that winter Sunday. Emily's partner, Marty, woke me up, showed me to the bathroom. Then they fed me dinner. When I left their home, I felt a tad bit human again.

Also sore. A week later, I'd taken Mr. Kim's offer, signed up for class. He'd put me in an intermediate class, which dealt my pride a major blow. "You have problem with some of form. Too many teachers. We straighten out quick enough." He gave me a wide smile, signed me up for the tai chi class his daughter taught. "Moving meditation good for person who cannot sit still. Whatever form, mind is at center of practice."

I placed the spade again, pushed it into the earth with my foot. A simple pleasure. Turning earth. Turning it over.

I was beginning to see connections. Some of my fault lines that shifted and rubbed together. Some stuff got pushed up by sheer force of movement by my tectonic plates. Like David Paria's arrival on my home turf. The same forward movement shoved it way below consciousness. Azar's death. What was grinding its way to the surface now had always been there. Buried. Waiting. Either to rise or sink when pressure built too much, when the movement of the plates increased.

I turned the earth, broke up the clod. Bill had been true to his word and outflanked the general. For now. Calls from first Bill, then Nathan, assured me the taps had been removed. For how long? I didn't trust the general. He was known for getting what he wanted.

With the taps gone, I'd quit writing the novel. When I'd told Emily, she'd surprised me.

"Good," she'd said. "You don't need to create fictional relationships as much as you need to create real ones here. There are some groups in Bloomington—"

"I'm not a groupie. I spent too long living in one humongous group. I enjoy the solitude."

"Do you?" Emily got up, pulled a postcard from a slot on her desk and handed it to me. "Marty and I have other plans, but you might enjoy this."

I read the invitation to a reading and book signing. Flipped it over. "At a bar?"

"In case you haven't noticed, most women's bookstores have closed. A lesbian author goes where her people are." She went to a bookcase and handed me a battered trade paperback. "She's good— knows how to write sex *and* relationships."

I'd gone to the reading and discovered how far off my game I'd gotten. I was used to cool-walking into a bar, selecting a partner and leaving with her after a couple of drinks. I'd lost my strut. I eased into the bar, perched on a barstool and kept my gaze on the bowl of peanuts.

I imagined a conversation.
"What do you do?"
"Um, retired."
"Well, what did you do?"

"I can't talk about that."

"Oh, okay."

End of conversation. My imagination had never done this to me before. I'd always been able to imagine what a woman would be like in bed after the first sentence she said. What she'd like. What would move her. I'd never imagined a fizzle.

The bartender brought me a beer and told me if I'd come for the reading, it was in the back room. Instead of the small room with a single lightbulb and crates of booze piled along the walls I imagined, I walked into a light, airy room that opened onto a back patio. Not one case or keg. Just stackable chairs in semicircular rows around a table.

I took a seat in the last row and sipped my beer. A petite woman was introduced, and I was surprised by her deep voice. Her first reading was hot. I could tell by the heavy breathing around me. The second, a twist in the love two women shared, choked me up.

I pushed my spade into the earth with all the force I could muster. I'd talked to a couple of women after the reading, didn't flirt. Didn't want to. I'd come home alone but with three more of her novels.

Turning it over.

* * *

I handed the borrowed book to Emily, sat down. Mentally started pacing. "You know, I used to be able to walk into a bar and pick up any woman I wanted."

"That's a good thing?" she asked, placing the book back in its place.

"Obviously."

She sat in her chair and stared at me.

"What? If I'd had an affair and been caught, I wouldn't be retired now. I'd be unemployed."

"You're talking about using women for your own pleasure. Not to mention objectifying them—pick something off the rack and wear it once. You donate to Goodwill?"

"Mutual pleasure. I always gave as much as I got." I crossed my legs. "What's this got to do with anything? You can't tell me when you were in the army, you didn't have a fling or two."

"I think you're full of shit."

I could feel the slap of her words and felt my face redden.

After five minutes, she broke the silence. "I think your college sweetie leaving you *hurt*. The first one always leaves the deepest scars because you've gone out on a limb. Then you found yourself in a macho culture. Love 'em and leave 'em. Girl in every port. You became a player. Well, Win, the game's over."

She let the silence absorb her words.

"Now that you can't use the military excuse anymore, you're bewildered. Wake up. You're a middle-aged woman, and you no longer have to fear exposure. The restraints are gone."

I stared at the carpet. It was nubby too.

"Look at me, Win. You fell in love. Yes, it ended tragically, but you found out what real intimacy is. Along with Azar's death, you're mourning the loss of that divine closeness with another human being. The old pickup routine isn't going to work anymore. It's not what your soul craves."

I met her gaze. "Do I have a soul?"

"Do you feel like you've lost it?"

"Yes."

Emily leaned forward. "Since when?"

I shrugged. "Since my first tour in Afghanistan. So much suffering. The women. Children. There wasn't a damn thing I could do about it. I had a mission. Orders. No time for hearts and minds."

"Do you feel you regained a bit of your soul in Azar's village?"

"Yeah. But then it got bombed."

* * *

Ruby Slippers was so different from the gay bars I frequented when I was young. The "back room" held a reading nook, complete with bookcases and a few comfy chairs. Who'd come to a bar to read? Evidently, a lot of these folk. The chairs were occupied both times I'd come.

Since the weather had warmed, I headed for the back patio. Julie, one of the co-owners, took my order for a burger and beer. She was one of those short, wiry women whose upper arms looked like taut ropes. I scanned the space for someone I'd met, but didn't recognize any of the half-dozen or so women. I leaned back in the chair, closed my eyes and felt the warmth of the sun like an embrace.

I felt a shadow and opened my eyes. Julie with my order. She surprised me by taking a seat next to me. "So, what do you do, Win?"

"Retired." I took a bite of the burger.

"Oh." She tilted her head. "From what?"

I finished chewing. She waited. "Marines."

Her eyebrows rose. "I know it's fashionable to say 'Thank you for your service.' But I really mean it. My sister was in the navy. She couldn't take it, didn't reup."

Before she could ask me where I'd served and what I'd done, I took the lead. "I know you're one of the co-owners, but who's the other?"

"James Gorman. He does the guy side, I do our side. Especially the programming."

"How'd you get into the business?"

She sighed. "I started at Olivia Records. Assistant to an assistant. But after a while, I helped book their artists' tours. Learned a lot about the bar business along the way. So when Olivia switched to the travel business, I took my money and opened this place with James."

"Why Bloomington?"

"Active women's scene and warmer winters than Ann Arbor. Since you want a bio, I'm single. My longtime lover missed the mountains, so she went back to Idaho."

I wiped my mouth with my napkin. "Not exactly a friendly place for gays."

"She won't be back."

I wadded up my napkin. "Sounds like it's still a sore spot."

Julie scowled at me. "I just have a prickly personality."

I laughed. First time in a long time. Shit, it felt good. "I'm going to have to remember that line. Works good—admit it before someone accuses you of it."

Julia's scowl turned into a mini-grin. "So, are you single?"

I nodded.

"I have to stick around for another couple of hours. Can you wait? We could go over to my place. I could fix you, er, something to eat."

"I just ate."

"Not what I have to offer." She waggled an eyebrow.

"Uh, I'm not looking for that kind of dessert, though I thank you for the invitation." I realized I wasn't looking for an easy score. Amazing.

Julie had been looking at me with her head tilted and one eyebrow lifted.

"Any good movies in town?" I asked. "I'd be up for a movie."

Her eyebrow rose more. "You don't look like a take-it-slow kinda girl."

"Well, I am." At least, I wanted to be. "If you're looking for an easy fuck, you'd better find someone willing."

"*Reaching for the Moon* is playing at the LGBT student center. Interested?"

I nodded. As she walked away, I wondered what I'd gotten myself into.

CHAPTER FIVE

Sarah

The glare from the TV cameras was blinding. I was grateful Tod Morrow, our prosecutor, made the statement and answered most of the questions. Standing on the courthouse steps, I watched the late spring clouds scudding across the blue sky, I wanted to be anywhere but here.

Tod finished answering his question, and one of the Indy reporters yelled, "Sheriff. Sheriff Pitt—how do you feel about the boys involved?"

The question took me aback. I took a moment to step to the microphones. "Feel? If you were a law enforcement officer, you'd understand what I'm going to say. We see any number of major crimes in our careers. It is our job to discover the perpetrator and find the evidence to bring charges and convict. We do our job. Where I have feelings? For the victim of that crime. For how one moment can change a life, and not just for the victim, but for the family and friends. A crime makes deep ripples in a community that can continue for years. That's what I *feel*."

Tod gave me a nod. "Thank you. That's all for now."

We turned and walked back into the courthouse and his office.

"What a left-field question. A damn paparazzi question for a crime so grievous," I said.

"I'm glad he didn't ask me. I didn't know I could feel such rage." He opened his office door for me, then sat down at his desk and sighed. "I wonder if Natalie can ever get over it. Not like the old days when photographs moved from hand to hand in a small circle. That girl's never going to find a place safe from her story."

I understood only too well what he meant. We'd pulled all the photos we'd found, but the possibility of missing some still lurked. I just wanted to run away from the whole sick business.

"Think I can sneak out the back door?" I asked, fingering the bill of my ball cap.

"Good luck. I plan to camp in here until all the reporters leave."

When I got to the back door, I put my cap on and removed my jacket. I made a head-down beeline for the Rise 'N' Shine, went through to the back alley and rapidly made my way to the back door of the sheriff's station. I met Caleb in the hall.

"How'd it go?" he asked.

"Tod did most of the talking. Anything happening here?"

Caleb shook his head. "Real quiet. When those kids turn themselves in, I suspect things will pick up considerably."

"I'd like to be gone by then." I felt like I'd done nothing these past weeks but live this case. I needed to be out walking the woods, listening to the whisper of the trees. Not living in the sordid depravity of my species.

He must have felt my restiveness. "Go home. Get some R&R. For once, don't check in tomorrow, Sarah."

I nodded, turned on my heel and headed for my car. I opened the windows and turned up the volume on the oldies station. The trees had unfurled their leaves, and a breeze excited their newfound freedom. Streams had returned to their beds and sparkled like fireflies at night. By the time I got home, I felt like I could breathe again.

I peeled off my uniform, put on old jeans and a soft cambric shirt. I left the tail out. Freedom could be found in small things. I headed out and down to the creek. I stepped carefully through the underbrush until I came to the rock that overhung the water. I settled on it, grateful that the sun had warmed it. I lay back so I could see only trees and sky.

The last few weeks had been brutal. Poring over photos no one should see, to identify bystanders and perpetrators, had made us all psychological messes.

Nathan shook his head when he brought in prints of the photos. Hard evidence. He'd pulled all the photos he'd found, put them in a virtual locked vault. We'd done the same with cell phones before returning them. "Going up north for a sweat lodge. Don't think I'll ever feel clean again," he'd said.

But the memory of the images would remain. For us, for the kids involved and for Natalie Elder. The worst were of the objects they'd placed in her vagina.

I was so weary of feeling dirtied, I was tempted to strip off my clothes and jump in the creek for a cleansing ceremony. But we had months to go before the trial, months of dealing with an exploitive press.

I had to stop thinking about the case. This was part of what I'd tried to explain to Emily. The kind of horrific crimes we had to investigate, the effort it took to rein in explosive emotions and keep to the facts. Especially when the facts were previously unenvisioned, even in nightmares.

I rolled my sleeves up and reached over to trail my hand in the water. The patterns of leaves and limbs shifted every moment as the current rippled over underwater barriers. If I was to heal from this, I'd have to learn to move around the barriers.

My mind drifted to Win. I'd stopped daydreaming about her, so the attraction grew in dreams. Erotic dreams where she'd explored the contours of my body. I didn't remember a face, so it could've been anyone. No, the hands were Win's.

I rolled onto my back and closed my eyes. I didn't know how I felt about the dreams. Should I be shocked at my response? It had felt so right. Had Natalie's rape skewed my attitude toward men? That didn't feel right. But who knew?

I could feel Win's kiss again, and this time, I didn't back away.

* * *

"Do you do, uh, cleansing ceremonies?" I asked. I'd felt better for a few days following the afternoon I'd fallen asleep on the rock, but since then the media coverage had exploded. "Nathan did a sweat lodge and seems to have regained balance."

"But you haven't?" Emily asked.

I swiveled my chair around to look out the office window to the square. Then untangled the cord from my land line. "I don't think any of my deputies who've dealt with the case have. Me included."

"How are the nightmares?"

"Your technique actually works. Every time it begins, I take it to another place."

"How often does it appear?"

I sighed. "I don't know. Not that often."

"You really know how to stuff those negative feelings way down to the bottom of your psyche, don't you? Never mind, no answer required. I'm not a shaman."

"It wouldn't do any good until after the trial, though there may not be one. Rumor has it they're going to plead out."

"Do you know how the young woman's doing?"

"I stay in touch with her mother, who says there's progress. Very slow progress."

"That's to be expected. They're getting good counseling?"

"I hope."

I hung up knowing I hadn't accomplished anything, but I felt better. I checked the time and decided it was time to go home, especially since I had to stop at the grocery. Dad was across the Ohio River, making his annual pilgrimage to kinfolk, so shopping and cooking chores had reverted to me. I was tempted to stop by the big-box store and pick up some frozen dinners. But Dad had spoiled me and I wanted something that wasn't cardboard. I drove to Rhomer's, a local grocery with a real live butcher. Most of the produce was local, in season and they had a nice gourmet section.

I was just turning into an aisle when I ran into a cart with a *clank*. I looked up to see Win. "Better watch out or I'll give you a ticket for reckless driving."

"With a shopping cart?" She smiled. "How you doing?"

I nodded, then acted on impulse, which was out of my normal. "You want to come over for dinner tonight? I'm cooking." I held up a package of lamb chops. "Tempting?"

"I thought Micah did the cooking." She shifted her weight to her other leg.

"He's visiting kith and kin in Kentucky."

She quickly changed back to the other leg. "I'd love to, but I've got a date tonight. I'm running late, but give me a call the next time you're doing lamb." She smiled and wheeled her cart around mine. Five minutes later, I saw her go through the checkout line.

Date. So much for impulses.

* * *

VICTIM COMMITS SUICIDE. The screaming headline was from the Indy paper. Lloyd had treated it more gently in the *Sentinel*. But how the press treated it didn't change the fact that Natalie Elder had hung herself from the balcony of her parents' home.

She left a note, writing in terse terms that her life was ruined, she'd never be able to outrun the story. Tod was weighing the addition of manslaughter charges.

We'd answered the call, found Brittany and her mother holding on only by the thinnest threads. Doc Webster had removed the body as quickly as the need for documentation allowed. What could I say to them? We'd arrested the bastards who'd orchestrated the rape. I couldn't promise them I'd kill the young men who'd caused Natalie's death.

Although I wished I could.

I took my rage and my Glock to the firing range and spent an hour drilling dummies, whom I'd named for each of the perpetrators. The dummies were dead and I was wrung out.

When this case had developed, I'd canceled all my campaign appearances. Charlene, a relative twice removed on Dad's side and my campaign manager, was flummoxed—her word. I told her to reschedule them in August and September. So I hadn't expected to hear from her for a couple of months. Then she left a voice mail saying we needed to "strategize."

Hell's bells, no way. All I wanted to do was curl into the smallest ball possible and roll away.

What I needed to concentrate on was what the sheriff's department could do to stop this behavior before it happened. I decided to call Jan Weberly in the morning. As the guidance counselor I trusted most at Greenglen High, maybe she had some ideas that we could move on. I knew they'd bring in extra counselors for Natalie's death, but I wanted to see if we couldn't do something that would change the course of behavior for these young people.

But for tonight, I wasn't going to think about it anymore. I just couldn't.

I picked five DVDs from Dad's collection, put the first one on, lay down on the couch and plopped a pillow behind my head.

During the night when I woke, I'd change the DVD and watch until I fell asleep again.

CHAPTER SIX

Win

I'd lied to Sarah. I didn't have a date that night I'd bumped into her at the grocery. Julie and I were dating, but not that night. I'd drive up to Bloomington once a week or so, and we'd see a movie or hear a band. With dinner before or after. We talked, but there was so little of my past I could talk about that sometimes we were left with a heavy silence. One that Julie rushed to fill with chatter.

Julie had asked me why I didn't invite her down to my house.

I'd said because there was nothing to do. At least not for two women holding hands. She'd said she was sure we could think of *something* to do.

She was getting restive. We'd kissed. She'd kissed my neck and run her hands over my breasts during a movie at the student center. Pulled me into a kiss and started to unbutton my shirt. I'd pulled back, stiffly removed her hand. "Not here," I'd whispered. She'd turned back to the screen and crossed her arms.

It was time to sleep with her or break it off. I hadn't been celibate this long, including deployments, since I'd first slept with Annie. I wasn't able to take the next step. Why the fuck not? I liked Julie. She made me laugh. But she got impatient so quickly. She had sharp edges that were abrasive at times.

Azar had been nothing but a soft haven in a harsh world. She would have been delighted with my home. Carefully picked up objects and asked for the story they held. I would have treasured her presence.

Sarah? I pushed away the thought. Julie? Maybe a couple of days away together would be a step to forming a real relationship. I initiated a search for a gay bed-and-breakfast or inn that wasn't too far away. The Rainbow Inn popped up. In West Baden. I emailed them and asked if they had any openings, weekdays, in the near future. The answer came back within minutes. They weren't into their busy season yet, rooms were open. Did I want to make a reservation?

Hold on, I replied. *Need to check.*

I picked up the phone and called Julie. When she answered, she sounded cranky and rushed. "Would you like to go on a short weekday vacation next week?"

Silence. "Well. I didn't expect this. Where? Please don't say the Wisconsin Dells."

"Rainbow Inn, West Baden."

"Next week?" I could hear pages turning. Probably her daybook for the bar. "It'd have to be Monday and Tuesday, and I have to be back by four on Wednesday."

"It's a date."

"You're a damn odd bird, Win. Got all huffy when I touched you. I was beginning to think you're a stone butch. You aren't, are you?"

"No. I like receiving pleasure as much as giving it."

My hand trembled as I set the phone on my desk. What the hell had I done? Three days together would be the acid test, even in romantically saturated surroundings. Wouldn't it?

I sent the email, printed out a map. Fled to my garden.

* * *

I opened the waiting room door as Emily opened hers. Her eyebrows lifted slightly, then she turned into her office. I followed, feeling like I'd lost two points for being on time and another for not having time to mess up the sandbox.

"So, what's upset you?" Emily asked as we sat down.

I leaned my head back, closed my eyes. I wanted to talk about the situation, but I wanted to ease into it. "I realized how much Azar would've loved my home." Even though I didn't want them, tears pushed for freedom.

"What brought you to that thought?"

Well, screw easing into anything with Emily. "Because I haven't invited Julie to my house. I realized I didn't want her picking up things I treasure. Making wisecracks about them."

Emily nodded. "So what did you do?"

"I invited Julie to a mini-vacation. Rainbow Inn, West Baden."

Emily steepled her fingers. "You'll sleep with her at a gay B&B, but not at home?"

I crossed my legs. "Yeah. I like her. She makes me laugh. But it's a rough humor." I recrossed my legs. "I've been trying to take it slow. Regular, old-fashioned dates, not diving into bed."

"Kudos, Win. You're trying to form an intimate relationship?"

I nodded. "I miss Azar so much. Sometimes, when I come in from the garden, I expect to see her. I start to say, 'Have you seen those tomato plants?' and realize there's never going to be a reply. Honest to God, it's crushing."

"You're still mourning, Win." She leaned forward. "Look, healing doesn't mean the damage never happened. What it means is that the damage wields less and less power over your actions."

"You think this is a dumb idea."

"I didn't say that. But it sounds to me like you're trying to build a relationship with a woman you don't want in your home. Sound weird to you?"

I looked out the window. Shit.

"The only advice I have to give is to be honest. With yourself. With Julie. Tell her what you're feeling—and if she's not willing to give you some space, then it's up to you. You can have a romantic getaway without consummation. Use the time to find out what she likes and show her what you like. Make it an erotic time without the pressure of bringing the act to completion."

"Oh, yeah. Julie's going to love that idea. Can I tell her it's yours?"

"Only if you tell her why you're in therapy, Win."

* * *

I'd been sweaty-palms nervous when I'd picked Julie up. She threw an overnight-sized bag in the back. That made me more nervous. I'd planned to take backroads down, enjoy the sunny weather and scenery.

She suggested a direct, quicker route. "I mean, I've been waiting to get some action going for eons."

"I like to see the country I'm traveling through."

"So you can plan a rapid retreat?" she asked.

"Exactly." I turned on the radio and told her to pick the station.

I'd stuck to my route through her increasing chatter about people I didn't know, trying to pick up a thread that would tell me what she was trying to tell me. I failed.

When we arrived, we were signed in by a poufy guy in a vintage Hawaiian shirt. I knew it was vintage because he told us.

He leaned toward us as if to impart wisdom or a secret. "We have a small hot spring at the back of the property. Wonderful place to unwind, if you know what I mean. But, no hard and heavy stuff. Makes it icky for everyone else. You know?"

I'd seen the sign to the hot spring when I'd parked. Thought it would be nice to relax after the drive. Maybe it would be a way for Julie to see my war-torn body before anything 'hard and heavy' happened. "Is it available now?"

"Nobody's got it booked for the rest of the day. I'll see your luggage gets up to your room." He plopped two large towels and robes on the counter.

We walked a pine-bark mulch path to the pool hand in hand. Her palm wasn't sweating.

"So you're a nature girl," Julie said.

"I spent a lot of my service outdoors. Indoors was much scarier." I never knew for certain who was on the other side of the door.

We arrived at the pool. The setting, maples and sumacs screening the pool, dappled sunlight, was serene. I felt my shoulders ease down.

"Do you want me to undress you, or is that something you'd rather do for yourself?" Julie asked.

I took a deep breath and looked at the pool. "I've been wounded a few times. I have scars. Shrapnel. A couple of bullets."

"God, I had no idea. Is that why you've been so fucking slow?"

"Slow to fuck? No. I want a relationship." I stumbled on the word.

For a brief second, she looked as if she was sucking a vinegar tit. "Whatever. Question still stands."

I turned fully toward her, opened my arms. "Just don't say I didn't warn you."

She closed the distance between us, kissed me while she unbuttoned my shirt. We were still on the same kiss when she took it off and unfastened my bra. She'd started on my pants when I pulled back. "You need to look at what you've uncovered."

She stepped back a tad. "Is that a bullet hole?"

"Yes." I took her hand and placed it where Paria's bullet had exited my body. I watched her face closely. "I have another down here."

I placed her other hand on my side. "One leg's pretty scarred by shrapnel."

She didn't leave her hands on the wounds long. They followed her gaze to my breasts. "The wounds don't hurt you anymore, do they? I mean, I don't have to be real careful, do I?"

"Not physically. No."

"Well, cellulite is disfiguring too. Don't worry about it." She brought her mouth to my breast and pulled down the zipper of my jeans.

The acid test. Maybe she didn't understand the wounds of war. What civilian did? Maybe she just didn't know how to handle the physical manifestations and was trying to make me feel okay about my body. But these trophies of war were only a symptom of what I'd brought home.

Okay. I finished taking my jeans and panties off and pulled her T-shirt over her head. This had just become a "fuck 'em and leave 'em" three days.

Well, shit.

CHAPTER SEVEN

Sarah

"What happened has a name: multiple perpetrator sexual assault," I said, looking at the mix of people around the table at the high school. "These assaults are often fueled by alcohol and/or drugs and most often occur at unchaperoned parties." I shook my head. "To be perfectly honest, I never expected to have to arrest our kids for something so horrific. Maybe the sheriff's office knows these kids aren't angels better than most. But it's the degree of violence that appalls me. The utter disregard of Natalie as a human being who was not only *being* hurt but would continue to be hurt in the most public of ways." I took a deep breath. "To say it simply, I'm not only outraged by their behavior but by their attitude. I cannot understand the kids we questioned, their indifference."

People squirmed in their seats, flipped through papers.

"It's the media," said one of the school's counselors. "The students are inundated by sex and violence and assume those images to be cool."

"And exert pressure on their peers to go along," another said.

"The video games they play—have you ever seen one?" asked the teachers' rep. "No respect for human life."

"Or women," chimed in another.

"I understand," I said. "But I can't arrest media producers. What I'm asking you is simple: what can we do to change the culture that's grown here? How can my department help?"

Silence.

"Sheriff's right," Emily said. "We can condemn media until the proverbial cows meander into the pasture, but it's not going to make a damn difference. It's parents' job to know what's coming into their homes. But, we can educate parents. Put together a 'sampler' of the violent games, present it with discussion points."

"Damn good idea," a counselor said. "While we're at it, we can do one for students."

Discussion continued, and though the principal was supposed to be running the meeting, I noticed Emily crossing off items on her list. Smart woman. When the meeting was finished, I caught up to her in the hall. "Nice job. Did we get through your list?"

"Mostly. You got the ball rolling, Sarah. Never heard so much bullshit. Some of those people were more concerned about covering their asses than making sure it doesn't happen again."

"Can we do that—make sure it never happens again?"

"We can sure as hell try." She paused. "I've got authorization to talk with the boys you charged. I'm going to try to profile them and the circumstances that moved them into action."

"So we can look for behavior like that before they rape?"

"There really isn't any predictive psychology," she said. "What I'm looking for is the particular pathology crossed with a precipitating incident. Sounds cold and clinical, doesn't it?"

I rubbed the back of my neck. "This is going to sound crazy, but I keep thinking there was so much malevolence behind what they did to her, it's almost like what happened in Africa. Rape used as a weapon of war."

She cocked her head. "The Janjaweed in Darfur, the Lord's Resistance Army in Congo?"

"Doing unspeakable things to women so the family and the tribe disintegrated." I fingered the emblem of my cap. "Now it seems as if McCrumb County has turned into a war zone."

"Then ask yourself the question: what triggered the war? Why this particular victim? As much as I know about the case, I've always thought she was targeted. You find out why and you may be able to add another charge."

She started walking toward the exit, then turned. "Talk to the sister. Alone. They were close."

* * *

The next few days, I tried to catch up with all the stuff in my inbox: a meeting with a DEA agent about tracking chemicals needed for making meth; finding a wife who'd filed for a protective order and then vanished; disentangling accounts of a multivehicle accident; investigating a report of excessive violence hurled at a deputy. Ducking numerous phone calls from Charlene, my overanxious campaign manager.

I hadn't understood Emily's cryptic remark, but I trusted her. I met Brittany at Beans aBrewing a few days later. I bought her an espresso, and we sat at a back table that needed a book of matches under one leg.

"I just want you to know how sorry I am for your loss," I began. "We're doing everything we can to put them away for a long time."

She nodded, turned her coffee cup around and around. "If it wasn't for thinking about changing majors, I wouldn't be home this semester. We wouldn't have gotten so close."

"It probably makes it harder for you in the short term," I said, "but in the long run, you'll value the chance to have gotten to know her in a new way."

"I miss her so much. Sometimes she could be a pain, but the truth is, she was a really nice kid."

"That's been my impression all the way through the investigation. Do you think she might've been singled out because she *was* such a good kid?"

Brittany took a quick sip, set the cup down with an unsteady hand. "No. I think she got targeted because she told Mark Zimmerman no. There's not a girl at that school who has the right to say no to Mr. Hero. He started spreading the rumor she was gay."

"Gay? That never came to light. Are you sure?"

"She showed me some of his tweets."

"Then maybe we can retrieve some of them. It would add a powerful premeditated motive, and it also falls under the statutes about hate crimes."

"Please don't. It would just make things worse."

"How?" I asked. She was dead. How *could* anything be worse?

"I won't testify at the trial. I won't." She set her jaw. "Natalie came out to me about two months ago. I'd never seen her happier and I knew something was up, but I had no idea. She was dating Christine Woods." She knotted her hands together. "She was madly in love, and I'm afraid she might've shown it at school."

I made a production of writing the name in my notebook. This was the kind of bombshell no law enforcement officer wants to discover after the fact. "I'm going to have to talk with Christine."

"Mom and Dad have had a hard time with the business during the downturn. They were just getting back to normal, and to find out now…" She hugged the cup. "I was trying to do the right thing, let her choose a time to tell them and I made a frigging mess. Nat's dead."

"Please," I said, covering her hands with mine. "It's not your fault. Don't you *ever* blame yourself. Your sister trusted you enough to talk with you. You were there to listen. There's no more you could've done, Brittany."

She sniffed and the tears poured down her cheeks. "I told her to be careful, not to broadcast it, but she said things were different than when I was her age. It doesn't help any that I was right."

* * *

Maybe it was just pure exhaustion or too much stress, but I found myself waking multiple times during the night—no Paria, no rape, just Win. Sometimes we'd be walking down the hall at Greenglen High, the old one, holding hands. We'd stop at my locker and she'd kiss me. Or we'd be stretched out on the rock by the creek, kissing, touching, kissing. Or sometimes, we'd be adults at her house and I didn't pull back. We'd kiss, long kisses full of desire. I'd take my parka off, toss it on a chair and our tongues and bodies would entwine.

I couldn't talk to Emily about this, nor Dad. But I couldn't stay on this treadmill much longer. I needed to talk to Win.

I touched my breast and wondered what Win's caress would feel like.

CHAPTER EIGHT

Win

I'd come home from three days of intense sex, physically exhausted but emotionally clear. Julie wanted sex. That was all. No trying to fit her life with mine, nor did she want me to fit my life with hers. That became clear when she avoided any serious conversation. For three days. Just sex and babble.

I'd missed Azar's lovemaking. The slow, teasing way she'd bring me to the gasping, groaning brink only to gather my senses together at another part of my body. Another slow build, and perhaps another before the moment of release when my body felt as if it were spinning on one point with all of the cosmos. As if the great Sufi masters were leading this great ecstatic dance with us in the center, at the center of a whirling universe.

I wanted so badly to feel Azar's hand in mine as we walked toward bed. Toward that dervish dance of complete surrender. The only one I'd ever known.

I slept a deep and dreamless sleep and didn't wake until ten a.m. When I had fortified myself with coffee, I found two messages from Emily. *"Due to the suicide of a high school student, all therapists with CET have been asked to attend to our high school students. For that reason, I'm canceling all my appointments for this week. If you need assistance during this time, please check my referral list. Please say a prayer, in whatever form, for these kids and those of us who are trying to help them."*

The second message said, *"Win, if you need an appointment, call. I'll get back to you as soon as I can."*

I took a look at the *Sentinel's* website and the story of the suicide. Restrained coverage, but I gathered a girl had been drugged and gang raped at a party. Had committed suicide. The coverage in the Indy paper was more explicit and graphic. Photos had been posted on Facebook and sent all over the net. God! What fucking destruction. Why did nobody stop them? Why the fuck would they photograph it for the world to see?

I was enraged. Ready to take after the whole high school, armed with a machete and righteous anger. This was like something I'd seen in the Sudan. In Congo. But that it happened here, in our heartland, was…I didn't know the word. I didn't think there was a word.

I saw a link to an Indy TV channel, followed it, and watched the first report. Some guy and Sarah, standing on the courthouse steps. Sarah looked drawn, seemingly permanent lines on her face that I hadn't seen before. When it came to her answer to a stupid question, I heard Sarah in every word. Maybe Micah and her granddad too. *A crime makes deep ripples in a community that can continue for years.*

I wondered what I could do for her. This had to be taking an enormous toll. Sarah had so few to share the load. Micah should be back from his travels, would help her any way he could. He knew the burden of the badge firsthand, years and years of the weight of it.

I wished I could hold her, let her cry. Lend her some strength. I wished I could give to Sarah what Azar had given me. A lightness that lifted my burdens as soon as I saw her. She always had a ready smile that shone from her eyes. Could always apply a balm to my spirit. That's what I wished I could give Sarah.

But I wasn't Azar. I couldn't get near Sarah until I had my libido under control.

I logged off, still enraged at the boys who'd sent ripples through this county and couldn't have cared less. If they cared, they'd never have raped a defenseless young girl.

The garden didn't need work, a long run bothered my leg too much. That left the dojang. I'd missed class and hoped Mr. Kim would let me slip into another one.

I needed to discharge.

Mr. Kim took one look at me and said, "Come back at three. In meantime, go drink soothing tea."

With a little over an hour to kill, I walked to Beans aBrewing and asked the barista for a "soothing" tea. She consulted with another young woman. They proceeded to concoct a cup of many teas and presented it to me with a hint of ceremony. I felt like bowing. I picked up a newspaper and looked around for a quiet spot. Instead, I saw Emily and Sarah at a table.

Emily waved me over. Shit. I put on my armor of good behavior and joined them. "I'm so sorry about the case," I said as I sat. "I've been out of town and just caught up on the news." I remembered Emily's message. "It must be hard on both of you."

They exchanged a glance I couldn't decipher.

"Win, what would've happened if you'd come out, all the way out, when you were in high school?" Emily asked.

The question startled me like a ruffed grouse flushed suddenly on a foggy morning. "Exile by the girls. I would've been the target for every jock who thought a good lay would cure me." Then I saw what the question meant. "Oh. The girl was gay?"

Sarah nodded. "We got confirmation from her girlfriend. It seems they weren't very closeted. Chris said that was mostly Natalie's doing—she was proud of the relationship."

"Shit. Kids think they're safe."

Sarah nodded. "I'd like your input, Win. As an officer of the court, I have a duty to push for additional charges. Prosecute it as a hate crime. Show how seriously we treat discrimination." Sarah looked out the window, her blue eyes almost the color of lapis. "But the family's already been through hell. The sister's carrying a load of guilt, and the parents are lost in a fog of grief. They don't need more publicity."

"She was targeted because she was gay? I'm getting that right?"

Sarah nodded. "We've found tweets and text messages that go to intent. All by the book, so the additional charges should prove out."

I took a long sip of my "soothing" tea. "Did her parents know?"

"No."

My heart sank. "I think you better call Solomon. I'm all out of wisdom, Sarah."

Sarah leveled her gaze at me. Accusatory.

"You'd have to tell the parents to let them decide, which would still add trauma." I glanced at Emily. "I mean if they didn't have a clue. It's not easy for parents, even now. People watch *Ellen* and *Modern Family* and figure everything's okay. It's not. Not here."

Emily nodded. "My practice is testament to the anti-gay sentiment in the area."

"Well, thanks, both of you." Sarah stood. "I've got some 'mullin' over' to do."

I watched her walk away. I liked jeans with a uniform shirt. What a lovely butt she had.

"So, you're doing okay?" Emily asked.

"Yeah," I said. "I know who to call if I want sex without any strings."

Emily examined me with that slit-eyed stare. "I'm sorry, Win. I know this was a risk for you."

I shook my head. "It's not a disaster. I realized how full my love for Azar was. I know I don't want to settle for less."

Emily nodded. "That's a really good step. Just be careful who you fasten your attention on."

"What?" But she wasn't going to say anything more. "I'm going to the dojang to work off some rage. Want to join me?"

"What anger?"

"At those boys," I said. "In fact, I'd like to give a martial arts demonstration on the kids who didn't stop it. If they'd seen what I saw in the Sudan, they couldn't have stood by. The aftermath is soul-searing. Like it should be here."

I saw something in Emily's eyes. An idea forming? Shit.

"I've got to get back to the school," she said. "Dealing with grief is one thing, but guilt is another. Sometimes I just want to say 'Live with it,' but instead I have to listen to them wallow. After the fact. Hell of a therapist, aren't I?"

* * *

Two weeks after graduation, I found myself in front of the girls of the incoming senior class, giving them what I'd introduced as a tour of the killing fields of Africa. The boys had come first and that had caught their attention. The girls cringed.

Nathan had helped me put together the visual parts of my talk; some images from Internet sources, some from my own prints. Emily and Jan, a counselor at the high school, had screened the images beforehand. With their advice, I'd taken out three or four. But the last one, no, it had to stay in.

I told the stories of the villages I'd found burned down by the Janjaweed in Darfur, the dead bodies of men and children. The women who'd been raped so brutally by the militia they just crouched and stared. I named the women, told what had become of them. Then I moved to Congo and the Lord's Resistance Army. The last image broke my heart. A woman who'd had a spear driven into her vagina, a man in fatigues standing next to her. Grinning.

"In Congo, sons were forced to watch their mothers' and sisters' rapes. You know why? Because it made them complicit. Their guilt kept them silent. Don't kid yourselves—rape is never about sex, it's about power. It's about control.

"Whether rape happens on the other side of the world or right here in McCrumb County, it's always about power. Not sex, not love. Power. Please don't think that drinking until you're blind drunk is cool. The women of Darfur weren't drunk. They were just living their lives. Trying to raise their children—or trying to be kids.

"Be grateful for where you live, what you have. Don't be afraid to stop a rape that you witness. Tell what you saw. There's nothing worse than the guilt that comes from complicity."

I asked for questions and was met by the rustling of a roomful of girls who didn't know where to start. Finally, one girl raised her hand and the dam broke. I met the flood and finally called a halt at noon.

As I packed up my equipment, I heard footsteps and looked up to see Sarah. I hadn't seen her enter the auditorium. "Hey, Sarah. Rough presentation. Hope like hell it does some good."

"I don't see how it couldn't. God! Those pictures. You saw those villages, Win?"

I nodded. "Operation Lightning Thunder in Congo in oh-eight. We never even came close to finding Kony. I'm glad I didn't have to stay long."

Sarah shifted her folio to her other hand. "We need to talk."

"Sure. Lunch? I'm starving—I was too nervous to eat breakfast."

"I was thinking about dinner. I'll cook. If you're busy tonight, give me an evening that'll work."

"Uh, tonight's fine. What can I bring?"

"Wine." She said it with a half smile.

"What kind does Micah like? I spent half my life on his wrong side, maybe a bottle of his favorite would help change the tide."

"Dad's uncle died. He's in Vincennes and will be for a few days. He's the executor of the estate. It'll be just you and me. See you around seven."

CHAPTER NINE

Sarah and Win

Sarah

The look on Win's face had been priceless: pure terror. It matched the feeling that was churning my stomach. Talk was okay, wasn't it? Conversation over dinner? I needed an explanation for my dreams, the continuing drama of courtship without closure.

The sex dreams shouldn't continue because my stress level was back to normal. The trial prep was in Tod's hands now. So was the decision about including the hate crime charges. Brittany's comment that her parents couldn't take another blow haunted me.

Blow. That's what finding out your daughter was gay meant. My mind kept tracking blow to gay to one kiss. I needed to speak my confusion, and who better to talk to than the woman who'd generated all my turmoil?

I left the office early, stopped by Rhomer's to pick up a few items. I'd decided to do Mom's lasagna rustica since a low pressure system had cooled temperatures. Besides, it would keep me busy chopping and cooking and not thinking.

Win

If I thought I'd been nervous this morning about giving the talk, I was a twit. This afternoon I'd pulled every outfit I had in my closet, trying to strike the right note for dinner. I didn't have a suit of armor. I glanced at my watch. If I was going to pick up wine, it was time to leave. I pulled my favorite jeans on, closed my eyes, and drew a shirt from the mess of them on the bed. White oxford cloth. Really intriguing, Win. I put it on, rolled up the sleeves, and lit out.

I drove the clerk at Rhomer's wine aisle crazy with my indecision. Finally he said, "Let me pick a white and red, fairly local, and if you don't like it, bring back the empties and I'll refund the full purchase price." How could I go wrong?

I drove up their long drive and parked by the barn. Fussed with my shirt. Checked the time. Took a deep breath and got out. Remembered the wine. Took another deep breath.

I tapped on the screen door and saw Sarah standing at the counter, tossing a salad. She turned, smiled. "Come on in."

Bottles rattling, I walked into the kitchen where I could read her T-shirt. An image of a Native American in a canoe on glass-like water. The background was cut in half, light and dark. It read, "Feeding the Spirit."

"Neat T-shirt, Sarah," I said, placing the bottles on the table.

She concentrated on the salad. "It's from Nathan. Said it was a reminder about taking time to find peace and quiet."

I put the white wine in the refrigerator and sat in the chair farthest from the counter. "Can I do anything to help?"

"Pour the wine," she said.

She was tenser than I'd ever seen her, her shoulders practically hiding her neck. I wanted to give her a shoulder rub, relax all those muscles that were so knotted. "How's the case coming?"

She put the salad on the table, turned and pulled a bubbling, aroma-laden dish from the oven. "The department's part is finished, evidence checked and rechecked. Now it's in Tod's hands to get the convictions."

"The hate crime charges?"

She pulled off her oven mitts. "I talked to her sister again, asked if it was something her parents could handle. She said a most emphatic no, so I gave Tod the whole story and told him it was up to him. I have the evidence if he needs it."

I eased the cork out of the bottle, sniffed. So far, so good. "You have any idea what he's going to do?"

"He's been 'thinking about' filing charges against the kids who took or posted the photos for distribution of child pornography. I suggested he try a Class C felony for vicarious sexual gratification from a rape. It carries a four-year sentence, but these kids could be out in six months."

"They'd still have a felony conviction." I poured a bit of wine in one glass, handed it to her.

"Right." She sniffed, took a small sip, swirled it in her mouth. "Wow—that's really nice." She turned the bottle to see the label. "Imagine wineries in Indiana. I can remember when California wineries were looked at askance." She brought the dish to the table and began cutting into it. "Mom's recipe for lasagna—hope you still eat sausage."

It smelled and looked delicious. My stomach was in turmoil, wanting food but quivering from nerves. What the hell did she want to talk about? Evidently not the rape case. Shit. Shut your mouth except to eat, Win.

Sarah

I had too much to drink and Win not enough. She rinsed the dishes while I got dessert ready. I'd planned to do coffee in the living room, but there was still a half bottle of white wine left. I put the bottle, glasses and dessert on a tray and tried to walk the straight and narrow into the living room. I put it on the coffee table in front of the couch. It was chilly enough outside that I lit the fire.

"Great dinner, Sarah," she said, rolling down her sleeves as she walked in. "Will you share the recipe?"

"Sure." I sat down on the couch, blood racing. I could hear my pulse in my ears. I filled the glasses and handed one up to her. For a minute, I thought she was going to sit on the floor. But she sighed, took the glass and sat at the other end.

She put the glass down and turned to me. "You wanted to talk about something. Now's a good time."

I took a big sip of wine, tried to take a deep breath but found my chest constricted.

"You don't need to get drunk, Sarah," she said softly.

Yes I did.

"Turn around, back toward me," she said. I did, felt the cushion tilt a bit, and then I felt her hands on my shoulders. Rubbing gently, kneading my muscles. She worked up my neck, concentrated on the back of my head and then back down my neck to my shoulders.

"Nathan's right," she said. "You need to feed your spirit. It's a wonder you haven't had muscle spasms. Or have you?"

"No. Just dreams." I grabbed her hand. "Dreams about you and... about us."

Win jerked her hands away and the cushion leveled. Shit, I'd blown everything. I had to say what I'd been thinking, without scaring her off.

I turned to face her. "I can't stop thinking about that kiss. And you."

Win

Sarah looked so scared, so fragile. If I extended my arm, I could pull her into another kiss. One not so brief nor innocent.

"I promised you that would never happen again," I said, trying to keep the shakes out of my voice. I felt to my bones how much I wanted her.

"But I want you to kiss me again." She took a sip of wine. "You said you never date straight women, but I'm not sure...anymore. I was, with Hugh. But I could give a hog's ass about the men I've dated since."

I was tempted to down the wine in my glass and carry her off to bed. "I don't understand what you're feeling, Sarah. I've known where my heart's attracted since we were in grade school."

"You never—"

"I had a crush on you from about sixth grade until we got into high school. I knew I couldn't afford to act on it. Besides, you were all excited about the guys you were dating." I smiled. "When Micah finally let you date."

"I want to know what it's like, Win. What it's like making love with a woman."

"This isn't an experiment, Sarah."

"It's making me crazy. Couldn't we—"

"I'll be glad to introduce you to women I've met in Bloomington. There's a bar..."

Sarah began to cry, tears running down her face despite the fact her eyes were closed. She started rocking herself. I couldn't take it. I reached out, pulled her into my arms. Stroked her hair. "What happens if I give you my heart and you decide it was a pleasant experiment, but you're straight?"

Sarah

"Would you give me your heart?" I asked.

Her voice husky, Win said, "I did a long time ago. I was amazed how at home I felt with you when you came over. You'd changed. But the old bond was still there."

"I know, I felt it too. I can't tell you how sorry I am about that afternoon. I just panicked."

"With good reason, Sarah. I've regretted that moment since it happened."

I pulled back a bit, examined her face. "Because it was awful?"

"No, oh shit no. Because of the way you reacted—like I'd hit you. You must know I'd never hurt you."

"Then..." I took a deep breath. "Then let's take it slowly, little steps. It's not all women I feel this way about or dream about—just you."

"Sarah, if it doesn't work out, what happens? Are we still friends? Can we be? If you find you like women, what's to say you won't go looking for someone else a little more exotic? What about your job?"

I didn't have answers to any of those questions, and I didn't care. I pulled her close and kissed her, softly at first, lips brushing lips. Then the pressure increased and I opened my mouth to taste her tongue.

Win

I pulled back. "I'm not kidding around, Sarah. I won't jump into this relationship. There's too much at stake. For both of us."

She put on the balky face I'd known so well when we were kids. "How the hell can I discover if what I'm feeling is real if you won't show me how to, you know..."

"It's taken me years, but I've finally discovered it's not about sex, it's about love. I fell in love, felt what Emily calls the divine closeness of two humans. I won't settle for less anymore. Are you ready to fall in love? With a woman?"

She touched my cheek. "I don't know, Win. Honest. But how am I going to find out? If you keep hiding from me, there's a real good chance I'll never find out."

I shrugged. "Dating?"

"Where? Go out to dinner and hold hands? Go to a movie in town and neck a little? I don't think so, Win."

"There's a bar in Bloomington. The LGBT center has movies."

"A gay bar? I can't, Win. What if somebody saw me there?"

"What if they did? Why would they be there unless they were gay?" I stood. "Think about it. Dating, falling in love should be joyous. If it's too much for you, we shouldn't start."

CHAPTER TEN

Win

I woke in my own bed, thinking last night had been a dream. But I remembered the pressure of Sarah's lips on mine. The way she'd pulled me to her. As I showered, I thought I'd never felt so confused in my whole life. I knew my feelings for Sarah had rekindled when I'd first kissed her. Glimpsed the pain and vulnerability beneath her shield of professionalism.

Fuck it. I didn't need a straight woman's curiosity to screw my life up more than it was already. Except Sarah wasn't just any straight woman.

I was drinking my first cup of coffee when the phone rang. Sarah. I said good morning with a shaky voice.

"I want to try your way. But I can't go to a gay bar, Win." She took a deep breath. "Maybe we could have dinner tonight at Boone's. I can't talk now, I'm at work for an emergency meeting with the state cops. I've no idea how long it'll take. When I get out, can I call you for an answer?"

"We need to talk, Sarah."

"I don't want to talk, Win. I don't want to think, I don't want to worry. I just want to exist in all these feelings, sensations. It's like a dam's broken and I've been swept away. I know there are dangers, things I can't see beneath the water, but I feel like I'm in a safe boat if you're with me."

"Shit, you sound like a teenager. Call me when you get free."

* * *

I drank my coffee in a swirl of emotions. I recognized fear. Not for me this time. For Sarah. If something developed, we'd have to keep the relationship secret. She was campaigning for office, for God's sake. Public scrutiny. Her SEAL opponent could be running ops on her. Where would we be safe to let the love grow?

Then my mind wandered to her body, long and lean with full breasts. Her hungry reaction to our kiss.

I couldn't concentrate on any one task. Between dusting and rounding up garbage, I discovered two calls from Bill on my burn phone. I sank into the chair, feeling the pit of fear in my stomach. I called him back.

"What's happened?" I asked as soon as he picked up.

"Scotty's still poking around, trying to find a way to reactivate you, but I don't think it's serious, Win. He's just a poor loser."

"They're the most dangerous kind." I started doodling on the phone pad. "So if my recall isn't impending, why'd you call?"

He laughed. "I got a call from the CELI director at IU. She's looking for someone fluent in Tajik and possibly Pashtun. Urdu would be a plus. Interested?"

"To translate?"

"To teach. In case you'd like to apply, I've emailed all the info, including military records you can disseminate. Not a whisper of special ops."

"Shit, Bill, I don't know. I've never taught. I'm not sure I could figure out how to do it."

"It's just like planning an op, only in most cases, less dangerous." He laughed again and hung up.

I opened my email and his attachments. Interesting, both for the job and the scrub Bill had done on my records. What the hell? I went to the Central Eurasian Language Institute job openings, printed out the job description and wrote a cover letter. I sent it and the sanitized résumé Bill had given me to the email address. I didn't think I had a chance. Hadn't graduated college. Though I made up for it with all the course work I'd done to get my commission.

At least it had taken my mind off Sarah for a couple of hours. I wondered what was going down. Why the meeting with state cops? Probably a drug bust. I'd seen how she worked with her deputies. By leading. Did Sarah have a good vest?

I looked at the calendar and realized today was my appointment with Emily. That scared me. This was so new. So unexpected. So dangerous in so many ways. She'd look at me with her eyes half-closed for a few minutes and say, "Who are you seeing?"

What the hell could I answer?

My phone rang. Sarah. My heart raced at the thought of seeing her soon.

"Win, we've got a big drug bust going down. Tonight."

The word hung between us.

"Keep your mind on the job, Sarah. I'll see you when we can."

* * *

Emily scrutinized me through lidded eyes and asked, "Who?"

Not quite the question I'd expected, but close enough. "How do you do that? What's with that funny stare?"

"You're avoiding, Win."

I squirmed in my chair. Ran my fingertips over the nubby fabric and thought of Sarah. Crap. "I can't give you a name. Not that I don't trust you. But I'd like to get her permission."

"This isn't sudden, is it?" Emily asked. "It's been building and it has nothing to do with Julie. Care to share?"

"I can tell you how I feel."

She nodded. "We can start there."

I told her I was falling in love. Shit, I actually said it.

"How does it compare with falling in love with Azar?"

I groped my memory. Tried to remember what that first kiss had done to me, what the growing feelings had been. How I'd missed Azar when I wasn't in her company. "I think it's about the same. Maybe because both women caught me by surprise."

"By surprise?"

"Would you expect to find a lesbian in a small Afghan village that basically existed in the seventeenth century? She took me by surprise with a kiss. The physical attraction was there from the first, but what I fell in love with was her spirit. Her essence."

"You're talking freely about Azar. Have you noticed?"

I nodded. "I'm remembering the good times we shared. Not her death."

"So this Ms. X took you by surprise too. How?"

I weighed my response. "I thought she was straight."

"Was she?"

I nodded.

Emily sighed. "I'm not going to lecture you about the pitfalls of dating a straight woman. You already know. But you're still in a fragile state of being." She recrossed her ankles. "How did she respond to sleeping with you?"

"We haven't. Slept together." I looked out the window so she wouldn't see the desire.

"Have you embraced? Kissed?"

"Both and she was fully participative."

Emily grinned, shook her head. "Honest to God, you're incorrigible. It won't do any good to tell you to ease back, will it? I can't help but worry about you."

"I worry about *her*. She's a public figure and this could destroy her career if it's discovered."

"Oh, hell." She smacked the arm of her chair. "You're romancing Sarah Barrow Pitt. Who's up for reelection. Who'd be out of a job and out of the county if she were discovered having a lesbian relationship. Nice going."

I stared at her. How the hell? I nodded numbly. I felt miserable. What Emily had said was true. But hearing it said out loud, that was something different than the whispers your mind forms. Those you can push away with visions of soft skin and full breasts awaiting your touch. My whispers. My touch.

"I'm going to suggest something," Emily said. "You'll probably hate it, but think about it seriously. I'd like to see you both together for couples counseling. Until that happens, I suggest you not sleep with her."

"I can't tell her I told you—"

"You didn't, Win. I see Sarah around and about, rather a lot in the past months. I knew something was up with her, I just didn't know who. To be less than candid with your therapist is death to the relationship. She knows that. She also knows this is all privileged information that I can't talk about." Emily closed her notebook. "She's always under scrutiny, but the intensity will lessen after the election."

"You want us to wait that long?"

"I didn't say that." She leaned forward. "But I want to be absolutely clear: you both need to talk about the dangers ahead. I'm offering to mediate that conversation."

"She doesn't want to talk about it. She just wants to be...happy."

CHAPTER ELEVEN

Sarah

The coordination meeting finally broke up, and I hurried to my office, closed the door and called Win. We had a brief conversation, with a warning from her to keep my mind on the job. This was a major operation and would net some of the big dealers of heroin and meth that were pouring into the county.

I didn't want to think about reelection, about the secret I'd have to hide. I didn't even want to think about putting the scum behind bars. I just wanted to think about Win and what might have happened tonight. Instead of being on a stakeout, I might've been in a warm bed, Win's hands turning me to a new life.

I heard a tap on my door and Caleb walked in. "Think we should go over the positions? Fine-tune them?"

"Yeah, I was just going to call you."

We sat down and hammered out a plan for our surveillance teams and who would go where best. Caleb could read my fretting and helped me work out the best plan.

We moved out before dark, the twilight blues making the few lights in homes we passed that much warmer. We arrived at the ridge where we'd watch for an eighteen-wheeler to pull into the parking yard of a ramshackle warehouse outside of the hamlet of Wakefield Ford. Night vision binoculars, on loan from the DEA, made the scene look like a green Hades. I wondered how many times Win had watched like this.

I caught a slight movement at the back of the building. I nudged Detective John Morgan, my partner this night. I pointed. We were running silent, only using cell phones to communicate.

"Looks like two men," he whispered.

I stared at the two figures, trying to figure out if they were armed. If they were ours. "Was anyone on the combined force supposed to be back there?"

"No. Should I call in?"

"Yeah. Let's be sure."

We not only had surveillance equipment, but two Mark 12s. Sniper rifles developed for the navy at Crane Naval Warfare Center, not too far from here in landlocked Indiana. Win had used this weapon in Afghanistan. I didn't know how she had survived this kind of tension year after year.

I watched the two men take positions behind stacks of pallets that had a view of the entrance. Again, I nudged John and pointed.

He nodded. "I think there are two or three more over there." He pointed to the other side of the entrance. "Command said they don't have anyone on the grounds. Hijackers?"

"This could be an interesting night. Give command a full update on what we've seen."

I watched and tried to focus on the night, the risks and the bad guys. The spring sounds of the night surrounded us. Underbrush rustling from small critters. The deep, muffled hooting of a great horned owl. I shivered, remembering relatives' stories about hearing one before death visited. If you counted the *hoo*s after the first, you'd know how many were going to die.

John's phone buzzed. He took the call with a series of okays. He turned to me. "Truck's ETA is ten minutes. Since there are suspects on the ground, they're pulling teams in closer. We're to stay here and keep a wide eye and the rifles ready."

"Hell, I wonder who we're supposed to shoot."

John had earned his sharpshooter's rating in the army. I'd hunted since I was nine and had kept up my skills at the firing range. But we were at least two hundred yards away, it was night and it would be hard to tell who was who. Double damn.

I went back to scanning the warehouse yard. The men there had remained in position, though one was smoking. I could see the flare of his cigarette. As I moved the binoculars to the other group, I caught a flare on the hillside across from us. I focused and could see a two-person team. Ours? They weren't supposed to be there. For the third time, I nudged John. "Our people aren't supposed to be there. Call it in."

I heard his voice, low and intense. He turned to me. "They think we're in the middle of a gang war. The semi has picked up a tail—big black SUV. There's another truck coming from the opposite direction they think are the buyers. Hinky setup all the way around."

"Do they know who the guys on the hill are?"

"Could be a team that got turned around—state cops don't know their way around our countryside. They'll call around and if the guys are ours, they'll signal."

I saw the lights of a truck coming from behind us. Box truck. It slowed, a passenger got out and opened the gate to the yard. The truck pulled in and extinguished its lights. I could hear the rumble of its diesel engine.

"I'm going to monitor the guys on the hill, you watch the yard," I said to John. The men on the hillside hadn't given any signal. But I could see, in shadow, their rifles. I slipped my own phone from my pocket, switched it on and linked to the command post.

The word came back, guys on the hillside not ours. "Positive?" I asked.

"Affirmative, Mama Bear," came the answer.

Within minutes, I heard the downshifting gears of a big rig. Headlights appeared as he slowed and swung into the yard. No SUV. Where had it gone? Was it waiting for the action to begin or finish?

The driver of the big rig turned it around with much clashing of gears. Not a professional driver. He cut the lights and the engine. As he got out and his passenger got out, the box truck guys walked toward them. Then Hades came true.

"Shots fired. Shots fired. Man down. Two men down." I signaled John to continue the coverage for command. I could see muzzle flashes from the hillside. Not our team. "Ask for clearance to fire, opposite hillside. Two men firing."

He nodded, passed the information. He put down the phone, leveled his rifle. "I'll take the one on the right?"

"Yes." The night vision scope brought my target into focus. Tricky shot at this distance, but there was no wind this night. I remembered

Paria, standing in my kitchen, ready to shoot Dad. I pulled the trigger, the man lurched, then lay still. I heard John fire, then curse.

From across the way I saw the muzzle flash, and flash again. Heard one bullet whizz by my head but didn't have time to finish ducking.

CHAPTER TWELVE

Win

The phone woke me at three fifty-seven a.m. I fumbled with both phones on the night stand. Not the burner. "Kirkland here."

"Sorry to wake you, Win. This is Micah Barrow. Sarah, she was doin' a drug bust tonight an'—"

"Is she okay?"

"Bullet caught her in the neck an' she lost a lot of blood. John said she asked for you repeatedly, so I thought it best to call. She's in surgery now. Doc said she had a real good chance, but she's gonna be weak as a newborn for awhiles. Surgery may last a coupla hours, so I apologize for wakin' you from a solid sleep. I just wanted to do what she asked."

"Can I keep you company?"

"Sure would 'preciate it, Win."

I threw on some clothes, drove like a maniac into Greenglen and to the hospital. I found Micah pacing the floor of the surgical unit. I paused, watched him. He was bent tonight, his shoulders sagging forward, his head down. He walked like an old man. I realized losing Sarah would destroy him. And me too.

I took a deep breath, tried to center myself. I walked toward him with my arms open. "Would a hug be hugely inappropriate?"

"Reckon it'd be most welcome."

He gave me a bear hug. I sank into it. He guided me over to a couch, and we settled side by side. He patted my knee. "It's gonna be okay. Close one, but we both know the risk. Reckon you dodged a bullet or two."

"A couple caught me. What happened?"

"Sarah and John—you met John Morgan? Don't matter. Sarah found two snipers on a hill 'cross from them. When the shootin' started, she and John set to stop them snipers. Sarah took her man out, John missed. That shooter returned fire. Sarah was duckin' down, bullet caught her right above her vest, went down into her collarbone. Ricocheted."

"Damn." I felt tears welling up.

"Artery was only nicked an' John had the presence of mind to keep his hand on it 'till the medics got there. Probably saved her life." He put his arm around me, pulled me close. I wept. Out of relief. Out of fear. Out of almost losing Sarah before we'd even had a chance to begin.

He let me cry it out, pulling me into him with both arms. God, he felt safe. Finally, I took a deep breath and wiped my face with the backs of my hands. "I'm a mess, aren't I?"

"Purty mess." He rose and took two cups of Beans aBrewing coffee from Jerry, one of the owners. "Thank you greatly, Jerry. You surely have gone above and beyond. We won't forget, son."

"Least I could do," Jerry said. "Sheriff is good people. If you need blood donated…"

"Let's go down to the nurses' station an' ask." He handed me a cup and walked with Jerry.

Good man. Between Micah and Elizabeth, Sarah had a sterling start at life. A lot to live up to. I sat down, took the lid off. Inhaled the strong fragrance. All I wanted to do was hold Sarah in my arms and tell her everything was going to be okay.

Micah returned and put a thermos on the table. "Refills."

"Amazing. How did he—"

"Him and Steve live out that way, heard the ruckus, came in to make coffee for the deputies doin' cleanup. Heard Sarah was here, called an' offered to bring some 'decent' coffee."

Did Micah realize Jerry and Steve were a gay couple? Did he care? I thought anyone would be a fool to underestimate Micah Barrow.

We sipped in silence, both lost in thoughts I was sure were very different. Why the hell had I insisted on stopping? I could see Sarah didn't want to. I sighed. Maybe, someday in the future, we could lie together. For a whole night, wrapped in one another's arms.

"Win, if this is too personal, you just tell me to butt out." He leaned forward, rested his arms on his thighs. "For bein' so furious with you when Paria was tryin' to kill you, Sarah sure has mellowed. Reckon part of it is your bein' friends since you was kids." He turned to me. "Since she visited your house back awhiles, she's been…up an' down. When I called her this mornin', she sounded so full of life. Said she wanted to talk to me when I got back. Said she was feelin' somethin' special. Betwixt you two?"

I had no idea what to say. Was she going to tell him about us? "Whatever she was going to say, it's her story, Micah. She'll tell you when she's awake."

He patted my arm. "You're right. Parent don't get over bein' a parent even when his daughter's a growed woman. Whatever makes her happy, Win, makes me joyous."

Was that his stamp of approval? Or just an admission of trespassing? I didn't ask because a deputy in a stained and muddy combat uniform clomped down the hall. I recognized him. Sarah's chief investigator, John Morgan. The man who saved Sarah's life.

Micah stood and embraced John. "She's not outta surgery, but they say she's gonna make it."

John wiped his eyes. "I got caught up in the after-incident report. Sorry, sir. I should've ridden in the ambulance. I—oh, God, I'm sorry."

Micah motioned John to sit down. "Sorry for what? EMT said you saved her life out there."

"I missed my shot. I missed the damn shot. Shooter returned fire and that's what hit Sarah."

"Son, if I crucified myself for ever' shot I missed since I been a lawman, I'd still be up on that cross, bleedin' somethin' fierce. You done the best you could. Can't ask nothin' more."

CHAPTER THIRTEEN

Sarah

I opened my eyes lid by lid and found the light too bright. I closed them. Where the hell was I? And why did I feel like three-day-old shit? I heard voices, but they seemed far off. I knew I was lying down, my body registered that much. Along with pain. My left shoulder, the whole thing, seemed to be the locus. I started to lift my left hand to explore, but it seemed to be caught up in cables or something.

I opened one eye again, took a quick scan of the room. God knew I'd visited these pale wards before. Hospital room. What had happened to land me here? Slowly it began to come back. Drug bust. Third-party shooters. John cussing. Ducking.

"Guess I wasn't quick enough," I muttered, not caring if anyone heard me or not, just seeing if I could still talk.

"Sarah Anne, you awake?"

Dad. No one else called me Sarah Anne. "Kinda. It's awfully bright in here."

I could feel the lights dim through my lids. I opened them. Dad hovered by my left side and a form stood behind him. "Hey, Dad. Guess I survived. John? He's okay?"

"Surely is."

"The bust?"

"Kinda messy. Haven't really kept up, but it turned out there was seller, buyer and a third party that intended to wipe out the other two. You guys hadn't been there, you woulda been countin' bodies for days."

My eyelids sagged. But I saw the form retreat. "Who else is here? Win? Is Win here?"

"Sure am."

She moved forward and I could see the concern on her face. I just wanted to stroke it, feel her close to me. Not in front of Dad. I hadn't told him yet.

She found my hand, leaned down. "You've got a lot of healing to do."

I smiled. That didn't hurt. "How long? How long have I been here?"

"Shooting was last night," Win answered. "It's about three thirty in the afternoon. Please take it easy."

She squeezed my hand, moved back.

"Best piece of advice I heard in a long time, Sarah Anne. I'm gonna go get the doctor so he can explain what 'take it easy' means."

After Dad left, Win came up to the bed again. "You scared the shit out of me. We should've been talking about...feelings and stuff. Instead, you were out getting shot."

"Freak accident."

"Accident, my ass. Combat."

"Have I told you you've got a beautiful ass?"

Win smiled, took a look over her shoulder and kissed me. I didn't want her to stop, but I knew this wasn't the place. She pulled back, held my hand again.

"How bad is it?" I asked.

"Doctors know more than I do."

"Tell me what you know. It hurts like hell all over my shoulder."

"Bullet went in above your vest, nicked an artery, then smashed into your collarbone, fragmented. Fragments wandered."

"Jesus, no wonder it hurts. I always said those damn vests need a collar." I heard voices in the hall and Win took the visitor's chair. The doctor came in and told me the good, the bad and the ugly.

* * *

Win hung out at the hospital most nights, Dad took the days. Dad brought in novels to read aloud, Win would pick up where Dad left off. When most people were asleep and the hall quiet, Win would say, "Want to talk a bit and then fool around a little?"

The talk was good, even though I felt so vulnerable. "Little" was the operative word on fooling around, kissing just about it. She wouldn't put me at risk of being discovered by an errant night nurse. It just left me wanting more and, when I dozed off, dreams about a fuller expression.

Caleb came in daily to give me a briefing. The investigation into our department's involvement in the bust was pretty straightforward. All our units had been in correct position and had followed the proper procedure. John and I had been given the green light because a wave of cops was ready to go in and the snipers could have cut them down. I'd gotten my shooter, not a kill shot, but serious enough to stop him.

Cards and flowers from all over made my room a florist's shop. I made the nurses share them with other patients at the end of every day. All my deputies stopped by, a lot of them uncomfortable with my hospital gown instead of my uniform. Okay, I reminded them what could happen to any cop. John had been a daily visitor until Dad had chased him out, saying, "Go catch the bad guys—much better way to atone for a missed shot."

After a couple of weeks, they wheeled me down to rehab and I began working on limited mobility for my shoulder. The exercises weren't fun and certainly didn't add much mobility. I had a rod where part of my collarbone had been. I had to be careful or I'd screw up the whole thing, go back to surgery and begin again.

I wanted out. I hated the smells, the noise and the constant traffic. I wanted summer and the smell of fresh-mown hay. To hear the bellowing of cows in the pasture down the road. To lie on my favorite rock on the creek and feel the sun's warmth on both sides of my body.

One night, Win walked in with a suspiciously large smile and a nurse with a wheelchair trailing behind. The nurse was smiling too.

They got me out of bed, into the wheelchair and flying down the hall with Win's long legs guiding me toward the elevator. "Where are we going?"

"I could've blindfolded you. Pipe down. Enjoy the suspense."

The elevator doors pinged open. We rode down to the first floor, then followed a hall to the chapel. "You want to pray?" I asked.

Win didn't say anything, just wheeled me through the door, down a side aisle and out a door I'd never noticed. I heard a small fountain and smelled roses. I took a deep breath, inhaling summer and roses.

The wedge of night sky shimmered with stars. "How'd you find this place?"

"Walks," she said, maneuvering my chair beside the fountain. "Long walks around the grounds those first few days, wondering if you'd really be okay."

I took her hand, kissed her calloused palm.

"We can't do anything out here, but I thought you'd like the night sky. Cloudless. Not as many stars as some places in the world. Still pretty enough."

Had Azar and Win spent time together, looking at stars in the thin air of Afghan mountains? I thought so and felt a twinge. I looked up and began naming constellations. Win added some. "Navigating through enemy territory, we use the stars. Same as travelers have done for millennia."

She sat beside my chair, took my hand and caressed it. "We've managed to create technology beyond the dreams of those ancient travelers. With it, more efficient ways to kill one another. Why does somebody's religion matter? Their color of skin? What the fuck does it matter?"

"Or their sexual orientation?" I asked softly.

"That too, Sarah. But being gay doesn't start wars."

We both stared at the sky, wrapped in silence, perhaps in our own thoughts. But she continued her slow rubbing of my hand. I wanted to move both hands to someplace more interesting, but along with the sky view, I saw hospital room windows, some lit, some in darkness. I hated the sneakiness, but I didn't know what to do about it. I didn't know so much.

"Win, what's it like?"

Since my eyes adjusted, I could see her look up at me. She had no idea what I was asking. Or else refused to acknowledge it.

"I love what we've done so far. You know, together. My body's never felt so alive."

"Even with a shattered collarbone?"

"You know what I'm talking about. Now answer me."

She kissed my palm. "I'll get you a book. It'll answer your questions. Without putting you back in the hospital."

"Win!"

She moved a hand to my shin and rubbed it gently. "I can give you a technical account, Sarah. But it's nothing you haven't guessed. The magic happens in the act. I'd like to wait to show you."

"With this damn shoulder, it could be months."

She looked at me, her eyes luminous where starlight reflected something inside her. "I was in therapy with Emily before we met up again. Getting better. Paria and all his crap got my PTSD going again. She does this dumb shit where she looks at me with her eyes half-closed and knows what's happening with me."

"What's this got to do with wanting you?" Then I remembered the way Emily had looked at me. "She knows? Did you tell her?"

"She put it together herself. I saw her the afternoon after we talked about getting together. I couldn't deny it, Sarah. I trust her. She needs to trust me."

I nodded. "I know she won't say anything to anybody, but it makes me feel weird. Exposed."

"Were you going to tell your dad?"

I took her hand in mine. "Yes. I was so happy and I wanted to share that happiness with Dad. I didn't think how it would make you feel because he respects you and couldn't care less that you're a woman."

"Are you sure that isn't wishful thinking?"

"Yes."

"Emily wants us to do couple's counseling with her before we, uh, take it further."

I was stunned. "You told her we hadn't slept together? But that we'd…"

"Declared interest." She wrapped her hand around my calf. "I need Emily. To help me understand myself. My baggage. So I can always be here with you. Not dodging bombs in my dreams. Not ready to kill you if I wake from one. If you can't do this, I understand. You have other dealings with her. Professional dealings." She leaned her head on my knee. "But I think she could help us make a good foundation."

Could I bare my soul to Emily and then go on with business when our paths crossed? I sighed and stroked Win's hair. "I don't know, Win. But I'll think about it."

When we got back to my room and the night nurse was satisfied I was unhurt, Win closed the door behind her. She came to the bed, kissed me softly and slipped a hand under my gown. I moaned. We kissed for a long time, her hand caressing my body, just not between my legs. Whenever I began to move, she backed off, worried that I'd hurt my shoulder. Damn the shooter.

CHAPTER FOURTEEN

Win

Though I'd taken Sarah outside to the tiny courtyard again, I hadn't repeated what happened after. I didn't want to set her progress back to her first days in the hospital. Her rehab was going slow. Much too slowly for her. That scared me. I'd learned, the hard way, to listen to the docs. My thigh had been blown apart, for all practical purposes. I'd been out of the field for almost eight months. Learning how to walk again. Learning how to maneuver over harsh terrain. I could've retired then, with medical disability. But I didn't. The damn bastards who'd blown up the Humvee would've won. Fuck them.

If I hadn't gone back, I'd have never met Azar. I knew one thing: Azar had opened me in a way that had never happened before.

Once, after we'd made love, she'd said to me, "Your petals are unfolding, one by one. And you are beautiful." I clasped her to me, my mind numbed and confused. "Don't be so afraid of being beautiful, Homa."

Homa. Her nickname for me. A mythological bird from Persia supposed to bestow great benefit to those who were crossed by its shadow. Not true for her. Also a great bird who possessed both male and female natures. That made sense to me, but I wasn't sure about the free-spirit meaning. I'd never felt like a free spirit, more like one bound to military protocols. Things I couldn't change.

A beautiful, powerful bird who never rested. Not me, no matter what Azar thought. Since Sarah had been brought in, I'd managed on naps in the late morning and afternoon. I couldn't shake waking at reveille. Nor could I stop watching Sarah sleep through the night. This bird was getting tired.

I watched Sarah come out of the bathroom, arm in a sling, managing. Mostly propelled by fierce pride. When she was settled in bed, I turned off the light above it.

"If you're going to tell Micah about us, I want to be there."

She studied my face. "Is that a bribe to get me to see Emily?"

"No."

"Will you come home with me tomorrow? We'll talk to Dad then."

My stomach churned. "You're supposed to be released at ten in the morning, but they're never on time. I'll come over to your house at one." The sheriff's department had arranged an honor guard to send her home. The newspaper would be there. Photographs taken. I didn't need to be seen with her.

She nodded. "You just hate standing around, waiting."

"Damn right." I moved to the bed, held her hand. "I don't want Micah to hate me for…spoiling his little girl."

She gave me a quizzical look. "Dad's not like that—unless you mean 'spoil' as in giving too many presents. He's always believed in moderation."

"Not the meaning I was thinking of, Sarah."

She pulled my hand to her breast, and I could feel the nipple tighten under the fabric. "He's always been protective, but he's not a bigot. Let's not borrow trouble. Let's just 'fool around' a little."

The door was closed. As she got better, the night checks had become fewer, then stopped. I wanted to strip off my clothes, climb in bed with her. Explore every feature of her body. Kiss her from crown to sole. But it wasn't time yet. Not for her shoulder. Not for Emily.

"Emily said you have to see her for after-incident clearance. I could take you and then nobody would be the wiser. Think about it. Good cover for us."

I slipped my hand under her gown and slid it from her breast down to her belly.

She responded immediately. "Oh God, Win!"

"I want to do this when you can fling your arms around me. Reach my butt and let me know what you want. What rhythm. That can't happen until you're physically ready. Shoulder healed. Trust me."

I withdrew my hand after tracing her inner thigh. Skin so soft.

She was breathing fast, her lids heavy over her eyes. She opened them and focused on my face. "Shit. This is extortion. All right. I'll see Emily. She damn well better find me ready to return to duty. In all ways ready for any kind of duty."

I kissed her softly. Didn't linger. I picked up the novel-in-progress. Opened it to Micah's bookmark. Began to read. My voice shook. I loved giving her pleasure. Awakening desire.

* * *

Micah had been great. Super. Had embraced me. Literally and figuratively. Asked me if I could stay with Sarah when he went back to Vincennes. "She don't think she's still hurtin', an' I reckon you know better. 'Sides, could be it's the only time you'll be able to be together, all quiet with nobody botherin' you. Reckon on leavin' tomorrow, be gone four or five days." He'd taken my hand. "You both gonna have a hard row to plow. Don't let the secret burrow deep in your heart, 'cause it'll eat up all the love, Winifred. Someday, even here, people ain't gonna care. You're just gonna have to wait 'em out."

I'd gone home. Packed conservatively, as if I was going to visit a spinster aunt. Just in case. The beginning of a long string of plan Bs, I was afraid. What had Emily said? That I was free of restraints. Shit.

I felt like Micah's stamp of approval was the only thing that mattered. I knew it wasn't, but hell, it was one big hurdle overcome.

The next big hurdle was Emily. Or more precisely, Sarah seeing Emily.

"She already knows, Sarah," I said as I settled on the couch beside her. My duffel was in the guest room. "So what's the big deal about hearing what she's got to say? She's lesbian. She understands."

"Maybe that's it," Sarah said, letting her head rest on the back of the couch. "It's like I'd be naked—she knows what we do."

"And what we haven't done?"

Sarah blushed. "Damn. I wish to God you'd just finish what you begin."

"So you'd know? If you really want to hook up with a woman?"

She was silent for a long time. "Because I want to experience that moment with you. My body's craving it and every time we kiss, I don't want to stop. Screw my shoulder. Take me, and then teach me how to pleasure you."

"I'll teach you everything I know. Emily's not going to change that." I reached over, traced her jaw.

"I know you need Emily, but as long as it's just you and me, it seems so right. I don't want her to take that away."

Internalized homophobia, whether she recognized it or not. I should've expected it. "Nobody can take away the way we feel. They can dirty it. Try and make us feel like shit. So far, they sure haven't succeeded with me."

She leaned into me, tucked her head under my chin. I couldn't see her face, but I could feel the turmoil in her body. I lifted her chin, kissed her. "Sarah, Emily can help you understand what you're feeling. I've been out forever, so I'm kind of thick when it comes to understanding whatever you're feeling now."

"All I want to feel is sexy and happy. I don't want people, even you, probing. We've got five days alone together, and all I want to do is spend them in bed with you. When else are we going to get a chance like this?"

"We can take a vacation—"

"Five days here. Just you and me."

"Cocooned in the family homestead," I said. "We have to leave sooner or later. You to work, me to my own home. Let me call Emily, set the earliest appointment possible."

She took a deep breath. "If I have to get naked in front of Emily to get naked with you, so be it."

Before she could change her mind, I called Emily. She had an opening the next morning at nine.

I told Sarah and sat on the couch. Farther away this time. "We're going to have to figure out how to immobilize your shoulder."

"I don't want anything immobilized."

"What is it with you? Horny as a cat in heat."

"Middle-age body, no regular sex in fifteen years and when I've had it, it was spectacularly unsatisfying. This is like when Hugh and I started dating. I mean, the arousal I feel when I look at you. I don't know what to say, Win."

"Pretty far from a sober sheriff."

"Yes, for five days, I get to be giddy. Then I have to assume the cloak of responsibility again. I just want to share this time with you. Be not-me." She reached over with her good arm and pulled me closer.

It was going to be a rough twenty-three hours.

CHAPTER FIFTEEN

Sarah

As we waited for our appointment, I raked the sand in neat concentric patterns around the rocks in the tiny garden. One, peanut-shaped and black, looked like something I would pluck from the creek. Its smooth middle would fit my thumb.

The concentration helped me stay in my chair and not run. I felt exposing myself to Em was the equivalent of standing on Courthouse Square and stripping off my uniform. The next time we met at a meeting, Em would see me naked again.

"It's all an illusion, you know," Win said.

I looked up. She'd been watching me. "What?"

"That we have control over anything. It's an illusion." She stared at the careful pattern I'd made. "Another client comes in. Changes it. Then another and another. The pattern you worked so hard to form is gone." She moved her gaze to me. "A 'routine' traffic stop. Two missiles shot into the wrong village. The pattern is lost. So is my notion of control."

The office door opened and Emily called us in. She'd pulled another matching chair into the grouping. A wrapped package with a multi-colored bow leaned against the back of one.

"For you, Sarah," Em said as she sat. "*The Whole Lesbian Sex Book*. I thought I'd better camouflage it as a get-well present."

I could feel my face heat up. "Thanks." I picked it up with my good hand and balanced its weight while I sat.

"I heard Micah was there every day, shooing people away when it got too much."

I nodded. Where was she going with this? Or was it just chitchat so I'd lower my defenses?

"Have you told him about Win?"

"Of course, and he's fine with it. Supportive."

"How many other fathers in McCrumb County do you think would be 'fine' discovering their daughter's fucking another woman?"

I felt like she'd hit me in the stomach with a baseball bat.

"If your partnership is uncovered, are you prepared to be called *fag*? *Dyke*? *Lezzie*? In public? Because you're a *public* figure."

I blushed. Win sat impassively, ankles crossed. "We'll be careful—"

"That's not what I asked you," Em snapped. "I asked if you're prepared to take that kind of abuse. What happens one day when you leave work and find those ugly words spray-painted on your car?"

"I'd review our damn security tapes and arrest the bastard."

"Then go your merry way?" Em stared. "Sarah, you have to be prepared for the worst. You have to admit what could happen. All those people who visited you in the hospital could run the other way if they found out you have a woman lover."

"Dammit, Em!" I brought my fist down on the book. "I know there's a bunch of crap out there. I investigated Natalie's rape, and her death. I know the ugliness. I'll deal with it if it comes. But all I want now is to be lighthearted. To feel open to a sexuality I didn't know I had. So, quit with the doom and gloom."

Emily stared at me, her eyes half-mast. Was this the weird stuff Win had mentioned? Was she scoping out my soul? I freed a disgusted breath.

"As much as you don't want to hear anything negative, the secret-keeping will take a toll on both of you. Especially until the election. If things get too hairy, will you come see me?"

I nodded.

"If you want to build a good relationship, you both have to contribute," Emily said. "I know Win's problem areas and how hard she's been working through them. Sarah, you can help her heal, or you can hurt her. You can't keep your stresses under wraps and think you're continuing to contribute to the relationship. You're going to have to be open with Win."

I nodded. "I can do that. I've been more open with Win than anybody in a long time."

"Well, just remember you said that," Emily said. "On another tack, I've seen your X-rays and medical records—I wasn't snooping, it's just so I can give the green light and you can return to work. I gather you two plan to jump into the sack as soon as possible."

"Jesus, Em. You want film?"

"Practical issue, Sarah. You want to go back for another surgery? Start rehab over?"

"No. Win's already harped on that."

"I can't figure out how to keep the shoulder immobile," Win said.

I shook my head, pissed off about the casual conversation about an extremely private act.

Emily shifted her attention to Win. "You're going to be guiding the expedition, I assume."

Win shrugged. "I'm not sure I've guided anything so far." She grinned. "Wild woman."

Emily grinned back. I felt the heat rising from my neck. Damn.

"Go through the book with Sarah, see what positions will take pressure off her shoulder. There are a couple of positions I could suggest, but I'm afraid Sarah would crawl under her chair." She turned to me, an irrepressible smile on her face. "Just remember, you can still have full sexual gratification while you protect your shoulder. As it heals, you can explore more."

"Okay, okay. I get it."

"Do you feel all right talking about what feels good with Win?"

"Yes."

"I've been concerned about you because I've never known you to rush into anything. You keep yourself controlled, measured. I've outlined the problems you may face, both now and in the future. Everything you said is strictly confidential." She reached forward, handed me a sheet of paper. "Your clearance. But promise me, if you need to talk with me, you'll call."

I folded the form.

"I know," Em said. "Before this, we were colleagues. Now you think you're my client. You're not. You came in as a partner of a client. Next time we meet, this conversation never happened. I'm not going to treat you as anything but a valued colleague." She stood.

I guessed we were finished. I stood up too. Emily opened her arms and we hugged. I sighed. "Thanks, Em."

"It wasn't too painful?" she asked.

I shook my head. "Not as bad as surgery but close to rehab."

She laughed. "Go to it, tiger."

* * *

Win kept removing my hand from her thigh all the way home. "Shit, Sarah, I've got to drive!"

I moved it onto my lap, then used it to adjust my sling. "It's just...I want to know what you look like, feel like." I fiddled with her radio. "Is there a gay station?"

"Oh, God. You're turning into a fiend."

"Isn't there any such thing? Special music?"

"Women's music. I don't have any with me, but when you come over, I'll have a whole stack lined up."

I knew I couldn't visit Win's often, nor stay overnight. Friends had dinner together, watched movies once every couple of weeks. If Dad was home, I couldn't see me excusing myself to go upstairs and make love with Win. Hugh and I never had. Maybe I was just a prude, embarrassed about sex.

Win piloted her truck into the drive and to the back door. She helped me out of the truck, opened the back door for me. Solicitous. God, she had to drop it or we'd never get anywhere. With Em's green light, that's all I could think about.

"We didn't eat breakfast, so you want me to fix something now?" Win asked.

"Just me. Let's go upstairs."

Win shook her head. "We've got homework to do. I'm worried about your shoulder. Let's go in the living room and look through the book."

She was so serious, I almost laughed. "I'm not going to be swinging from a chandelier."

"How do you know that?" She took my hand and led me to the couch.

Win studied the drawings with intensity, but my interest was a different kind. I noticed my breathing was getting ragged.

"This might work," she said, pointing to a sketch of two women, fully engaged.

I took the book out of her hands and pulled her closer. "We'll invent something. Maybe I can just leave my sling on."

"That might work, but you still can't put pressure on the shoulder." She removed the sling, unbuttoned my blouse and eased it off. I wouldn't be able to wear a bra for another month, so she had a clear view. She kissed my mangled shoulder, then cupped my breasts, kissed them lightly and sucked them softly. Time slowed into an exquisite dance of touch and tongue. I'd never known the range of pleasure Win gave me.

"Don't I get to play tit for tit?" I asked.

She stripped off her T-shirt and bra. "Touch me whenever you want, Sarah. As long as it doesn't take you away from your own pleasure."

I sucked in my breath. "They're beautiful and there's no sag."

"Not enough there to sag."

I moved my hand to her breast, ran a finger around the areola and watched her nipple grow rosy and tighter. I kissed it and then sucked slowly, gently. I moved my kisses up to the hollow of her neck, then to her lips.

As she kissed me, I ran my good hand over her breasts, echoing the rhythm of her kisses. When her mouth moved lower, I threw my good arm around her, felt the muscles in her back. Her hand returned to my thigh, moved to the other one when I opened my legs. Brushed my crotch. Moved up to my belly while she sucked on one breast. I kept pulling her to me.

She unzipped my jeans, then pulled back. "I think it's time to go upstairs. If you're ready."

Yes, yes, yes.

CHAPTER SIXTEEN

Win

I'd led Sarah upstairs, then to the mountain. So to speak. Took side paths, but always doubled back to her growing passion. She came in an explosion of sound and movement. As I lay beside her, breathing in her scent, I thought of the image I'd always carry with me. Sarah, opening the window when we'd first come into her bedroom. The curtain fluttering over her breasts. The sun a bright diagonal that ended at her open jeans. Turning. Looking at me with such sweet desire. Trust. Nervousness an underlying thrum.

"It's heating up," she'd said. Grinned. Walked to me. Leaned against me. "I'm too aroused to be scared. So do your magic, Win."

I'd wrapped my arms around her. We'd stood that way for minutes. Slightly rocking back and forth. I'd felt her spirit and mine merging.

Now the sun was almost down behind the trees to the west. I was in a sleepy stupor. Also hungry. I eased out of bed, dressed and went downstairs to the kitchen. I opened the fridge, hoping for eggs and bacon. I saw a covered casserole. With a note tucked into the lid.

Reckon you might not feel like cooking food. Heat @ 350 for half an hour. Another one in freezer. Love, Micah

I steadied my breath. Sent him my thanks. Put it in the oven. Micah was a mystery to me. When I was a kid, he'd kept a close eye on me. With reason. I wasn't a wild child, but had to admit to a rather fond attachment for pranks. He'd clamped down on those with more serious repercussions. Just gave me his patented stare for the rest. "'Member, Win, what you think is fun can hurt people. Think of that afore you do somethin'."

I hadn't exactly taken it to heart, but the advice had stopped me from doing a couple of dumb capers. In high school, my pranks left behind, he'd welcomed me into his home. Even gave me advice about going into law enforcement. Little did he know the path he'd set me on.

The one thing I was sure about Micah Barrow was that he was genuine, through and through.

I heard a car on the drive and pulled back the kitchen curtain. Paria come again? No, a sheriff's cruiser. Caleb Habstadt, Win's chief deputy, got out. Tugged up his duty belt. I glanced in a mirror. My hair was disheveled. But then it usually was. I finger-combed it and hoped for the best.

He tapped on the back door and I opened it.

"Hey, Win. Glad to know you're on the job," he said with a smile. "Micah said you'd pulled duty while he's finishing up in Vincennes. Bet Sarah's plenty cranky and I don't envy you."

Not cranky at all. But I couldn't give an explanation. "She's asleep. I think her rehab exercises wear her out."

"Sarah can push through almost anything—don't you let her work out too hard."

I lifted an eyebrow. "Stop her from doing anything she's decided on? Are you kidding?"

He sighed. "Yeah, well." He handed me a file folder. "Blotter from last night and today. I've been trying to keep her up-to-date. I keep wondering if I should."

"I'm sure she'd be really testy if you didn't. So I thank you." I wondered if I should ask him to stay for dinner.

"Tell her I said hi and not to worry about the department. We're managing." He winked. "Barely."

I watched him turn the cruiser around and head down the drive. Heard a floorboard creak by the hallway. Turned. Saw Sarah in a robe. Without her sling, her Glock held in both hands. Paria would haunt this house for a long time.

"I heard the car—should've looked out the window." She set the Glock on a counter and walked to me.

We embraced and I kissed her. Opened her robe to get her arm back in the sling. That accomplished, I caressed her naked body. Kissed her again. Then drew back and retied the robe.

"Dinner will be ready in about twenty minutes," I said. "Courtesy of your dad."

She sniffed. "One of his curries. Hope he didn't experiment too much—sometimes he gets carried away with his new culinary skills."

"Sit and I'll make a salad." Surprisingly she did. "How's your shoulder? You didn't hurt it, did you?"

"Not that I'm aware of. You planned well." She smiled, ducked her head. "When are you going to let me return the gift?"

I found a salad, already prepared except the dressing. Shut the refrigerator door. "Your shoulder makes that a bit problematic. You want help getting dressed?"

"Why get dressed just to get undressed again?"

"Visitors?"

"No. This is my home and I'll be damned if I can't wear what I want. We'll have to worry about crap like that too soon. Besides, I'm convalescing, and an old flannel robe is appropriate."

I looked at her as I transferred the salad. I could see most of one breast and more of one leg. "Without anything underneath?"

"I may never wear a bra again. I like being 'unbound.'" She grinned.

"God woman, you've been possessed by a hussy."

"Feels wonderful." She got up and went to the cupboard. "I've been thinking. I still own the cabin at Red Hawk Lake. Mary Cloud's rented it since Hugh died, but I'm sure I could ask her for a few days now and then. Want to go fishing?"

"Anytime."

"I haven't been back since I left that night. It's time. I think I've known it for years but couldn't get the energy to do it."

"Sarah, we don't have to—"

"I'm ready to go back to the cabin for a visit. Thanks to you. You've brought me back to life." She turned and got out plates, one by one.

I hurried to help her. She stopped me, slipped her hand under my T-shirt. Then her other hand moved to join in. She massaged my breasts. Kissed me.

"I have much more mobility than you give me credit for." She raised my shirt with her good hand, moved her mouth to my breast. Her free hand moved down to my stomach. "We could do it here if you sit on the counter. It said so in the book."

The timer went off. I drew a shaky breath. "Time for dinner."

* * *

We actually ate dinner. Sarah turned out to be as ravenous as I was. I washed dishes and Sarah dried. Comfy. Domestic. I hadn't brought music, but a DVD. I handed her the last dish and let the water out of the sink. "You up for a movie?"

"You know what I'm up for," Sarah replied.

I shook my head. "I always knew you were single-tracked, but this…" I kissed her forehead. "I brought a lesbian love story. *The Touch of Spring*. Beautiful story."

"Do they ride off into the sunset together?"

"I'm not going to tell you the ending. Come on in and watch it. I'll tell you what I like while we watch."

"It's porn?"

"No. It's a love story. But there's one scene…"

I ran upstairs to retrieve the disc. When I came back down to the living room, Sarah was already settled on the couch. Robe demurely closed. I sat down beside her, put my arm around her shoulders. Carefully.

I'd watched this movie many times, first on videotape. I'd bought a DVD when I'd returned here. Watched with envy. Wondered at the love those two women discovered. How it grew. Feeling the lack of it in my own life. Now I could share it with Sarah.

"Do I have to be good?" she asked as she settled into me.

"Yes." I was amazed by her lustiness. Her desire. This wasn't the Sarah I'd grown up with. Or maybe she was. Only the passion then had been channeled into wandering the woods and fields. When we'd grown up, she'd had all the intensity I experienced now. Directed in a different direction—toward honoring the sheriff's badge.

"When was this made?" she asked.

"Late eighties, I think. Why?"

"It could be today, here."

"I know, Sarah. Sometimes change stays underground for a long time, then bursts through and blooms."

"Depends on the soil, doesn't it?"

I kissed the top of her head. We watched the film in silence until The Scene. Her breathing increased.

"Go back—play that part again."

I did. Three times.

"Do you like that?" she asked, touching my thigh.

"Yes." My voice was husky. I'd liked it so much that the first time Azar did it, I'd cried.

I closed my eyes. Azar. I'm on a new life adventure, love. Guide me in this. Guide Sarah. This is so new to her, she needs someone standing beside her.

I remembered one night Azar had touched my face. "Homa, you have no idea how big your heart is. If things don't work out—if I can't make it to America—you will discover your heart is big enough to love again." I hadn't believed her.

"Start the scene over," Sarah said.

Her voice brought me back to a living room in McCrumb County. Both women trusted me. Took huge risks to love me. I hit the button.

When the movie was over, she turned to me. "I'm so afraid I can't..."

"Bring me to orgasm?"

"Yes."

I pulled her close and stroked her hair. "It really doesn't matter that much now. If we're both on social security and you still haven't managed, I will be cranky. Promise."

"But—"

"It's not about orgasms. It's more than that. It's about forming a bond. Maybe being open. Something emotional that I've felt for one other woman."

She took my hand. "I have, for a man. What does that mean, Win?"

"No idea." I intertwined her fingers with mine. "I've known a lot of women who didn't come out until middle age. Some had been married, some not. Maybe it's hormonal." I kissed her fingers. "Having avoided emotional bonds until I met Azar, I'm probably not the person to ask about it."

"I don't want to ask. I don't want to analyze." She kissed me, her tongue insistent, probing. "I just want to do. You. Tell me—no, show me—what to do to make you a puddle of a woman like you've made me."

CHAPTER SEVENTEEN

Sarah

Our uninterrupted days together passed too quickly. It amazed me how hungry I became for her body. I found new ways to set her moaning and learned to sense her quickening response.

"Just wait until I have full mobility," I'd said one morning after breakfast.

She'd grinned and lifted herself onto the counter. "Screw full mobility."

Since she only wore an oversize Navy football jersey, it wasn't hard to accept the invitation. Whatever inhibitions I'd had were vaporized.

But it hadn't been just physical exploration. I'd found myself talking about Hugh in a way I never had before. I think Win found she could talk about Azar in the same way. She'd also spoken about some of her war experiences, horrible times, things that had scarred her. I hoped hearing her own words helped her bring "her demons out of the cave." I wasn't sure what she meant by that phrase, but I understood the feeling behind the words.

Dad called on our last day. "Two hours out, Sarah. Fair warnin'."

I laughed, then gave the warning to Win. She'd quickly led me upstairs. By the time he got home, we were demurely sharing cooking chores. It was crushing to watch her drive away.

"Ain't gonna ask how it went, Sarah Anne," he said. "You got yourself a glow." He kissed me on the forehead.

I smelled her scent when I went to bed and felt desire shake me so hard I wanted to ask her to come back. Maybe we shouldn't have had so much time together. What the hell were we going to do now? I wanted to feel her next to me, touch her, feel her touch on me. I finally gave up around three a.m. and went down to the front porch. Dad had put our rockers out, and I finally rocked myself to sleep. The lightening sky woke me up.

I went up to face one of the hardest things for me to do alone: shower. The first time in five days I'd had to. This time, it took me half an hour to maneuver. I tried to put my uniform shirt on, couldn't quite manage it and had to call Dad.

"You goin' back to work?" he asked.

"Yeah. Doctor hasn't cleared me for anything but desk duty, but I need to…"

"Keep busy." He nodded. "I'll drive you in. An' pick you up for your doctor's appointment. Be a half day, but I reckon that's enough to keep you busy. Bring home paperwork needs doin'. Mebbe that'll help tonight."

When I walked into the station, I got a standing ovation. It was gratifying, but I was embarrassed by the attention. Caleb walked me to my office. "Want to have our usual morning meeting?"

"Yes. Please. I've missed them, Caleb. Missed getting into a case up to my elbows."

"Are you going back on the campaign trail?"

I shrugged my good shoulder. "I've been ducking Charlene. I had the nurses trained—if they saw her coming, they'd call, and by the time she got to the room, I'd be asleep."

"Doesn't sound like you want to be reelected much."

Be a lot easier for Win and me if I wasn't. "It's complicated, Caleb." I sat in my chair, and Caleb pulled a chair up to my desk. "I love this job, but the responsibility never goes away. This is the first time I've been away from the job since I was elected. It was hard to hand over the reins to you. You understand?"

He nodded.

"It's something you'll have to reckon with when you take over."

"That's a long time in the distance, Sarah."

"Yeah, sure. Let's get me caught up."

He ran over the current cases while I took notes. Writing with my pad on my lap wasn't easy.

"And," he said, handing me a thin file, "this is something that don't add up. New family moved to the old Kingman place. Bought the place, not rented. But their neighbor, uh—"

"Luke Feinhold?"

"Yeah. He came in two days ago. Didn't want to make a complaint or anything, but he voiced a concern. Said the guy who bought the place don't have a job and there's a lot a traffic in and out some nights. Thought it could be a poker game or something, but they didn't stay long enough."

"So you're thinking what I'm thinking?"

"Drug distributor. Could be a meth lab. I've put it under surveillance. We'll know more today, but we're going to have keep up surveillance to build a case."

"Dammit, Caleb." I slammed my good hand on my desk. "I'll bet half the buyers already have a jacket with us. We arrest them and they're back on the street in a year and a half." I ran my smarting hand through my hair. "Good job, Caleb. Keep me up to speed. I've got a doctor's appointment later today, so call me at home if anything breaks."

"You're not cleared for ops."

"I'll talk to the doctor, see if I can get clearance to ride along if any of this proves out."

He looked skeptical but nodded.

* * *

I sat at my desk, doing the duty roster and flaking away to think about…stuff. Distracted by life.

When I'd had my appointment, the doctor was pleased with my recovery but wouldn't sign off on any police busts. "Just to ride along?" I asked. He ignored me.

When I got home, I found Charlene camped out on the front porch. She badgered me until I let her set up a few appearances, beginning next week. "You're gonna get a lot of sympathy votes, Sarah, so be sure to wear your sling." I could've strangled her with it.

My days at the station grew in length. So did our surveillance of Mark Jarek, his wife Susan and their two kids. We photographed his visitors and I was right. Some of them had rap sheets going back to when they were juveniles and I was a rookie. We were sure the shed in back was the meth lab. At least the kids weren't allowed in the shed, but if they were cooking, they'd spread the poison into the house. We got a warrant to tap their phone and computer traffic and waited to build the case. It angered me that more poison was filling the county, but we couldn't tip our hand.

I called Win and she called me, usually late at night. Some of it was pillow talk, some just talk about the day. She'd applied for a job teaching language at IU and was due to go in for an interview soon. I hadn't realized she was proficient at so many Middle East languages. She'd said, "I can say 'I want you' in fifteen different languages and more dialects." When she began, I'd shushed her.

I knew the sheriff's department couldn't hire her when she was sleeping with the boss, so I was glad she'd found something where she could use her skills. Still, it would've been nice to work with her and see her most days. She'd invited me for dinner Friday night—and included Dad. When I'd passed on the invitation, he said, "Thank her for her generous invitation, but I reckon I really don't wanna be a third wheel."

"Fifth wheel."

"She got two more comin'? My, my. But I'm too old. Probably have a heart attack." He'd gone back to reading his newspaper, hiding behind it to laugh. He hadn't seen my blush.

Caleb tapped at my office doorjamb. "Got a minute?"

"Sure." I cleared the top of my desk.

He dropped into a chair. "We gotta stop Jarek."

"I agree, wholeheartedly. We have a good line on his distribution routes?"

"Yeah, just finished the last one." He brushed his mustache with his finger. "We could do ops Saturday night. That's when he gets most of his traffic."

"Okay. But he may have ten to twenty guys there, so we're going to have to call in the state cops on this one."

He nodded. "What about DEA?"

I drummed my fingers on the desk. "I'm not comfortable with the way some of their agents operate. They're cowboys, used to acting alone. See how many cops the post can give us first."

He nodded again. "Know what you mean, some scary dudes in DEA." More mustache fiddling. "You not planning to roll on this one, are you?"

"Why shouldn't I? I won't be in on the action, but I sure as hell want to be there." I stared at him, willing him to see what I saw. "These are my people, Caleb, going into combat. What kind of leader would I be here, monitoring the action from a safe distance?"

"A wounded leader, still healing," he said. He held up his hand. "At least think about it. No one here is going to think less of you."

"I would."

CHAPTER EIGHTEEN

Win

"So, how would you like to take care of a wounded warrior, Win?" Bill asked. "Named Destroyer, called Des. Think you met her in Kabul."

"A dog? Real sweetie? But would tear a terrorist apart without fear?"

"The same. I'd feel better if you had someone at your back."

"Why? What've you heard?"

"Nothing concrete, so don't get yourself in a lather. Tell you more when I drop her off. Going to be home tomorrow?"

"Yeah. But I don't remember saying yes to a dog."

"Under that rough exterior is a heart that could never say no to a dog in need. See you early afternoon."

He hung up. I wondered what the hell had just happened. I'd never had a dog, though I'd always wanted one. Mom had said no. Allergic. Bullshit. She just didn't want to be bothered.

Since I'd come home, I'd been thinking about getting one. A hunting dog. Not a ferocious dog used to disarming the enemy. If it was just me, no visitors, it'd be no problem.

What had he heard? I'd felt my spider senses tingling a couple of times lately. But I checked, thoroughly. Didn't find anything. I marked it down to hypervigilance. Something I didn't need anymore. Something that would find me hunkered down. Waiting for an attack that never came.

Just to be on the safe side, I went into Greenglen to the pet store. Left my bank account behind as I headed home.

I heard a truck coming up my drive at noon the next day. Sounded a lot like the shiny red one the general had driven. Grabbed my Glock, just to be sure. Same truck, only about ten years older, dinged up and white. Bill got out of the passenger seat. Stood where I could see him. I put the Glock in a kitchen drawer and opened the door.

"So?" I asked.

"I want you to meet Jo Campbell," he said.

I watched as a petite woman got out of the driver's side. "Nice place, Des will love it here," she said.

"Jo is the best trainer I know," Bill said. "She'll help Des get adjusted. To you, and to retirement." He looked at Jo. Then me. "Ready?"

She went around to the back of the truck, motioned me to follow. Des was in a crate, looked curious. Not threatened.

"You met the dog?" Jo asked.

"Yeah. Spent a few days with her. Well, in the same billet. Right before I went into the mountains. A couple of years ago. Will she remember me?"

"Let's find out." She unlatched the crate secured in the bed, put a lead on Des and helped her down.

The dog had had a swath of fur shaved on her side and I could see a long, narrow wound. "Shrapnel?" I asked.

"Yeah. Guess you've seen that before."

"We match, except mine is on my thigh. Should I—"

"Just stand still. If she comes up to you, hold out both hands, palm up. Close to you."

Des scented, looked around. Then at me. Her tail began to wag. She walked up to me, Jo behind her, lead firmly in her hand. I held out my hands. She took another step forward, sniffed gently, then put her paws on my shoulders and licked my face. I took her ruff in my hands and kissed her back. She was grinning like crazy, tail going like a beat box.

"I've never seen that before," Jo said. "You must've made quite an impression on her."

"We'll never tell, will we, girl?" I grinned at Jo.

"I'd like to take her around the property so she gets all the scents now. Okay?"

"Sure."

When Jo was out of range, I asked Bill what news he had of the crap-assed general.

"I can't get a good line on it, Win, but I heard he's hired somebody to keep an eye on you."

"Shit!" I banged my fist down on the truck's hood. It hurt.

"He really can't touch you unless you're doing something illegal."

"Maybe not me."

"You're involved with someone?"

I nodded.

"Everybody knows you're gay. You kept it out of sight for a lot of years, but it's not going to hurt you now." Bill's eye grew large. "Your lover?"

I nodded. "Involved in a campaign for public office."

"Oh, man." He ran a hand through his buzz cut. "You think he might use any intel he gathers to force you to work for him?"

I nodded. "It's called blackmail. But the thing I don't understand is why he wants me. War's winding down, we're pulling out. What can I give him that he doesn't have access to already?"

"I don't know it for a fact, but my guess is he's got a private stream of intel and he wants you to evaluate it."

"About fucking what?"

Bill shook his head. "I'm almost tempted to ask you to take the job to get the evidence."

"No."

He put his arm around me. "I wouldn't do that to you. But Jesus, I'd like to nail the bastard." He released me. "Just keep your head down for now. I wouldn't meet with your lover, at least not here, until I give you the all clear."

I groaned.

"This must be serious."

I nodded. "Very. I'll do anything I can to protect her."

"I'm going inside to do a sweep for bugs—"

"Bugs? He bugged my home?"

"That's what I'm going to find out, Win. Stay out here, please."

He pulled a briefcase from the front seat and disappeared into the house. I could see him walking around the living room, then he disappeared from sight. I felt the anger balling up my fists. All I wanted to do was pound Scotty into the damn pile of shit he was.

I bent over and rested my hands on my thighs. Tried to calm my breathing. Emily thought I was paranoid? Ha! It'd be an interesting session this week. And, oh my God, Sarah. We hadn't been together since I'd stayed with her. Had some asshole been lurking outside Sarah's house? Taking photos? Is that what Scotty was after? Shit, shit, shit.

I heard a rustling. Jo and Des broke into the clearing where her truck was parked. In front of *my* home. *My* sanctuary.

I pulled myself together. "Good walk?"

"Yeah, think she got to know the terrain. You have a fox's den or something down by that creek?"

"No. Why?"

"She alerted, but it didn't seem the threat was current."

Scotty's man?

"I've got some stuff in the back for you," Jo said. "Want to come and look?"

I hoped I hadn't duplicated everything. Just wanted to be prepared. I walked around to the back of the truck and looked at a small box. "This is it?"

"Yeah. The blanket she's been sleeping on during her recovery, some toys, though she doesn't seem particularly attached to them. I didn't bring bowls or stuff like that, figured you'd have something you could use."

"I went to the pet store. We should be fixed for supplies."

She handed me a sheet of paper. "These are behaviors Des may display and basic remedies for them. She should be okay with people who are friends of yours. I'll show you how to introduce them to her."

She did. All I could think was that the introduction wouldn't be the problem. Or even having Sarah around. It was when we got in bed. After her demonstration, I posed the question. "What about lovemaking? I mean, it's physical. Noisy."

She looked me up and down. "Ease into it. Let Des see you physically interact with your lover—you know, kiss, caress one another. She how she reacts."

"Des reacts?"

"Uh, yeah." Jo grinned. "Anyway, keep the noise to a minimum until she's used to both of you rolling around in bed. Are you that loud?"

I looked at the woods surrounding us. "Anything else?"

She kept the grin on her face and handed me another sheet. "The commands she knows."

I scanned them, glad to divert. "All in English? Do you think she could learn them in another language?"

"Um. Don't know." She reached in a pocket. "Here's my card. Give me a call when Des is settled in, and I'll come back and work with you. Does your lover live with you?"

"No."

"Then take it even slower. Let Des get used to her before you go to bed. For sex. Sleeping's all right. Sleeping would be good." She laughed.

Bill chose that moment to reappear. He motioned me over. "No cameras, but you've got two listening devices, one by the couch and one by your bed. I've trapped the broadcast signal and I'll see if I can track it down. We need to know who's doing it, Win. So please don't mash them under your heel."

Crap. I felt the anger grow again. "You better do your tracking really fast. That pollution isn't staying in my house long."

* * *

For the rest of the day, I worried how I could deliver the news to Sarah. She'd want to charge into the fray. She could arrest the eavesdropper, but nothing would stop him from spreading the news about an affair. Especially if he was still in the service and under orders. I needed to find the guy. Maybe Nathan could help. But that was later. First Sarah.

With my second cup of morning coffee, I ran a search for grant applications for cops, filled out a couple and printed them. So far, Des had been super. We'd have to go for a ride eventually. Was now too soon? I wanted to see Sarah when I said our date was off. Des was the perfect excuse. Especially if she saw the dog and her wound. I called and told Sarah I had some stuff to drop off. "Will you be there?"

"Oh, yeah," she said. I loved the throaty sound of her voice.

Then I called Micah and asked him to meet me for coffee. I could hear the curiosity in his voice, but he didn't ask. We set a time and I hung up. If the mic caught these calls, I hoped they'd sound innocent enough.

"Okay, Des. Wanna go for a ride?"

She cocked her head the way smart dogs do. I put the lead on her, locked up. Opened the door to my truck. She leaped in and sat on the passenger side. I could hear her thinking, *Such a slow human.*

When we arrived in Greenglen, I pulled into the parking lot behind the sheriff's department. "Are you going to be a good girl? Not bite any of the people?"

She snorted and I laughed. Actually, she was used to being around people with guns. Spending time in offices. Waiting for the next assignment. One of the hardest things she had to learn was that there wasn't going to be another assignment. I rubbed her under her jaw. "I don't know about you, Des, but I'm glad I'm retired. That it's over."

We made it through the long hall. Threaded our way through the bullpen. Des was cool. The people who watched our progress weren't. I thought it was her healing wound that caused the unease. I tapped on Sarah's doorframe and delighted at the way her face lit up when she saw me. Then she saw Des.

"A wounded warrior to keep me company," I said. "They called, asked if I'd take her in. She's been retired. It helps that I know what she's been through. Much better than a civilian family."

I instructed Sarah what to do as I made the formal introduction. Des wagged her tail, sniffed Sarah's hand. Her crotch. Oh, Des.

"I'm going to have to cancel our date." Sarah's features settled into her cop face. "She's just settling in. The physical part might...I don't know. Set her off. I don't want you hurt."

"Oh. Yeah." She sat back down at her desk, going all brisk. "Probably for the best. We've got a big drug bust going down Saturday night and the more planning we can do—well, the fewer mistakes we can eliminate before they happen."

"Like snipers who weren't supposed to be there?"

She nodded.

"You're not going on the raid, are you?"

She gave a one-shoulder shrug. "There's been discussion about my staying here. I don't see the harm in riding along."

"Jesus, Sarah. Anything could—"

"That's where good planning comes in."

I wasn't going to make headway. I could tell by the set of her jaw. A beautiful jaw. I handed her the file I'd printed out. I wanted to take her in my arms and make love on her desk. But I left.

Micah was waiting for me in Beans aBrewing. I left Des in the truck, parked where I could keep an eye on her and passersby. I ordered a plain cuppa and sat at Micah's table. I sketched my story of intrigue, the reason I couldn't see Sarah until I made sure no one was keeping me under surveillance.

"Well, hell and damnation," he said. "Anythin' I can do?"

"Explain to Sarah." I took a sip. "I broke our date. I hate this, Micah, but until it's over, Sarah and I have to stay apart." I finished my coffee. "Take care of her Saturday night—she's planning on going on the raid."

"She'll need a driver," Micah said. "I'm 'bout the best there is."

CHAPTER NINETEEN

Sarah

We kept up surveillance on the Jarek place, listened in on his conversations, read his text messaging and emails. He was going to have one hell of a party on Saturday night. We huddled with Major Galt, our state police liaison, and he okayed the plan. But he didn't have enough men available.

"You're going to have to call the DEA, Sarah," he'd said. "Otherwise, we'd be stretched way too thin."

"I'd rather call the FBI—they're disciplined."

He'd nodded. "But if you do that, you're not going to get cooperation from DEA anytime in the future. As long as you're steering the boat, it should be all right."

So we'd left it at that. I'd called DEA, asked for four agents and gotten them. They'd come in Saturday morning, look at the plan and get their assignments. I still had a niggling concern about their presence.

When Win had come, all thoughts of drug busts disappeared and I couldn't help but think about Friday night. Our first time together since she'd stayed with me. My psyche ached for her and so did my body. Then I saw Des, beautiful and bright-eyed, and I couldn't believe the scar she bore. When Win said Friday night was off, I'd wanted to cry.

Shit! How long would it take for Des to get used to me? Please, dog, not long.

I ran my gaze over Win's lean body, her breasts high under her T-shirt, and remembered the feel of…I couldn't go on this way, I had to concentrate on work. Then Win and Des were gone. I hadn't even told her how much I missed her.

When Dad picked me up, he looked upset. He told me the reason on the way home.

"Shit!" I said, regretting the expletive as soon as it was out of my mouth. "We could put a deputy on Win's place—"

"Nope. This is Win's war, *not* yours, Sarah Anne. She knows the players an' has a military ally. 'Sides, you don't have the manpower to put anyone on surveillance."

"But—"

"No buts. I figure if you want to help Win, you'll stay out of her way." He pulled into our driveway and parked by the back door. He put his hand on my arm before I could get out. "Sarah, I know you'd do anythin' in the world for her. An' I respect that. But if she had a brain tumor, would you operate?"

"She's being stalked in a county of which I am sheriff." Dad stared at me, probably trying to figure out what I'd said. "Can we talk about it? Maybe some alternate plan that won't involve the department."

"We can talk 'till the geese fly south again, but it ain't gonna change Win's mind, nor mine. She knows what she's doin'. You gotta respect her skills, Sarah Anne."

"She shouldn't have to go to war again alone."

"She ain't alone. Got a colonel on her side. She's got Des. An' she's got us, cheerin' on the sidelines. Know you hate sidelines, but sometimes it's best all around. Oh, an' speakin' of sidelines, you ain't gonna be part of the Saturday operations." He got out and met me at the back door. "Not unless I drive you."

* * *

Twilight again, and another drug bust. I hated everything about drugs. The whole culture that destroyed lives, made users useless. Most of all I hated the sellers who hooked kids. We had evidence that drugs and alcohol had fueled the party where Natalie Elder's rape had occurred.

I didn't understand the high people sought—were their lives so damn empty?

Or maybe I did, just a little. The high Win gave me filled me, overflowed into areas of my life that had been parched for a long time. I was hooked on Win. But I didn't pay some scum for my fix, it sure as hell wasn't synthetic and it didn't waste me.

"Gonna take the Hamlin Crik Road," Dad said. "Then we hike 'bout a mile. Think you can make it?"

"My legs are fine. That'll put us right across the road from Jarek's place. You let command know?"

"Yep. Got night binoculars and a rifle. You think you can fire your sidearm?"

"I took practice three days ago. Not my best score, but adequate. The new holster helps a lot, makes drawing my weapon much easier. Besides, we're sideliners."

Dad snorted. We bumped down the rutted Hamlin Creek Road, and even though Dad took it slow, I could feel every jolt. By the time we got out to begin our hike, I felt a dull ache from my collarbone to my shoulder socket.

Full dark, but also full moon, so the path through the woods was clear before us. Dad took point, and by the time we reached the perch Dad had sussed out this morning, my shoulder felt stiff but didn't ache anymore. We settled in, and I propped my back against an old sweet gum tree. Holding the binoculars with one hand was tricky, so Dad spelled me.

Night sounds, including the silent flight of an owl above my head, quieted me. I let my thoughts drift since we probably had a couple of hours before the scumbag contingent started arriving. I knew Win would stand beside me if I was in trouble. Why the hell wouldn't she let me return the loyalty? There was something Dad hadn't told me, or she hadn't told Dad. Why had she attracted a stalker? One attached to her old commander? A military matter, Dad had said. I couldn't figure it out. Damn. I just wanted her—her company, her conversation and her lovemaking. I could feel my nipples hardening just thinking about our last time together.

"Did you tell me everything about Win's situation?"

"Nope," Dad said. "An' I ain't gonna. Leastways, not now. Keep your mind on why we're here, Sarah Anne."

I sighed as noisily as I could. Dad was right, I had to keep my mind on the business at hand or I could get both of us killed. These were not the boys and girls next door of yesteryear. They were contemptible felons who belonged behind bars for life.

"Stop wool-gatherin', Sarah. Our guests are beginnin' to arrive."

We watched, gathered license plate numbers and waited some more.

"Think that's it?" he asked when we hadn't gotten any more traffic for ten minutes.

"Should be one more." I called command. "Any more incoming?"

"Nothing on the road inside our perimeter. Should we wait?"

"Set the roadblocks. Let's keep to the plan. Wait for the go until John gives the signal Jarek's returning to the house with the goods."

We waited another fifteen minutes, then my phone buzzed and the text appeared: GO. I raised the night vision binoculars and watched as our men worked their way to the house, surrounded it and burst in through front and back doors. All going to plan.

Five minutes later the phone rang. John. I put it on speaker. "Sarah, Jarek isn't here. He came in from the shed, the goods are on the kitchen table, but he's gone."

"Basement? Attic?"

"Looked in the basement, but there's no way he could've gotten to the attic before we busted in."

"Root cellar, the entrance is openin'," Dad said.

"Hold on, John." I raised the binoculars to where Dad was pointing. "Think he's coming up from the root cellar...yeah. There's supposed to be a DEA agent right in that area—where the hell is he?"

"They're all in the kitchen with the meth."

"I'm in pursuit." I turned off the phone, tucked it in my pocket and stood. "Backup, Dad."

I sprinted down the slope, ran across the road to the continuation of Hamlin Creek Road. Where he had a car parked? Where his wife and kids were waiting for him? I took my arm out of the sling and reached for my Glock. I dodged branches as I plunged into the woods. I wasn't running flat out because I needed to listen for his footfalls. They were loud. I could hear him panting. I closed the gap between us.

"Police." I fired a warning shot. "Stop and put your hands up."

He followed directions. "Oh, man, I just knew somethin' was up."

"Your hands." I was holding my weapon with both hands, and my shoulder was hurting. I needed to lower it a bit. "Kneel down. Now!" I waited a beat. "It would give me great pleasure to put a slug through your heart, or better, your head, and save the county the cost of housing you. Believe me, nothing would give me greater pleasure right now."

He knelt, his hands still up.

My left hand was trembling. "Now lie down, hands first. All the way down."

I heard someone behind me.

"It's me, Sarah Anne. I got it from here."

Dad moved around me, held the rifle to Jarek's neck and carefully placed a boot on his back. "You make one move an' I shift my weight. You're lucky an' you die. Unlucky, you end up slobberin' the rest of your life an' unable to wipe yourself." He cuffed Mr. Scumbag.

I'd never heard Dad talk like that. He'd meant it and I'd meant every word I'd said. What the hell was happening to us?

CHAPTER TWENTY

Win

My burner phone buzzed. The text message said: *Go outside. Need to talk.*

I opened my front door, let Des out. Walked to my truck. The phone buzzed again. "Yeah, Bill. What's up?"

"We need to meet, your choice of a secure place. Remote, if possible. I'm in the area."

I thought. I'd been out to Nathan's a couple of times since I'd been home. A wonderful old cabin in the woods. With a satellite tower behind it. "Let me make a call."

I hung up, called Nathan. Then called Bill back. "I need gas. Can you meet me at the Stop 'N' Go on SR 48? Follow me from there?"

"Yeah. ETA?"

"Fifteen minutes."

I hung up, pulled a blazer over my T-shirt. Grabbed my Glock. Des had grown to love our rides. She jumped in as soon as I opened the door. She was becoming an important part of my life. She made me laugh. And, unlike Julie, wanted something permanent.

After I filled up my thirsty truck, I watched my rearview mirror for Bill. When I pulled off the highway to a county road, I saw a nondescript sedan follow me. A few minutes later, I turned up the rutted track to Nathan's cabin. Des joined me when I got out. We waited for the engine I heard coming closer.

Nathan opened the cabin door and I could see a rifle held close to his side. "Friends?"

"I sure as hell hope so." I waited until the car drove in and the front doors opened. Bill emerged from the driver's side, a laptop in his hand. A gorgeous Eurasian woman stepped from the passenger side. A woman I'd known from a number of hookups on leave. Bangkok. Singapore. Hawaii. What the hell was Bill up to?

He grinned. An evil grin from where I stood. "You remember Pan?"

"You don't look happy to see me, sweetie," she said.

"Just surprised," I responded. She hadn't aged a bit. Flawless skin. Big latte-colored eyes—if latte was made with gold. Tight butt. Large breasts. A delightful temptation from head to toe. I began my introduction to the group. "This is Des."

When I finished, we started for the cabin. The skirt of her uniform caressed her butt in a most delicious way. "You still flying for Singapore Air?"

She smiled at me. "Sure. What else can I do?"

"How do you know Bill?"

"He's my boss, sweetie."

I felt my stomach flip. Since when? We entered Nathan's cabin, half from the nineteenth century, half from the twenty-second. Nathan busied himself in the kitchen.

I turned to Bill. "You've got a lot of explaining to do."

He nodded. "Pan's been on our payroll for years, been a great asset. After your first, uh, encounter, she said you were the most tight-lipped person she'd ever met. We made no more inquiries."

"Fuck you."

"It's why I trust you so much, Win." He jangled the change in his pocket. "Anyway, if Scotty thinks you have a lover, I thought we might divert attention from the local area. He's had a camera installed in your bedroom."

"He what?"

"We picked up an addition to the broadband he's transmitting on. Camera. I had one of my men check the other day when you were out. I'm sorry. I know that was an invasion."

"Invasion? You have a fucking flair for understatement." I started pacing, tried to relax my hands from the fists they'd formed.

"It's fastened to the frame of that photograph of the Hindu Kush. Not wide-angle. Focused on the bed and motion activated."

I wanted to smash the bank of electronics that lined Nathan's rough-hewn wall. I wanted to smash Bill's face. But most of all, I wanted to kill Scotty. I took a deep breath. Counted to four. Let it out.

"I am sorry. For all of this," Bill said.

I nodded. I couldn't manage to get a word out.

"Anyway, I thought Pan might be able to help you. I want you to look at some stuff I've 'collected' from Scotty's work."

Nathan brought tea in, two mugs in each hand. "This is very soothing, Win," he said as he handed me one. "My Auntie Clair's recipe."

I took a sip, didn't feel calmed, but I appreciated Nathan's concern. "What stuff?"

Bill opened his laptop, brought up a file. "Can you translate?"

"You want to put it on one of my monitors?" Nathan asked. "Easier to read and it's safe."

"You sure about the safety?" Bill asked.

"Get your best hackers—they won't get into my network." Nathan smiled and walked to his console.

I sat in the other chair and looked at a page displayed on a monitor. I fell back into an old, familiar role. "Interesting. You have history on this stream?"

Bill clicked a few keys. I started at the beginning, about six months ago. I read on, taking notes on the text. Half an hour later, I sat back. "They're talking about a shipment. Nothing concrete that tells me what it is. But the first is a native Pashtun speaker, the second isn't." I looked over my notes. "The shipment is due in this country in the next week on an army transport. Make sense to you?"

"No clue to what the shipment is?"

I looked over my notes. "I don't think it's a person. More like a package. Does that help?"

"My analysts didn't pick up on that, so yeah."

"How's this connected to Scotty? What the hell does it have to do with me?"

"I'm guessing he wanted a good translator who's under his thumb," Bill said. "He wanted you because he knew you'd pick up the subtleties and give him insight to the dealer."

"So Scotty's the nonnative speaker?" Bill nodded. "Who's the other one?"

"Fazal Gul Khan."

"From Jalalabad?"

"Yeah," Bill said. "Ring any bells?"

"Warlord. He's gotten fat and rich during the war. Wars. Has deep ties to the Pakistani Taliban. But you must already know that."

"I do, but I wasn't sure you did. That's a bit south of where you were located."

"He has a long reach, Bill."

"So, knowing who the two correspondents are, can you give me anything more?"

I thought. "I doubt they trust one another. Whatever the shipment is, both are going to have a fail-safe plan to pull out. Even at the last minute." I turned back to the screen, scrolled back through. "Whatever the shipment, Scotty must feel he's got enough pull to get it on the transport."

"Drugs?" Bill asked.

"It'd have to be the mother lode. Something more valuable. Is Scotty a collector?"

"We can check, but I haven't heard anything."

"If you want, I can dig," Nathan said. "I don't hack, but someone who's harassing a friend? Who may be undermining this country? Not a problem."

"Nathan's worked with law enforcement," I said. "If he works it, none of the feelers you put out will get back to Scotty."

"You're welcome to stay and watch," Nathan said. "I've got everything I need but the man's whole name."

Bill gave him a long, level look. "Son, you're working on a matter of national security. That means I can okay your snooping. It also means if you ever talk about it to anyone, I'll send you to Gitmo."

Nathan's face was impassive. "You want to start now?"

Bill turned to Pan, tossed her the keys to the car. "You and Win work out the details, then hit the road."

* * *

I walked Pan to the car. She leaned against me. "I been looking forward to this assignment." She ran her hand under my blazer and to my breast.

I gently took her hand and removed it. "It's not like that anymore."

Her thin eyebrows rose. "What? You come home, get religion, go straight?"

"No. I met someone."

"You in love? *You*, Win?"

I nodded. "She's why I'm doing this at all. I need to protect her from snoops. I'm not going to say anything more about her."

Pan smiled, that beguiling smile I remembered so well.

"We going to have to do something to convince them I'm your super-duper lover. When I drive up, I will plant a big one on you. In case there are eyes on us. Where are the mics?"

"In the living room by the couch and in my bedroom."

She rubbed my hand. "Remember, you glad to see me. Surprised and tremendously pleased. You going to have to do me."

"No."

"Faking not going to work. So, I have a surprise ready for you. Sweetie, enjoy. Then I plead for a nap, we sleep until dark. Bump around under sheets, then eat."

She got in the car, slid the window down. "You can still screw me good? Yes?"

With her body, who couldn't?

I whistled for Des, got in my truck and followed Pan's car down the drive. She took a left and I took a right toward home. My thoughts raced. Why did life have to get so damn complicated? Pan and I had shared some torrential sex in the past. I still remembered her dancing around a hotel room in Manila in nothing but stiletto heels and attitude. With toys.

All that before I met Azar. Before Sarah and I became lovers. Shit. Pan thought fucking her didn't count as long as she didn't do me. I wasn't so sure about that. She had the best body of any woman I'd been with. Always loved to experiment. I'd have to be senile not to get aroused by her. Was that betraying Sarah? Who I was doing this for. Shit.

Des sensed my tumult. She lay down on the seat and put her muzzle on my thigh.

"You want to get in my pants too?" I ruffled her fur.

When I got home, I took Des for a walk. Not so much for her. In fact, I think she'd had enough excitement for the day. What was I going to do with her when Pan came? What had Jo said? Let Des see you physically warm up with one another. Something like that. I'd have to explain to Pan. This whole thing was becoming too much.

What the hell was Scotty really up to? It must be close, time-wise, or he wouldn't put a man on me. He must have thought my lover would be coming over soon. If that was true, he could've assumed it was Sarah. I'd stayed with her. But he didn't have photos. He would've used them by now. Damn him. To hell, but never back.

When I took Des inside, she immediately settled on her bed and went to sleep. Maybe that's what I should do. Go to sleep and when I woke up, this would be over.

Pan showed up a little after four.

"Surprise!" she said, raising her arms. She swayed toward me. Slid her hands under my T-shirt. If I hadn't looked surprised before, I did then. She began to kiss me, her tongue tattooing mine. I leaned into her. Wrapped my arms around her. Kissed her back.

"Um," she said. "Maybe we better go inside."

"I have to introduce you to my dog." I went through all of it again. Des looked at me like I was crazy. Maybe I was. And maybe there was someone watching.

She retrieved her suitcase and we went up the stairs, arms around one another. She paused by the couch. "I sure hope you don't have other plans, Win. I missed you so much, I take vacation time."

I nuzzled her neck. "No plans that I can remember. Would you like a tour of the house?"

"Would very much like to see bedroom."

I shook my head. Grinned. Led her toward it. Paused outside the door and whispered in her ear. "If we do preliminaries by the door, the camera won't be able to see us. Mad dash to the bed, under the sheets. I really don't want to be gawked at by unknown males who are jerking off."

She nodded and we went into the bedroom. Des followed, curled up on her bed. Snorted.

Pan put her bag by the door, stood still. Out of the range of the camera. She unbuttoned her blouse, button by teasing button. Opened it. I didn't know whether to laugh or swoon. Her black lace bra had cutouts. She dropped the blouse. Unzipped her skirt. Let it fall. She had nothing on but a black lace garter belt and stockings. "You like?"

"Oh, yeah." I managed to croak that out, but I couldn't have said anything else.

"Take off my hose, please?"

I undid the garters on one leg. Began rolling the stocking down. Knelt. Brushed my hand over her thigh. Skin so soft it begged for light kisses. She raised her leg. I took off her shoe, finished with the stocking. Started on the other leg. Felt my pulse quicken. Her legs were beautiful, long, muscled just enough. When shoes and stockings were off, the garter belt followed. I ran my hands along her thighs. Placed my hands on her butt and pulled her to me. I moved my hands up her back and unfastened her bra. Let it drop. Stood and stared. "Luscious" didn't even begin to describe her. I pushed back her long, straight hair and kissed her neck, her lips. While my hands caressed her breasts. Stomach. Belly.

She pushed me back. Relieved me of my clothes in record time. Then she pulled me close, rubbed her body against mine. Whispered in my ear, "Time to dash, Win. Or you want to do it here? I like it standing up. Remember?"

Oh, did I. I grabbed her hand, ran to the bed, pulled back the top sheet and dove in. She fell on top of me. I covered us. Felt the rush of desire. Pure lust.

CHAPTER TWENTY-ONE

Sarah

Lloyd had done a long interview with me about the drug bust for the *Sentinel*, much longer than I could sit still for. I'd had him interview Caleb and John for their perspectives. The one thing I'd asked him to print was that this wasn't the cure of the disease. I gave him detailed lists of behaviors, both for neighbors and family members, that might indicate drug activity.

Lloyd examined one list. "Hard to tell between drug behavior and just being a moody teenager."

"That's the problem."

When I walked into the task force meeting the high school had called, I got a round of applause. I hoped I was gracious, but I gave them the same message: for every meth lab we closed down, another popped up.

My shoulder hadn't suffered any lasting damage from the bust, just sore muscles. So I was surprised when someone tapped me on it as I walked down the high school hall. I flinched.

"Oh God, Sarah. I'm sorry," Emily said.

"It's all right, you didn't hurt me."

"Just jumpy?"

"Yeah, I guess." I started to walk again, Emily at my side. "I think I need to talk to you."

She stopped and looked at me. "About work?"

I nodded.

"I have time free tomorrow morning. Ten o'clock?"

"Fine. I'll see you then." I started walking to the exit and found her keeping up with me.

"Can I ask for a little more info?"

"I'm not sure—the bust, I think. Maybe being sheriff. I'll try to get my thoughts organized before tomorrow morning."

But I couldn't. I kept going back to the moment I stopped Jarek. I'd been ready to pull the trigger, maybe more than ready.

When I settled in Emily's chair, I laid it out for her. "Are the stresses of this office making me into a murderer? He was unarmed, not resisting arrest. I could've shot him then and there."

"If that had happened, what would you have done?"

"What do you mean?"

Emily shot me a look. "Would you have covered it up? Turned yourself in to your chief deputy? What would you have done?"

"I don't know, I didn't think beyond the moment." I recrossed my legs. "I just wanted to blow him away."

"But you didn't. You had an impulse, but you controlled it. Is that the first time you've had that thought—to 'blow away' the perpetrator? Or otherwise punish a criminal?"

I nodded. "I've always been by the book, and the book says you don't harm the criminal, no matter how heinous the crime."

"Micah's book?"

"Yeah. But it's just good police procedure, Em. I want a clean case, one that I can present in court without explaining excessive force or anything resembling it."

"What stresses are you experiencing now?" She held up her hand. "Let's see. Drugs are pouring into the county as well as being produced locally. They're connected to the party Natalie went to. Then there's the campaign which you don't want any part of. Anything else?"

I shook my head. "Well, I haven't seen Win in a while. I miss her."

She stared at me. "I understand Micah was with you when you made the arrest."

"He drove. Doctor won't let me drive yet. I was just there to watch, coordinate if necessary. Dad ended up as my backup." I looked out the window. Clouds were moving in from the south, the trees swaying from the gusts. "I couldn't ask my deputies to go into danger without being there."

"Even though you were lucky to be able to raise your gun? Your dedication is admirable."

"Is that sarcasm?"

"You bet it is." She closed her notebook. "Sarah, you've been experiencing doubt about the job, about the toll it's taking on you. But you won't let go, keep pushing yourself to do the best job possible, even when it's not possible. That's an essential, internal conflict. You've got to solve it. Then you'll know whether you've got to worry about your impulse control."

I felt what she'd said was true, but it was a blackberry thicket for me. "Will you help me solve this?"

"I don't know," Emily said. "Win's my client. I can't break confidentiality for either one of you, if I take you on."

"But you did the Paria after-action report while you were seeing Win."

"Two separate issues and, if I'm correct, you weren't dating Win at that point."

"Em, I'm not going to anyone else for help. It's you or the blackberry thicket."

* * *

Emily suggested I look at my campaign as a platform to get the word out about drugs and the horrible toll they took on individuals and families. "After all," she said, "it's the parents who believe their kids couldn't possibly do drugs who do the most damage."

I tried to get my thoughts ordered, then wrote a new stump speech that concentrated on what our citizens could do to help us rid the county of drugs and the people who pushed them. I tried it out on the Chamber dinner. It got a good reception, and I saw Lloyd scribbling away, taking notes. The next day, he presented my suggestions in a long article, posted on the *Sentinel's* website.

I handed over the drug bust evidence to the DA, though some tests hadn't come in from the state lab yet. Leslie and Vincente had worked overtime to get their testing done in their now-completed new lab on the third floor. We hadn't been able to buy any additional equipment, but at least they didn't have to worry about being flooded out. Maybe Win could find some grant that would get them what they needed.

Win. I couldn't talk to Emily about Win, I understood that. But who? Even though Dad had welcomed her with open arms, I was reluctant to share my interior life so fully. I sure as hell wasn't going to tell him how much I wanted her in my bed.

From talking every night, our calls had dwindled to two or three times a week. Was Win regretting our relationship? Getting cold feet? I hadn't come out and asked her, but I'd probed. Yes, Des was adjusting to her new home. I was waiting for "adjusted."

I felt the distance between us and I had absolutely no idea what to do to close it.

I left the office at five thirty and still had two hours of sunlight left. The doctor had finally cleared me to drive, but advised against any driving that would cause abrupt movements. "No car chases, Sarah."

Time before twilight for a drive in the country where the air smelled sweet from grass cutting. The spring had been wet, streams and creeks singing their songs for anyone who'd listen. I pulled onto an old road that ran by Logan's Creek and switched off the engine. I listened to the water's deep bass notes and the soprano trills.

I also debated stopping by Win's, worried that she might not want to see me or she might think I was checking up on her. Dad had said I couldn't fight Win's war, whatever it was, and that I should trust her skill and training. I did. I just wanted to see her. At least I could take a detour home, do a drive-by.

Once the decision was made, I felt better. Until I pulled into her drive and saw a car parked in front of the house. I braked. The car felt wrong, maybe because it was a rental. Someone from out of town. Someone from her past? An old lover?

Why in God's name would I jump to that conclusion? I sure was lacking in faith in our relationship. Why? I felt ashamed and just a tad bit humiliated, sneaking around like a suspicious spouse. If Win was fighting something from her past, I didn't need to complicate her concentration.

I backed out.

I didn't notice much of the scenery as I drove home. Her sudden stalker might've been a sheer coincidence with the arrival of an old friend she'd never talked about. Who was her visitor? Why hadn't she told me she had company?

I tried to push the doubts down, but found myself following the same scent around and around the same tree.

I pulled into my drive, parked and tried to sort my feelings before I went in. I called Win. It rang, then went over to voice mail. I hung up. Don't try a case with circumstantial evidence unless the evidence is substantial. That was a principle for law enforcement that I should take to heart, to matters of the heart.

I went in and found a note from Dad. *Gone over to Dog's. Dinner's in the fridge.*

I felt relief that I didn't have to hide my emotional state from Dad and crushed that he'd abandoned me.

CHAPTER TWENTY-TWO

Win

I told Emily the whole story. Scotty. National security. Pan.

"I've screwed up everything," I said, leaning back in the chair. Exhausted. Pan had stayed two days.

"All of your activity with Pan is on tape?"

"Only the first time. Nathan managed to disable the camera remotely. Made it look like the camera got a loose wire or something. I'm the one with a loose wire. I never should've said yes to the plan. Never."

"You thought you could withstand the temptation?"

"I thought when the time came, she'd fake it. I should've known better." I pulled out my wallet, took a folded snapshot and handed it to her. It had been taken on the Thai coast. Both of us were in bikinis. Pan's ample attributes were obvious. I was the angular one.

Emily took a long time, then handed it back. "You were having a good time."

"I needed a break." I leaned back again. "Leave was a time I could forget everything else. Just sex. No regrets."

"Do you think it might be possible that Pan, returning when you're under stress again, unlocked some of those old feelings? Let you escape into a memory of escape?"

"Probably. But I enjoyed every minute of her."

"Did thoughts of Sarah enter your mind?"

I nodded. "But I'd push them away. Told myself I was doing it for her. Truth is, I was doing it for me."

"You certainly are a judgmental bitch," Emily said. She waited.

"Look, I'm not going to get in a discussion about judgment. I used it all the time at work. About a person telling the truth. Lying. The soundness of a plan. The judgments I made, sometimes in an instant, had weight. Repercussions. Am I judgmental? Damn straight I am."

"Nice filler," Emily said. "How gray was your world then?"

"Fifty shades. When I was on leave."

Emily smiled, rubbed her thumb on her thigh. "I like you in the bikini, Win."

Was she coming on to me? Shit!

"You have a great body. Small breasts, but full."

"What are you doing? Hitting on me?"

"If I were?" Emily asked.

I stood. "Why would you say something like that? I don't want to do this anymore. No more games."

"Is that what you think I'm doing? Playing games?"

"I don't know what you're doing. Shit. I don't know what I'm doing."

"Sit down. I wanted to gauge your reaction. Sorry." She watched me. "We're here to figure out why you feel the way you do. Why you do what you do." She leaned forward as I sat down again. "I could hand you what I see of your patterns. They might be useful for a while. But when you come to the realizations yourself, they have meaning far beyond a current situation. You begin to understand yourself."

"Tectonic plates. They keep moving." Pushing stuff up. Burying other material. But the plates were connected by their meeting points.

"Care to share what you're thinking?" Emily asked.

I got up, went to the window. I leaned my head against the pane. "You're trying to get me to realize that seeing Pan triggered an old reaction. One I used to avoid thinking about combat. Pan was a way to avoid stress, forget everything but skin and sweat and..." I pushed away from the window. "Maybe that's what happened. But what I experienced now was plain old lust."

"Lust that pushed Sarah and your feelings for her to the far back burner?" Emily asked. She stood too. "I'm not living in your shoes, but I understand. Marty and I have been together almost thirty years. We've both strayed, attacked by a good case of lust."

"You're still together. Is that the lesson?"

"I don't know if that would be true if our occasional forays into other people happened at the beginning of our relationship. Are you going to tell Sarah?"

I walked over to my chair. Sat down. Buried my head in my hands. "I've got no idea. I know it would really hurt her. I keep seeing her face when I visited her office. How she got all bright and shiny."

I felt Emily's hands on my shoulders. "It's all right to cry." She began to knead them gently. "Let the guilt flow out. Then we'll look at what's left."

* * *

I got a text from Bill on my burn phone. *Come to Nathan's, 2:00. Can you leave Des at home?* I called him. "Why leave Des?"

"To guard the home front. Can you make it?"

"Yeah. You're making progress?"

"See you."

I snapped it off. I should be used to Bill and his cryptic nature by now. He was the best CO I'd had. Able to see patterns others couldn't. But with Bill, it was always need to know. I'd find out what this was about when he was ready to tell me.

I got Des's list of commands, saw there was one for "stay and guard." I ate lunch, gave her the command. I swear she said, "Aw, hell."

When I got to Nathan's, no other car was visible. Didn't mean Bill hadn't already arrived. I waited for Nathan to come to the door. When he did, I got out and followed him into the cabin. Bill was sitting in the second chair in front of the bank of network gear.

I walked over to him. "You ever spring something like Pan on me again, I swear, I'll hunt you down like Al Qaeda."

He had the bravado to grin. "That woman's a handful. But the diversion worked, Win."

At what cost?

"Your friend here is worth his weight in platinum. He's done a lot of digging."

Nathan took the other chair, hit several keys, and a monitor sprang to life. "These are the general's collecting purchases."

I looked at the list. "Chinese jade. It'd be possible to get stuff through the Chinese border, take it through the Wakhan Corridor and then down to Jalalabad. If Scotty scored big, Fazal Gul Khan would be the man to arrange transport."

Bill nodded. "What do you know about Afghani gems?"

"Small mines, mostly in the mountains." I ran a hand through my hair, trying to remember what I'd heard. "Emerald, sapphire and ruby as I remember. Plus aquamarine, amethyst, topaz and a bunch more I can't remember. You think that's what he's bringing in?"

"Yep."

"Is that illegal? Some of the Chinese jades are probably stolen, but gemstones?"

"The gems are legal only if he bought them and can produce the paperwork." Bill swiveled his chair toward Nathan. "Show her what you found."

The monitor changed and what looked like some incident reports appeared.

"They're reports from a number of mine owners in the northern provinces," Bill said. "Gems disappeared either en route to Kabul or from the mines themselves."

"So he's gotten his hands on hot merchandise. Why didn't he bring this stuff back with him when he came stateside?"

Bill turned back to me. "He thought he was going back to Afghanistan."

"Why *is* he here? He hasn't retired. He's still got his rank."

Bill pursed his lips. "He's being investigated."

"For?"

"I've already said too much." His face closed down.

"How long until I can resume my life?"

"We'll have him when the transport lands and he claims his ill-gotten gains."

"*How long?*"

"Soon. Nathan got an electronic bead on his hired-hand stalker." He glanced at his watch. "Our MPs should be picking him up right about now."

"It's over?"

"As over as it can be for now. You still be careful, Win. General Scott Lester has a goddamn pattern of landing on his feet."

CHAPTER TWENTY-THREE

Sarah

Win called Sunday night, her voice warm and relaxed. "You're sounding better," I said.

"I feel a bit human again. Not like a hunted animal. Tell you about it when we meet—which is why I'm calling. I'm still not comfortable with you coming here. Might be devices around the house we didn't find."

"Devices? You're sounding paranoid, Win."

"I'm not. My stalker is behind bars awaiting court martial."

I sat down at the kitchen table. I was ready to go up to bed and I begrudged this intrusion. Win sounded back to normal, yet I had no idea what she'd been through. "You need to tell me what happened."

"I will. But I don't want to do it over the phone."

"When, then? Where?"

"I thought you might have an idea. When's your next day off?"

"Tuesday. But Dad will be home."

"Maybe we could go up to Indianapolis. I can look—"

"No." I felt awkward, but I wasn't ready to go out on the town yet, not openly.

"Do you want to break this off, Sarah?"

"No." I sighed. "I'm not sneaking out of the county every time we want to meet." I softly thrummed my fingers on the table. "My cabin. Des would like it, plenty of room to run and terrorize small animals."

"The cabin where you and—"

"Yeah. I'll have to call and see if Mary can let us have it."

"We shouldn't push her out. Maybe I can—"

"I need to do this, Win. I need to go back and reclaim the place. I'll send you a map."

"Draw one on paper. I'll come by tomorrow and pick it up. You do work tomorrow?"

"Yeah. Better idea—I'll pack a bag, keep it in my truck and you can follow me. I'll leave at three thirty. Okay?"

"Confirm with your tenant. Call me back."

She hung up and I was left with swirling emotions. I called Mary and she said fine, she'd been wanting to go visit her cousin. Would four days be enough? I'd said thank you and then called Win back. "We can have it for four days, counting from four Monday afternoon. I can't take four days off, but I could take Wednesday. I can take the early shift for the rest, come back to the cabin. That is, if you're interested."

"Interested? Jesus, woman. I'll be parked on the street by your parking lot. At three thirty." She cleared her throat. "I've missed you, Sarah."

The next morning, I packed a small duffel and hung extra uniform shirts in a clothing bag. I took them downstairs and Dad watched me as I put them by the door.

"You runnin' away from home?" he asked. "Or from the job?"

"Mary Cloud's going to visit her cousin and I thought it was time I faced the ghosts."

He cocked his head. "Only 'bout fourteen years tardy. Good for you, Sarah Anne." He flicked his newspaper, groped for his glasses in his pocket. "You goin' alone?"

I took a deep breath. "I'm meeting Win."

He nodded. "You know this is your home. You can tell me to skedaddle anytime."

I took another deep breath. "This has been your home longer than it's been mine. I'm not kicking you out, Dad."

He put his glasses on. "Just sayin'. You do what's comfortable for you. Your mother an' me got a tad nervous when you got to be 'bout ten, eleven."

"Too much information, Dad."

He just chuckled and started reading his newspaper.

I drove to work looking at my interior landscape. Why the hell had I doubted Win? Irrational jealousy? Or some inner warning? I just didn't know. Why had I felt her call to be an intrusion? That I couldn't fall back into my increasing loneliness? Was I already ready to settle back into my work-only life?

Seeing the cabin, being back inside where I'd shared my life with Hugh, would bring clarity to my feelings. I was sure of it. Would Win fit into what had been a closed world for me?

CHAPTER TWENTY-FOUR

Win

I'd heard the hesitancy in Sarah's voice. At least at first. Then, in pure Sarah style, she'd made a decision and hit the gas. To where? Four days together? My heart and my body said yes. All the training I had said maybe—but beware of the curve ball.

I called Emily and asked if we could change times for my appointment. She asked her favorite question: why?

"A getaway with Sarah for a few days," I responded. "My threat level has been reduced to yellow."

"I'm glad for that, but wish it were a green." She must've been flipping through her appointment book. "I don't have any openings except Thursday morning."

"That's fine. Sarah's got to go into work Thursday. What time?"

"Into work? Interesting. Okay. Eleven, Thursday morning."

"What's interesting?"

"Are you going to come clean about Pan?"

I started transferring my dishes from the drying rack to the cupboard. "I don't know."

"She'll know something's wrong," Emily said with a sigh. "But, I have something for you to think about. Why do you feel the compulsion to tell her? To relieve your conscience? To obtain forgiveness? Before you tell her anything, you'd better answer the questions. Honestly. Be clear about your motivation. See you Thursday."

She disconnected, and I was left feeling a pang of fear in the pit of my stomach. The word she hadn't used was *absolution*. Was that what I wanted from Sarah? Sprinkle a bit of water on my head and the sins were washed away. Sins? I'd never looked at sex as a sin. Couldn't have afforded to. Not as a gay woman. I'd be condemned to hell for being me. Even the excesses hadn't bothered me. Recreation. With women like Pan.

The burn phone buzzed. Nathan. "Hi."

"Two things. Bill wanted me to pass on a message. Your general never showed to pick up his merchandise. It seems he's in the wind."

"Shit. Shit, shit, shit."

"Bill said he thought the general is fleeing to a country that doesn't have an extradition treaty. Probably has cash stashed all over." Nathan paused. "I can install a pretty sophisticated home security system. It doesn't have to be intrusive and it might let you sleep easier."

I thought I had a pretty good security system. Her name was Des. "Let me think about it."

"Think quickly, Win. If the general's going to come after you, it's going to be now." I heard him sigh. "I do have good news. I removed all the footage the camera had caught. You're clear in that department."

"Thanks. You don't know how much I appreciate it. It's gone for good? I mean, they can't reconstruct it?"

"Not one byte left, and he hadn't sent it anywhere yet. I also went in and wiped selected sections from the audio. I had to leave enough for evidence, but it's pretty innocuous."

"Define 'innocuous.'"

He laughed. "TV, cleaning house, some conversations but nothing, er, racy."

"I owe you big, Nathan."

"No problem. I know you'd have my back if circumstances were reversed. You always did."

I finished with the dishes, packed clothes, set my bag by the door. Des eyed it with bright eyes. I took her out for a walk. I worried about Scotty. But by not meeting Sarah here, I thought I could keep her safe. If the MCIA investigation had been going on for some time, Scotty must have picked up a whiff. Would he abandon his plan for me? Or figure I'd tipped them? Especially since his snoop had been arrested. Shit. Still, I could pick up a tail on rural roads. I wouldn't lead him to Sarah. Even if I had to cancel. Double shit.

All the worry about Scotty was simply a bass line to the tune that was playing in my head. The melody was guilt with a counterpoint of motive. Did I really need Sarah's blessing to clear my conscience? I'd never needed anyone's before. Not in love. Not in war.

I stopped, took a deep breath. Truth? I wanted Sarah's blessing because I had betrayed her trust. At a time when her trust was as fragile as a seedling. Betrayal was the sin I recognized. Hated. No one could absolve me from my own betrayal.

Des nuzzled my hand.

"Time to go?"

Her ears flicked forward. She started back up the trail we'd followed. Woofed.

I glanced at my watch. It was time to leave if I was going to be in a parking space in Greenglen at three thirty. I looked at Des. "You're really going to keep me on the straight and narrow, aren't you? Why couldn't you've done that when Pan was here?"

Des snorted.

CHAPTER TWENTY-FIVE

Sarah and Win

Sarah

I ducked out of the station early and walked over to the Rise 'N' Shine. I figured we needed some food, though thinking about the time we were last together, we hadn't eaten much. I smiled, remembering. The back door was propped open and I walked in. "Aunt Tillie?"

Tillie poked her head around the corner of the walk-in refrigerator. "Too late for lunch, Sarah. An' you should know that."

"I came to see if you could pack up some food for me," I said. "I'm going down to the cabin for a couple of days."

"'Bout time. 'Course, you shouldda gone down there an' faced your ghost before he gained so much power over your life." She got a cardboard box from the pile by the door. "Go up front, take the weight off an' I'll have somethin' for you in a few minutes. Coupla days? Two? Three?"

"Maybe three."

"Go set."

I slid into the closest booth and thought about ghosts. Had Hugh become a ghost for me? Was I so afraid of what the cabin meant to me that I'd never returned? Probably. It had begun as overwhelming pain that I couldn't face, didn't think I could endure. Mom and Dad had moved my things and Hugh's from the cabin, and it had taken me years to go through the packed boxes. Mom had labeled them in her beautiful handwriting, and some were still in the attic.

About three months after Hugh's death, Nathan had contacted me and suggested his sister, Mary, could act as caretaker. She was an herbalist and the land we, no, the land I owned was rich in good medicine plants. I'd said fine. At the end of the year, Mary said she wanted to rent the cabin from me. "It's only fair," she'd said. "I can't live off you for free."

I'd bitten my tongue because her people, the Miami, had lived on this land long before the Europeans had invaded. "A dollar a year," I'd said, and refused any more.

Though I'd left the furniture there, I wondered how Mary had changed the place in the intervening years. She wouldn't see it as a museum for Hugh.

"All ready, Sarah," Tillie called from the kitchen. "Come an' get it so I can get outta here an' put my poor feet up."

Win

I watched as Sarah loaded a box into the back of her SUV and closed the hatch. She looked around. Saw Des hanging out the window. Nodded. I followed, keeping an eye on the rearview mirror. No GPS attached to my truck by unknown cretins. I'd disabled the truck's. I hadn't detected anyone tailing me from home. But if someone saw me leaving, they could've run it like an op. With spotters. I didn't think Scotty still had that kind of pull. But he had a lot of old friends.

I left some space between Sarah and me. Not so far that she could lose me at a turn, just far enough that I wasn't obviously following her. With each turn, I checked to see who else had turned. Either they were running a super-good op, or no one was tailing me.

It came as a relief. Allowed my thoughts to head in a direction I didn't want to go. Pan. I couldn't lie to Sarah. But I couldn't tell her the truth. *Betrayal* was an ugly word. Conjured images of Benedict Arnold and an Appalachian Trail-hiking governor. I thought Emily was right. I'd escaped to escape. From the pressure of Scotty's coercion. For his own fucking purpose.

I'd run away. From the purpose I'd begun with—to protect Sarah from exposure. Instead, I'd blown off steam in a way that was familiar to me. Shit.

I was so lost in thought, I almost missed Sarah's turn. I slowed, turned down a road that was basically two narrow lines of dirt amid the grasses and lined by trees. I saw the glimmer of water off to the west. A meandering road. Ten minutes later I pulled up behind Sarah. Next to a really old cabin, well-maintained. The cabin sat on a bluff and the lake glittered below.

I got out and Sarah embraced me. We stood together for a long time. Finally, she stepped back. "Welcome to Red Hawk Lake."

I saw the tears in her eyes. "I'm going to take Des on a perimeter walk. I thought you might like some time to…be inside with the memories."

She nodded. "I need to do that. But please, don't be too long."

Sarah

I'd wanted Win to walk inside with me. But I knew I needed to do this alone to see if Hugh's ghost still resided, or if he'd gotten tired of waiting for me to say goodbye. I opened the plank door, stepped on the wide boards that glowed in the setting sun. Memory and the present merged. I almost expected to see Hugh's uniform jacket hanging on a peg by the door. Furniture had been moved, a rag rug had been replaced by another. Nothing lasts forever.

I took several steps forward. Nathan, on one of his forest rambles, had found this falling-down remnant of the past. He'd shown me and Hugh the place, gauged our reaction, then given us the deed to the cabin and twenty acres as an early wedding present.

"Figure it'll take six months for you to stabilize it and another six to make it liveable." He'd grinned. "So you better schedule the wedding for a year from today."

One year later, on a rainy fall day, Hugh had carried me across the threshold of our marriage. Into the pioneer cabin forgotten in the woods a hundred years, to a friendly fire in the hearth that Nathan had left the reception early to light for us.

The past would always be present here, but maybe I could forge a new future.

"Hugh, if you're still here, bless us, Win and me. I feel for her what I felt for you, and even though it's bewildering to me, I want a future for us together. Can you help me make this a haven for us?"

The setting sun streamed through the window and reached across the room to a Baccarat vase. Hugh had bought it for me our last wedding anniversary and told me it should always remind me how beautiful I was. It sent prisms of light throughout the room, and I thought I had my answer.

Win

After our walk, I perched on a boulder where I could watch the cabin. Sarah stood for a long time in the middle of the room. She was talking. To Hugh? Then she walked into an addition that jutted out the side. I could see the bed. She ran her hand over the quilt on the bed. Then she folded down the quilt and the sheet beneath. Plumped the pillows. I watched her go back into the main room, look around one more time. The front door opened and she stepped out.

A breeze ruffled her hair. She looked beautiful. Des looked at me, then took off down the hill. I followed down the rough terrain. Des stopped in front of Sarah, tail wagging like a crazed metronome. I slowed down as Sarah knelt to hug her. Kisses were exchanged.

Sarah looked up from the love fest. "I thought you might be close behind." She stood, held out her hand. "Would you like a tour?"

I held her hand as she showed me the main room. Told stories about pieces of furniture. About restoring the cabin from the falling-down wreck it had been. Building the addition in the way the original had been built. I thought about all the sweat and love that had gone into this home. Hers, Nathan's, his relatives'. Hugh's. No wonder she'd been afraid to come back here. Talk about raising ghosts.

"Do you like it?" she asked.

"It's wonderful. Warm. Welcoming." I put an arm around her waist. "I can understand why it took you so long to come back."

"Can you? Really?"

I nodded. Kissed her on her forehead. "I need to get my bag."

"Oh, the food! Tillie packed a box. Let's go find out what she packed."

I took my bag out of the truck, walked over as Sarah rummaged through a cardboard box. "She gave me enough for a week."

I handed her my bag, picked up the box. "I, for one, am hungry."

"So am I, Win. So am I."

Sarah

After we'd eaten, Win cleared the table and did the dishes. I watched the way her body moved, the smoothness of her motions. It felt so right. So why the hell did we have to hide out?

"I brought some CDs," Win said as she stacked the dishes in the cupboard. "Anything to play them on?"

"I don't know, we had a CD player, but in all the time since..." I got up and walked over to the living room area. "Yes, it's still here.

Looks like Mary uses it." I looked through a stack of Native American flute music, wondering if the CDs Hugh and I had listened to were in the attic, still boxed up.

Win hung up the dish towel, walked into the bedroom and returned with a stack of CDs. "Some of my favorites. Cris Williamson's first, *The Changer and the Changed*. Meg Christian."

"Sit down first, tell me about your stalker. After all, I'm the sheriff." I sat on the couch, patted the cushion. "Tell me why you didn't want me involved."

She sat, put an arm around me and kissed me softly. "The stalker was a marine. Sent on a mission by the general. He'd planted microphones and a camera, Sarah. If you'd come and he'd recorded us..."

"Blackmail? By an officer?"

"The general wanted something from me I couldn't give." She took my hands. "I can't give you details. The investigation's ongoing. Scotty's in the wind."

"You're in danger—"

"Probably not, Sarah. Bill sent a bodyguard for me when the danger was high. She's gone."

"She?"

"You're a sheriff. A woman can't be a bodyguard? Pan's a really good agent. Took me years to find out she was an agent."

There was something else Win wasn't saying, but I didn't want to press. That she had chosen to leave me out of the loop was disconcerting. But at least I'd identified the car parked in front of her house.

"It was a military op, Sarah."

"You think we're safe here? I mean, it's so isolated."

"All the better to make love. Besides, we have the best early warning system in the world." She looked at Des. "She won't let anything happen to us. We need to proceed slowly, let Des get used to our lovemaking."

Des snorted and curled into a tight ball by the fireplace.

Win

I took her hands, kissed the palms. "So, how's your mobility?"

"Much better," she said, leaning over and kissing me. "I'm guessing sufficient for most things."

I laughed. Got up and put the CDs in the player. Returned to the couch. Wondered at the woman awaiting my touch. I kissed her softly, unbuttoned her uniform shirt. Watched her shoulder as she took it off. Definitely more mobility. I kissed her neck, the scars that had formed on her shoulder. She still wasn't wearing a bra, so it was easy to keep on going.

She moaned when I slipped my hand into her pants and caressed her belly. "No fair, Win. You've got to lose some clothes too."

I'd worn a shirt so she could unbutton it, not have to take it off over my head. She made short work of that. And my bra. Very good mobility, I'd say. "Slow down, Sarah. We've got all night."

"Tomorrow and the day after. Too bad all that food's going to go to waste."

"Not all of it," I said as I unbuckled her belt. "One thing I've learned—you've got to keep up your strength."

She laughed. Sighed. "I can't believe this. I feel so at home with you, here. I never thought I'd feel this way again." Her hands went to my breasts, massaging them in a circular motion. Light at first. Then with more intensity.

I pulled her close. Cupped my hand around the back of her head. "Thank you for bringing me here." I kissed her. Ran my hand down her back. Moved it around to her side. Stomach. Moved my lips to her nipple. Felt her hands on my breasts echo the rhythm.

"I like the music, Win. Think we can still hear it in the bedroom?"

"Oh, yeah. But first, let's strip out here. So Des will know, you know, it's okay."

"She's sound asleep, Win."

Sarah

I lay next to Win, watching her chest rise and fall in sleep, wanting to touch her but knowing she could think I was the enemy if I awoke her. She'd warned me the first time we'd slept together to only call her name to wake her, not to touch her.

A phrase kept running through my mind: *so right, so right.* It felt so right to be here with Win, in a familiar bed, watching her sleep. A stab of moonlight crossed her belly right above her pubic hair. I was so tempted to run my hand over her skin.

I sighed. Win was the most complicated person I'd ever known. Though I hadn't realized it when we were kids, it was true back then. When she'd come out to me, I'd been surprised. Well, more than that. I hadn't really understood. She liked girls? Well, so did I. But I didn't want to date girls and I couldn't imagine sleeping with one.

Win could. She'd tried sleeping with a couple of guys and found it gross. I'd been a virgin and the pressure from the guy I was dating was turning me off. Further off. It wasn't until I met Hugh our freshman year in college that desire had awakened.

Through all the years, Win had known herself. What she wanted, what she couldn't abide. She'd hated hypocrisy. I wondered how much conflict her shadow life had caused her.

I closed my eyes. I wondered how much of the shadow life I could live—hiding our relationship, meeting only on scheduled days or nights in this quiet cove of McCrumb County. Maybe a few times at Win's. She gotten used to hiding, hadn't she? I thought that Win flaunted her sexuality where she could, with other lesbians. Probably a woman in every port and fort, then she pulled her cloak of androgyny around her when she was at work. Nathan said if she'd stayed in, she might have retired with stars. He said she was cool under threat and commanding.

I'd seen only passion and vulnerability. Win had shown me a part of her that maybe only Azar had seen. If their secret had been discovered, would she have made it out of that village alive? She'd risked willingly because of what she felt for Azar. Love.

Was I willing to risk for Win? Not my life, just my job.

Love.

CHAPTER TWENTY-SIX

Win

"Winifred, wake up!"

My eyes popped open. I saw Sarah standing by the bed with a steaming mug. Smelled coffee. Looked out the window.

"It's light out," I said. "What time is it?"

"Eight thirty, sleepyhead," Sarah said. "I've been calling your name for ten minutes." She set the mug on the nightstand and sat on the bed. "I thought you always rise with the dawn. Guess I'll have to figure out other ways to wake you up." She leaned over and kissed my breast.

My nipples stood at attention. "I haven't slept this late since I joined up."

"What, I exhausted you last night?"

"Utterly." I put my arms around her waist. She'd put on a nightshirt that had a moose pattern on it. I thought about unbuttoning it, but I had to pee. "Let me get some coffee in my system, Sarah." I ran my hand through her hair, brushing it back off her face. "You're getting more silver in your hair. Job stress or me stress?"

"I have no idea. I don't spend a lot of time in front of the mirror." She leaned over again, kissed my other breast. She let her tongue linger. "There's a storm heading our way, and I thought you might like to explore the lakefront. So get up and join the day." She ran her hand down my body. Stopped at my muff. Grinned. And got up.

"Tease," I said as I rolled out of bed.

The trail to the lake was a series of switchbacks, well-trod and steep. Des was a blur bounding down to new adventure. I followed Sarah, who was following muscle memory. A lot of memories. I felt no jealousy about her life with Hugh. Just glad that she'd found a good person to love and share her life with.

The trail ended at a cove complete with a skiff tied to a small dock. Sarah pointed to the opposite end of the lake. "You see the two cabins? Our only neighbors. The Jacksons and Clarks. I don't know if John will be back this year since he lost his wife this winter. The Clarks don't come until August."

I could barely see the cottages through the trees, though both had substantial docks that jutted into the water. "How far away are they? Two miles?"

"A little over that. Unless they use binoculars, they can't see us."

"So we can go skinny-dipping?"

"No, the water's way too cold for swimming, even in late summer. Nathan thinks the lake was formed by a meteor strike because it's so deep and there's nothing else that explains the depth. His people say Thunderbird created it."

"Well, it's beautiful."

Sarah pulled me to her, kissed me. "Thanks for giving me a reason to come back here. I didn't realize how much I'd missed this place. I always feel such a sense of peace, of belonging to something bigger when I'm here."

I wrapped her in my arms. "Being with you is such a gift."

She kissed me, slipped her hands under my shirt.

I wasn't comfortable with making love out here. Not on an open dock. We needed to slow down or go back to the cabin. I pulled back. "Can we go fishing?"

Sarah looked embarrassed. "Yeah, but not today. Feel how muggy it is? See that bank of clouds in the northwest?"

I looked but could only see a smudge over the ridge line. "Not a metaphorical storm coming, I hope."

"Real one, should be here soon." Sarah sniffed. "You can smell the ozone."

I sniffed. Nothing. "Do you have a root cellar?"

"That's the snuggest cabin in the world. We'll be dry, cozy and safe." She sighed. "But a metaphorical storm could hit anytime."

I let my arm drop and examined her eyes. "Because of us?"

She nodded. "I love being here with you, and I've said that to you. It's just…"

"If someone discovered us? It'd blow your world to bits?"

She leaned against me. "Oh Win, I don't want to think like that. I told you, I just want to be here and now. I don't want to think about repercussions. Dammit! I shouldn't have to."

I rubbed her back. "That's the price for living in McCrumb County. I keep saying, things are changing."

"Bullshit. Last year, this crazy guy started sending letters to the editor, awful, hateful letters. One suggested that all gays be rounded up and sent to concentration camps."

"I think that was already done in Germany."

"He got cheered on by a lot of people. Lloyd said he printed the letter to get discussion going about the changing status of gays. That's not what happened. I read the letters he didn't print. The vitriol was overwhelming."

"I'm sorry that you had to read that garbage, Sarah. Sorry you had to see the hate. But it's no use denying that it's real." I kneaded the back of her neck. "The only thing I can do to solve the problem for you is walk away. I will if you want me to."

"No!" She put her fingers on my lips. "Don't say it. Don't even think it."

We stood on the shore, embracing. As close in spirit as our bodies? I wasn't sure. That put clouds on my horizon.

"Let's go up and eat lunch," Sarah said. "That way, when the storm hits, we'll be comfy in bed."

It poured torrents. Lightning struck close. The wind tossed branches against the cabin. By the time it was over, we were sated. Ended up on the couch in front of the fireplace, watching the fire. With the passage of the storm, the temperature had dropped. At least outside. Sarah was ready to begin again.

* * *

I sat in Emily's office waiting. Already destroyed the order of the sandbox. Two days and nights with Sarah, in the shelter of the cabin, had demonstrated what an eager learner she was. I loved falling asleep with my arms around her. But our conversation at the lake haunted me.

The office door opened. Emily yelled, "Next."

Crap, I didn't need a cranky therapist. I walked in, closed the door. Sat in my chair. "Next? Really?"

She grinned, opened her notebook. "So, how's the time with Sarah? You are taking it easy with her shoulder?"

"She's gained a lot of mobility. Believe me." I stretched out in the chair. "She's got so much sensuality that I never expected."

Emily did the slit-eyed business. "You're happy, but worried. About Pan?"

"I thought about what you said. Decided my guilt was my prime motivator. That she didn't need to be hurt so I could feel absolved. I told her Pan had stayed with me, that Bill had sent her. As my bodyguard."

Emily laughed. "The word 'bodyguard' just assumed an entirely new meaning."

I played the nubby game. "Sarah's worried about the fallout if we're discovered."

"She should be. Should that happen before the election, I doubt if she'd find herself in office for another term."

"That's fucking stupid. The people of McCrumb County are fucking morons." I leaned my head back. "I think she doesn't understand the difference between coming out to yourself and telling the whole fucking world. I haven't had her experience. I don't know how to help her, Emily."

"What are you afraid of?"

"That it'll eat at her until she won't take the chance anymore."

Emily nodded. Wrote something on a page and reached across to hand it to me. "This woman was married for nearly thirty years. When her husband died, she was devastated. Then she found her balance in the arms of a younger woman. Have Sarah talk to her."

I took the paper. Folded it. "That's all I can do? Have her talk to somebody else?"

"You said yourself that you don't have the perspective to help her work through this."

"What if I talk to this Paige instead? Ask her what I can tell Sarah?"

Emily raised her eyebrows. "Like a game of telephone? I don't think so. Arrange a meeting at Ruby Slippers. Sarah needs to know there's a community out there, although she may be scared of that too."

"She's terrified."

"Win, you sought a community of women who were like you. Sarah may be at the point where she's willing to say she's attracted to you, maybe even in love with you. Maybe she's not at the point where she's willing to say she's lesbian."

"She hasn't really come out?" I asked.

"*'Really'* is a relative word. It's hard to say where she is unless I ask her. You're welcome to set up some couple's sessions. But first, take her to Ruby's."

"Scare the crap out of her?"

"In a hostile environment like this county, finding a supportive community can change the dynamics. Tell Paige I sent you, meet her first, explain the situation, particularly Sarah's vulnerability. Make an assessment, Win, and then act on it.

"Now, tell me about the threat you're still under and how it's affecting you."

CHAPTER TWENTY-SEVEN

Sarah

I sat at our kitchen table and watched Dad make dinner. When I'd come home, toting my duffel bag and warm memories, he'd given me a hug, then held me at arm's length. "You got the glow again. Win's good for you an' I'm glad. 'Bout time you got somethin' to think 'bout other than work."

Then he told me how much damage the storm had done. Straight-line winds and lightning. When Caleb had called, Dad had said I was in Indy at a rehab specialist. I wasn't in Indy, but I thought Win qualified as a rehab specialist. Still, I felt guilty for not even thinking of checking in with the office.

I rubbed my hand over the surface of the table which had stood in every Barrow homestead since the second one. Tung oil, rubbed in at the change of every season, hid the scars a bit and made it glow like honey. Scarred but beautiful, like Win.

"What makes you so open-minded?" I asked.

Dad turned from the stove. "I always reckoned I was a pretty ornery sonofabutt. You mean, how come I ain't gettin' out my shotgun and goin' after Win?"

"Yeah. You grew up in this county, just like the people who'd tar and feather me and Win."

He turned back to the stove, gave the pot a final stir and put the lid on. "Guess 'cause my Daddy was that way. An' Momma. You ever realize your Great-Uncle Bob was gay?"

"No—really?" Or was this a tale to make me feel better?

"Really. He never married, which coulda been a cause for talk. But he musta dated every woman in the county. Had a reputation as a ladies' man. All the whilst, him an' George McGarrett was carryin' on under the noses of all them righteous folk."

"George? I knew they were friends, but I never connected the dots." I turned and looked into his eyes. "They lived in the shadows."

He sat across from me. "Yep. Sarah Anne, I ain't gonna tell you your path with Win's gonna be easy. An' it's probably a good idea to keep your walkin' together secret for now, leastways, from some folk in the county."

"Remember the hornet's nest that the fake reverend stirred up? You read those letters too."

"I did, but I kept thinkin' the folk what cheered him on was few in number. An' no pastor, not even them what are real conservative, sided with him."

"They still preach homosexuality condemns a soul to the fires of hell for eternity."

"Mostly just them fundamentalists. Father Nowicki don't preach against much, talks mostly 'bout how to love other folk." He traced the grain of the wood with his hand. "Foundations. As far as I can understand it, Jesus Christ come to bring the good news, an' the Old Testament don't matter so much, but bein' good to folk does. That's the foundation my daddy taught me, an' I hope I taught you. Now's the time to see how good I taught you."

* * *

"How good I taught you" echoed in my mind as I tossed that night, sleep elusive and my shoulder aching. I'd slept immediately and soundly with Win next to me. My shoulder hadn't bothered me at all. Every time I thought about our affair coming out, I broke out in a sweat. I'd always kept the personal and the public separate in different boxes. Even my mourning for Hugh had been in private.

I'd never thought much about homosexuality. Except when Deputy Marvin Howard had been killed, prefaced by the letters his killer had sent the *Sentinel*. As it turned out, the murder had little to do with Marvin being gay and more to do with a smokescreen his killer had needed.

I hadn't known Marvin was gay and Dad had. Even after that incident, I pretty much ignored the issue. I'd heard the arguments about gay marriage and come down on the side of marriage equality, *equality* as the operative word. I'd had no clue that the issue would land much closer to home.

I gave up on sleep about three a.m. and I debated calling Win. This internal struggle was mine. She was sure where she stood and she stood there proudly. Why couldn't I join her? Why couldn't we just run away, forget about the bigotry and start a new life together in a place friendly to gays? Upstate New York was pretty country and we could get married.

Married. I never thought I'd think about getting married again. Never. Could I really share a future with Win? Make it a "'till-death-do-you-part" life? I knew this initial euphoria would cool. It had with Hugh, though we'd always had a healthy sex life. I didn't think the frequency and intensity Win and I were experiencing could last until one of us died.

At four thirty, I got up, slipped downstairs as quietly as I could and made a pot of coffee. Neither of us had said those words, *I love you.* I thought I loved Win, but maybe it was just a swirl of hormones and new experiences. I'd never questioned falling in love with Hugh, but then, our love hadn't been forbidden. I could hear Win's reply: *who's fucking forbidding love?*

Maybe those folk were more fringe now, but I knew in McCrumb County there were plenty of people who didn't want to think about it. If they did, they thought it was a perversion, no matter how many loving gay relationships were portrayed on TV. They weren't evil people, but had learned the lessons of whatever church they congregated with. They weren't about to bow down to the golden calf of popular opinion. I understood and had always thought it was all right for them to hold their own opinions. I still believed that. I just wished they could change the way they looked at homosexuality.

A little before six, I called Win. "Did I wake you up?"

"Um. But I would've been up soon." I heard some rustling. "Move over, you bed hog."

My heart did a flip. "Who are you talking to?"

"Des. Who else?"

"You let her sleep on the bed?"

"I think she knew I missed you and just wanted to provide a warm body so I could sleep." She yawned. "So did you call to check up on my fidelity?"

"No, I just wanted to hear your voice. Maybe I should get a dog too."

"Hard to get to sleep, Sarah?"

"I never did."

There was a long silence. "Worried about us?"

Yes, I wanted to say. Why pass on a load of crap that I had to sort? "Just missing you. Maybe we could have dinner at your place—I can't stay the night, but we'd have some time together."

"I don't want you to come here until the bastard's under arrest."

"You really think he's that dangerous?"

"I know he's dangerous. But what I don't know is if he blames me for getting caught. If he does, it could be bad news."

"What can I do?"

"Nothing. Military matter. But how about we go out one night this weekend?"

"Where the hell can we go out?"

"Let me worry about that." Her voice was throaty and low. "We can neck in the truck."

CHAPTER TWENTY-EIGHT

Win

When I got home from the cabin, I found Nathan sitting on my front stoop. Des wagged her tail. "What are you doing here?"

"I want to walk you through the system I've installed," he said as he stood. "Don't look at me like you'd like to shoot me."

"I told you I'd think about it."

He shrugged. "It's in, so let's go learn it."

"How'd you get in?"

"Look Win, I'm not the enemy—but you've got one. I'm trying to help."

"Don't you ever break into my house again, Nathan. Or I will shoot you. Or Des will eat you." Her ears pricked forward, and I hoped *eat* wasn't a command on the list. "Show me."

He went to a disguised keypad that he'd built into a wall. Close to the door, but unless you keyed in, the alarm would go off. He ran through a number of different options, including motion detectors and yard lights. "You don't have to run these all the time. I imagine you get deer and other critters at twilight."

"You mean I can scare the shit out of them?"

He grinned. "Now, where's your computer?"

I showed him my laptop and tower.

He took a thumb drive, downloaded a couple of programs to both. He opened one and I could see us on the screen. "I've got cameras monitoring doors and vulnerable windows. Nothing in the bathroom or bedroom. I've also got a program where if someone crosses an electronic trip wire at the base of the drive, it'll send you a warning."

"Person as well as car?"

"Yep. If you're not home and Des starts barking, it'll send a warning to you. All of this is accessible on your regular phone, but not the throwaway. Oh, and if you're in real trouble out there somewhere, hit seven, then the pound sign. It'll beep me, give me your location. I can forward that information to the sheriff's office. Questions?"

"Where'd you hide the RPG?"

"If you can get me one, I'll install it," he said with a perfectly straight face. "Now I've got to get going. A lot of storm damage to my network."

"You did this when you had—"

"Did it before the storm, but I wanted to get you online today." He smiled at me. "I want you to be safe. Bill and Sarah are doing their part, and this is my contribution to the cause."

He packed up the gear he'd brought. "I'll continue to monitor your phone and computer. If you have any problems, call me on the throwaway phone. Sleep sound."

I thanked him all the way to his van.

I ran through everything he'd shown me. Set the motion detectors and the lights. Then headed to bed. Slept soundly. Until Sarah called.

Her voice sounded ragged. Sleepless night? Worrying about discovery?

I got up, fixed breakfast, turned off the systems. Went outside with Des. It had gone from seventy-five to fifty degrees in a matter of two hours during the storm. It was still chilly. I thought about lighting a fire in the fireplace, beginning a new novel. Or maybe finishing the first one for my own enjoyment.

Then I thought of the woman named Paige. I waited until nine to call her. She sounded youthful, energetic. We arranged a meeting. Three at Ruby's.

* * *

I walked into Ruby's a tad before our meeting time. Picked up a beer at the bar and said hi to a few familiar faces as I made my way to the patio. I looked around. Only one woman sat alone at a table.

White hair gelled into a spiky version of Ellen's latest 'do. I hoped she was Paige.

She looked up. "Win?"

I sat at the table. "Thanks for meeting."

"Hell, you had to do the driving. Where in McCrumb County do you live?"

"About twenty miles outside Greenglen. Ten miles from Clayton Corners."

"Nowhere." She moved her chair under the shade the umbrella provided. "Now, tell me about your woman."

I liked this woman. Straightforward and honest. No wonder Emily had sent me to her. "I need to be assured that what I tell you is confidential. No casual conversation topic."

She made the Girl Scout pledge sign. "Hope that was right. They kicked me out the first year."

I laughed. God. It was a good thing I hadn't met Paige first. I took a sip of my beer. Followed a bead of sweat down the side of the glass with my finger. "She's the sheriff of McCrumb County."

"Sarah Pitt?"

"Shhh."

"Oh hell, Win. Nobody here's going to break the silence. Besides, nobody knows what we're talking about. She's running for reelection, isn't she?"

I nodded.

"You're her first?"

"Woman, yes. She was married. He died."

"Ah, now I see why Emily gave you my name. Similar circumstances, but Win, none are identical. So whatever I say, you've got to determine whether it applies to Sarah or not. I'm not a public figure, just a professor. Vi is much younger than I."

"Sarah and I grew up together."

"You have an adolescent thing? Experimentation?"

I shook my head.

"Why the hell not?"

"She was my friend and I didn't want to ruin that. I knew she didn't feel the way I did about girls."

"Then why now?"

Why? Because I wanted her to know she wasn't alone. "I kissed her once in the winter, we kissed again in the spring, we slept together in summer. I initiated the first kiss."

Paige flagged a waitress, ordered another round for us. "So she's as swept away as I was."

"I don't know how it was for you, but Sarah's been fully engaged. She's feeling the pressure of hiding our relationship. It's complicated because, um, it seems some unfinished business followed me home."

"You're seeing someone else too?"

"No. Nothing like that. I was in the military." I listened to birds chirping as they fought over crumbs on the ground.

"Do you love her?"

"Yes. But I haven't told her. I didn't want to put extra pressure on her."

The waitress put two cold beers on the table and left.

"Does she love you?"

"I want to say yes. But I think she's afraid to say anything."

She shook her head. "Fear seems so much a part of women loving women. Especially in that bastion of rednecks called McCrumb County. How about dinner at my place on Saturday night?" She watched the birds flutter as one hit the jackpot. She brought her gaze back to me. "Does she want to come out?"

"I don't know. We haven't really talked about it."

"Why is it people always avoid the conversations they should be having?"

CHAPTER TWENTY-NINE

Sarah and Win

Win

"So why are we going to dinner in Bloomington?" Sarah asked as she climbed in my truck.

She looked really nice tonight. Navy linen trousers, a white blouse that draped over her breasts without disclosing the lack of a bra. "I thought it would be nice to introduce you to some friends." I pulled out of the drive, still scanning my rearview mirror.

"No, I mean the real reason." She put her hand on my thigh. "Tillie hurt her back at work and Dad's staying with her tonight. The house is ours and we could've rescheduled. Why's it so important to go to dinner?"

Honestly? I wasn't sure, but I didn't have another answer. "Paige is a late-bloomer too. I thought you might like to hear her story." I pulled over to the side of the road. "I know sneaking around's weighing on you. Talking about stuff helps."

"With strangers?" She folded her arms. "Couldn't you've asked if this is something I want to do?"

"I should've." I wanted to fold her into my arms. This wasn't the place. "But the sex isn't going to carry us down the long road."

"You're getting bored?"

"No. I'll never get bored with you. Ever. I promise."

She turned to face me. "How can you make a promise like that? You've never had a long-term relationship."

That stung. I put the truck in gear. Hit the gas pedal hard. Was that part of what was going through Sarah's mind? That I'd tire of her? Or that she was the expert on the long road?

"Slow down, Win."

I looked at the speedometer. Slowed. But the questions kept sounding alarm bells in my head. Was she tiring of the sex? Not that I could see. Tiring of me? The secrets I carried? Was I pushing her to speak when I offered only silence in parts of my life?

"I'm sorry." She touched my arm. "That was a low blow."

"Way below the belt." I made the turn onto SR 50. "I should've asked. Sometimes it's really hard to get any answer from you but no."

She took her hand back. We rode in silence the rest of the way.

I parked in front of the address Paige had given me. "You don't have to go in. I'll make your excuses."

She opened her door. "I'll try this, but I have a long habit of silence."

Sarah

Paige Hanover was a character. Blunt to the point of rudeness, but saved by a wicked sense of humor. Maybe the twinkle in her eye that preceded a comment allowed me to relax. Her lover, Vi Smythe, was a Brit and seemed very proper.

When we finished dinner, Vi asked Win to help clear, and the two headed down the hall to the big kitchen. Paige led me into the living room, a large room done in Mission furniture to go with the Craftsman style of the house. I remembered rooms like this from visiting relatives' homes when I was a kid. When I had to be on my best behavior, though Mom and Dad never said so. I'd always been more comfortable in the kitchen.

Paige lowered herself into a leather upholstered chair. "My arthritis seems to kick up a bit in the evening, which is why we usually make love in the afternoon." She put her feet on an ottoman. "Win hasn't told me much about you, so if you will, fill in some blanks. This is your first time with a woman?"

I nodded. I needed to say something, but what? "I've known Win since we were kids, and I knew she was gay, but I never envisioned… this."

"You never fantasized about going to bed with a woman back then?"

"No. Should I have?"

This got a belly laugh from Paige. "There's no list that you need checked off before you screw a woman. Some, like Win, know their orientation from the get-go. You and I? Different birds. So let me tell you mine.

"Vi seems very buttoned-up and proper. Ha! I first met her in a graduate seminar I was giving. She flirted outrageously, but I wouldn't cross that teacher/student line. I was on her doctoral committee, and as soon as she'd passed her orals, she invited me out to dinner. I'd been a widow for almost four years, and though I'd had a few brief flings, I enjoyed being courted so exuberantly. It was a very good restaurant. She drove me home, walked me to the door.

"I said, 'Thank you very much for a wonderful evening, but I'm not inviting you inside until you graduate.' Can you imagine? So she kissed me on my front stoop. A long and lovely kiss. It changed the world for me. I was sorely tempted to open the door, but we managed propriety until graduation. Is anything in your story like this?"

I shook my head. "Win kissed me, apologized, promised it would never happen again and stayed away."

"But you couldn't stop thinking about it."

"No, I couldn't. I began to wonder what it'd be like."

"To have sex with Win? It's still hard for you to say, isn't it?"

"I feel like I'm sitting here naked and you know everything we've done."

"I probably do, although with Win, perhaps not." She crossed her legs at the ankles. "You've never had an animus toward lesbians, but you didn't want to know what they do to one another in the privacy of their own bed. Right?"

I nodded.

"Now that you do know, you're scared to death everyone will know every intimate detail. That embarrasses the hell out of you."

I nodded again. "I know it's dumb. I can't remember feeling this way when I married Hugh."

"Lesbianism is exotic for most people and erotic for most men. Jon once admitted that he'd like to watch me get it on with another woman. But for most, having sex with another woman is something for behind closed doors. Preferably, closed closet doors. While straight people profess to not want to know, they wouldn't mind watching. When that thought occurs, they push it away with vehemence.

"It's a vicious cycle, Sarah. I really think most women have erotic thoughts about other women. Most get stuffed down, put away and the door closed. I'm mixing my metaphors. But let me ask you this: do you like having sex with Win?"

I swallowed. "Yes."

"Has Win gone down on you?"

I felt heat rise from my neck and covered my face. I managed a nod.

"I can see you liked it." She chuckled. "Lighten up, Sarah. I don't know any couple who doesn't. When combined with good vaginal stimulation, it's unbelievably good. Orgasm nirvana."

My blush wasn't fading.

"Do you like going down on her?"

Damn, this woman was crazy if she thought I was going to share this stuff.

"Sarah, it's nothing to be embarrassed by. I have a good friend, been friends with her for years, who's straight. She did for me what I'm trying to do for you now. When she asked me if I enjoyed going down on Vi, I had about the same reaction as you do now. I was mortified. She looked at me and said something like, 'What is wrong with you? We've always talked about sex with our husbands, shared experiences and tips—why is this any different?'"

I felt the tears slipping away from my control. "I don't want it to be, but it is different. Yes, I love going down on Win. I'd never give Hugh a blow job. I loved him, but I never would."

Paige brought over some tissues, sat on the arm of the chair and patted my back. "You're one conflicted broad."

Win

I could tell Sarah had been crying as soon as I walked into the living room. Glanced at Paige. She gave me a sneaky thumbs-up. Sarah seemed okay now. Paige could be brutally honest. I liked that in her. But Sarah?

I glanced at my watch. "It's a long drive. We should hit the road."

Paige rose, Vi moved to her side, gave her a quick kiss. I envied that moment.

"Please come back," Paige said. "I've enjoyed having you both here. It's always nice to visit with country cousins."

She gave Sarah something—her card? Walked us to the door.

When we were in the truck, I pulled Sarah to me before she'd put the seat belt on. "Thank you for coming."

"Thanks for bringing me. Paige is...instructive." She kissed me, her open mouth an invitation. Which I took advantage of. I buried my face in her neck, inhaled the scent of her shampoo, moved my hand to her stomach. Moved it gently, feeling the fabric beneath my fingertips. I kept waiting for her to stop me. After all, this was a public street and any passerby could see what we were up to. But she didn't.

I leaned back, my head against the window. I took a deep breath, removed my arm and my hand. "Woman, you're one hell of a roller-coaster ride. We *are* in a public place."

She moved to her seat, buckled the belt. "I know, Win. I know we need to talk, and that sometimes I make you crazy. Hell, I make me crazy. Paige made sense to me, but shit, can she shock. Right now, drive. I want to get home—you can stay the night, can't you?"

"We're going to have to pick up Des." I started the engine, pulled into the street. Reached for her thigh. "I can stay, if you'll tell me what you and Paige talked about."

She laughed. Stretched out. "About how much I enjoy it when you go down on me."

I hit the brakes. "You what?"

"And how much I love to go down on you. Now drive, so we can do both."

Sarah

Win woke up early, slipped out of bed to go to the bathroom. I felt my nipples tighten as I watched her brush her teeth. The way her back muscled down to a high, firm butt. I got out of bed, tiptoed behind her and reached for her breasts as she saw me in the mirror. I kissed her neck, ran her nipples between my fingers. Her body arched as I ran my hands over her stomach, and then her belly.

"Let me brush my teeth and then we can shower," I said to her image in the mirror.

Win turned around, a silly grin on her face. "Are you sure you have enough hot water?"

When she opened my legs and ran her fingers between them, I forgot about brushing my teeth. We did run out of hot water.

"So," Win said to me as she finished breakfast. "What did you and Paige talk about besides sex?"

I blushed again. "Hell, Win. You're beginning to sound like Paige. She's so…"

"Blunt. Not willing to mince words." She pushed back from the table. "Unlike you."

I began clearing the table. "We talked about why I'm so reluctant to talk about us."

"Because you're ashamed," Win said. "Otherwise, why keep what we do together so buried?"

"No. I'm not ashamed. Paige made me realize I'm mediating everything I feel about you through an outside lens."

"What will the neighbors say?" Win asked as she poured another cup of coffee. "I don't see how that's different."

I filled the sink and dumped our plates in the suds. "I don't like talking about sex and never have. Mom gave me 'the talk,' and I squirmed all the way through, even though she did a really good job. Hugh and I never talked about what I liked. Or what he liked, except once when he asked me for a blow job." I wiped my hands on the dishtowel, threw it on the counter. "I tried but I just couldn't do it. He was apologetic and said he never should've asked. That kind of shut down the conversation." I took a deep breath. "Then you breeze into my life and show me what you like, how you like it and take the time to find out what I like. I'm never ashamed of us, Win. But I get embarrassed talking about it."

"I shall call you Prude," Win said, her voice unsteady. "Sarah, we've only begun to play."

CHAPTER THIRTY

Sarah

I went into work and Win drove to her house. That's the way it would be. For how long? Brief, intense meetings and then longing. My mind straying to the things we'd done, the delicious passion we'd shared.

I looked at my calendar and duty roster. I changed my shift on Saturday to the early one. Paige had said I needed to take a step forward and visit Ruby Slippers in Bloomington. Enjoy a good band, have a chance to dance with Win and meet some good women. The very thought of dancing in public with Win scared the shit out of me, but maybe we could just drop in and eat. Before people started arriving for the evening, we could leave. Baby steps were better than no steps.

The question Paige asked, right before Win and Vi came in, was screwing me up. "Do you identify as a lesbian, Sarah? Or a woman who just happened to have fallen for a woman?"

Identify as a lesbian? Hell no. The only identity I claimed was as a law enforcement officer. No doubt, if I walked into Ruby Slippers with Win, everyone there would assume I was lesbian. I didn't even understand what the word meant. I understood what the sex part meant, orgasm nirvana, as Paige had named it. I realized people applied labels by who shared our beds. But Win had talked about sex as only a part of her psyche. An emotional bond between women was something I understood and took for granted. Mom had a large circle of women friends, and I knew she loved them. So, had she been lesbian? And Dad never noticed? Hell.

I looked up at a tap on my door.

John Morgan walked in and sat across from me. "I've heard rumors that the one guy who escaped our net has opened a new meth lab. The guy's name is Larry Fellows and he's appeared on our watch list a couple of times."

"We can't get warrants on rumors. We need more, John."

"This is like Catch 22."

"It is Catch 22. Put him on the watch list again and whatever data you've got."

He nodded, pushed himself up. "I'll take whatever I can get. Rumor has it, it's a mobile lab in an old RV."

"I've heard you've been spending a lot of time down at the rifle range."

"I wasn't as sharp as I thought I was," he said, ducking his head a bit.

"Let it go, John. Each one of us knows we could take a bullet every time we go on patrol. This is the only time I'm going to say this, so listen up. It wasn't your fault. Not. Your. Fault. Now go get some bad guys."

After he left, I wondered if what I'd said was true. Did we bring to consciousness the thought that we could die every time we put the badge on? The thought was something always there, but shoved down beneath the layer of immediate demands.

My desk was covered with immediate demands.

* * *

Last year's drought and searing heat had fled. So far this summer we'd had more rain than had fallen since 1893, and wave after wave of cold fronts had brought Canadian temperatures to southern Indiana. Sunday night, I lit a fire in the fireplace and put on one of the CDs Win had left. This time, I listened to the lyrics. Songs of loss, of coming out, of soaring. I really liked the music and wondered why I hadn't heard it before.

Tillie's bad back had finally been diagnosed as a slipped disc, and Dad had been spending a lot of time with her. His schedule shifted according to her needs and when her neighbors could fill in. I didn't feel I could have Win over tonight, even though the odds were Dad would stay at Tillie's.

Maybe a little distance from her touch would help me think things through. I didn't think I'd ever thought about Stonewall until I happened to be in Bloomington during a gay pride parade and a float had memorialized the event.

I'd looked the other way. It hadn't been my business, certainly not my issue.

Now? I just the hell didn't know. It was a bewildering maze with corridors opening to unknown directions. I stood at the entrance, afraid to take a step in any direction for fear of taking the wrong one. At the heart of the maze Win waited, ready to lead me out.

CHAPTER THIRTY-ONE

Win

When I got home, my alert level zoomed up. Everything looked okay, but I couldn't shake the feeling that something was off-kilter. I checked the system logs. Lights had gone on three times last night. I looked at the images. Deer twice, both right after it got dark. The third time showed nothing. Shit. After I blew up the image, I went back over it. No animal, but it looked as if a branch had fallen. That made sense. I was still uneasy.

I took Des out for backup, walked to the garden. Played gardener while I examined the branch. Old, with a broken end. Could have fallen. Could've been tossed to check the system. Was I getting paranoid again? Imagining threats where none existed? I pulled weeds. Watched Des, who was sniffing around but didn't seem anxious.

When I'd finished, I called Des and went back inside. I started to call Bill, but thought if Scotty was still at large, he might well have hacked Bill's phone line by now. I decided to go into Bloomington and buy new phones, one for me and one for Bill. While I was at it, I'd see if Paige was free for lunch.

Paige said yes, and so, after setting the system, I began the drive to Bloomington. Keeping an eye out for a tail. I'd learned to trust these feelings of danger. They stood me well in my career. Here at home,

I was trying to neutralize them. This was a strong suspicion I had no viable evidence for. Back to crazy.

I bought two new burn phones at Wally World, then navigated the streets of Bloomington until I parked in Ruby's parking lot. Paige was waiting at the same table.

"So, you and Sarah have any time or inclination to talk?"

I nodded, scanned the menu. I'd seen a waitress approaching out of the corner of my eye. The waitress turned out to be Julie.

"Haven't seen you in a while," she said. "Thought for sure you'd come back for more by now."

Fuck her. I snapped the menu shut, handed it to her and ordered.

"My, my," Paige said as we watched Julie walk away. "Never would've put you two together."

"One weekend. When I was trying to stomp down my feelings for Sarah."

"That one didn't work, did it?" She leaned toward me. "Though I respect Julie enormously for making this place possible, I don't like the way she treats women."

I waited five beats. "How important is it that Sarah identify as lesbian?"

"I like you, Win. On your own, you're a strong, centered woman. When you're with Sarah, you tiptoe."

"I'm protective. Maybe feeling guilty for having initiated this whole thing." I glanced at Julie taking another order at another table. Flirting. "I wanted a relationship. Being back at home, no more globetrotting. I wanted to settle down."

"Openly?"

"Too many years in the closet." I blew out a long breath. "But I'm still in there. This time, with company."

"You're out in this community, Win."

"Doesn't change the equation. Even if I could be out, live with somebody, McCrumb County would be problematic. Some days, I wonder if I should've come home at all."

"Where else you would like to live?"

"In the mountains. Maybe Colorado. Somewhere with real mountains." I began shredding the paper napkin, taking out my frustration on an inanimate object.

"So, did you and Sarah talk?"

I nodded. "A little. She identified part of the incongruity she's facing."

"Incongruity, my foot." She snorted. "I doubt very much that she identifies as lesbian. Probably doesn't matter much now, at least it didn't for me. But she's going to have to face the question sooner or later."

"How important is it? For the relationship? I don't really give a shit."

"You may not now," Paige said. "But how long are you going to be content living separately and pretending you're 'just friends'—a year? Five? The rest of your lives?"

I didn't have an answer. Didn't need one because Julie brought our lunch. She placed Paige's plate in front of her, handed me mine. "Don't forget to save room for dessert, hon. My office is small, but very accommodating." She rubbed my shoulder as she left.

"Shit. I can't believe I ever…"

"She was probably on good behavior," Paige said as she placed the napkin on her lap. "You, my dear, would be a lovely trophy for her." She winked. "As far as Sarah goes, listen when she wants to talk, but don't push. For all of her confusion, that woman has a spine of steel. Don't get her back up."

When lunch was finished, I drove to Bill's house, parked down the road a bit. As he drove up about dinnertime, I flashed my headlights at him. He pulled up.

I handed him the phone. "I'm getting that feeling again. Any word on the general?"

"Nope, but we're working hard. Anything I can do to help, let me know."

I also stopped by Nathan's. We went over the logs together.

"Looks clean, Win. I'll monitor closely, but if he's on foot…"

"Scotty doing his own dirty work? I doubt it." He still might have minions. "I'll walk the perimeter with Des in the morning."

"Be careful, Win."

* * *

I slept with one eye open that night. The lights only went on once, right at twilight. I snuck to the window, saw a doe and fawn. I still couldn't relax. Hypervigilance, Win. Watch out or all the bogeymen will come back. I did twenty minutes of deep breathing. Felt calmer, but if I had hackles, they would've been up.

I woke a little before dawn, made a pot of coffee. Waiting for it to get light enough to check for footprints or some other clue that someone had been on my land. If I found nothing, I could go back to feeling like I was home.

The trip wire on the drive pinged. I reached for the gun that was holstered at my side. Watched until Nathan's ancient Jeep stopped out front. He rolled down his window and waved. I disarmed the system and opened the front door. "What are you doing here?"

"Thought I'd walk the perimeter with you." He got out toting a backpack. "I brought some more toys."

I set the system, locked the door. Walked down the drive with Nathan at one side and Des on the other. He'd had the reputation as an expert tracker since he was in high school. I'd gone hunting with him once and I was a believer. But he shouldn't stick out his neck this far.

I stopped. "We've got to divide up duties. I can't look for footprints at the same time I'm looking for a sniper."

"Sniper, huh? You concentrate on that, but my guess is someone was testing the system. You know who?"

"My general. Or someone he hired. It's got to be tied to that situation. I haven't ticked anybody else off since I've been home." Had I?

At the back of the property, off a fire lane, Nathan stopped. "This may be it."

"May be what?" I asked as I looked at a solid screen of trees.

He walked over to a gathering of saplings, pushed them aside. I saw a deer path. "Well, hell."

He led, I followed. He stopped again and pointed. I peered over his shoulder. A partial boot print coming in this direction.

"Not enough to make a cast, but it looks like a men's size nine or ten. At least he isn't here now."

He started up the hill again. When we got close to the top, he pointed again. "Looks like he watched for a while, then went a bit closer."

I could see the back of the house. Shit.

Nathan took a few careful steps. "You find anything in your yard that shouldn't have been there?"

"A branch?"

"Show me."

We walked into the yard, the lights went on. Nathan took what looked like a remote control from a pocket. The lights went off. I showed him the branch.

"I think he tossed it from the top of the hill, testing the limits of surveillance. From what I've seen, I think he was here recently. Prints are fresh. Were you home this weekend?"

"No. I went into Bloomington for dinner Saturday night. Stayed over."

"What time did you leave?"

"Afternoon."

"He must be watching your coming and going," Nathan said. "Figured you might be gone long enough to check it out. When it got dark and he saw the lights go on with the deer, he tested the system."

"You think he's a pro?"

He nodded. "But not someone used to the woods. He left too many signs behind."

One boot print? Some crushed weeds?

"He didn't drive on the fire lane, but it looks like he headed farther down it." He closed his eyes. "Foley's Knob. It's the highest point around here, and he could use glasses to see you come and go. There're a lot of trees between you and the glasses, but he could definitely see you drive out."

"Then he saw us leave."

"If he's still there and still looking, I can find out. Unless you're afraid I'll scalp him before you question him."

"Nathan, quit. I'm afraid he'd kill you."

"I can move like air."

"Yeah, well if he's ex-Special Forces, he can feel the air shift. Maybe I can figure out a way to smoke him out. Until then, don't go near the Knob."

"Then I'll set up another trip wire with a camera. Go on in the back way and sit tight. System's off, leave it that way until I get back."

Thirty minutes later I heard a tap at the back door. Nathan came in, put the backpack down. He opened my computer, tapped a few keys, and a picture of the trail we'd been on came up on the screen. "If he comes back, we'll have an image."

He walked me over to the front window. Pointed. "See those trees sticking up over there? Foley's Knob. I can look around, see if I can find his transportation."

"Too dangerous, Nathan. Please. I'm the warrior and you're the shaman. Let's stick to our strengths."

"Shaman? Well, I'm going to have to do some magic to get my poor old Jeep out of here without being seen."

CHAPTER THIRTY-TWO

Sarah

I'd worked hard all morning to get all the paperwork off my desk. Responses to the grant proposals were coming in, all thumbs-up so far. But that meant allocating these new funds, finding quality materials at the cheapest possible price. We needed to stretch the money until it yelped. I wished I could put all this on somebody else's desk, but Caleb was up to his neck with a string of burglaries and the roving meth lab.

My cell rang. I didn't recognize the number. "Sheriff Pitt."

"My God, you sound official," Win said. "I was all ready for a sexy greeting. Low, sultry voice filled with desire."

I checked outside my office, and the coast was clear. "What are you wearing?"

Laughter pealed down the line. "Shit, Sarah, that's the best you've got?"

"I'm not used to sounding sexy."

"Hmpf." Win sighed. "Actually, I called to say I can't make it to the cabin tonight. My stalker seems to have returned. There's no way I'm leading him to a remote place like that."

"Damn. Double damn."

"I know, I feel the same way. Thrice over."

"You know, I was just thinking I wish I had help in allocating the monies from the grants. We could put you on as a consultant. I could really use your expertise."

"I could come in for a meeting before class. In about an hour?"

"That would be great." I lowered my voice. "More than great."

"In your office?"

She disconnected and I laughed. I wrote up a list of the grant monies we'd received and what they were supposed to be used for, printed it out and put it with the catalogs I'd gathered. Then I went back to clearing out my inbox. I couldn't wait to see Win, but we couldn't even share a kiss here. Hell, I hated hiding like this. Maybe we could find someplace private, somewhere not the cabin, not my house, not her house.

It ticked me off that Win was keeping me at a distance with this stalker again. Hell, that's what the sheriff's office was for, serving and protecting all citizens of McCrumb County. We could catch the sonofabutt, put Win's fear to rest and meet at her house.

An hour later, Win and Des walked into my office. They both looked beautiful. Win sat across from me, Des settled by her side. "So, what's my project?" she asked.

"You wrote such good grant proposals, that money's coming in and I have to decide how to disperse it." God, I sounded like an idiot. "What I'm looking for is good equipment for the least amount of money. I made a list. Here are the equipment catalogs."

Win took the list and scanned it. "I think you can get a lot of this from the military. Cheap. I don't need the catalogs, I'll do it all online." She looked up. "What I'll need is purchase order numbers and your authorization so I can just place the order. Some of this stuff goes pretty quick."

I handed her what she needed. "Let me know if you need anything else."

We shared a long, searching look. It took everything I had to stay in my chair, not walk around the desk and sweep her into my arms and kiss her forever.

"So what class are you taking?" I asked.

"Uh, teaching. Mr. Kim's finally let me in the advanced class. With that comes the opportunity of teaching a beginner's class that covers my tuition."

"Mr. Kim? That tae kwon do place down on Walnut Street?"

"Dojang. Yeah. You do any martial arts?"

"I took basics at the academy, but that's a long time ago."

"Why don't you come down, watch my class," Win said as she rose. "The Kims all leave for dinner at five. My class ends at five. I have the key to lock up." She took a step toward the door. "They have showers. Lots of hot water."

* * *

"We need to talk more," Win said as she unbuttoned my shirt.

"I like this kind of nonverbal communication." I undid her white jacket.

"Why do you wear a damn undershirt?"

"Since I'm still not wearing a bra, it gives me some camouflage."

"Not for long." Win pulled my T-shirt over my head and dropped it on the bench. She pulled me to her, her arms strong around me.

I leaned into her, knowing I could stand this way with her for a lifetime, knowing that I loved her. I slipped her pants down, she started unbuckling my belt. Within two minutes, we were in the shower and she was soaping my body. Win was right, we didn't run out of hot water.

As I toweled her off, I asked, "Is there enough hot water for another shower?"

She glanced at the clock. "We better get a move on it, students will be here for night classes."

"Why don't you come over? Des is here, Dad's with Tillie."

She rubbed down my back. "Are you good at picking up tails?"

"Yeah. You're worried about your stalker?"

"What if I drive out, you follow me at a distance. See if anyone's tailing me."

"If he is, I can arrest him, but then we won't get any time together because I'd have to book him, and that takes forever." I kissed her neck, ran the towel over her butt.

"You can't arrest him because he's on the same road I am."

"I'll shoot him."

"No. Get a license plate. I'll give it to Bill."

"But you'll stay?" I kissed her shoulder.

"Yes." She pulled back. "Now stop hustling me and get dressed. Otherwise you're going to have to explain why you're naked to a whole bunch of students."

CHAPTER THIRTY-THREE

Win

Sarah left first, out the back door. When the first students showed up, along with the younger Kims, I left. In a routine I'd gotten used to, I began to search for a GPS attached to a wheel well. I checked every morning, though my truck had been parked in the garage all night.

None this time. I started the truck and pulled away. Sarah was going to begin her tail three blocks away. Nobody pulled out behind me.

I hadn't seen anybody behind me since I left Greenglen. I turned into Sarah's drive, parked behind a shed where my truck would be invisible from the road. While Des ran around the yard, checking everything, I waited by the back door until Sarah turned in and parked.

She walked up to me, pulled me close by the front of my shirt. She kissed me, long and slow, her hands running freely over my body.

"No tail," she said as she opened the back door.

"Good. He's just got eyes on my house."

She stopped with her duty belt in her hand. "What's going on, Win? I had your back tonight, I can be there for you. You don't have to fight this war alone."

I took the duty belt, hung it on its peg. Put my arms around her. Just stood, feeling her closeness. "I'm starving. Can we eat something while I tell you?"

"I called for a pizza on the way and he should be here any minute."

I was afraid to kiss her. Afraid I couldn't stop and the pizza guy would deliver to a naked and aroused sheriff. I just held her. Buried my face in her neck. Nibbled. Thought about what a miracle this love was.

We heard tires on the gravel. I grabbed her service pistol. Stood behind the door. Des was on alert. Sarah opened it, greeted the guy. I could smell the pizza. "Clear," I said to Des. Watched her relax.

We didn't do much talking until the pizza was reduced to greasy smears and threads of cheese on the bottom of the box.

Sarah collected the detritus, closed the box, put it on top of the trash can. "Now, I want to hear what the hell is going on. All of it, Win."

She sat across from me. I began with Scotty's visit.

"My God—could he really do that? Put you back in battle?"

"He could recall me, but it wouldn't be for battle." I continued with the story to the last alarm. "The testing of my security system didn't feel like Scotty. Too physically present—you know?"

"I don't understand why that general's doing this, Win. Revenge? When he could be hightailing it out of the country?"

I shook my head. "Makes no sense to me. But now you know, could we retire to the living room? Listen to some music?"

"You don't want to talk about this anymore?"

"No. We weren't tailed here. Tonight we're safe."

She rose, came over. She stood behind me and cupped my breasts. Leaned over and kissed her favorite spot on my neck. "Let's just go upstairs to bed."

* * *

Breakfast was silent except for an occasional "Pass the maple syrup." Sarah was chewing on something other than her waffles. Which was fine. I was tired. Amazed at her receptivity to try new things last night.

Since I'd planned to return home, I hadn't brought my laptop. Now there was no way I could check on my house. I really didn't want to walk into a trap. I could go to Nathan's. Or maybe just call him. One thing I had with me was my new burn phone. Scattered thinking, Win. Pull it together.

"I think we need to go to Nathan's, have a war council," Sarah said. "First, we need to find the guy who's camping out on Foley's Knob. Trace if he's connected to your general for some nefarious purpose, or another assassin ready to kill you."

"We can't do anything without letting Bill know," I said.

"Then invite him. Nathan's the best tracker in the county, and he taught me. We need to know if the guy's still there, and if he is, why."

"If he's not?"

"Then we need to find out what he did while he was up there," Sarah said. "You have no real evidence who he is or what his motivation is. For all you know, he could be a traditional stalker and madly in love with you."

"Highly improbable."

"I think he'd be a fool if he wasn't attracted to a beautiful woman like you."

On her way to the sink with the plates, she kissed my neck. On her return, she rubbed my shoulders. Soon, her hands found their way around front. She slipped them under my T-shirt. Caressed my breasts with a feather touch. "Let me do you down here, in the chair."

"What about the war council?"

She looked at the wall clock. "It's six thirty, let's set it for nine thirty. You call Bill and I'll alert Nathan."

She got her phone and tossed me mine. Bill said he had to juggle his schedule, but he'd be there.

As she disconnected, she looked at me. "Now where were we?"

I stood up, turned the chair around and stripped off the T-shirt. "I'm all yours."

She walked to me, I removed her robe. Stroked her butt. Kissed her with increasing passion. I pushed my thigh between her legs, began moving her.

She pulled away. "I thought I was doing you, in the chair."

I grinned. "I got carried away. You have any silk scarves?"

She look puzzled. "Do they have to be silk?"

I shook my head. Sat down in the chair. "Two long ones, if you have them. The other two can be any length. I'll be here when you come back."

She raced upstairs. When she returned, I was sedately sitting in the chair. Legs spread. "Let me show you how to tie my arms."

Her eyes widened. "Is this bondage, Win? Like in the book?"

"Very mild. I get so aroused with you, I start taking over. I know it happens, but I don't mean to. This puts you in charge."

I showed her how to tie one arm to the back of the ladderback chair. She took care of my other one by herself. "I've never let anyone tie me up, Sarah." I leaned forward as much as I could. Kissed her hard. "This is an act of faith, in you and in us. This is my surrender."

As she tied my ankles to the chair legs, I wondered if she understood what I said. How hard it was for me. Because I knew I had control over so few things in my life.

She straddled me. Kissed me lightly, and her fingers played with my nipples. She kissed my neck. Whispered in my ear. "Tell me what you want, how you want it. If you're scared of losing control, I'm terrified of having it. Thank you for trusting me, Win. I love you."

CHAPTER THIRTY-FOUR

Sarah

I drove Win's truck to Nathan's in a daze. The past couple of hours had been a major shift between Win and me. I'd had the power of bringing her whenever I wanted. I'd come too, riding her and without penetration. Utterly amazing. When I'd untied her and we went upstairs, she'd taken me in such a tender way I almost cried.

I glanced over at her, and saw she was sound asleep with a slight smile on her face. No matter what we faced in the future, I'd never forget this morning.

We bounced up the track to Nathan's and she woke up. Des grumbled.

"Back to the real world," she said, the trace of a smile vanishing.

"Win—"

"Shhh. We'll talk later. Right now, we need to concentrate on the business at hand. I want to be free to live my life. To welcome you to my home without having to worry about who's watching and listening."

Nathan greeted us as we got out and stooped to give Des a greeting. Inside, he showed us the results of the system at Win's over the past twenty-four hours. "Here comes the interesting part."

We watched as a man pushed through the leaf screen that hid the deer path. Dressed in camo gear and wearing a sidearm, he paused and looked around. Lifted his head.

"I'll be damned," I said. "Willy Nesbit. Why the hell is he doing surveillance on Win?"

"This is the guy who's running for sheriff against you?" Win asked. I nodded.

"Wait and watch," Nathan said.

He switched to another camera that overlooked the "nest" Nesbit had used before. He installed something on a tree, then turned around and left.

"Directional mic with transmitter."

"He's eavesdropping?" Sarah asked. "Why?"

"You can ask him when we find him," Nathan said. He swiveled his chair around to face us both. "He's still up on the Knob. We can nab him now, before this gets any more weird."

Win shook her head. "A Navy SEAL is the most lethally trained fighter in the world. It's too damn risky. We don't have the arms. The only way to get him—"

Nathan stood up. "Before we go into the how, let me ask you a question. Are you two having an affair?"

Win's eyes opened wide.

"Yes," I said. "I wouldn't call it an affair. I'd say I fell in love with Win and we express that love in the way any couple would."

Nathan smiled, hugged me. "I'm glad for you, sis. It's been a long time since I've seen you so happy." He turned to Win. "I remember when you had a huge crush on Sarah in middle school. Sure took you long enough." He hugged her too. "You two don't need my blessing, but you've got it, should you want it."

We both said thanks, and then Nathan settled down to his plan, which was basically sneak up on Nesbit and get the draw.

"Before we go to the plan, I'd like to know if there's a chance Nesbit is working for Win's general. Or if he's just trying to sink me."

"I haven't picked up any communication between Nesbit and the general," Nathan said. "But Nesbit's been burning the lines with Mac."

"Rob McKenzie, our former sheriff," I said to Win. "He had two terms between Dad and me and almost destroyed the sheriff's department with patronage and graft."

"You think Nesbit's trying to get evidence of our relationship?" Win asked.

"I've talked to him a couple of times," I said. "He appeared to be a relatively sane human being. But that's something Mac would do, leak photos or taped conversations."

"As far as I can tell, his surveillance has only been going on ten days or so," Nathan said. "Only added audio yesterday."

We went back to arguing the best way to take Nesbit down. I thought Nathan's plan would work, especially if Win was willing to provide a diversion.

"A diversion? Really? I'm a trained sniper," Win said.

"With you driving up, maybe driving down the fire lane and poking around, his attention is not going to be on his immediate surroundings," I said. "That'll give us the opportunity to take the last few yards."

"If he doesn't blow you away first."

"Win, he has no reason to fire at us," I said, exasperation creeping into my voice. "If he sees us, his best option is to get out of there. What he's doing is illegal, he knows it and I'm quite sure he doesn't want to be arrested at this stage of the campaign."

We heard an engine drawing close. I unholstered my weapon, stood by a window. A nondescript sedan pulled into the clearing.

"Clear," Win said. "That's Bill."

Nathan opened the door for him, and he strode into the room like he was on a parade ground.

"You must be the sheriff," he said, briskly shaking my hand. "Heard good things about you." He handed a thumb drive to Nathan. "Win, we found two recent communications. See if you get the same translation as we did."

Two brief messages lit one of Nathan's monitors. Win sat at one station and began writing on a tablet. "This second one's a bit tricky. I assume both came in from Fazal? And you didn't find replies?"

"Fazal, yes. No replies."

"The first is to cancel the shipment. He's upped the 'fee' for delivery. The second is to use a prearranged place. But I'm a bit at a loss where."

"Any guesses?"

"I can work on it. The reference is to Persian mythology. But damn, I don't know what it means to either Fazal or Scotty. That's the key, what it means to those assholes."

"You will work on it?" Bill asked.

"Yeah. No guarantees. And not right now."

Bill put his hand on her shoulder. "I think this is why Scotty's after you. He wants not only a translation from you, but for you to figure out where the damn shipment is."

Win turned in her chair. "It's got to be prearranged. Why the hell wouldn't he know?"

"Number one, Scotty's sloppy in a lot of ways. Maybe he wasn't paying attention when Fazal set it up. Or, number two, this is a test. Scotty doesn't figure it out, he doesn't get his booty."

Win's eyes lit up. "My money's on the second."

Bill nodded.

"I know this is important," I said, "but could we take a couple of hours to run a local operation to nab Win's stalker?"

Bill looked at Win. "Your stalker is in the brig awaiting court martial."

Win sighed. "This is a new one. Doesn't have any connection to my service. Makes me feel like a magnet for punks."

"Can I come with?" Bill asked.

I glanced at Nathan. He gave a slight nod. "Yeah, but you're going to have to stay back. We're going to arrest an ex-SEAL. Could be a lethal situation, and I won't be responsible for you, nor do I want to worry about your safety. Deal?"

Bill scowled and then nodded.

* * *

Bill rode with Win and Des and had volunteered to be part of the diversion. Once they'd pulled into the fire lane, Nathan and I worked our way up the backside of the Knob. If I hadn't known Nathan was there, I wouldn't have known he was there. I wasn't as good, but my missteps were small ones, not noticeable in a thriving woodland setting. Nathan took the left, I took the right, and the plan was to simultaneously step from cover, weapons fixed on Willy Nesbit. I'd stopped at home and donned my uniform shirt and duty belt. Nathan carried his deer rifle. Not heavy armament, but we hoped surprise would protect us.

We were almost there when we heard Nesbit. "Dammit, Mac, I can't record anything if there's no one home. But we may get something interesting soon. She's just arrived and I think she's with a MCIA colonel. They're poking around the deer path I used. Let me call you back."

I nodded to Nathan and we both broke out of the brush at the same time. "Police! Keep your hands where I can see them," I yelled.

Nesbit rolled over to face me and slowly raised his hands when he saw my Glock aimed at his heart. "What the fuck?"

"You've been busy, Mr. Nesbit. Surveillance, which falls under the stalking laws, not to mention federal electronic eavesdropping laws." I got my handcuffs, told him to roll over and cuffed him while Nathan covered him.

We signaled Win, led him down the Knob and met up with them at the foot of Win's drive.

"Why in God's name would you do this to me?" Win yelled. "You, of all people, should understand. When I'm finally home and trying not to jump at every shadow."

Nesbit hung his head. "I'm sorry, Ms. Kirkland."

Bill marched up to him. "Sorry doesn't do it, Nesbit. What the fuck is behind this pathetic attempt to intimidate one of my people?"

Nesbit straightened up, squared his shoulders. "Your people? I was told Ms. Kirkland was a national security risk."

"*Security risk?*" Win yelled. "Do you have a fucking brain? Do you have any fucking evidence that I have ever done anything other than serve my country to the best of my ability? Who the hell told you I was a traitor?"

I stepped between them. "Easy answer. Mac. We heard you talking to him."

"How the hell did you get up there without me hearing you?" he asked. "Jesus, you really blindsided me."

"What's the story with Mac?" I asked.

He went back to staring at the ground.

"We have photos of you trespassing on Win's property, photos of you installing an illegal listening device without warrant and we have the device. We can file felony charges for the latter. Certainly would end your campaign early." I kicked his shin. "I don't want to win a second term by default. Talk."

"The media will have a field day with this," Bill said. "Ex-SEAL does illegal surveillance on wounded warrior who fought in Afghanistan. There's a nightmare for command. Have you thought what this is going to do to your pension?"

"Look, I didn't want to do this, but Mac said Ms. Kirkland was going to sell high-level intel to Al Qaeda through this woman at IU. If I got evidence, he thought it'd be a big bust with lots of good publicity."

"Shit," Win said. "I may get a teaching position at CELI. With Bill's backing. I have an appointment with the head of the Middle Eastern major tomorrow. Are you stupid or just out to win an election?"

"I didn't even want to run, but Mac said it was my duty," Nesbit said.

I took a deep breath. "We have a conundrum, Mr. Nesbit. I don't want to arrest you, but you've broken the law, so I can't really let you walk away. Any solution to offer?"

"Think hard on this, Willy," Bill said.

Nathan stepped forward, his rifle held casually in the crook of his arm. "If I understand law enforcement practice correctly, some infractions can be overlooked in exchange for information. If Mac wanted you to do this to a war hero, what's to say he won't ask you to do the same to anybody else in the county? If you pass on all his requests and instructions, perhaps this could be resolved. Sarah?"

I nodded. "That would work. I doubt if you know this, but Mac almost destroyed the sheriff's department when he had the office— ask anybody in the county. The feds were investigating, state police, state's attorney's office, whole kit and caboodle."

"I'll drop out of the election," Nesbit said. "I swear, I don't want to do this." He turned to Win. "You know how hard it is to be home and not be paranoid. He put out these theories that just made too much sense, especially after all the sheep-dipping I went through. I should've known better. Blame it on my own paranoia."

Win examined his face. "Apology accepted."

"Don't drop out of the election," I said. "Let the people decide who's fit for the job. Just promise to pass on any requests Mac makes of you."

Nesbit nodded. "On my honor."

Though that was dubious, I unfastened the cuffs. "Gather your gear and get out of here."

Nathan watched him go, then turned to Bill. "Ready to go back to work?"

They piled in Nathan's truck and Win and I were left at the bottom of her drive.

"Would you like to come up to my house? Have coffee, sun tea, or me?"

CHAPTER THIRTY-FIVE

Win

We walked up the drive hand and hand, Des dancing around us. Dashing into the brush and quickly coming back. I unlocked the door, went to the panel and shut off the alarm system. I felt suddenly shy. Maybe from finally having Sarah back in my home. Maybe from my performance this morning. In her kitchen. Shit! Anybody could've come to visit, and there I would've been. Naked and tied to a kitchen chair.

But mostly, Sarah had witnessed my total surrender.

"I was beginning to think you had a mistress stashed here," Sarah said, pulling me toward her.

We kissed, gently, tentatively. I didn't hug her too hard. My breasts were a little tender. That wasn't all. I wanted to ask her what she'd seen when I'd been so naked. Soul naked. But I was afraid. Time to do some serious lovemaking or talk.

I pulled back. "Want to talk? About this morning?"

She nodded, her eyes showing the same fear I felt. We settled on the couch with enough space between us to keep the fire at bay.

"You said you loved me," I said.

"I do. I've felt it growing. I wanted to be sure before I said it out loud. But when you, you know…You gave me control over your body, and I think you opened all of you to me."

"I surrendered? Let you storm the walls?"

"Your walls. You came again and again, and we were so together. I've never felt anything like that before. Not between us, not with Hugh. It was like melding into one another." She grasped my hand. "I think it was possible because you trusted me completely."

Yes, I had. It scared the shit out of me. I'd handed Azar my soul, and I couldn't go through a loss like that again. "I love you too, Sarah. I have since I started seeing you." Here came the hard part. "Your work is so dangerous. You could've died on that drug raid. I'm so afraid of losing you."

"Like you lost Azar?"

I nodded. Traced her fingers. "The time after her death was so dark. Even though they ordered me out, I stayed in the village. Months. Working like a madwoman to rebuild what we'd destroyed. I slept in Azar's bed every night, smelled her scent. Cried. I think I went mad."

"I can't imagine your pain. Hugh and I knew the risk, but Azar didn't." Sarah rubbed her thumb over the back of my hand. "That's the first time I've been shot, Win. Paria was the first person I fired on. Usually the job isn't that dangerous."

"One traffic stop. It can all change."

"I know." She put her hand on my cheek. "We don't have any guarantees, Win. You've lost Azar and I lost Hugh, and I doubt either one of us thought we'd make it through the grief. Now we've found one another. I've been so lost in this emotional swirl, like being in the middle of a tornado, I haven't wanted to think. I know I need to because it isn't fair to make you hide."

"Sarah, I couldn't hide being lesbian if I screwed half the men in McCrumb County. I'll stay in the background until after the election. Because you're a damn good sheriff. Be prepared to talk about it in November. Maybe with Emily?"

She nodded, pulled me close, began to unbutton my shirt. "This time, I want to hand control to you."

"I hate to tell you, but I've pretty much had control all the time we've been together."

"I get that, Win. That's not what I'm talking about." Sarah unbuttoned another button. Slipped her hand inside my shirt. "But I want to be naked on your kitchen chair, at least metaphorically."

"You want me to tie you up?"

As she nodded, a slight flush crept up her neck. "I've never seen your bedroom—does the bed have posts? Would that work?"

I shook my head. "You don't need to do this, Sarah."

"I've come every time we've made love, but I don't think I've ever come like you did this morning. It felt like wave after wave after wave."

I traced her cheekbone with a finger. "It was wave after wave after wave. I felt like I was drowning. Then I'd come up again. I'd hold on to you."

She nodded. "I want that with you, Win."

"You don't need to be tied up to feel that," I said. "You have to trust me—and yourself. Ask me to stay still. Move. Whatever will bring you."

"I'm learning that too." She kissed me while she slipped both hands to my back and unfastened my bra. She pushed it up and cupped my breasts.

I forgot the soreness and pushed against her hands. "Sarah, please. Listen to me. You surrendered to me when we first got together. You put your trust in me to show you the way. I'll love the hell out of you. I'm not tying you up."

She withdrew her hands. "I'm all yours."

I finished unbuttoning my shirt, took it off, dropped the bra. "Stand up, Sarah."

When she complied, I removed her duty belt. Unbuttoned her shirt, took that and the T-shirt off. "Turn around."

Her eyes widened. Finally she turned around. I began to caress her breasts. Ran my hands down her body. Unsnapped her jeans, unzipped them, put my hand down her panties and touched her clit.

She drew a sharp breath. Pushed down on my fingers.

I withdrew them. Pushed jeans and panties down until she could step out of them. Turned her around. Began kissing her mouth and worked my way down while both hands kept busy.

"Remember, Sarah," I said as I kneaded her butt, "your job is to be receptive. Feel the pleasure, but don't go after it. Let me bring it to you."

I led her into the bedroom, sat her on the bed. "We'll ride the roller coaster as many times as you want. Just tell me when you want to get off. Get your feet back on terra firma." I kissed her temples, eyelids, her lips. "I love you, Sarah."

* * *

As the dawn grew brighter, I watched Sarah sleep. Her breath tickled my chest. I wanted to touch her, caress her. I wondered when her shift started today. If I could change my appointment in Bloomington to late afternoon. Stay, have Sarah join me for dinner. Dancing. I sighed. Probably not. She couldn't afford to be discovered now. When? How many terms would she run for? How many years could we hide? Until we were old women when people assumed sex was dead for us?

I felt some movements in her hips. She smiled in her sleep. Dreams of last night? I could bring her awake in full bloom. I glanced at the bedside clock. Almost time to get up. I brushed my lips across her nipple. Got a small moan. Went back and took it in my mouth. Her hips thrust upward. I ran a hand down her body. Her eyes opened.

"Oh," she said. "Oh. Am I dreaming?"

I kissed her, opened her legs. "Are you ready for this?"

She took my hand and guided me in. She came quickly and thoroughly. We lay together, her eyes closed.

"What time do you have to be at work?" I asked.

She groaned. Looked at the clock. "We have an hour before I have to leave." She smiled. "Plenty of time to make this mutual." She put one hand on mine between her legs and slipped the other into me. "Think we can do this together? At the same time?"

"We can give it a damn good try."

So good we ran late. Breakfast was coffee.

"Can you take me home? I have to pick up my car."

"Of course, but I need to be in Bloomington by nine." I glanced at my watch. "Let's go."

She was silent on the drive. Dozing a bit. Waking herself up when her chin hit her chest. No wonder. It had been a remarkable night. Morning.

"How do you feel?" I asked.

"Exhausted. Exhilarated. Thinking about calling in." She sighed. "But my desk is always piled high on Wednesdays."

"You could come into Bloomington," I said, touching her thigh. "Have dinner tonight."

"Where?"

"Ruby's. Just dinner. No dancing."

"I don't know, Win. I…"

"Just a thought. If you're not comfortable, don't."

"I never thought I'd be comfortable with some of the things we've done," she said, holding my hand. "Hell, I'd never imagined some of the things we've done. But out in public is still something I'm uneasy about."

I'd dropped her off with a kiss. Headed for Bloomington and a job interview with Dr. Kemat Fitzgerald. I should've done research on her, had meant to. But with the intensity of the past few days, it had slipped my mind. So I wasn't prepared for the older beauty I found when I'd opened the door to her office. Dark eyes, black hair with streaks of silver, comfortably dressed, yet very feminine. Her perfume was something I'd smelled before and it teased my memory.

She got right down to business, asking me a series of questions in a number of Persian-derived languages and dialects. When she closed the leather notebook where she'd scribbled notes, I felt like I'd been through a round of speed-dating.

In English, she asked, "Where do you think I'm from?"

And I clearly heard that illusive accent I'd been hearing. "Egypt. You're a native Arabic speaker."

"Very good, Ms. Kirkland. Very few people hear that. Listening to your replies, I would have thought you were from Tajikistan or northern Afghanistan." She leaned back in her executive chair and folded her hands together. "Why do you want to teach?"

"I'm not sure I do. I've never taught and I'm not sure how to approach it." I paused, thought of Azar and the villagers. "But I love the languages. I love the countries I've been in. Most of all, I love the people. I'd like to be able to share what I've learned with people here."

She opened a file drawer, fingered through a number of folders and pulled out sheaves of paper. She put them on the desk and pushed them across the desk to me. "These are course syllabi which you can use for organization of your knowledge, but do not feel you have to follow them slavishly."

I looked at her. "You mean, I have the job?"

"Of course." She laughed. "Most of the people I've interviewed could barely understand the questions I asked in Tajik, much less the shadings you responded to. I'll send you a contract and class schedule by the end of the week. Do you have any scheduling preferences?"

"I'd like to keep Monday nights and Tuesdays free. Is that possible?"

"Of course." She made a note, stood up and we shook hands. "The Institute sponsors a get-together on Friday afternoons once the semester starts. I will send you the time and location and I hope you will be able to join us."

As I walked back to my truck, syllabi clutched in a sweaty hand, I wondered what the hell I'd gotten myself into.

* * *

"You look like this has been a good week for you, Win," Emily said.

I grinned. Told her about the job. Told her about catching our stalker. That Sarah had finally been able to stay the night at my house. "She's been amazing."

"Good sex, huh?"

"Oh, yeah." I wasn't going to describe our adventures. "Plus, we talked. She's open to couple's counseling. After the election. I asked her to meet me at Ruby's for dinner, but she's still shying away from a gay bar."

"I hope Paige sowed some good seeds, though they may take a while to germinate." She shifted her weight in the chair. "I'm trying to get you both to examine the idea of a long-term relationship, once the initial excitement wanes. You're doing well with the PTSD, Win— just remember, some event could throw you back into that old warrior state."

I told her more about my stalker, the sense of paranoia I'd felt when I began to feel his presence. "But I didn't do it alone, Emily. I asked for help. Nathan. Bill. When Sarah offered, I accepted."

Emily took notes. "That's an important step, Win. What about your general? Is he still in the picture?"

"He's gone to ground. But we think we know what he wants from me. I should've started working on some research, but I've been occupied by Sarah. She said she loves me."

"Must've been some really good sex—not that I'm doubting her sincerity."

"I trusted her with control."

"You did bondage with her?"

"Very mild."

"My, my. Win, you amaze me. I never thought you'd be the bottom in erotic play."

"I never have been before. But I will be again, for Sarah. It was awesome."

"Did you get to be top for her?"

I nodded. "But without any bondage. It's been a good week."

"Too good? Are you waiting for the blow to hit?"

I exhaled a long breath. "Yes."

CHAPTER THIRTY-SIX

Sarah

Charlene, my overenthusiastic campaign manager, sat across from me in the visitor's chair. "They want a debate, an' my God, Sarah, you just can't say no, you just can't. They'd say you were afraid to debate, that you were tryin' to hide somethin'."

"Who's 'they'?" I asked when she ran out of breath.

She looked at me as if I'd asked who God was. "Uh, the Chamber's sponsorin' the debate on August fifteenth at the high school. In the gym. Everybody's invited. Should draw a good crowd, an' let people see how smart you are, an' show 'em what a good job you're doin'."

"Let me ask this another way, Charlene." I leaned back in the chair. Charlene wasn't a dummy, by any means. She was a savvy Machiavelli behind the candidate. "Who approached the Chamber with this idea? Can you find out?"

"Suppose so, but you need to accept this challenge now. We ain't got time to tippytoe around, smellin' roses an' missin' the skunk. Been callin' you for days, tryin' to let you know 'bout this. If you'd picked up right aways, I'd have an answer for you now."

"My fault, Charlene. I apologize. I turned it off Monday afternoon and haven't turned it on since. Days off are valuable to me." I couldn't even remember where I'd left my cell. Win's house? "Do me a favor, call my number."

She did and I heard a buzzing in my top drawer. I took out my cell phone and thumbed through the messages. A lot from Charlene, one from Lloyd, two from Dad and one from Willy Nesbit.

"Say yes to the debate and that I think it's a wonderful opportunity for the people of McCrumb to learn about the law enforcement issues we face." I kept the phone in my hand. "That do it?"

She gathered her large purse, tote bag and plastic shopping bag. "I'll find out the who, but we already know it's Mac. What I really have to find out is why."

"Thanks, Charlene. Again, I'm sorry."

"Somedays I wonder if you want to be sheriff at'all," she tossed over her shoulder as she left.

Me, too, Charlene. I marked the date on my calendar and, sure she'd left for good, played the message Willy Nesbit left. *Mac's furious I didn't get anything. He's not going to quit, so watch your back. He's talked people into a debate, probably wants to explode a bombshell. Let me know what I can do.*

Interesting. I had the "who" and the "what." He was looking for dirty business, and I'd be damned if I'd hand him something to blow my career to smithereens. Win and I would have to go back into hiding. I texted back: *Keep ears open.*

Mac's "associates" were ex-lawmen and wealthy businessmen. The guys he'd sold the department to for electing him. I wondered if they were too old, too lazy and too drunk to mount a threat. Better not take chances, no matter how much I hungered for Win.

I called Dad. "What's up?"

"Hello, Sarah Anne. Thought mebbe you fell into the rabbit's hole. Just checkin' in. Tillie's not gettin' better, an' I'm takin' her to the hospital."

"You need help?"

"Sure would 'preciate it. You got time now?"

"I'll be right over." Well, so much for catching up. I told Dory where I was going, ducked into Caleb's office and told him I hadn't made much progress with the paperwork.

"No problem, Sarah. It's been quiet."

"Too quiet?"

He nodded. "We had a line on the RV, but they'd moved it by the time we got there."

"A leak from this department?"

Caleb scrunched up his face. "Don't know, but I sure as hell hope not."

"See if Nathan can help. Have him look at the department's phone records so we won't need a warrant. Call it an audit."

Between Dad and me, we got Tillie to the hospital where her doctor was waiting. We hung around until she was settled. That she came at all meant that she thought she was dying. Tillie didn't surrender to anything or anyone.

As we left, I told Dad how sorry I was that I hadn't helped him take care of her.

"I actually enjoyed bein' with Tillie," he said, fingering a key on his key ring. "She got to rememberin' when Lizbeth was growin' up. Stories I never heard afore. Enjoyed thinkin' 'bout her runnin' 'round, gettin' in trouble." He handed me the key. "Tillie wants somebody to check on her house. Thought I could stay there or you an' Win could meet there. Nobody'd ask questions if they saw you, an' Win could duck in the back. Interested?"

I looked at the key. "I think Mac's still trying to get dirt on me, and I'm not sure if this wouldn't make it easier. It's in the middle of town."

"Don't you let Mac back you into a corner, Sarah Anne. He's nothin' but a lazy sonofabutt, an' you can run circles 'round him. An' you got the Silver Fox at your back."

I laughed. "Silver Fox, eh? Appropriate, to say the least. You stay there. How many days do you think they'll keep Tillie?"

"They wanna do surgery, but Tillie don't want no cuttin'. We'll see."

"She's going to be climbing the walls. I don't envy your job."

* * *

I got back to the office, dove into the paperwork piles and had finished them by the time I quit. I drove home and called Win. I told her about the offer.

"It doesn't sound safe. Anyone could see me in the neighborhood. Sneaking in the back door."

"That was my feeling. I wonder if we're both getting paranoid."

"We've both been spied on. That's not paranoia, Sarah. That's fact. Believe me because I have a hard time keeping the two straight sometimes."

"I'm just adding to the confusion. I miss you." I sighed. "Any word on the general?"

"No. I've done the translation but I haven't figured it out. Got a meeting with Bill tonight. Oh, and news. I got the job teaching at CELI."

"Wow. Congratulations. Do I have to call you something special now?"

"Love. Say *love* instead of Win."

"I miss you, *my love*. Good night. I'll be dreaming of you."

I debated calling Em tonight. I needed to talk to someone who'd understand, who wouldn't push me in one direction or another. I called. She told me to come over to her house.

"Are you sure? I mean…"

"Come," she said. "Marty's out, and I'm just roaming around, looking for something to occupy time until she gets home. You and I are old friends, Sarah. I probably shouldn't have taken you on at all, but since I have, don't make me go into the office when I don't have to."

A half hour later, I pulled into her driveway. She flicked on the porch light and stood in the doorway, a welcoming figure.

"You look tired, but, hmm, fulfilled."

"Paperwork day always makes me look tired," I said as I followed her to her study. "The problem is 'paranoia versus facts.' Win and I have had a lot of pressure thrown at us from outside. It makes the relationship that much more fraught."

"Fraught?" she said as she sat in a chair angled toward the couch.

I sat down and leaned back. "If the good folk of McCrumb County found out I was sleeping with a woman, they'd show me to the nearest border. You know the kind of homophobia that's nurtured here. Remember, the representative who wants to put man-woman-marriage-only in the state constitution is from this district. He *is* mainstream for this area. I'm not imagining this, and as I remember, you told me the same thing when Win and I had an appointment together." I banged the arm of the couch with my fist. "Natalie Elder's dead because she was targeted. Why? She was gay."

She sighed. "You've got a lot of anger, Sarah. Where's it coming from?"

I closed my eyes. Where indeed? "Part of it is being forced to hide. It's not fair to Win. I'd like to take her to Founders Day, march her up on the stage at Pioneer Park and give her a kiss."

"Quite a fantasy," Emily responded. "What's the rest of the anger?"

I took a deep breath and tried to gather my scattered thoughts. "Natalie. What they did to her was appalling. Hideous."

"Do you relate to her in a particular way?"

"I don't understand—oh, because I was thinking about Win?"

"Give the lady a cigar. You were reexamining your own sexual identity. I think you understood the vulnerability she felt, even though she showed a bravado you couldn't. Does that sound right?"

I nodded and wiped away the tears that had sprung from nowhere. "Win had a crush on me, back when. If she'd acted on it, that kind of persecution could've been directed at us. Oh crap! I hate the bigots and their poison. And…maybe I've been a passive part of it."

Emily handed me tissues, then sat back and scrutinized me. "Where do you want to be in five years?"

I dabbed my eyes. "Win asked me what I wanted the next chapter of my life to be the first time we kissed. I had no idea then, and I'm not sure I have a better answer now. I want to be with Win, I'm certain of that."

"Living together?"

"Yes."

"Where? Win's put a lot of herself in that house she built. It's pretty much self-sustaining, with solar panels, a small wind turbine and other stuff I don't remember."

"I don't know. Why don't I know?"

"You've probably been busy with other things." She raised an eyebrow. "You need to do some thinking about this, Sarah. Micah's getting older. And I have another question: how many terms are you going to run for? Doesn't McCrumb County allow more than the state statutes?"

"I don't know, Em. I mean yes, our limit is four terms. But I've had a hard time running this time, if you'll remember."

"So Win may have to wait another four years, or perhaps an additional twelve years, to be in a more open relationship? You think she can wait?"

The tears came again. "I know she's part of my future if she wants to be. I know I'm asking a lot of her, but Em, I was sheriff before Win came home. It's what I've wanted since forever. I'm not sure I can throw that away either."

"Talk this over with Win, find out what her expectations are." Emily raised a hand. "I know, you're in the overwhelmed-with-passion stage, especially since you're new to the life. But the more talking you do now, the more future problems you avoid. Keep as open to Win's thoughts as you keep open to her in bed."

CHAPTER THIRTY-SEVEN

Win

"I've got the translation, Bill, but damn if I know what it means," I said as Bill balanced on a stool behind me. I pulled up the message. "It means 'the package rests in the lair of the White Demon.' Want a short lesson on Persian mythology?"

"No, but if I don't, I won't understand?"

"Doubt if you'll understand anyway. Div-e Sefid, the White Demon, is one of a host of demons. Most are black. Some theorists think this reference refers to white people who invaded from the north. Or a specific northern prince. In this case, Div-e Sefid could refer to General Scott Lester. Hell if I know where his lair is—do you?"

"Lair? Shit no." Bill shook his head. "You said before that this might be a puzzle Fazal set up? If Scotty wants the package, he has to figure it out?"

I nodded. "Look, Fazal might not have sent anything at all. He may be sitting on top of Scotty's shipment laughing."

"Then where the hell is Scotty?" Bill stood, started pacing. "He's off the grid, no credit card use, no phone calls."

"He had a stash," I said. "Cash or credit cards in another identity. Burn phone. It'd be easy for him to put that together."

"Where'd he stash it?"

"Where was the last place you tracked him?"

"Camp Atterbury."

"Shit. Then his hidey-hole is close. He have property in the county?"

"Nathan couldn't find any, at least, not in his name."

"If he doesn't own it, maybe he rents. A lot of people in the county rent out rooms or houses or sheds. Keep it under the table. But Bill, if the package is at his 'lair,' how could he not know?"

"Then where the fuck is it?"

"Maybe we could enlist the local constabulary," I said. "Have Sarah put out a BOLO with an observe-only."

"I don't want to involve local law enforcement in military matters," Bill said with a shake of his head. "There's got to be another way."

"Not unless you deploy the troops to do a door-to-door." I shut down the computer. "Sarah will help, won't ask questions. I remember the truck he drove and a partial plate. She can also run the plate in the state database. How bad do you want to get him?"

Bill paced for a while, back and forth until he made me dizzy.

"It's not illegal! He had me under electronic surveillance. What's the problem?"

"Will she just inform us? Not try to arrest him? I really don't want civilians involved."

"Sarah's not a civilian," I said as I stood up. "She's a damn good cop, and if she weren't, I'd be dead."

He perched on the stool. "I told you Scotty's under investigation. Big stuff. We need to nab him clean."

"I still think local eyes are better than being blind."

"Okay. But eyes only. No arrest, no pursuit. And preferably, no record." He grabbed his jacket, headed for the door. He turned. "By the way, congratulations. Dr. Fitzgerald is thrilled and looking forward to your presence on campus. She says you'll be a wonderful role model for grad students."

"Of what not to do with your life?"

He left, I set the alarm system, and then I called Sarah. I told her the basic facts, asked if she could put out a BOLO.

"What's the vehicle?"

"Cherry-red F-350, but I only got a partial plate." I gave it to her and heard computer keys clacking.

"Win, I'm not seeing anything that matches. Could he have stolen or switched a plate?"

"Always possible, although that would be an extra risk for him."

"I'm just ready to leave, so I'll have Caleb run all the red F-350s in the county. Would that help?"

"Anything would help, but tell Caleb to keep it quiet. This mess has...repercussions."

"Will do," Sarah said. She didn't hang up.

"What time is your shift tomorrow?" I asked.

"Afternoon. Why? Are you coming over?"

"Not a good idea, Sarah. But maybe you could come over for dinner. We could talk."

"That's all? Talk?"

"I didn't say that was all I'm offering. But if you can't make it—"

"I'll pick up a pizza on the way over. See you in forty."

* * *

We didn't let the pizza go to waste, although I was tempted. I told her a little more about Scotty's message while we ate. "Maybe I'm not making the right connection."

"What other interpretations would the White Demon have? What's the whole story?"

I told her the story of the challenges the hero, Rustam, faced and overcame before he came to the White Demon's cave. "Rustam slew the White Demon and tore out his heart. Nice story to go with the pizza."

"It's the classic hero's quest story," Sarah said, wiping her hands and wadding up the napkin. "What if it's not a location, per se, but a challenge? What if this Fazal sees himself as Rustam? He intends to kill Scotty? Does that make any sense?"

"Yeah. Convoluted, but fits both players."

"A grudge between them? Revenge? Anything like that in their history?" Sarah asked.

I took another bite and watched Des sit quietly and drool. "Fazal has a reputation as being one sick bastard. Utterly ruthless. Kind of like a mob godfather, only with a finger in every pie between the Afghani and coalition governments. If Scotty double-crossed him, he would see it as a threat to his honor."

"It still leaves the question: where's the lair?"

As soon as we finished, I called Bill with the new interpretation. "I'd check with the State Department or CIA and find out if Fazal's on the move."

"Makes a weird kind of sense," Bill said. "I remember some trouble between them a couple of years ago. Scotty had two of his men picked up for interrogation. They never came back."

"We still need to find the 'lair,' Bill. I don't have a clue." I clicked off and went to the couch where Sarah had already settled.

"Maybe we should set up a PI agency," I said as I sat next to her. "We make a good team."

She leaned over and kissed me, ran her hand up my thigh. "What are we going to do, Win? As much as I fret about being sheriff, I feel like I've been born and bred for the office. I really like putting the bad guys away, and I'm good at it."

"I'll wait, Sarah. At least, for this term." I kissed her softly. "I lived most of my life in the shadows. Now nobody cares who I sleep with." I could feel her go stiff in my arms. "Don't talk about being fair. Life isn't. I want to be with you, Sarah. For a damn long time."

She leaned her head on my shoulder. "I want to be with you. But I'm already tired of carrying around this fear of discovery. I'm looking over my shoulder all the time. Any advice?"

I realized I'd been holding my breath. I let it go. "I don't know. I got used to hiding. First high school. Do you realize how much coming out to you meant to me? You were my best friend. You accepted me as I was. An affirmation of who I was. Like Micah's acceptance of us now."

Sarah nodded. Burrowed deeper into my shoulder. "Same with Nathan."

"Living openly with Annie freshman year meant a lot too. A circle of friends."

"Gay friends, Win. I remember," she said. "A closed circle who'd never hang out with me."

"I know." I ran my hand through her hair. "Back then, it was about circling the wagons. You'd find the women at Ruby's welcoming, even if they think you're straight."

"Shit, Win. The thought of going there makes me so nervous." She groaned. "How did you survive hiding in the military?"

I stroked her hair again, tightened my arm around her. "I never had a relationship. I fucked women, they fucked me. Period. I didn't want to know them. Their histories. Their hopes or dreams. It was just sex." I kissed her forehead. "I'm not proud of it."

She reached up and touched my lips. "If that's what taught you how to make me so crazy in bed, it wasn't wasted time."

I kissed her. Long, building. Held her. "I'm not going to push you, Sarah. I know your job is a way of life for you. All I want to do is fit in somewhere."

She kissed me, slipped her hand under my T-shirt. "I love it when you don't wear a bra."

"We'll figure it out, Sarah. Where we belong in McCrumb County. Together. I'll tell you when I can't hide anymore."

She squeezed my nipple. "I hope you'll never have to say that. I want to be with you, Win, now and until we're both collecting Social Security."

CHAPTER THIRTY-EIGHT

Sarah

I had an idea at breakfast and wondered if I thought too much about work. At work, I wondered if I thought too much about Win. I watched her make waffles, loving every fluid movement. The oversized Colts shirt hid her butt, but couldn't alter my memory of it. As smooth and round as her breasts. Time to shift gears or I'd be molesting her while she cooked.

"Can Bill get satellite images?"

Win turned and looked at me. "I'm sure he's been going over them."

"Think he'd share?"

"I'll call him as soon as we've finished breakfast. Scotty could be long gone. Should be if he has any gray matter left." She plated the waffles, added the sausage and brought the plates to the table.

"So," she said as she sat across from me, "we could view them at Nathan's. Be a lot easier on the monitors he's got. What time do you have to be in to work?"

"If I'm at Nathan's looking at sat images, I am at work."

Win called Bill as I took the dishes to the sink. She asked if it was possible to send Nathan sat images from over the past week. She nodded. "Thanks." She started to disconnect, but I heard Bill's voice.

She put the cell back to her ear. Nodded several times. "Thanks. I'll tell Sarah."

"Scotty's been communicating with Fazal. In English. Bill wants me to thank you for the idea. Fazal's on the move. They don't know where."

I nodded and walked back to her. "Shit, I'm tired of miscreants of every stripe." I pulled her T-shirt over her head, took her butt in my hands and pulled her close. I slipped my hand between her legs and felt her wetness. Her eyes were closed, her head thrown back. I kissed her neck, she whispered, "Counter? Or just standing up?"

* * *

We decided to drive to Nathan's separately. I called the station, told them where I'd be and asked Caleb if he'd managed to cross-check trucks.

"Yeah," he said. "Nothing in the county I could find, but I asked surrounding counties to check their databases. Krueger County came in with an affirmative. Address don't check out, though."

"So the general could be living in the southern part of McCrumb?"

"I told patrol down there to keep an eagle eye."

"Thanks, Caleb. I'll be in as soon as we finish with the sat photos."

Rivers and streams were still running high, and the corn, not yet knee-high, swayed in the slight breeze. Darker than spring, the trees were clothed in their summer green. The land was settling into its growth.

As I drove into Nathan's clearing, Des ran from the woods to greet me. I got a big lick and a wolfish grin. We walked into the cabin to find Win and Nathan already scanning photos. I told them what Caleb had found, and we did the southern part of the county first.

"There," Win said, pointing. "That's it. Red cab parked by those trees." She moved the cursor. "Latitude 39.099039, Longitude 85.271826."

I took a close look. "Can you pull out a tad, Nathan?"

Nathan clicked his mouse and looked at me.

"Recognize the barn?"

"Only round barn left in the county," he said, enlarging the image again. "There's Shasta Bridge. McCleary place." He flipped back through images of the week. "Parked under the trees and hasn't moved."

"I'll get Bill—"

"Hold on." I called Dad and explained what we'd found. "Could you call Kevin McCleary and casually inquire about the truck?"

"He an' the family's on vacation," Micah said. "Left two days ago for Pigeon Forge. I run into him at the barber's, an' he was all excited 'cause the whole family was gettin' together, even the boy in the navy."

"The truck's been there longer. You remember what vehicles the McClearys own?"

"They took the RV. Got an Explorer, mebbe two years old. An' an old F150 what serves most of his needs."

I thanked Dad, disconnected, called the station and had them run the license plates for McCleary's vehicles. "Put out a BOLO on both vehicles with an 'observe and report only.' Caleb, tell patrol to be careful. This guy is armed and dangerous."

I disconnected and looked at Win. "Any ideas?"

"None, unless he's heading for a border and didn't want that truck traced. I've no idea what he's still doing in this area. If he *is* still here." Win took a deep breath. "If he disappears, he's home free."

Nathan cleared his throat. "I've been doing some digging on General Scott Lester." He got a thick file from a drawer. "Maybe you both should go over the material."

CHAPTER THIRTY-NINE

Win

We walked to our vehicles hand in hand, and when we stopped at my truck, I kissed Sarah. She pulled back after a few seconds.

"We can't sleep together anymore," she said.

I felt like she'd slugged me in the stomach. I couldn't say anything, just stared. Felt like the world's axis had flipped and landed on top of me.

"Not forever," she said, taking my hand. "Just until we nail this bastard or are sure he's out of the county. I need to be clearheaded, and you, my dear, provide nothing but distraction. I find myself thinking about you at work when I should be making decisions and directing the department."

"It's because it's so new to you, Sarah. It'll wear off. The breathlessness."

"Not soon enough to catch your general."

She leaned into me and I put my arms around her. "You shouldn't even be involved. I'm sorry I brought you into it."

"I know this county and I know the people who live here." She tightened her arms around me. "I'm sharing all intel with Bill, and when it comes time to take the general down, it's out of my hands. But I've got ways to look the military doesn't. Trust me?"

"Of course." I kissed her forehead. "But Scotty's a real snake. Well-trained by our government. Spent his whole career in intelligence."

"Then who better to take him down than some country bumpkin sheriff?"

"You think he'll underestimate you? Shit, it's such a big gamble, Sarah." I held her at arm's length. "Will you at least see me? No fooling around?"

Sarah groaned. "We'll see." She kissed me, not so lightly this time. "This is not going to be easy." She gave me a quick hug, then opened her door. "Anyway, Bill's sending pics of your general with a variety of facial hair, and some of Fazal. I'll forward them to patrol."

"You spot either one of them, call Bill. Promise?"

She nodded. "I wish you weren't staying out at your place by yourself. You've got no backup but Des."

"Des is plenty. Besides, we don't have any evidence the general is still interested in me."

Des nuzzled my hand. Her sign it was time to get moving. "I'll call tonight."

She nodded, fired up her engine and took off.

I sighed. Sarah didn't know how guilty I felt for bringing all this crap home. First Paria, now General Scott Lester. Two rogue agents who felt no compunction about playing by the rules. I'd put her in danger. Not once, twice.

When I got home, I packed a bag for me and a box for Des. I called Micah. "I'm worried about the situation," I said. "These guys are trained assassins and prime scum, Micah. I'd like to stay close, keep an eye on Sarah."

"Sarah Anne be happier if you did, under different circumstances. Tillie fought off them doctors, so she's back at home an' I'll be over there. We got a guest room for propriety. Come on over, an' if Sarah balks, the title on the property's still in my name."

* * *

Micah and I were eating dinner when Sarah came home. She had a slight meltdown when she saw me, but it fizzled under Micah's steely glare. After dinner, we watched a little TV, then Micah left for Tillie's. Sarah and I were left on the couch, the middle cushion between us.

She snapped off the TV and turned to me. "You outflanked me."

"You said you didn't like me 'all the way out there by myself.' Where else do I have to go?"

"That's not why you're here, Win."

"I've been thinking. Have you formed a task force to catch the general?"

"No, I've just been working with Caleb and John Morgan."

I moved my arm to the back of the couch. "How about you form one? Call Bill, have him give a briefing. Make me a consultant."

Her eyes widened. "Would Bill do that? Come and share federal secrets about a rogue general?"

"No. He doesn't share secrets. But he'll come to talk about how the general will react to external conditions. Bill knows him a lot better than I do."

"Profile him," Sarah said with a sigh. "We could do with help, but we've just begun the search. Patrol is showing his picture around at real estate agents, groceries, gas stations. We should have a rough idea in the morning where to concentrate a search."

"That's where Bill could be handy. With your permission, I'll call him."

After a moment, she nodded. I called, outlined the plan. "No, no state cops. You want—" I heard as close to a bellow as I'd ever heard from Bill. I looked at Sarah. "What time?"

"Nine a.m.? That'll give me time to gather reports from patrol and Bill to get down here."

I passed the word, he agreed and we disconnected. "Done. So, are you going to sign me up too? It would go a long way to explaining my presence here. Closer to the action. Strategy sessions."

She put her arm on the back of the couch. "It really pisses me off that we have to make excuses to have you stay here. It's pandering to bigots."

"Getting pissed wastes energy. I understand the pressure. Some people only see the sex. Not the love. Scares them. The biggest homophobes probably recognize something within themselves. The rest? Follow their pastors with fire and brimstone licking at their heels."

"I'm still pissed, Win." She rubbed the back of my hand. "I think I had a crush on you, way back when."

I shook my head. "I would've known."

"I don't think so. But I've been trying to figure this thing out. Remembering. I thought about you a lot, even after you came out to me. Hell, Win, I didn't even know two women could fall in love, much less have sex. After you told me, I talked to Mom."

"You told her I was gay?"

"No. Just asked about homosexuality. She said some women could love women without feeling romantic, others felt a romantic attachment. She also said she couldn't understand why people condemned two people for loving each another."

"She never asked why you were asking?"

Sarah shook her head. "But I thought a lot about what you told me. I imagined kissing you." She entwined her fingers in mine. "That's about as far as I could imagine. Then."

"Maybe not a crush on me. A crush on the idea."

"Maybe. Did you love Annie?"

I closed my eyes, tried to remember my first lover. "I was infatuated. Besotted, really. Because I'd fantasized about women for so long, and there she was. In my bed."

"How did you meet? You never told me, and I just started seeing you two together."

I laughed. "We were in English Lit together, and one day after class, she came up to me. This hippie woman. Long, curly hair, long skirt, tank top with an open cotton blouse. No bra, big breasts. She asked if I wanted to join her study group. I asked her who else was in the group. She said, 'You and me, babe. Let's go study.'"

"Wow. I never would've had the courage to ask anybody out back then."

"She was experienced, Sarah. From New York. There I was in my button-down shirt and chinos. She knew. I think she also guessed I was a virgin as far as women went. She swooped down and took me to her apartment. We had sex that afternoon and I was in thrall."

"Like me? Now? But you knew, didn't you? That you belonged in her bed? That you were lesbian."

I rubbed the back of her hand with my thumb. "I can't give you answers, Sarah. But what I do know is that you're a caring human being with a big capacity to love. Name your identity on the sexual continuum when you're ready to embrace it."

"You make it sound easy and it isn't. I know I loved Hugh, and I know we had good sex. What you and I do is so real and yet, so different. There's no stopping point, just a roller coaster ride that can go on as long as we both have energy."

"Well, the coaster ride's out of service for now. You hung the sign up. Remember?"

"Yeah, yeah, yeah. Which means I can take it down too."

"You said you weren't comfortable having sex in your dad's home. Remember?"

She nodded. "But we could mess around awhile."

I sighed. "I can't flip switches like that, Sarah. A kiss good night is about all I can afford."

"Afford?"

"Before desire overwhelms what sense I have left." I stood up. "I'm going up to bed. Alone."

She stood, wrapped her arms around me, nuzzled my neck. I could feel my juices flowing. I held her tight, kissed the top of her head. We stood that way a long time.

CHAPTER FORTY

Sarah

"I can't go into why the federal government's interested in asking General Scott Lester a lot of questions, but I can tell you he's a high priority," Bill said as he looked around our conference room table.

Caleb, John, Mark Goodrich, head of patrol, Win, Nathan, and Dad sat around the table with me. Caleb was ready to take notes if Bill ever said anything worth writing down.

"We didn't get a whiff of the game Scotty's running until six months ago, and we now believe he's been involved for over ten years."

"Spill the beans, Bill," Win said. "You're putting these people in jeopardy if you don't tell them what's going on."

Dad nodded. "Ain't nobody in this room gonna give away secrets, an' I sure as hell don't want to walk into somethin' blind. Heard tell we got this Fazal guy might be wanderin' 'round the county too. Need-to-know, Bill."

Bill glared at Win, began pacing, and then nodded. "I'll give you as much intel as I can."

"You got any idea why the general's usin' McCrumb County for his base?" Dad asked.

Bill stopped pacing, resumed his place at the head of the table. "Camp Atterbury. He's got buddies there and it gives him access to… things he needs."

"Aw, shit!" Win said. "The things he needs are aircraft and the crews."

"Smugglin'?" Dad asked.

Bill nodded.

"You gonna tell us what?"

"Weapons out to the Middle East, heroin in," Win said. She looked at me. "David Paria was one of his first recruits. I knew the ring, I just didn't know Scotty headed it."

"What kinda weapons?" Dad asked. He sounded like a bulldog growling, and except for the jowls, kind of looked like one too.

"About anything you can think of," Bill said. "Handguns, machine pistols, semiautomatic and automatic rifles. He has a network of straw buyers all over this country. He'd get an order, distribute the purchases, gather them together and ship 'em out."

"Where to?" Caleb asked, his pencil poised.

"Africa at first," Bill said.

Win snorted. "To Somalia, to Darfur and the Janjaweed, Congo and the Lord's Resistance Army. Then he branched out to the Near East. Al Qaeda is a major purchaser. He also upped the ordnance. RPGs, all kinds of rocket launchers and rockets." She'd been looking straight at Bill, now she gazed around the table. "A lot of stuff stolen from National Guard Armories. I also heard he'd made a big score. Enough to retire on after he split the profit with his network. What has he come into possession of, Bill?"

I watched Bill's Adam's apple bob a couple of times, then he shook his head. "Can't say, folks. Orders."

I glanced at Win and saw her eyes widen with horror.

"A dirty bomb?" I asked. "Or whatever they need to make one?"

Bill sat down and stared at the tabletop.

Dad shoved back from the table. "You know there's somethin' like that in McCrumb County an' you don't bother to tell the duly elected law enforcement officers of that county, then you can go to hell. An' don't bother comin' back." He stood and began to march out of the room. Notebooks shut around the table and my people pushed away from the table.

Bill stood up, pounded the table. "Wait. For God's sake, wait."

Dad paused at the door.

"I couldn't tell you because I had *orders* not to. It's not my fault you people are too smart for your own good. We're not sure what he has, but we suspect it's some kind of thermonuclear device and don't know if it's armed or not."

"*Some* kind?" Caleb asked. "Holy shit, man! What the hell are we talking here?"

Bill cleared his throat. "You've got to keep this in this room. You can't tell friends or family. No one. I have to insist. I won't go a step further until you swear."

Family. Mine was here, but I looked at my people. Caleb had a wife and two small children, John's wife was expecting her first and Mark's daughter was pregnant with his first grandchild. Bill expected that they keep quiet, not warn their loved ones. I glanced at Win, saw the pained look on her face and knew she was thinking the same thing. That she knew there was no alternative, not if we didn't expect a mass exodus from McCrumb County.

Dad nodded, sat back down. Everyone else returned to the table, but all had brows furrowed, frowns, tight shoulders.

"This is probably a small device," Bill said. "But no matter how small, I can't minimize the danger. I know what I'm asking, and I know you people didn't sign up for this. I can't tell you how sorry I am to have to ask you to keep this quiet."

"A matter of national security," Win said, with as close to a spit as she could come without doing it.

Bill gave a tiny nod.

"What else can you tell us?" I asked.

Bill examined each face. "It was assembled by a man the FBI's been watching, a right-wing nut. They didn't think he was far enough along to worry about."

Dad turned to Bill. "What'd the FBI miss?"

"Might as well ask what they didn't miss," Bill replied. "We picked up on this guy when he contacted Scotty a few months ago. We were watching Scotty, FBI had the other guy, but we never connected with them. Scotty and his buddy both disappeared about the same time. We did pick up on Scotty when he got back in Indiana."

"Are you sure this isn't a setup?" Win asked. "He's gone, then poof! He's back where he probably suspects you're watching him. Doesn't make sense, Bill. Is the FBI sharing their intel?"

"Some. When Scotty got back, he put the word out he had something to sell. Bids began. Big money, Win."

"I don't get it, Bill," Nathan said. "If you're monitoring his phone, why don't you know where he is?"

"He disabled the GPS," Bill replied. "He keeps his calls so fucking short, we can't triangulate cell towers."

"Interesting," Nathan said as he jotted down notes.

"Well, while you is playin' spy games, think the rest of us should go through the canvass reports," Dad said. "That is, if you wanna find the general."

* * *

Dad pulled me aside after Bill left. "Sorry for the histrionics, Sarah. But I figgered you was bein' quiet 'cause you needed to work with the MCIA. If I reckoned wrong, I'm more than sorry. I never forget you're the sheriff. You wanna dress me down, you're entitled."

"I enjoyed the entertainment, Dad. You're right, I couldn't afford to alienate Bill. He's got all sorts of strings he can pull for us. Now, let's go look at all the reports."

"One more thing. I gotta go over an' help Tillie, gonna stay the night."

"You don't have to do that for us."

"Got nothin' to do with you. Tomfool woman's thinkin' she's Superwoman, got more'n a twinge in her back now. Gotta keep that woman off her feet or she'll be back in that hospital."

We spent the afternoon going over the reports and the county map. We'd winnowed the search area down to the southern part of the county, but it was still a large area. Bill said he'd send the latest satellite images to Nathan as soon as he got them. We'd begun the process of getting the plat maps of the area from the county recorder. It would take her a while to pull the plat books, so we broke for dinner with the intention of coming back in. Time seemed to be ticking in a dangerous way to me.

I called ahead and Win and I walked to the Pizza Shack, not my favorite place but close. We walked into the redolent scent of garlic and basil. After I waved at Bobbi to let her know we'd arrived, we settled in a back booth. Win looked tired, but spectacular. Her shirt was still crisp, but I wished she'd unbutton it another two or three buttons.

Win leaned forward. "You have the most lascivious look on your face, and you're staring at my boobs. Cool it, Sheriff, or there'll be talk."

"Dad's staying at Tillie's. She evidently hurt her back again and is refusing therapy. Probably tried to move the stove in the diner."

Win smiled, her eyes lit up. "Best news all day. I mean, sorry about your aunt. But this might be time to take down the 'out of service' sign for the roller coaster. Although, I don't want to interrupt your concentration. Seriously."

"I heard the coaster's ready to roll, and I've been in high concentration mode all day. I need a break."

The pizza came and as we ate, we talked about the case. "Do you really think he has a you-know-what?"

"Don't know, Sarah. But it's a possibility. It'd be a damn good way to keep the law from getting too close."

"Afraid of what he'd do to the county?"

"Yep. He's got a habit of bluffing. On the other hand, I wouldn't put it past him to make a huge deal, damn the consequences. He's probably got his exit strategy in place."

Win started to shred a napkin, and I could read the tension in her body, ready for action, hating the waiting.

"I wonder if I should send everybody home, come back in early in the morning. Plat maps won't come until the morning, ditto for the satellite images. I'm about cross-eyed and the pizza's making me sleepy."

"We only have one sector to finish, Sarah. Let's get it done."

"What if we miss something because we're all too tired?"

"That's the benefit of having a task force. What one person misses can be picked up by somebody else. We're almost done for tonight." She gathered the pieces of napkin and put them on her empty plate.

"I think my subconscious is rebelling at the thought that something could endanger all the people of this county. Sheriffs shouldn't have to deal with shit like this." I picked up the bill, counted out the money and we went back to the station.

By the time we got home, we were too tired to do anything but strip, drop into bed and fall asleep.

CHAPTER FORTY-ONE

Win

Our lovemaking in the predawn hour was liquid, as if a single touch was a gift. I knew it was. I think Sarah realized it too.

"We passed a milestone last night," I said as she made coffee.

"By not making love?"

"Yeah. Just feeling you next to me was enough. Being able to hold you in sleep."

She leaned against the counter. "I felt the same way, safe and not alone. Does that mean we're an old married couple now?"

I walked to her, kissed her slowly with passion licking my heat. "We still have a lot of exploration ahead." If we both live through this. The next drug bust. The next traffic stop.

She must have felt my body stiffen. She ran a finger over my jaw. "What?"

"I want us to grow old together."

The coffeemaker shrieked three high, piercing beeps.

Sarah poured two mugs, filled a thermos with the rest. "You come up with any new thoughts about bomb/no-bomb?"

I took the mug, stared into its dark, reflective surface. Wished I could use it for a crystal ball. "We need the FBI file."

"You think they'll give it up?"

I shrugged. "How sure are you of the two sightings from your canvass?"

"Sure as I can be without seeing him myself. Why?"

"He's a master game-player, Sarah. Don't ever forget it. He lays out an op as if it were a chess board. Sees all possible moves, plans accordingly. A lot of his strategy has always been smoke and mirrors."

"You think we don't stand a chance."

I examined her face, the crinkles around her eyes as she frowned. "No. To the contrary, I think you and your people are something he never factored in. That's our advantage. He knows Bill is looking for him, but not the sheriff's office. That's a hell of a lot more eyes than he's counting on." I thought back to the way Scotty had set up ops I'd been involved with. "I wonder where he bought his burner phones."

"Plural?"

I nodded. "I'll bet he bought two, at least. One for him, one for the nut job in Pennsylvania. Probably sent it to him through the mail. Maybe FedEx."

Sarah's frown grew. "How do you know that?"

"Experience. Bypasses the need for couriers."

"I'll never know what you went through, will I?"

"I'll share what I can, Sarah. But you're going through something like it now. Try not to get stressed out. Stay your methodical, procedural self."

"That makes me sound boring." She took my mug, set it on the counter. Kissed me, ran her hands over my body. "I know we don't have time now, but a little messing around might help me make it through the day."

* * *

The intel came in hot and heavy. The recorder hand-delivered the plat maps. I suspected she'd been up most of the night to finish the task. On her heels, Nathan walked in with a huge monitor and a laptop. While he set up his equipment, Mark Goodrich called our attention to patrol's new canvasses. Three more sightings, all at night, all at gas stations with pump payment. He'd been noticed because he was driving Kevin McCleary's old truck.

"How did patrol miss him?" Sarah asked. She held up her hand. "Too few deputies, too much land to cover. I'm sorry, Mark, it was frustration not criticism."

"I feel the same way, Sarah," Mark said. "Started to chew out a deputy, then knew it was just damn luck the guy slipped through. I've moved a couple of deputies down to that district. Okay with you?"

"Yeah, but we don't have the budget to replace them." She ran a hand through her hair. "Could you cook up a reason to ask the state cops to cover?"

"Awful cases of food poisoning? Our guys ate at the same place?"

Sarah nodded and Mark went to his desk.

"One problem down," Sarah said. "Like a chess board, huh? I feel like I started the game late."

"You did," I replied.

Nathan popped his head around the doorframe. "Ready when you are."

"You heard from Bill?"

"He's on his way," Nathan said. "Sounded stressed, but said go ahead and start."

"That's big of him," Sarah said, rising from her desk.

When we walked into the conference room, everyone was there. As I took my seat, I scanned the faces of the people gathered. Instead of the fear and unease I'd detected yesterday, I saw determination. Good people who'd gathered their resources and were ready to face the unknown.

"Did everybody, patrol included, get the description and license plate numbers for the McClearys' trucks?" Sarah asked.

Heads nodded in the affirmative.

"I'd like to know what's in the McCleary's' garage," she continued. "If he's driving McCleary's F150, what's to prevent him from switching out the Explorer?"

"I can check," Micah said. "His garage has two windows in the back, an' there's a path from the county road to the McCleary's' backyard."

I marveled at the man. He seemed to hold all of McCrumb County—history, geography and people—in his head.

"Okay, you've got it, Deputy." Sarah grinned. "We've had three additional sightings, all early in the morning. Mark's put extra patrols on the southern district, and we'll have heavier coverage at night. Questions?"

"You need gas that much, you're doing a lot of driving," Caleb said. "Why haven't we picked him up on the sat photos?"

"He knows when satellites are taking pics," I said. "He's staying put during those times, moving a lot at night."

"Good time to look at sat images." Sarah signaled Nathan, and he brought up the first of many.

We found several that *could* be the truck. Hard to tell from up above.

"Are they clustering?" I asked. Got befuddled looks back. "Are the locations somewhat close together? Forming a cluster?"

Caleb had been charting the sightings. He showed me the map. "Close enough to be a cluster?"

I nodded. "The arrows indicate the direction he was heading?" Caleb nodded. "Then I suggest we break into two groups. One keeps working with the sat images, the other goes to the plat maps and finds structures where he could hole up." I drew a light circle around the area where the cluster was. "Inside this circle."

Micah and Mark volunteered for the plat map group, Caleb and John for the sat group. I looked at Sarah. "I'll keep with this. I'm used to looking at satellite images."

She nodded, went to the other group. As we found other possibles, we gave the other group the locations. They were grouped around large plat maps at the other end of the table, Micah pointing a gnarled finger at structures and naming the place.

We were almost finished when Bill came in. He looked at the two groups, raised his eyebrows at me.

I walked over. "Cluster sightings, ground and air. We're almost finished with the sat images. They're working with plat maps inside the cluster circle."

"You got them shaped up this quick?" he said with a grin.

"I didn't do shaping, Bill. These people are pros and they know this county. Their homes are here."

He motioned Sarah over. "You have a place we can talk?"

"My office."

When we were settled in Sarah's office with fresh coffee, Bill rubbed his eyes and sighed.

"A lot's happened overnight. The PA state troopers found Curly Erlich, the bomb maker. Dead, hands bound, single shot to the back of the head."

"Execution. Where?" I asked.

"Real close to the Ohio border, not too far from I-70. Body wasn't hidden. And the truck showed residual radiation."

"He transported a bomb, the buyer picked it up, killed him." I backtracked. "But if there was a radiation leak, what the hell kind of a bomb is it?"

214 S. M. Harding

"Good question, Win. The troopers notified the FBI, and they did a sweep of his house. Found the workshop in the basement. The guy was his own machinist, for the love of Mike. Workshop was loaded with radiation. He may have built his own containment unit." He rubbed his eyes again. "Am I making any sense? Been up all night and just flew back."

"Yeah. So the radiation could either be from raw materials or a leaky bomb. I was really hoping this was a bluff."

"You and me both, kid." Bill tried to stifle a yawn. "Sorry. I'm getting too old for this shit. You any closer to finding Scotty?"

"Narrowing in," Sarah said. "Unless you have any more surprises for us, we should check in with the plat map crew."

Bill nodded, got to his feet. We went back to the conference room. Both groups were gathered around a plat map.

"Think that may be it," Micah said. "Been thirty years since I been down that road, but if I'm rememberin' rightly, used to be an old farmhouse 'bout halfway up the hill. Drive in was close to half-mile. Kids used to use it for a party house, but when we found a body out there, they stopped goin'."

"Well, this is the latest plat map," Caleb said. "It still shows a structure there. We need to get the transaction details from the recorder. I'll go call her."

"Details, please," Sarah said.

"Only structure ain't occupied nor fallen down in the area is this one," Micah said, stabbing his finger at the map. "Land transferred four years ago, Caleb's trackin' down the buyer. House stood empty for a lot of years, Sarah. Take a passel a money to get that place livable. 'Cept to all the critters was livin' in it."

"Nathan, can you pull up the latest sat image on this area? Zero in on this farm?" Sarah asked.

"Yeah," Nathan said. Hit a number of keys in rapid succession.

An image appeared on the monitor. All trees.

"There's the road in," I said. "Maybe part of the roof. Wait. There's another structure behind it. A garage?"

The group took a closer look.

"Think mebbe you're right," Micah said.

"I know a trail up the back of that ridge," Nathan said. "Used to do some hunting down there. Guy with binoculars could get good intel from the top."

"Too dangerous, Nathan," Sarah said.

"Could be booby-trapped," I added. "At one time, Scotty didn't sit behind a desk. He was out in the field on special ops."

"I know that land and I know how to avoid traps," Nathan said. "Also know how to make them. I won't take foolish chances."

"I'll go with you," I said.

"No," Sarah said. "This guy's probably sitting on a bomb. If he—"

I looked at Nathan. "Since we're both only consultants to the sheriff's department, do we have to take orders from the sheriff?"

"No," Nathan said solemnly.

"This is too dangerous!"

"Look, Sarah, I'm not the ghost in the woods Nathan is, but I've done ops like this more times than I can remember. I'll provide backup for him, keep my eyes peeled for electronic surveillance. That's more Scotty's speed than booby traps. We'll be safe."

She locked her gaze with mine. I held my breath. Finally, she nodded. "All right, head out, but for God's sake, be careful. Have Caleb get you vests and some heavy firepower." She turned to Micah. "You too, Dad. Vest and rifle. Please, stay safe."

* * *

We got our equipment. I changed into old fatigues, boots and flak jacket. Sarah and I stood in the hall to the back door. Her face was a study in worry. Des whined, but lay down and silently vented her frustration with a huge yawn.

I turned to Sarah. "We'll be okay. I wouldn't have volunteered if I didn't think we'd get in and out safely. Promise I'll be back."

"You can't promise that, Win."

Micah and Caleb walked toward us. Both wore vests.

"I'm going with Micah," Caleb said. "A lot safer for both teams if they're teams." He grinned. "Don't look like you've lost control of the department, Sarah."

Both men laughed and walked on through the door. I could feel the tension radiating from Sarah's body. She looked at me. Threw her arms around me.

"Sarah, we're at the station."

"I don't care. I'm so scared you won't come back, and if people around here can't accept a hug between us, well, hell."

She hugged me harder and I put my arms around her.

"Stay in touch, use your cell phone," she said.

I pulled back. I wanted to kiss her so badly. "We don't want to lose the light. Man your post, Sheriff. You're the hub of this whole wheel of law enforcement."

I saw Nathan's Jeep. Took a deep breath. Kissed her on her forehead. Walked to the door without looking back.

CHAPTER FORTY-TWO

Sarah

I watched Win march off to battle, Mark 12 slung over her shoulder. The sight broke my heart, and it took every ounce of discipline I had not to stop her. I watched until she got into Nathan's Jeep and he drove out of sight. As I turned, I saw Dory at the end of the hall. I wondered how long she'd been standing there and realized I was afraid to ask.

"DA's office called," she said, handing me a slip of paper. "Tod sounded like he might explode. Call him back ASAP."

Plea bargain for those boys? My heart sank. "Okay."

"Hard to see the people you love walk into battle, isn't it?" Dory asked. She touched my shoulder, leaned in. "I seen the way you perked up when Win come back. You been happy, first time in years. She'll come back, Sarah."

She patted my shoulder and went back to dispatch. I wondered if I had a sign on my forehead that said "I love Winifred Kirkland."

"Come on, Des, it's our job to wait." I heard the click of her nails on the old pine boards.

Bill was waiting for me in the office. "This department is remarkable. I've never seen such a well-oiled machine. Just thought I should say so."

"Thanks, Bill. I think our people are top-rate." I sat down behind my desk. "I need to make a call."

Bill started to stand, but I motioned him back down. I dialed Tod Morrow and he picked up on the first ring. "Please don't tell me those boys plea bargained their way out of prison time."

"Definitely not," Tod said. "The leader of the group made additional charges possible in his deposition. Said they thought they were doing Natalie a favor—if she got laid good, she'd forget that silly girl she was fucking. That's a quote. His lawyer couldn't shut him up. So, would you send all the documentation over for the hate crime charges?"

"With the greatest of pleasure."

We hung up and I got the two binders of materials. "Be right back." I took them to Dory, asked her to have them copied and then taken to the DA's office. ASAP.

"Good news?" Bill asked.

"The best," I said as I returned to my desk. "Additional charges for a group of boys who raped a young girl because she was gay."

"Shit. What the hell's wrong with people?" He crossed his leg, ankle resting on knee. "I know Win's felt the lash of bigotry. One of the best operatives we've ever had, but if she'd been found out, we'd have lost her service to this country." He rubbed his ankle. "She'll be back, Sarah."

I wondered how transparent I'd been. Did everyone know? I cleared my throat and glanced at my watch. "We should hear from both teams in forty minutes, when they get in place."

"You mind if I wait with you?"

"I wish you would. Neither operation should be dangerous, but I always get hyper when my people are out. Any news on Scotty?"

"More data coming in from Pennsylvania. Some tire tracks near Erlich's truck, and they figure it's the killer's vehicle. They're running them now."

"If they identify the vehicle, would you have them send us the prints? I can't see Scotty taking an old truck that far. I bet he borrowed the Explorer. Would the cargo area be large enough?"

Bill nodded. He took out his phone and sent a text. "Done."

I got coffee and gave him a cup. "You didn't order Win to kill Scotty, did you?"

"No. First of all, I can't order Win to do anything. She's out and won't be recalled. Second, I wouldn't. We need him alive for his intel. If anyone was going to take a shot at him, I'd be the one."

"Sorry, it's just Win left with a sniper rifle."

"It's probably what she was used to carrying in the field. She talk much about her experiences?"

I shook my head. "Just the drone attack on the village where her team was staying."

He raised his eyebrows. "I was going to say I'm surprised, but I'm not. I get the feeling you two have become close."

"We've been good friends since first grade, interrupted only by her service."

His eyebrows inched up. "Then you ought to know. I don't think the drone attack was an accident. I think Scotty wanted to get rid of her because she'd done so much damage to his network."

"My God." My heart sank and I felt numb. Then anger swept over me. "If somebody kills him in McCrumb County, I swear to God, I'm not investigating."

He gave me a look that I could only read as a warning. "I can't prove anything, but I suspect he changed the coordinates. What he's done to our troops, again and again for his own profit, is treason. For that, I hope he abides in the lowest region of hell for eternity," he said with a grim scowl. "What I just told you—that's between you and me. Right?"

I nodded. How could I keep the knowledge that the drone raid was set up to kill her? How could I not?

* * *

Bill stretched out on my couch, Des beside him, and I tried to work through my paperwork. Futile. I kept glancing at my watch, wondering where Dad and Caleb, Win and Nathan were.

The first message came five minutes after I thought it should. Dad. "The Eagle has landed. We're at the edge of the garage and there ain't nobody home. Hold on."

I put it on speaker and motioned Bill over. I held my breath as a rustling filled the air. Dad must've put the phone in his pocket. "Yup, Explorer's here. Dirty, an' Kevin never'd put it away like that. We're gonna move around to the front."

"Dad, don't."

More rustling. "Lock's off the door. Caleb brought a Geiger counter an' we're gonna take a look." I heard ticking, then it increased to frantic pace.

"Dad, get out of there! Caleb, vacate—that's an order."

"We're out, Sarah Anne. But I think this was the transport vehicle for the bomb. You want us to hold the fort 'till the marines land? We can do it outta sight."

"If you would, we'd be most grateful," Bill said. "How far is that place from the farmhouse?"

"Twenty, twenty-five miles."

"Are you worried marine activity might alert him?" I asked.

Bill nodded.

"Stay put and out of sight," I said to Dad. "I'll call Bubba's Wrecking. They can pick it up and take it—where?"

"Up to Camp Atterbury. We'll sneak it in the back way," Bill said.

We disconnected. I called the tow truck operator. He wasn't happy until I told him the government was picking up the tab. "About time they put some tax dollars back in my pocket."

The phone rang again. Win. "We're at the base of the hill. No traffic on the trail in a long time. We're on our way up."

"Be careful, Win. Please."

"We will. Tell Bill to get his act in gear."

I looked at him.

"They'll be fine, Sarah. Is there anyplace around there we could use for a staging area?"

"Like what? A field, a barn?"

He thought a moment. "Barn would work. We'll use National Guard troop transports. Got a place?"

"Yeah, about a mile and a half down the road. Close enough?" I called the Jacobs, asked them for permission and warned them not to tell anyone.

Bill listened, nodded and placed a call. "You have coordinates for the barn?"

"Jesus, no. It's a farm. Let me see if I can get something off the Internet." I went to a site I'd bookmarked a couple of months ago. Thought about the nearest town, plugged that in and got those coordinates. "This is about three miles away. I can give directions to the barn."

"Let me get this going." He barked coordinates and orders and then hung up. "Want to be closer to the action?"

"Yes." I got up and headed out the door. Stopped. "Sorry, sweetie. Stay, Des." She glared at me, then jumped on the couch.

The call came when we were halfway there. "We're in place," Win said. "Nathan's taking good photos, but I'm going to send you what I've taken with the phone."

"Win," Bill said. "Any back way out?"

"Not unless he hotfoots it cross-country."

"Send the photos and then do some hotfooting yourself." He turned to me. "What's the name of the barn?"

I took the phone. "Win, tell Nathan our rendezvous site is the Jacob place, their barn. He'll know where. We'll meet you there. Leave now. Please."

"Ma'am, yes ma'am." She hung up.

"It's okay," Bill said. There was a grin in his voice. "Win won't blow an op just to stop you from bossing her around."

CHAPTER FORTY-THREE

Win

"He's getting ready to take off," I said, putting the binoculars away. We'd watched Scotty come out the back door of the farmhouse with a rolling suitcase. "Damn."

"This is when we leave, Win. We'll let Sarah know, but that man's nervous and I don't like nervous men who are heavily armed." Nathan looked at me. "I don't want to bring that bomb down on the county. He won't move until dark."

I nodded. We headed back down the hill. I called Sarah. "We're down the mountain and ready to rendezvous. Looks like the fucker's getting ready to bug out."

"Thank God you're all right. We're almost there," Sarah said. "ETA three minutes. Jon's ready for us—he said pull behind the barn."

Nathan took a left into a farm drive and pulled behind the barn.

"You really are a ghost in the woods, Nathan. You should think about training Special Forces."

He laughed. "Enough on my plate, Win. Plus, my skills go back generations—a different way of walking and a different way of thinking."

"Whites don't get it," I said. "I understand."

"Can't make generalizations. Micah and Sarah are skilled because they've been connected to this land for five or six generations. They love the land and respect it."

I thought of the wild country of the Hindu Kush. I probably knew it better than I did McCrumb County. I heard another vehicle turn into the farm and Sarah's Escape slid around the corner, parked next to us.

Sarah tumbled out and ran around to my door. "I was so scared, Win."

"Piece of cake, especially under Nathan's guidance," I said, raising an eyebrow. "Cool it."

Sarah let go of my door, straightened her face. "I'm just glad both of you are out of there."

Bill walked over to Nathan's side and handed him his phone. "Boys have landed at your coordinates. Would you guide them here?"

"Sure." Nathan got out of the truck, walked a few paces away.

"Thanks for not killing Scotty," Bill said to me.

"It was tempting," I replied. "But I figured you'd send me to Gitmo if I did."

"How do you get him to talk without a lawyer shutting him down?" Sarah asked.

"His actions have put him under the sway of the Patriot Act," Bill said. "I have to ask you to keep quiet about this op."

Sarah nodded, though a small frown marked her forehead. She didn't like the exclusion of due process. I didn't blame her, but I sure as hell didn't agree. Not under these circumstances.

Nathan handed the phone back. "They're here. Let me download the photos I took. I tried to get as much coverage as I could."

He and Bill huddled over the laptop. I heard the rumble of an engine, and Jon Jacob trotted out and opened the doors to the barn. A troop transport swung into the barn.

A tall, muscled man dressed in black walked out of the barn and shook Bill's hand. "Bill. Win. So, what've we got?"

Bill introduced Harlan to Nathan and they looked through the photos.

"Hey Win," Harlan said, turning to the truck when they were finished. "Good to see you again. But I thought you were out."

I grinned, knowing he hadn't intended the double entendre. "Just lending a hand."

"You want to run over these pics with me?"

I got out, pointed to features I knew he'd think important.

When we finished, I walked back to Bill. "I'm not leaving now. I'm going with. You owe me, Bill."

He flashed a look at Sarah. She shook her head. What? He was asking her permission?

"Win, you're not active military, and you need to stay out of this," he said, a vein pulsing on this forehead.

"I won't take no, Bill." I could see him waver. "I promise I won't kill him. But I'm the last person he'd expect to see. Surprise element you need."

"You kill him, you're dead," Bill said.

"If Win's going, I'm going with," Sarah said.

"No!" Bill and I said together.

"Yes. I. Am." Sarah gave Bill her steely look. The one she'd learned from Micah. The one she'd practiced twenty years on felons.

I felt Bill wavering. "She's more stubborn than I am. She'll guarantee I won't shoot him. I don't want to be locked up in the county jail. Besides, if I'm worried about her safety, I'm less likely to cause trouble."

"To hell with both of you," Bill said.

* * *

We moved out after Harlan briefed his men. One contingent east, one west and two snipers for the perch. Sarah's vest had been replaced with a flak jacket. One with a collar. Still, I was scared to death for her. We worked our way through the cover of the dense woods, then toward the drive. The only way out. Shit, what a cocky bastard he was. When we got in position, we settled down. He wouldn't leave until dark.

When dusk began to fall, a couple of guys broke cover to lay stop sticks on the rutted driveway. Covered them with leaves. I didn't think Scotty would see them in time.

As the dark deepened, Harlan got a message from the perch. "He's in the truck. Truck's started." Harlan gave the other unit the command to move out. We moved to the edge of the drive, though still in among the trees. I could hear the truck's engine.

"Can I take point?" I asked Harlan. "Seeing me here will take him off balance."

I grabbed Sarah's hand. Squeezed.

I couldn't see Harlan's face, but I heard his breathing. "Bill will probably kill me, but I think you're right. Just time it as close as you can. We'll spring it as soon as his attention's focused on you. Take care, Win."

I waited until I saw the headlights. Until the truck hit the stop sticks with two pops. Slithered to a stop. I stepped out of the cover of the woods, weapon ready. I took two quick shots, blew out his headlights. "Get out, Scotty," I yelled.

The door creaked open. "What the fuck are you doing, Kirkland? Playing cowboy one last time?"

One guy appeared at his side, weapon trained on his head. Another on the passenger side. Scotty slid out, hands raised. He was slammed against the truck and cuffed.

I took a deep breath. Walked up to him. "You're worse than pond scum."

"You won't get out of this alive, Win."

I shrugged. "Have a great time at Gitmo."

* * *

The ride back was quiet. I knew Sarah was still worrying about the bomb. Bill's bomb techs were still disarming it. She was also reliving the moments when I stepped from the woods.

We got back in Greenglen in the station's parking lot without Sarah saying a word. Nathan pulled in behind us.

"We're going to have to hang out at the station until the all clear comes in. You staying, Nathan?"

He nodded. "Whole thing makes me doubt the sanity of the human race."

"I've doubted that for a long time," I said. "What if we order dinner in for the task force?"

"Good idea," Sarah said. "But it means we won't get home until late."

She wanted a little close time. Now. I took her hand, entwined our fingers. "We're here, we're together. The rest can wait."

Nathan threw his head back and laughed. "Thank God! I thought you were going to make me stand guard outside your office."

Sarah threw him a look. "That can still be arranged."

Sarah left again to arrange dinner with Tillie's diner. As a favor, because they didn't stay open for dinner. Sarah was probably picking up the tab.

I understood her restlessness. Waiting for the conclusion of any op was hard. Dinner came around seven, and though everybody tried to enjoy it, the tension in the room was as thick as the gravy they'd sent with the mashed potatoes.

Sarah's phone finally rang. She put it on speaker and everyone leaned in. Bill's voice came through strong. No one missed the tone of jubilation.

"Mission accomplished."

Whoops went up around the table. Des barked.

"The bomb?" Sarah asked, the strain still in her voice.

"Bomb techs took it apart. It's on its way to Camp Atterbury in a safe containment unit. Go home. Get some sleep. We'll debrief in the morning. Many thanks to all of you—job well done."

Sarah looked at me. "Let's go home." Des was on her paws in an instant and woofed.

I was going to follow Sarah, but she insisted on driving us both. I knew something was percolating, but she wasn't willing to share. Yet. I hoped.

When we'd parked by the house, she looked at me for a long moment. "Dad's at Tillie's tonight, and I want to be with you so much if he came home, I'd kick him out."

We got out, went in the house. Des took off for her bed away from home—the couch in the living room. Not a good habit for her to get into.

I took Sarah's duty belt off, removed the Glock. "You want to go upstairs? Or do our debriefing down here?"

"I'm exhausted and so wired. Part of me is still confronting that greedy bastard and his goddamn bomb, part of me is still frantic because he could've killed you and part of me is just numb."

I put the Glock on the kitchen table. Wrapped my arms around her. Held her tight until I could feel tears falling. I hung on tighter.

Finally, she wiped her eyes and took a deep breath. "I was terrified he'd kill you."

"You kept your cool."

She ran both hands over her face. "It seems like it's taken a lifetime for us to get together."

I pulled her to me, hung on tight. "I know this love has taken you by surprise. But things will level out." I kissed her again. Then held her at arm's length. "You were kind of public at the station. Are you sure about that?"

"Dory knows, she figured it out for herself. Same with Bill. If it's so obvious, why should I try to hide?"

"For all the same reasons that existed before. Dory, your dispatcher?"

"Institution at the station."

I sighed. "Anyone who knows you well will be glad for you. They see your happiness. But those people who are homophobic will still tear you apart. Let's keep a low profile until after the election. Then you'll have more space to figure things out."

"I'm already tired of hiding. I don't know how you could've done it all those years." She put her hand on my chest. "I know, you had a career you loved. So do I. But the ante keeps going up in McCrumb County. More drugs, more senseless crimes to feed the habits, Mexican gangs. Now a bomb. What's next? Shit! I'm beginning to wonder if this is what I want to spend my life doing."

"You're the only one who can answer that," I said. "I know the challenges. I know the stress. But announcing you're queer to the county now isn't a good move."

"It feels like bait and switch."

"Hey, you're still the same sheriff. The same person."

"Am I?"

"Yes. Just with a little different experience." I grinned.

Her hand on my chest moved to my breast. She leaned forward and kissed me, tongue and fingers playing the same rhythm. I wanted her to think about something else. I took her hand in mine. "You've had good reactions with the people you know. How about meeting some strangers who are already on our side?"

"Bloomington?"

I nodded. "You won't be different in their midst. You'll be one of the family."

"When?"

"Let me see who's playing this weekend. Okay?"

She nodded. Untucked my long-sleeve T-shirt and ran both hands to my breasts. Her tongue licked one while her hand began undoing my pants.

"Are you sure you want to do this in the kitchen?" It was more of a groan than a question.

"Yes. Here. Now. I want to be in you so I can be sure you're alive. That this isn't a fantasy. When you come, everything feels real."

* * *

I woke early, watched Sarah deep in sleep. No wonder. Last night had been a release for both of us. But mostly Sarah. For all the tension and fear she'd carried all day. I'd enjoyed every innovation she'd brought to our lovemaking. Sarah had flowered. Shed inhibitions. Become a lover I wanted to please in every way. I knew I was pushing her about Ruby's, but I wanted to slow dance with her in a room full of women. Kiss her when I felt the impulse. Know that others on the dance floor would cheer us on.

Ruby's felt safe to me. Greenglen didn't. I eased out of bed, fired up my laptop and checked the schedule at Ruby's. I didn't know the band on Saturday night, but Friday night featured a woman who sang ballads in a beautiful alto. I'd caught her a couple of times in San Francisco, had a CD. I went ahead and made reservations for the show.

"You're beautiful naked," Sarah said in a sleepy voice from the bed. She stretched. She held her arms open to me in invitation.

I slid in beside her. Ran my hand over her body. Thigh, belly, breast. "Can you take off for Bloomington Friday night?"

She pulled me down to her breast. "I'll tell you after we've had some loving."

I ran my tongue around her nipple. Then stopped. "Tell me now."

"Why?"

"Because I'll have to cancel the reservations."

"That's not why." She touched my breasts. "You're afraid I'll back out, but I know it's important to you. As it happens, I have the early shift. I can leave at three—if I get everything done."

"I just want to share the experience of being with women who like naked women in their beds." I returned to her breast.

"Oh God! Are all of those women going strip me with their eyes?"

"Would that please you?"

"Noooo. Well, probably not." She locked her gaze with mine. "I don't know how to act, and I think that scares me. You know, do I have to be a femme to your butch?"

I laughed. "Do you have a slinky dress?"

"No. In fact, I can't remember the last time I wore a dress. Do you have one?"

"Yeah. I bought it in Shanghai for a ball in DC. Plunging neckline and a slit up the side."

She groaned. "I'm serious. I read the whole book, and there's talk about butch and femme stuff. But I don't feel less a woman when I'm with you, even when I'm doing you."

I kissed her belly. "There are women who identify mostly as male. It's a gender thing for them. Butch women. There are women who like a more passive role. Femmes. But most women at Ruby's act just like you and me. There's no special handshake. No password. All you have to do is dance with me. Kiss me back if I kiss you. Or kiss me if you want to."

"Hell. I know you're trying to make me feel more comfortable, but it's not working."

"Think about what I said. Stay open in the moment. We'll be fine." She nodded but I knew she didn't buy it.

CHAPTER FORTY-FOUR

Sarah

The paperwork from our small part of the general's takedown took a lot of the next day, and a meeting with Tod took up the rest. He was also pressing charges against the kids who'd put the pictures on Facebook. I wished him well, and maybe he could change the culture with prosecution. I thought we needed to dig deeper. The high school task force was still coming up with ideas and beginning to implement some changes.

I left work Friday feeling caught up, drove home preoccupied with what I should wear. I didn't really have "dress-up" clothes. I walked into the house to find Dad in his chair, listening to Bach. "You finally get away from Tillie duty?"

"Nope. Just takin' a break. Gotta be back for dinner duty an' she don't like my cookin'."

"Dad, you don't have to stay away. Win and I are going into Bloomington for dinner. I think she wants me to stay at her place tonight."

"Sarah Anne, I ain't stayin' away from home 'cause I'm worried I'll catch you two smoochin' or somethin'. I'm stayin' with Tillie 'cause she's family an' needs my help right now."

"I give up." I threw up my hands and grinned. "But you better be careful or you're going to walk in on two naked women making love on the kitchen table."

He groaned. "You don't gotta tell your father stuff he don't want to hear. Now go on and get ready for your date. Sure as the devil can't wear your uniform dancin'."

I went upstairs and opened my closet door. Stared. Gave up and took a shower. I came out of the bathroom to find Win sitting on my bed.

"You look lovely," she said with a grin. "But I took the time to pick out an outfit."

She looked great. A linen tunic top with thin black stripes and linen trousers. Cool and fresh. "I don't have anything like what you're wearing."

She pointed to the bed. It held a newish pair of jeans, a crisp white shirt and linen blazer. "Really? Jeans are appropriate?"

"Jeans are fine," she said with a smile. "But in the meantime, if you don't get dressed, I will ravish you right now."

I swished my hips. She came to me, kissed me like she meant it, then stood back. "Your Dad's home."

"He doesn't care as long as we don't do it naked on the kitchen table."

"Oh shit!" She laughed until she had to sit back down on the bed.

I went to the bureau and pulled out new underwear. A push-up bra and bikini panties. As I put them on, she whistled. I blushed. I finished dressing, slipped into sandals.

She looked at me, top of head to toes. She unbuttoned the top two buttons of the blouse, stood back and gave me a thumbs-up. "Let's go."

We listened to the woman who was to perform tonight on the way into Bloomington, and I had to admit I liked her voice and her songs. Win parked down the street from Ruby's and grinned at me. "Ready for the gauntlet?"

"I guess. You're not going to do anything special, are you? Pull out my chair for me when we're inside?"

"No. You're a perfectly strong woman who can manage chairs for yourself. Shit, where are you getting these ideas?" Her face lit up with a smile. "This isn't like a first date with a guy who's on good behavior because he wants to get in your pants."

We walked into a light, airy room. The walls and tin ceiling were painted white, the long back-bar shining light oak. Tables and chairs from an old ice cream parlor filled the right side. The place was filling up with women who looked like Win and me. I followed Win as she led me into another room in back that had an open wall of windows. Beyond that I could see a patio with tables that had umbrellas. Trellises lined the back walls, plants twining upward. A hostess greeted us at the door, showed us to a table and handed us menus.

"So far, so good?" Win asked.

"I don't know what I was expecting."

"Probably red velvet wallpaper and voluptuous half-clothed women. But that's a whorehouse, not a lesbian-feminist bar."

"I didn't mean that like it sounded, Win. I just didn't know what to expect."

She lowered the menu. "You can't paint pictures of what you haven't seen. Imagination will only enhance your fears, Sarah. Now, what would you like to order?"

We settled on pasta dishes, and I had a chance to look around. A nice, comfortable place with obvious couples talking quietly. One large table had a group of young women, laughing at a joke, relaxed and enjoying each others' company. "I don't know why I was so skittish about this."

"It was an unknown," Win said. "It's not like you to be afraid of something. So I figured once we were...more familiar, you'd trust me not to take you into danger."

I wanted to kiss her then. She read it in my eyes, took my hand.

"So where's the dancing?" I asked.

"In the back room. The room between the bar and here. They'll put small tables around the walls. Leave dancing space in front of the stage."

I looked toward the room we'd passed through and could see people moving furniture. "Have you ever danced with someone here?"

"No. Slow dancing is special. Or should be. Between two people who're building a life. A way of being close in public. To share the radiance."

"God, Win. You're talking like a poet."

After dinner, we moved to a small table in the corner of the back room. She put an arm around me and I snuggled into her. It amazed me I could feel so comfortable with even this small show of affection in public, even if the public was all women. I turned to kiss her and found she was looking at my newly formed cleavage. "Down Win. Would you settle for a kiss?"

She took my chin in her hand, pulled me close and kissed me. I felt free of a burden I hadn't even known I'd been carrying.

Win waited until halfway through the set to ask me to dance. The floor was pretty full, but we managed to find a free corner. She took me in her arms, pulled me close and began singing along with the performer into my ear. It was a song of longing and desire, and I could feel the heat rising in my own body. I understood what Win had meant, that this was an eroticism that lit the dark dance floor.

* * *

I raked the sand in a circular pattern and heard Win laugh. "I know, control is an illusion."

"You're the one who always tidies that sandbox, and I'm the one who's experienced a strong impulse to throw it out the window." Win reached out and touched my hand. "What a pair we are."

I squeezed her hand. "I like order. Control and order are two different things."

"Are they?" Win asked.

Em's door opened and she said, "Come on in."

Win took my hand, we walked into the office and settled into two chairs, still holding hands.

Em gave us a long, silent stare. "Glad to see you both." She turned to me. "You feel much less twitchy than the last time you were here. What's happened?"

What had happened? No one thing, I was sure. The trust we'd built up through sex. The openness I felt when I came, damn the vulnerability, because I knew Win was there with me. The way we could talk with one another, guard down, free to say anything. I knew we'd pick up the thread of order and control.

"No single thing," I said.

"The sex is obviously good," Em said. "Which is important when you're new to the life. Sometimes it's hard to ask for what you want, or say what you don't like."

Win snorted. Em grinned.

"Damn, I'm outnumbered," I said. "Sex is part of it, but everything I've found in Win lets me trust her. I love her."

"You must trust her to go to Ruby's over the weekend," Em said. "I remember you saying you found a place like Ruby's intimidating."

"How'd you know we went into Bloomington?" I turned to Win. "Did you tell her?"

Win shook her head.

"Marty and I went in for the show," Em said. "You only had eyes for Win. Didn't see us, did you?"

"No." What she said made sense. Once finished with dinner, we'd headed inside and acted like any other couple in love.

"And I'd wager you didn't see your deputy."

"My—who?"

Em shook her head. "Not my job to keep tabs on your people, Sarah. But how do you feel now that you know someone from your department saw you?"

"Exposed, particularly since you won't tell me who it was," I said.

"You know intellectually if one of your people was there, she's lesbian too. A bond, not a threat. Right?"

I nodded. "Intellectually. It was such a nice place, and the women—"

"She imagined hooker haven with a painting of a naked lady over the bar," Win said. "Butches and femmes out of the fifties."

Em laughed, a full-throated chuckle that continued to a belly laugh.

"I'm glad I'm providing entertainment for you both," I said, feeling silly about my own imagination. "The important thing about that visit was that Win asked me to trust her. I did."

"You're absolutely right," Em said. "Yet when I told you I was there, your protective shield went up a bit. When I mentioned the deputy, fear kicked in. Am I right?"

I nodded. "I have to be careful, Em. You know that."

"What would happen if you were called out as having a lesbian affair during the campaign?"

"Shit." I took a deep breath. "I'm hoping to get through the campaign without it coming out. Besides, if I could, I'd marry Win, so it's not just an affair." I looked at Win and thought I saw her tearing up. "I would, Win."

"Look, I'm not trying to make either of you paranoid," Em said. "Last thing I want. But I think you need to face the possibility. Remember, Mac hates you. He'll use anything he can."

"I don't get it," Win said. "Why's he so dead set against Sarah?"

"Because I defeated him the last time he ran, and he thinks he was just up against the Barrow dynasty. He doesn't carry any guilt for what he did to the department."

"He's a bitter man and a blamer," Em said. "The dangerous kind. Anyway, I don't want to spook you. It's a real delight to see you together, to see Win healing and to see you happy. I'm delighted you found one another. My only suggestion is that you talk over the possibility of exposure and what you want to do about it."

CHAPTER FORTY-FIVE

Win

I kissed Sarah in the hall outside Emily's office. She was already looking over her shoulder. "Can you come over tonight? I'll cook."

She nodded. "What time?"

"Come from work. I washed the uniform shirt you left. Even ironed it."

"Ironed? No kidding." She kissed my cheek. "Be there around four."

I watched her walk down the hall to the stairs. When she disappeared, I phoned Emily. "Can I talk to you for a minute? You have another client?"

"Between clients. How about you take me to lunch?"

We met at the Beanery, another vegetarian restaurant. I ordered a wrap but had visions of burgers dancing on my taste buds.

"So what's bothering you?" Emily asked.

"This Mac. We got one guy he sent to surveille me, but you think he might've sent someone else?"

"Possible for Mac's profile. But there's a rumor floating around, about Sarah and another woman. No hint of your involvement. I think Mac's shooting in the dark."

"Hitting the target." I pushed away my untouched lunch. "Shit."

"I don't think he has more than a rumor going, no proof he can show."

"That's damage enough. Sarah thinks he's going to pull something at the debate."

Emily frowned. "You two need to decide in advance how you're going to react. Whether Sarah denies it completely or—"

"Comes out and ends her career."

"It may not come to that. The people of this county like her and have a lot of respect for her family's contribution." Emily finished her wrap. "Tell me, Win, how would you feel if Sarah denied your relationship? Or if she outed you?"

I was glad I hadn't eaten. "She can't out me. I'm already out. Awful if she denied me. But I'd understand. I've been there. Had to sleep with officers to 'prove' I wasn't gay."

"You never told me that."

"It's something I'm not proud of. But something I had to do if I wanted to stay in the service."

"It's disgusting and unimaginable for men who're supposed to defend our country's values."

"You really are naive, Emily."

* * *

I stopped at Rhomer's Grocery, picked up most of the ingredients I needed for *Korma Nadroo*, a lamb stew with onions, spices and lotus roots. No luck with the lotus roots, but I thought I might be able to substitute with jicama.

I started cooking as soon as I got home, thinking about the last time I'd made this. With Azar. Over a cooking fire. Maybe I should break it off with Sarah. For her good, not mine. It would've hurt like a devil's prod, but I would've done the same for Azar. Maybe should've. No, there was no way I could've protected her from a drone attack. Our presence there should've been enough protection.

But Sarah? I realized it wasn't my decision. It was *ours*. As a couple. We'd have to talk it through. Damn Emily.

Sarah arrived a little after four to a joyful greeting from Des. Sarah sniffed. "What are you cooking?"

"An Afghan dish I think you'll like."

She looked at my kitchen. "Damn, you really did cook!"

"Order will be restored when chaos has taken its course." I pulled her to me, kissed her. "We have at least an hour before it's ready. Would you like to practice lesbian love in the interim?"

"Practice? As in 'makes perfect'?"

"Practice, as in 'do.' It's already perfect."

I unfastened her duty belt and draped it over the couch. Unbuttoned and untucked her uniform shirt. Was surprised at the lack of a T-shirt. The push-up bra was a surprise. "Nice."

I draped the shirt over the duty belt. I began kissing her, running my lips down her neck to nestle in her cleavage. "Where would you like to do this?"

She pulled my T-shirt up and off. Her hands went to my breasts. There was an urgency in her touch. "Right here. Right now." She kissed me, deep, insistent. She peeled off her jeans. "Take me standing up, Win. I just want to feel you inside me."

Afterward, we lay on the couch, legs entwined, her head buried against my shoulder.

"I'm not going anywhere, Sarah. Promise." I kissed her forehead. Stroked her arm.

"What if I have to send you away?" She put a hand on my cheek, looked me in the eye.

"The election? Are you having second thoughts?"

"No second thoughts, Win. None." She kissed me. "But what if this starts to unravel?"

"What if you have to stand up before the county and swear you're not in a lesbian affair? Do what you need to, Sarah. Just remember, it affects me too. If you claim our relationship, I'll be known as the sheriff's bitch."

She caressed my cheek. Ran her fingers down to my lips. "I don't think I can deny the truth."

My timer on the stove went off. "Dinner's ready. I want to talk this through with you. Could we eat first? Talk about how your day was? Something normal?"

"Yes." She kissed my breast she had cupped in her hand. "Would you hate being called the sheriff's bitch?"

"I'm nobody's bitch."

CHAPTER FORTY-SIX

Sarah

Field corn grew above my head, the silks barely turning brown. Harvest time, this year, would be in October instead of the drought-induced August reaping of last year. As I drove toward Greenglen, I saw a couple of farmers beginning to take in their sweet corn. Nothing like an ear of Silver Queen to make my mouth water. The first ears of the season was one of the passages of country time that I looked forward to. Sparing major storms, farmers should have a good crop this year, and we all needed it. Farmers made the economy, and a good harvest might mean more funds for the sheriff's department.

My phone rang and I pulled over on the berm. A familiar number by now because Willy Nesbit had kept his word: he was a mole in his own campaign. "Hey, Willy. What's up?"

"Not sure, but Mac's up to something. Don't know what, but he's planning on springing it at the debate."

"Crap." My fear had proven out.

"Sarah, I just want to say, if I'd known what a scumbag he is, I never would've run. I'm only hanging on because I promised you."

"Thanks for the heads-up. Really, I mean the thanks."

"I don't know why I didn't tumble to him right away. A bit frayed, I guess, trying to be a civilian."

We disconnected. I sat by the side of the road, watching the corn silks move in the light breeze. Damn. My record as sheriff was so clean I didn't need to polish it. Ditto my life. The one thing Mac could produce? The lesbian sheriff. Win was the only part of my life I had to hide, and that was the one thing I couldn't do, not if the accusation was made, or the question asked.

Win and I had been careful, keeping our meetings to twice a week. We'd only gone in to Ruby's once since, met for an early dinner when I'd had a meeting in Bloomington. We'd been alternating Win's home and my cabin on Red Hawk Lake. Both of us watched for tails, had Nathan keep an eye out for electronic snooping. We'd been careful, though it was a hell of a strain on both of us.

I slammed my fist on the steering wheel. "Damn him."

It wouldn't do any good to cuss Mac, but I felt a little more in control. Win would laugh at that. I knew she was right, but it was the sheriff's lot to control a county hell-bent on breaking the law.

Monday afternoon, and as soon as I checked in with the station, I would be heading to the cabin. I sent a fervent prayer to the universe that I could get away. Win and I had exchanged keys, and, at least for summer, Mary would follow the powwow trail. It gave her an income and allowed an alternative to the isolated life she led at the cabin. She'd offered to move, knowing that we needed privacy, but I'd declined. She needed to follow her path as a healer.

Hugh's memory shared the space with Win most gracefully. I was beginning to put the two lives I'd lived, was living, together into a whole.

I pulled back onto the road and walked in the back door of the station fifteen minutes later. Dory handed me a couple of messages, and after a quick scan, I put them on my desk for tomorrow. Caleb tapped on the doorframe.

"Get outta here," he said with a grin. "We've got everything covered. Go."

I did, keeping an eye on my rearview mirror all the way down to the cabin. Win's truck was tucked under a tree, and I spotted a new charcoal grill in a level space with no branches above. Good idea. Good woman.

She opened the door and took my breath away. In cutoffs, T-shirt and bare feet, she was the most beautiful woman I'd ever seen. I opened my door, took my extra uniform shirt and bag out and walked into her arms.

"Honey, I'm home," I said.

She took both hanger and bag, and smirked at me. "You think we're that domesticated?"

"I hope not."

"I did a silly thing. Bought hot dogs. My brother's favorite when we were kids and he'd pester Mom every night. When I was twelve, I swore I'd never eat another one. But I saw them in the grocery and I couldn't resist. I even made Mom's potato salad. Weird, huh?"

She put my stuff in the bedroom and took the charcoal outside. I flopped full-length on the couch, weary with worry. Why the hell should I have to watch for a tail when I went to meet my lover? She'd be my wife if we were married. Or would I be hers?

"Fire's started," she said as she came in and sat on the portion I'd left her.

"Fire's been started for a long time now and doesn't show any sign of diminishing." I pulled her down to me.

"We only have twenty minutes until the coals are ready," she said. "I don't want to rush this." She sat back. "So what's wrong?"

"Am I that transparent?"

"Only to me. Maybe your dad too. Talk."

"You just want me to grumble about my day so you can have hot dogs ASAP."

"If I had to choose between eating ever again and making love to you once, I'd choose you." Win grinned. "So stop avoiding and tell me what's wrong."

"Later," I said. "After dinner and after…Promise. Right now, I just want to…well, you know what I want to do."

* * *

We didn't end up talking about Willy's call until breakfast. I told her as much as I knew.

"I think you're right, it's about us," she said. "But I'll bet you he doesn't know about me. He's going to throw shit on the wall to see what sticks."

"I just wish I knew what he had up his sleeve. I can counter moves when I see them coming."

"Hmpf. What do you think special ops are? Preparing for all that's known, guessing at what's unknown and making strategies for both." She took her bowl to the sink, rinsed it and turned to me. "We could have Nathan hack his phone calls."

"No. I won't have him break the law so I can win the damn election. Let's just see what Willy can find out."

"You trust him?"

I nodded. "I'm not sure why, but I do. Maybe because I can imagine the crap Mac told him to sign him up."

"Had somebody told me shit like that when I first came home, I would've believed it."

"He hadn't been home long, Win, probably didn't know how rotten Mac is."

"I checked on his service record," Win said, crossing her arms and leaning against the sink. "Outstanding record, Sarah. Not one blemish. He made SEAL 6."

"The guys who killed Bin Laden?"

"Some of the guys in SEAL 6. I talked to one of his COs, who gave him a glowing recommendation. I know how these guys talk. Obfuscate."

"Recommendation for what? Your own mercenary company?"

"New SWAT team for McCrumb County." She grinned. "I had to have some reason to dig. Since you won't hire me, I thought I'd better line up some recommendations."

I took my bowl to the sink, nudged her aside with my hip. "So, if we got married, who'd be the wife?"

She wrapped her arms around me. "Both of us."

CHAPTER FORTY-SEVEN

Win

After Sarah left early the next morning, I cleaned the cabin and removed all traces of our rendezvous. Then I headed to Nathan's.

As I drove up the track, I saw smoke from the stovepipe floating like a halo over the clearing. I stopped, turned off the engine. Waited. This time, he appeared from a trail leading into the forest. Motioned me inside with a big smile.

He gave me a hug, held me at arm's length. "What's the matter?"

"The damn campaign." I told him the whole story, though "whole" was a skimpy tale. "Sarah made it clear that you can't hack, but there's got to be a plan B. I don't want you to break any laws, but I don't want Sarah blindsided either."

"Me neither. Well, as the provider for Rob McKenzie, I can check to see that his service is operating at peak." He went over to his computer bank, hit a few keys. "Now, I can't open his email or listen to conversations. But, I can look at his logs."

I looked over his shoulder. "What I'm looking for is a series of emails or phone calls to a person he doesn't have usual communication with."

He hit a couple of keys and a series of phone calls were highlighted.

"You have a reverse directory?"

"Don't need one. That's the Reverend Manfred Brown, one of those fire and-brimstone preachers."

"Rabidly antigay?"

"To put it mildly. Calls have been going back and forth for about two weeks. Anything special happen two weeks ago?"

I shook my head. "We've been careful when we meet, Nathan. The folks at the other end of the lake haven't been around except on weekends."

"Let me nose around, Win." He hit another key and other accounts began scrolling down. "I've lived here my whole life, and I know a lot of people who'll talk to me."

I nodded. "I feel so useless, Nathan. In a way, I brought this down on her—"

"You didn't bring anything down on her, Win. She fell in love, and I say, it's about time. What's causing this is a slimy politician and a bigot. Let's keep our eye on the ball."

I nodded again. "I know you're right, but when I have to stand by—"

"Can it, Win. Trust me to carry this part of the load. I love Sarah too."

I took a deep breath. "How come you two have never gotten together?"

"Incest," he said. "Sarah and I started playing together as soon as we could walk. Elizabeth was best friends with my mother, Micah and Dad the same. It'd be like romancing my sister."

"Too bad, you'd be a cool couple."

Something in his eyes shifted for a second, and I wasn't sure if I'd hit a nerve or given him an idea. "Okay, you need anything from me, holler."

* * *

Two days until the debate in the gym of Greenglen High. I hadn't heard anything from Nathan. Sarah hadn't heard anything more from Willy, except he was still working on it. I wanted so much to hold her, comfort her, make her forget the stress. But I didn't think it was smart to get within two miles of her.

I'd tended my garden, worked with Des and generally puttered. I kept tracking back over the times we'd been together, trying to figure if anyone could've seen us. I knew my perimeter was secure, so that left the cabin. Our trip into Ruby's for the concert. Emily had been there, had also noticed one of Sarah's deputies. Could she be the leak? Was this woman in the opposing camp? I could ask Emily.

She thought I was making enough progress, especially since the nightmares hadn't returned after my special ops foray with Bill, that we'd moved the appointments to every other week. Emily read auras, I read body language. I called and Emily slotted me in for this afternoon. She might kill me when she found out the purpose of my visit: find out who was the female deputy.

I brought Des along for the ride. Way too hot to leave her in the truck. I'd no more opened the waiting room door than Emily's office door opened. She waved me in, met Des. She sat and crossed her legs. "What's on your mind?"

"I may be here under false pretenses, but I didn't know who else to ask." I told her Mac was planning something to spring on Sarah at the debate, but I didn't know what.

"You think it has to do with your relationship with Sarah?"

"Otherwise, her record's so clean it could blind you."

"How do you feel about that?"

"God, you sound like a shrink."

"Maybe because I am," she said.

"I kept thinking that if I hadn't come back home, she wouldn't be facing this now." I held up my hand. "Wait before you give me the lecture. I talked to Nathan, and he said if I wanted to blame someone, how about the pond scum who's willing to expose her private life? I've thought a lot about that and think he's right."

"Okay, you think he's right. How do you feel?"

Shit. What a persistent bitch. "I feel like I walked into 1950. It shouldn't matter who she sleeps with as long as she's a good sheriff. She is."

Emily recrossed her legs. "How do you feel about being the lover of a woman who could lose her career because of you?"

I got up, started to pace. "How do I feel? Wonderful, because I love her and she loves me. Awful, because she should have the right to decide what she does for a living. Furious with this goddamn fucker who's trying to get revenge for his own ineptitude and greed. Grief. If she loses the job, she loses part of her identity."

Emily's eyebrows shot up. "Sit down, Win. Now, what did you come here to ask me?"

It was time for my eyebrows to travel upward. "Who was the deputy you saw at Ruby's?"

She thought for a minute, nodded. "I gather you're not going to out her? Not even to Sarah?"

I made a cross-my-heart.

"Leslie Ryburn. A CSI."

"You think she could've outed Sarah? Or maybe said something accidently?"

Emily shook her head. "Definitely not. Leslie's loyal to Sarah because Sarah's the one who encouraged her and provided the classes she needed to qualify. Not your leak, if there is one."

"It was a possibility." I sank into the chair. "I feel like shit not being able to protect Sarah."

I felt even shittier when Nathan called to say he had things under control. He asked that I not sit in the front row.

CHAPTER FORTY-EIGHT

Sarah

"I want to see you tonight," I said. I switched the phone to my other ear so I could steer with my good arm.

"I don't think that's a good idea," Win said. "The debate's tomorrow."

"I just need to be held."

"Is that all?"

"Fuck you. I'm on my way over." I hung up.

I steered up Win's drive with both hands, thinking she'd have to get a load of gravel before winter came. When I crested the top, Win stood by her open garage. Her truck was nudged into the edge of the forest. Des wagged her tail beside the tall, beautiful woman I wanted to melt into, meld with. I stopped, turned off the engine, leaving my Escape in the middle of the yard.

Win walked toward me, shaking her head. She leaned in the window and kissed me. "I went through a rebellious stage. My second year as an MP. Got so tired of hiding. Almost cost me everything. Please put your car in the garage, Sarah."

I did as she asked. When we were inside, she pulled me to her by my duty belt and held on tight. She stepped back, took off the belt and led me down the hall to the bedroom.

I came quickly, and though it took my breath away, I felt as if I could breathe again. We lay together, breathing, mostly still clothed. She kissed me lightly and began to withdraw. I clamped my hand on hers.

"When I feel you inside me, you're touching my center. I feel brave."

Win's eyes teared up. "I love you, Sarah." She kissed me softly, settling her head on my chest.

When she finally began to move, I came just as quickly, again and again. We finally stripped, and I returned the grace. Finally exhausted, I noticed night had fallen, and I heard Des clicking around the kitchen.

"Hungry?" she asked.

I realized I was. I couldn't remember if I'd eaten lunch or not. "Yeah, though I hate to leave this haven."

She kissed my breast, then pushed up and out of bed. "If Des doesn't eat soon, she'll start nibbling on us." She grabbed the two robes that hung on the back of her door, threw one to me and put on the other.

Win threw together a couple of ham sandwiches on rye, and we both wolfed them down, almost as fast as Des had eaten her dinner. I felt sated and safe.

As Win cleaned up, I searched through her music. I wanted something slow and lyrical and romantic. She pulled me onto the couch after I put a Margie Adams CD on.

"I want you to listen to me," she said, pushing my hair off my forehead. "We all have wanted to kick the traces at one point or another. You have to ask yourself who you are and what you want in life. Being sheriff is part of you. I'm part of you. I want to be part of your life as you're meant to live it. Get used to the shadows, Sarah. Someday we'll be able to live in the light. Just not yet."

* * *

Win fed me breakfast in the early dawn, then shooed me out. "I'll be there, but not up front, Sarah. Keep your balance—God knows, you should be centered by now."

I was pulling out of the drive when she stopped me, gave me a quick kiss.

"Do whatever Nathan tells you to do. Don't forget, he's in charge of this op."

"Yeah, yeah, yeah."

When I got home, Dad was calm, finishing his breakfast and looking cheery. "You're in on this too? Whatever 'this' is—Win wouldn't tell me."

He took a sip of coffee. "Best you not know, Sarah Anne. Just answer the questions Lloyd asks to the best of your ability an' ignore sonofabutts. You don't got to answer to them."

"What expression would you like me to assume when the metaphorical bomb blows?"

"Me an' Nathan be sittin' in the front row." He shook his head. "It's under control, an' I ain't tellin' you nothin' more."

He wasn't going to break his code, so I went upstairs to shower and change into a fresh uniform. I was going to have to get new underwear since what I had was scattered here, at the cabin and at Win's. I knew I couldn't afford to think about her today, not until after the debate, so I began to run through the latest county statistics in my head.

They were good stats and improving every year. I was proud of the team I'd built and the way we worked together. I couldn't stand the thought that team would be dismantled by another sheriff.

Dad rode with me to the station, disappeared when I went inside to get some work done. I thought he was off to do his part of the "op." Damn.

At eleven thirty, Caleb poked his head around the doorframe. "Time to go shake some hands, Sarah."

I took my Glock out of the drawer and put it in its holster. I figured if I didn't like a question, I could shoot the speaker.

We started at noon sharp, Lloyd moderating with questions readers sent in, as well as his own. Willy's answers were short, sometimes one sentence, and mine were to the point, but cited statistics I knew as well as the back of my hand. Evidence.

Finally, Lloyd opened the floor to questions from those present.

Dog, owner of Dog's Pound, stood and asked how I'd managed with all the cuts in county funding. "What with the drought an' all, most of us ain't got two pennies to rub together."

"Neither do we," I replied. "We'd like to do a number of undercover drug operations, but I don't have enough people to cover patrol as it is. The only hiring we can do is to fill retirements. It stretches us thin, but we've managed to do a couple of major busts by joining with the state police and DEA in a joint task force. We've also gotten a number of grants from various branches of the federal government.

"The bottom line is that it's hard to serve the people of McCrumb County with a severely curtailed budget, but we put our heads together and continue to find ways."

Lloyd asked Willy how he'd face the budget.

"About the same," he said.

A short, bald and overweight man rose from his seat at the back of the crowd. Lloyd nodded at him.

"You are nothing more than the Whore of Babylon! The Harlot of Sodom and Gomorrah!" The words echoed in the gym. "You are whoring yourself with another woman! Tell me how, when you are supposed to be a model of morality for these people, you can stand before them today and flaunt your homosexuality? Your perversion? Your deviance? When you call the wrath of God down upon your soul—"

"We catch the drift of your question, Pastor Brown," Lloyd said.

Fr. Nowicki from St. Catherine's rose. "Excuse me, Lloyd."

He turned to the people and I could tell he was winding up for a sermon.

"You all know where my church stands on homosexuality. But I fail to see how what Sheriff Barrow-Pitt does—*or doesn't do*—in the privacy of her own home is anybody's business but her own. I cannot see how it affects the duty she is sworn to do for the people of this county. We don't live in the times of the Crusades, nor the Inquisition. We have free speech. We also have separation of church and state."

I was sure Pastor Manfred Brown was set to go off again, but the Methodist, Presbyterian and Anglican ministers stood in rapid succession and echoed Fr. Nowicki's sentiments.

"Haven't churches learned anything from the Inquisition?" Reverend Martin asked. "We Christians were responsible for the horrible torture and deaths of close to a million people on *accusation* only." He turned toward the back, looked around. He spotted the pastor sneaking away. "My God, man, this is the twenty-first century!"

Evidently, the pastor and Mac hadn't expected the interference. Well played, Nathan and Dad. I knew they'd been together in this.

Since Pastor Brown's back was rapidly departing, Lloyd thanked everyone for coming. It was over.

Nathan jumped onto the stage and walked rapidly toward me. "I'm going to kiss you, so please look like you're enjoying it or my rep's gone."

I was surprised how soft his lips were.

"Uh, thanks," I said when the short kiss was over.

He put his arm around me and leaned over. "Was that as weird for you as it was for me?"

I laughed. "Yeah, bro, it was."

The crowd sounded like a swarm of bees. A lot of people came up, shook my hand, asked questions about specifics of my answers. They exchanged greetings with Nathan and Dad, who stood on either side. My wall of protection.

I didn't see Willy and figured he must've left. He'd been low-key on stage, the bottom note of a piano. Then I spotted Win, leaning against the bleachers with a big smile on her face.

CHAPTER FORTY-NINE

Win and Sarah

Win

Sarah met me at the cabin Saturday evening. I opened my arms, and she stumbled into them. We stood in the doorway, wrapped around each other. Finally I let go and we walked in, hands clasped as if we were holding on to life.

"Coals are about ready," I said.

"Are you going to roast me like the preacher? Fire of perdition and all?"

"Never." I took steaks out of the fridge and turned off the oven. "Salad makings are ready. Set the table while I'm grilling?"

When we finished dinner, we walked down to the lake. Kept to the shadows in case anyone was home across the lake.

She held me tight. Buried her head against me. "I wanted to kill that damn self-righteous prick. If he's a true representative of God's word, then I don't want anything to do with God."

I rubbed her back. "Who the hell is he?"

"Has a small cinder block box called the Family Praise Tabernacle in Ridley's Station, and has maybe ten members."

"Sounds like Westboro Baptist Church. Rabidly antigay, no matter who they hurt."

"Yeah. But he's let the genie out of the bottle, which was Mac's intent."

"After the priest and ministers, the genie may have lost his potency."

"Mac's not going to quit. I only have two more speeches scheduled, one at Founders Day, the other with the Chamber."

"Safe places?"

"Chamber, yes," she said, leaning against me. "They're much more concerned with the economic bottom line for the county."

"Founders Day?" I asked, holding my breath. "It could well be a replay of the pastor, plus his congregation."

"Nothing I can do if they apply for the right permits." She touched my chin, kissed me, pushed her body into mine. "Let's go in, Win. Forget the crap and celebrate this love between us."

"You can't hide your head in the sand." I brought my hands around to her slim sides. "You've got to face the battle, not avoid it. Figure your strategy."

"Dad pushed me into making a decision about running, but what I've realized is I love this job, despite all the stress and worry, and I don't want to lose it. But..."

I knew what she'd left unsaid. She didn't want to lose me either. "Classes start soon. I've rented a studio apartment in Bloomington."

"Can I come and visit?"

"I teach Wednesday through Friday, but I can use the apartment for prep time on Tuesdays." I touched her hair. "Getting chilly out here. Time to go in."

She took my hand and we headed up the bluff.

Sarah

"I'd like to go back to your shooting, Sarah," Zoe McClanahan said as she flipped through her notebook.

"I don't," I replied. "Look, the possibility of being shot, or killed, is always with us. There's not a law enforcement officer in McCrumb County that doesn't know it when we strap on our sidearm to go to work. But we can't dwell in that knowledge. It would paralyze us."

"All right, then," Zoe said as she closed her notebook. She noticed the surprised look on my face. "I'm not a tabloid reporter and have no interest in your private life. I'm a journalist. Used to be, that meant people with integrity."

"Still does, around here." I rose from my desk. "I appreciate the chance to talk about what I've done in office and what I still want to do."

"That's my job. Send me your latest stats when you get them compiled, would you?" Zoe pushed out of her chair, stopped with her hand on the door. "Off the record—so far off it'll never see print— who do you think is behind the pastor's agitation?"

"Mac." I shrugged. "No evidence at all, and even if I had some, I can't charge them with anything. You repeat this, I'll dog your tail good."

"That one of Micah's expressions? He's got the most charming smokescreen of any law enforcement office I've ever known." She opened the door. "Thanks for your time, and we'll keep to the facts."

I watched her leave and sat down at my desk.

Win was installed in her studio in Bloomington, working hard to keep ahead of her students. We spent Tuesdays together, though I usually didn't go in Monday night, nor did I spend the night with her. I missed waking in the morning with her body beside mine. I felt comfort with her there, though comfort could turn rapidly to the erotic when she woke.

"Only until November, Win."

That was my mantra. I looked out at Courthouse Square. Leaves on maples were beginning to turn, and the temperatures were cool at night. Once Founders Day was over, the end of the gauntlet would be in sight.

Only to begin again in four years, if some felon hadn't killed me by then.

Win

"What've you heard?" I asked.

"Pastor ain't applied for no kind of permit," Micah said. "Don't mean he ain't gonna show up with his congregation in tow. Mayor said if that happens, his cops'll get 'em outta there."

I nodded. Much better the Greenglen PD escort them out than deputies. "I just wish Sarah would think about what might happen, plan for it."

"She can't. She's doin' good puttin' one foot forward at a time." He rubbed his jaw. "I know what she wants to do—come outta the closet, damn the consequences. But Win, she's inherited the McCrumb County sheriff's gene. She cares 'bout the people of this county, cares 'bout the job she does for 'em. So, she keeps puttin' thinkin' 'bout it off. She loses, she don't have to think no more. She wins, she's got some colossal thinkin' to do. You understand?"

"More than you know. I know how draining it is. One boot at a time."

Micah hugged me. Rubbed his chin again. "Thinkin' 'bout growin' a beard, make me look distinguished. What do you think?"

"A big, bushy, long thing?"

"I said 'distinguished.' Keep it trimmed, though I'll be damned if I go to the barbershop every week. So?"

"Are you going to wait until after the election?"

"Guess I should. Don't want to look like no reprobate."

I grinned.

"Try not to worry. Keep your mind on your job, enjoy the time you spend with Sarah. An' don't go takin' the law into your own hands."

He kissed my cheek and walked away with the stride of a man thirty years younger.

I could smell woodsmoke in the air. A harbinger of winter. Founders Day was a fraud. The two families who settled here hadn't come in late fall. They would've starved. They'd come in spring, early enough to build cabins and plant crops. The fraud had been perpetrated by the Chamber of Commerce sometime after WWII because they figured they could pull in more tourists who were in the area looking at fall foliage. Funny how we build tradition on fraud.

Courthouse Square was dressing itself in flagrant colors for visitors. Sarah and I had tomorrow together before her speech at Founders Day. I wished I could tell her everything would be okay, but I had a feeling in the pit of my stomach. Nathan hadn't picked up any chatter from Mac. Maybe I was wrong. Maybe the pastor had been embarrassed and crawled back under his rock. But in my experience, creeps like him didn't feel shame.

Sarah

I lay in Win's arms, desire rising again. Would I ever feel sated? I fervently hoped not. I ran my hand along her skin, from breast to hip. Goose bumps followed in its wake and she smiled. I leaned over so she could have my breast while I continued to explore. I felt the rhythm she wanted as she sucked my nipple, heard it in my own breathing and the blood pounding in my ears.

It amazed me how I'd learned to pick up on little clues for what Win wanted, and in the same way, how I'd learned to show her what I wanted. The sounds we made now rarely contained words. It stunned me that I could fall so deeply in love, and be so sure Win was the only path I could take home.

As the sun slanted its passage through the window, we stayed in bed. At times, languor replaced passion. Just being close, feeling her next to me, was enough for the moment.

"Any chance you can spend the night?" Win asked, propping herself up.

"I don't know—I don't want to get caught coming home in a rumpled uniform," I said. "I don't want to get caught, period. That damn pastor's been too damn quiet. So has Mac."

"Still no permit application?"

"No." I rolled over on my back. "I don't want to bring those people into our bed. They don't belong here."

"I keep telling you, nothing can ruin this except us." She caressed my cheek. "I brought a uniform shirt. It's hanging in the closet. Hope I didn't use too much starch."

Win cooked and did laundry. "Do you do windows too?"

"No. But I can do you."

Win

I almost cried when Sarah left that morning. Not like me. It had been a comfort to have her next to me when I woke. The crack she'd made about windows? I realized I'd been doing a lot of the cooking. I'd done her laundry. Shit, I'd have to butch up my image.

Friday night we'd had a hard freeze and I'd lit the first fire of the season. Snuggled with Des on the couch. As much as I loved my canine companion, she did not compensate for Sarah's absence. Nothing did. Except perhaps the exhaustion I felt on Friday nights, back in my own home, the week's teaching finished. Hardest job I'd ever had. I didn't want to see student evaluations at the end of semester.

Saturday morning, the sun twinkled on the hoar frost as I drove into town. Parking on the Square didn't exist today, so I parked at the far end of the sheriff's lot. After all, I was a consultant. Des and I walked over to Tillie's and ate a leisurely breakfast while I read the latest print issue of the *Sentinel*.

Zoe had done a nice piece on Sarah a few weeks ago. This week she'd done a short follow-up with the doctors and nurses who'd tended Sarah after her shooting. The sidebar was a quote from Sarah about what every cop faced. Every day.

"Yes! Tell them what it's like, Zoe." Des woofed and Tillie gave me one of her patented looks. I'd told her Des was my service dog, and she'd only grudgingly allowed her in. The first time. Since, we'd become semiregulars and Des had worked her magic. Truly magic, because Tillie had started serving Des treats with my order. This was the first time Des had opened her mouth except to eat.

I finished my coffee and took Des out into the beauty of a fall day with trees at their color peak. A reviewing stand stood in front of the courthouse. Bleachers had been erected across the street and on the east side of the Square. The parade would come down Market Street from the west, past the stand, up East Street and then on to Pioneer Park. For more leaf-peeping, food, crafts, demonstrations, reenactments, a flea market and more food. Sarah's speech would be after the mayor, historical society director and a county commissioner. Right before the parade.

Where would a sniper set up?

I escaped the thought. Took Des for a long walk through the town. When we arrived back at Courthouse Square, I noticed a commotion at the far end where the floats were lined up. Sometimes just the presence of a dog like Des quieted things down. I slipped past the barricade and walked toward the noise.

"You can't be in the parade 'cause you didn't sign up for it. Now turn this rig 'round and scat!" Big man, red in the face underneath the mountain man beard and mustache. Pointing away.

"Anybody can be in this parade, you miserable sinner. I demand my rights."

I recognized the short, bald guy standing on the float in front of a cardboard log church. Even in a black suit, the vest straining across his belly. And the fake beard. It was the look in his eyes. Pastor Brown. I called dispatch, relieved that Dory answered. "You might want to give the GPD a heads-up. Pastor Brown's trying to join the parade and there's a mountain man ready to use his ax."

"Lordy, Win. I'm on it—and you stay out of it, hear?"

"Yeah, yeah. Over and out."

I walked around to the back of the float, saw some female congregants dressed in pioneer gear, long dresses and sunbonnets. It looked as if they were preparing to hand out fliers. I smiled and was handed one.

The top was crudely lettered: WHORE OF BABYLON!!! HARLOT OF SODOM!!!

Beneath was a picture of Sarah, naked and in the arms of a woman. I took a closer look. The woman was heavier than I, with long curly hair. Then I examined Sarah's body. Definitely not hers. Then I noticed Sarah's face. The same photo of her that appeared on the sheriff's website. Photoshopped! Once you really looked, it was a lousy job.

I giggled. Couldn't help myself. When I looked up, I saw two Greenglen police officers rousting the pastor and his float. I dialed first Micah, then Nathan. Time for a powwow.

CHAPTER FIFTY

Sarah

Dad strode into my office, closed the door and put a flier on my desk. I glanced at it, then took a better look. "Hell."

"Win, smart woman she is, figgered a way to deal. You point out the manipulation of images an' remind folk your face come from the department's website. Then point out the image of the two women has to come from pornography. An' ask what the preacher been watchin'."

I looked into Dad's eyes. "I'd love to stop hiding."

He nodded. "Reckon so, but wouldn't you rather do it on your own terms? Think on it, Sarah. I'll abide by your decision."

He kissed my forehead, opened the door. I watched him greet deputies on the way to the street door.

"Double shit." I knew Dad was right, neither affirm nor deny, just point out the smear. I took a second look and laughed at the piss-poor job they'd done. "Crap."

I wanted the opinion of someone who wasn't close, who understood the danger and wouldn't minimize it. I thought of Leslie, on duty today upstairs in the new lab, working on a tough fingerprint case. I picked up the flier and started upstairs.

Leslie was hunched over a computer monitor, running partial prints. She turned and smiled. "I'm not meeting with much success."

"I wasn't expecting an easy answer," I said as I pulled a chair to the desk. "I wanted your opinion on this." I handed her the sheet.

Her face clouded, then her eyebrows went up and she started to giggle. "Awful job of photoshopping." She laid it on the desk. "I saw you at Ruby's a while back."

I glanced at her, not sure of her reaction. She was smiling, a small tug-up of the corner of her mouth.

"You and Win are a stunning couple," Leslie said. "Nobody could keep their eyes off you two. Sparks, for sure."

I swallowed hard, and felt the heat creeping into my face.

Leslie swiveled her chair. "This flier's crap and people will see it for what it is."

"I'm not so sure."

"Hey, you're talking to a woman who came out to her devout Baptist parents. It wasn't easy for them at first, but they've come around. The more of us who come out, the more people will see we don't have horns or carry pitchforks."

Touché, Leslie.

"Vincente knows about me," she said, returning her gaze to the screen. "He kept trying to fix me up with his male cousins. When I got exasperated, he figured it out. Now he's still trying to fix me up with his cousins—of the female variety."

I snorted. I could well imagine Vincente playing matchmaker, though he'd never tried to fix me up with either male or female relatives. Maybe he couldn't decide. "You think I ought to approach this with humor?"

"No! It's not funny, Sarah. It's bullying, plain and simple. Call this guy out for the creep he is." She looked at the flier again, then scooted over to another computer. She got on the Internet, typed in "lesbian porn," went down a list and clicked a link. A really ugly site came up. "This is for guys who get off watching two women. All fake, not a lesbian in sight. Peg and I used to watch these for laughs." She hit one title and the cover came up.

"The same women as the flier?"

"Yep. *Vixen on Vixen*. Really trashy. The guy didn't get the image from the website. He had to have been watching."

"I don't know that I have to do more than suggest where this came from. Thanks, Leslie." I rose.

Leslie turned back to her computer. "I'm sending this to Zoe."

* * *

I looked out over the assembled crowd who were waiting for the parade to begin. We couldn't have ordered a more perfect day with powder-puff clouds drifting in the deep blue sky, the temperature in the high sixties and the glory of autumn at its ultimate. I could smell a light aroma of woodsmoke in the air, probably a remnant of last night's chilly temperatures.

People were getting restless, and I could see kids in the bleachers across the street beginning to bounce around. I glanced at my watch. The county commissioner had been droning on for twenty minutes. Finally, he ended to polite applause.

I stepped up to the podium.

"I'd been planning to talk about Constant McCabe and his son, Remedy, the first two sheriffs of McCrumb County. About what they faced as law enforcement in the 1820s.

"But, if you haven't seen this, you will." I held up the flier. "This is bullying. The kind that makes unsubstantiated accusations without thought of consequence. There's always consequences, sometimes ones that ripple through a whole community. My department's been working with the high school to turn around attitudes about bullying, but perhaps we should've begun with the adults.

"I do not appreciate having my head attached to the body of a porn star. I don't like porn. It makes objects of the people involved, and once a person is an object, the bully appears with an excuse to do any kind of damage that makes him feel good.

"What would Constant or Remedy McCabe have thought of this? My guess is that they'd think we don't have the same sense of honesty and integrity, the same sense of community we once did. I think they'd be disgusted with us.

"Now let's get the parade rolling."

CHAPTER FIFTY-ONE

Win

I watched Sarah work her way through the crowd at Pioneer Park. So far, I hadn't seen anybody twitch at shaking hands with her. All of McCrumb County had to be assembled, plus a thousand or so visitors. The park was packed and the festivities spilled out into the streets around.

I'd also watched the four young women in bonnets who tried to pass our their fliers. Most people refused them. Those who took them laughed, wadded them up and threw them in the nearest trash container.

So far, so good.

I glanced at my watch. Another half hour and I could take off. Des was completely bewildered by the large crowd, the excess attention she got and the ever-present aroma of roasting meat. I'd been resisting the temptation for both of us, but I figured some barbeque pork ribs could be the reward for keeping my eye on the crowd all afternoon. Des agreed.

I'd just settled at a table with Des looking up at me with soulful eyes. I'd have to share the meat because I sure as hell wasn't feeding her bones.

Nathan sat down next to me. "Nice move, Win."

"What?"

"Sarah's speech," he said, picking up his bratwurst sandwich. "Good idea, puts that old lunatic on the defensive."

"He should be run out of town on a rail." Des whined. I pulled off some meat and tossed it to her. "But that kind of fire-and-brimstone homophobia does more good for us than harm. Makes people uncomfortable."

I grinned. For the moment, life was good.

* * *

Sarah didn't arrive until five thirty. Looking thoroughly exhausted. She took off her jacket, cap and duty belt before she collapsed into my waiting arms.

"Rough day," I said as I pushed back her hair. "But I didn't see anyone treating you like a leper."

She leaned back. "I'm exhausted from shaking hands and making small talk. But you're right, no one spit on me." She wrapped her arms around me, then rested her head against my shoulder.

"Are you hungry?"

"Part of running for office is sampling every local food. I'm stuffed, tired, dirty and glad to be in a safe harbor."

"You want to take a shower? We'll have a beer and talk when you're finished."

She sighed. Trudged to the bedroom. I thought about calling Paige to set up a luncheon date tomorrow, then second-guessed myself. Whatever we did, we'd have to do it together. I knew Sarah wouldn't appreciate me charging to her rescue—unless she said "Help."

Twenty minutes later, she walked into the living room in a robe, her hair still wet and slicked back. "I feel better, Win. How do you always know what'll make me feel good?"

"There were times in Iraq when I would've killed for a shower." I brought two beers and sat beside her on the couch. "Talk to me."

She took a long drink. "I wish you'd just say, 'Stand up and be proud!'"

That wasn't going to happen. So what was? I put an arm around her. She sank into it. "So, what did you feel when you saw the flier?"

"Terrified. Enraged. Then I took a second look and started laughing. Hell, I hope I never look like that when we're making love." She snuggled closer. "I don't, do I?"

I laughed. The photo they'd attached was Sarah making like a mean lawman. All she needed was mirrored sunglasses. I took a sip of beer. "So how did you feel about all the people who sought you out today? They did, you know."

"It's a nil game as far as I'm concerned," she said. "The photo was clearly faked, so they felt sorry for me. They thought I was a victim of a scam."

"You were."

"The pastor's scam, yes. I keep coming back to the truth. I could've pointed out the faked photo and then told the truth. I feel like I had an opportunity today and I blew it."

Complicated issue. Complicated woman. I don't think I'd realized how much Sarah needed integrity to breathe. "So, have you thought about identifying as lesbian?"

"Oh, Win, no. Not now."

I felt her frustration. But maybe if she got a handle on that issue, the rest would follow more easily. "How do you feel at Ruby's?"

She looked up. "I like it, Win. I love dancing with you. You know what Leslie said? She said we were a stunning couple."

My eyebrows shot up. "Your CSI? You talked to her?"

Sarah nodded. "When she said that I blushed crimson, cursed with Mom's gene."

"You notice other women's bodies?"

"Sexually? No. I'm too wrapped up in yours." She took another sip. "Do you?"

"Of course. Long habit. I notice hips and butts and eyes."

"Not breasts?"

"So you are noticing." I grinned.

"A little. Maybe." She pulled me down to her, kissed me. Her weariness was gone.

I returned the kiss with increasing passion. So much for talking.

CHAPTER FIFTY-TWO

Sarah

I watched Win dig into a pile of pancakes, her relish apparent in every movement of her body. Rather like last night. I dug into mine before my grin could turn into a smirk.

When all that was left was coffee, I took a deep breath. "Last night, after you fell asleep, I started thinking."

"You could think after that?" Win asked.

"Only when I was sure you were asleep." I finished my coffee and got ready to take the plunge. "I realized I feel guilty about us."

"You're just realizing that now? When you've been using the word 'caught' since we first got together?"

"Well, getting caught doesn't mean...I guess it does. Win, I have no idea where it comes from. Mom and Dad were never homophobic, and the only prejudice Tillie has is people who use credit cards."

Win examined my face. "It creeps in through the culture. When we were growing up, nobody talked about it. It's only been in the last ten years or so that entertainers could come out and continue their careers. In the meantime, we absorbed nothing but negative messages. It's called internalized homophobia. I don't know a lesbian who hasn't felt it. Well, women our age."

"How did you get over it, Win?"

"I don't think it's something you 'get over.' Instead, you learn to recognize it. Evaluate it. Like Emily had me do with my paranoia when I started seeing her. What's a real threat. What's a projection of my imagination." Win began clearing the table. "You know when the sodomy laws were repealed in Indiana? Nineteen seventy-six." She licked her fork. "What would you like to do today?"

"I brought the book, it's in the car and I have some questions." I immediately began to blush.

"Oh man. Well, let's see," Win said with a wicked smile. "You already know about fisting. Anal sex? A butt plug can enhance vaginal penetration. I don't like something stuffed up my ass, whether it's a dildo or fingers."

I buried my head in my arms and heard Win roar with laughter. She came up behind me and put her arms around me.

"Did I miss any of your questions?" she asked.

"Hell, I have no idea. Are you trying to desensitize me?"

"Your red neck tells me I'm not succeeding." She turned me around, raised my chin so I looked into her eyes. "We've nothing to be ashamed of, Sarah. Straight couples do all of this stuff and don't think twice about it." She traced my jaw, lightly, like a butterfly. "I keep telling you, being lesbian isn't all about sex. It's about heart."

* * *

We arrived at Ruby's when it was still light, sat on the patio and ordered. The woman who took our order flirted outrageously with Win and barely looked at me. Did I want her to? I'd found myself checking her out. Did they pump estrogen into the air?

After dinner, we moved into the back room, waiting for the lights to go down and music to begin. Win's arm encircled me, and I pulled her to me, my tongue quickly finding hers.

"You're a brave woman," Win said when the kiss finally came to an end. She ran her hand through my hair. "For your questions. Your willingness to try something new."

"I was just curious, and I knew you'd...explain everything."

"You mean demonstrate." Win laughed as I began to blush. "We still have the rest of our lives to explore."

"The rest of our lives. I can't take much more sneaking around."

The lights went down, the DJ came onstage. Win pulled me to my feet and we began to slow dance. I pressed into her body.

She nuzzled my neck. "For right now, let's just enjoy the freedom to dance together. Along with a bunch of other women. This is heaven, Sarah."

CHAPTER FIFTY-THREE

Win

Our lovemaking was different that night. Sarah couldn't be sated, either giving or receiving pleasure. When she came, I saw the tears slipping down her cheeks. I watched her over breakfast. While her body was eating, her mind was elsewhere. Eyes unfocused, forehead wrinkled up as if she was asking why.

"What's up?" I asked.

She startled. Sighed. "It doesn't matter," she said, laying her fork on the plate. "What the county thinks. What matters is how I feel—right?"

"You lost me in translation. How you feel about me? How you feel about your job? How you feel about being exposed?"

"All of the above."

I began to clear the table. "I signed up knowing that as long I was a marine, I couldn't come out. You ran for office with no notion how your world would change."

"I found myself standing at a podium, giving a speech that was irrelevant."

"What you said wasn't irrelevant—bullies flock to gay people. Especially gay kids."

"I know and I'll never forget Natalie Elder."

Sarah was driving me crazy, mentally pacing one long loop. So I packed a day pack, map and handed her an extra pair of hiking boots.

"What are the boots for?" she asked.

"Hiking. It'll help clear your head." I massaged her shoulders. They were like two rocks on either side of her neck. "You have a favorite hiking place?"

She glanced out the window. "It's cold out. We could build a fire here."

"Not cold at all when we're moving," I replied. I kissed the nape of her neck. "Boots."

We ended up in Versailles State Park where the autumn was breathtaking. Hiked five hours. Picked up a pizza on the way home. Nothing like pizza and beer in front of a roaring fire after a brisk day outside. With Sarah beside me.

"You were right," she said, balling up her napkin and closing the lid on the pizza box. "I feel much better. How did you know?"

"Experience." I gazed at the fire. I pulled her into my lap, ran my hands down her back. Felt her shoulders with my thumbs. Much more relaxed.

She looked me in the eye. "If someone asks me outright, I can't lie."

"We keep going around and around, don't we?" I stroked her hair. "Sorry. We'll just sit here and enjoy the fire and cuddling."

"That's all?" She laughed and pulled my sweater up over my head.

The fire was embers. We lay on the couch, her head on my chest, my legs wrapped around her. She hadn't cried tonight. Hadn't been so hyper. Had been utterly lovely.

"I wished we lived together," she said, her voice husky. "It would be heaven to come home from work to this. You know, pizza and beer, a roaring fire and you."

This was a complicated love. "I can't see you leaving the homestead."

"I'm the end of the line, for the Barrows, I mean. Hugh and I always postponed having kids."

"You regret it now?"

"Yeah, I do. To be honest, I didn't want to put my career on hold. Then he was dead."

I kissed her forehead, her cheek. "We could have kids."

"That boat's sailed, in case you haven't noticed."

"Adoption."

She propped herself up on an elbow. "You're serious, aren't you?"

"I love kids. Spent as much time with kids as I could. Afghani kids are so joyous. Maybe we could offer a couple of them a good home."

"How long have you been thinking about this?"

"Long time. Before I came home. Before I fell in love with you."

She kissed me. "That would be something—the gay sheriff, her beautiful partner and two Afghani kids."

I kissed her back. "Only two?"

CHAPTER FIFTY-FOUR

Sarah

This was the last meet-and-greet before the election, in a comfortable old home in Greenglen. Tree-lined streets, soft glow of yellow-orange from windows, families going about their business without drawing the curtains. I smelled woodsmoke in the crisp air and turned up the collar of my Windbreaker. This was the American heartland that Norman Rockwell would've painted if he'd ever left the East.

I felt such a sense of being an outsider, locked out of the living rooms and barred from opening the curtains. Maybe I was just tired after a long day of chasing the phantom RV that we thought was a mobile meth lab. Weary of chasing a ghost that always seemed a step ahead of us. I'd formed a small task force within the department to spend the majority of their time jumping ahead of the RV. I'd asked them to exclusively use their cell phones and designated a code for patrol. I prayed the dealers weren't getting their information from within the department.

I walked up the cement steps, the walk and onto the porch. I tapped on the door, which was immediately opened by Charlene, anxiety clearly written on her face.

"Thought you'd forgot or chickened out, Sarah Anne."

"Long day, I'm tired, Charlene, and if I had my druthers, I'd be at home with my feet up."

"Well, missy, wipe the ornery off your face and put a smile on," she said in my ear as she ushered me into the living room, where twenty or so people were drinking coffee. Someone pushed a cup into my hand. I spotted my hosts and walked across to thank them for having me. We chatted a few moments, then they started to introduce me to people I didn't know.

All went well, good questions from many, and I was getting antsy to get home. My duty belt felt like it weighed a half-ton.

"This is the Reverend Luke Rodale of the Third Church of the Brethren," said my hostess.

I reached out to shake his hand, but was met with empty air.

"Sheriff, I surely do wish you'd clear up that little matter Pastor Brown brought up this summer."

I saw red. All the frustrations of the job, the fear I'd harbored, the pressures to be perfect, the criminals I'd faced combined to paint a red scrim between me and the room.

"Oh, Luke, please—"

"She hasn't answered it yet," Luke said, shaking his head.

"What *is* the question?" I said, taking a step forward. "Am I gay? Am I lesbian? Is that what you're asking?" I took another step. "It's none of your damn business. I was elected to uphold the law, not your specific morality. It's not against the law to be gay and hasn't been for forty years, and while homosexuality may offend your sense of morality, that's irrelevant to the office I've sworn to uphold.

"And while I'm at it, Natalie Elder was targeted by those young men because they thought she was gay. You want to talk about immorality? That rape and its spread on social media are the most immoral acts I've ever witnessed. Have you preached about it? Begun working with the schools to root out such wickedness? What are you doing to stop such perniciousness that's taken root in our county? What?"

I took a deep breath. I'd been shouting and everybody was eyeballing the scene. "Don't talk to me about morality, Mr. Rodale, when prejudice and bigotry are preached from the pulpit."

"Ma'am, you still haven't answered the question," Luke said.

"So why don't you ask it?"

He shuffled his feet, looked at the carpet. "Are you a lesbian?"

I put my coffee down, the cup rattling in the saucer. The red was becoming crimson. I stepped up to him, leaned forward. "I don't know."

I glanced at my hostess, gave her my thanks and left, the total silence following me out the door.

CHAPTER FIFTY-FIVE

Win

Sarah had been jumpy all day. Driving Des crazy. She'd spent the night at her house with Micah, voted as early as the polls opened. Then come to me. This was the first time we'd been together since she'd seen red and exploded. Her words, not mine. Today, while I'd found her in my arms frequently, we hadn't made love.

"He asked me outright, Win," Sarah said during one of her bouts of pacing. "I couldn't come up with yes. I'm a thorough coward and I hate myself for it."

Nothing I said gave her comfort, just my arms around her.

Evidently, word had spread quickly. Her deputies were standing fast behind her. Caleb had sat down with her the day after, told her there were still some jackasses in the county, but not in the department. All of the deputies wanted to take out a full-page ad in the *Sentinel* supporting her. Of course she said no, citing the statute that addressed elections. Caleb ignored her, and though there wasn't one mention of the sheriff's department, every deputy signed it. It wouldn't be hard for anyone in the county not to recognize most of the names.

After a dinner which she'd barely touched, she left for County Democratic Headquarters to await her fate. She'd wanted me to come with. I said no. If she lost, I'd console her. In public. If she won, God knew what I'd do to her. She said she'd call when the results came in. I started pacing about eight thirty. No word from Sarah. Did that mean it was too close to call? Shit.

I gave Des her final walk for the night. Lit the fire, got myself a beer. I knew that Sarah had answered the reverend's question honestly. Right now, she didn't know. I'd had friends in the service who'd faced the same dilemma. "Win, does this mean my sexuality has done a U-turn? Forever?" "Win, I haven't felt like this since high school, so consumed with lust. Will it last?" "Win, I'm so in love with Naomi, but I'm not attracted to you—does that mean I'm not lesbian?"

My answer to all was, "Time will tell." After the first flash of passion had dimmed, they'd gone on to other lovers. All with women. That's what terrified me. After our exploration of Sarah's sexuality and with her questions answered, would she move on to another woman? Leave me with only memories? I'd end up a bitter old woman, living alone, and die without anyone caring. Shit.

I got up for another beer. Heard the ping of my warning system. Nine forty-five was late for a visitor. Shit, I didn't have visitors. Which was why no one would find my body until months later. "Fuck it, Win."

I watched the monitor as the lights went on. Sarah's SUV. Why the hell hadn't she called?

I met her at the front door.

She pushed into my arms. Kissed me hard. "Fuck me, Win. Fuck me hard."

"You lost?"

"No. I won. It looks like a landslide."

"Whoopee! Great, Sarah." I closed the door and led her inside. Got two beers and brought them to the couch. "See, the people of McCrumb County have some sense."

We clinked bottles, she took a sip, put the bottle on the table.

"Win, I don't know if I'm in or out of the closet, I just want you in me and me in you."

I felt my eyebrows lift. I brushed my hand through her hair. "You were hoping you'd lose."

"No...well, I don't think so. Hell, I don't know which end's up." She closed her eyes and I could see tears welling up. Slipping down her cheeks.

I pulled her to me, wiped them away with my thumb. "How about we make mad, passionate love tonight? Get rid of the doubt, the anxiety. The gerbil wheel of thought. Just celebrate tonight with our bodies, not our minds?"

"But—"

"We'll talk tomorrow." I kissed her, held her face in my hands. "Now, we'll do our own celebrating."

We both slept in the next morning, finally roused by Des's insistence on going out. While I waited for her to come back in, I started the coffee. I heard the shower, was tempted to join her. God, what a woman.

Des whined at the door and Sarah walked into the kitchen. I let Des in and looked at Sarah for a clue to where she was this morning.

"What a night," she said with a wicked smile. "It certainly helped me…unwind." She kissed me on the cheek.

I poured her a cup, leaned against the counter. "You want to talk or not?"

"Not." She put the mug on the counter, moved to me, undid the tie on my robe.

I retied it. "Then let me talk. You know what scares me? I'm terrified of losing you—"

"I'll never—"

"Hush up, Sarah! Just listen." I immediately wanted to reach out, pull her to me. Say sorry about a million times. But I needed her to hear me. "I love you. No doubt. You love me, now. But when the hot passion begins to fade—don't. Just listen. This white-hot condition won't last. If we're lucky, it'll settle into something deeper. Soul-deep, Sarah."

"Why are you saying this?"

"Because you're wondering if you're lesbian. I'm just telling you things will change between us. When they do, you may be looking around for someone more exciting. Get that rush again."

"You think I'm lesbian."

I shrugged. "My guess is yes. It's up to you to claim that identity, or turn away. What I'm trying to tell you, if you claim it and get comfortable with it, our relationship will change. I've never wanted to push you out on a ledge. But I think you're coming to it now. Immersing yourself in sex isn't the answer." I pulled her to me. "Sometimes not a bad substitute. Never a solution."

She wrapped her arms around me and we hung on to each other like we were standing in a strong wind.

"I love you, Win," she said. "I'm sure, as sure as I was with Hugh. The forever kind of sure. I know things change, they did between Hugh and me. Do you mind me talking about him?"

"Of course not. He was the love of your life, Sarah."

"Until you. Everything else in my life may be crazy, but I'm sure of what I feel for you." She kissed me lightly. "You know what I'm afraid of?"

"You're fearless," I said, my lips brushing her hair.

"I'm afraid I'll lose you because I can't come up with answers—if I'm lesbian, how far we can come out—and you'll run out of patience."

"Not going to happen."

"I'm going to hold you to that." She looked to the living room and our clothes still scattered there. She found her pants, rummaged in her pocket. She walked back to me. "I love you and I want to spend my life with you." She opened her hand. A worn gold band rested on her palm. "It was Mom's. Dad couldn't bear to...It held too many memories for him. He gave it to me a couple of weeks ago and said, 'Tell Win to make a honest woman of you.' So, will you marry me, Win?"

My legs almost buckled. I felt my world turning upside down. Tears forming. I was so choked up, all I could do was nod.

She slipped the ring on my left hand. It fit perfectly. "Maybe we can take a vacation this winter, New York or Massachusetts, and make this conventional and formal."

We kissed, softly, briefly. Almost like the first time we kissed. Except I didn't pull back abruptly and she didn't have a panicked look on her face.

Bella Books, Inc.

Women. Books. Even Better Together.

P.O. Box 10543
Tallahassee, FL 32302

Phone: 800-729-4992
www.bellabooks.com

Printed in the USA
CPSIA information can be obtained
at www.ICGtesting.com
JSHW082154140824
68134JS00014B/235